"Why?" she asked. "Why would y

"Let me show you, Vivien."

He reached across and snatched her up in a hard grip, pulling her across the intimate space and into his lap.

Clutching the thick wool fabric of his coat, she gazed up at him.

"Wha . . . what are you doing?" she stammered.

"I'm answering your question," he murmured, the dark rumble making her shiver.

Then he moved, tilting her back over his arm as he swooped in to kiss her. His mouth fastened over hers. Not gently, either. He plundered her lips, demanding entrance with a masculine arrogance that swept past her resistance in one skipped heartbeat . . .

Books by Vanessa Kelly

MASTERING THE MARQUESS

SEX AND THE SINGLE EARL

MY FAVORITE COUNTESS

HIS MISTLETOE BRIDE

SECRETS FOR SEDUCING A ROYAL BODYGUARD

CONFESSIONS OF A ROYAL BRIDEGROOM

AN INVITATION TO SIN
(with Jo Beverley, Sally MacKenzie, and Kaitlin O'Riley)

Published by Kensington Publishing Corporation

SECRETS
for SEDUCING a
ROYAL BODYGUARD

VANESSA KELLY

ZEBRA BOOKS
KENSINGTON PUBLISHING CORP.
http://www.kensingtonbooks.com

ZEBRA BOOKS are published by

Kensington Publishing Corp.
119 West 40th Street
New York, NY 10018

All Kensington titles, imprints and distributed lines are available at special quantity discounts for bulk purchases for sales
promotion, premiums, fund-raising, educational or institu-
tional use.

Special book excerpts or customized printings can also be
created to fit specific needs. For details, write or phone the
office of the Kensington Special Sales Manager. Attn.: Special Sales Department. Kensington Publishing Corp., 119 West
40th Street, New York, NY 10018. Phone: 1-800-221-2647.

Zebra and the Z logo Reg. U.S. Pat. & TM Off.

ISBN-13: 978-1-4201-3122-2
ISBN-10: 1-4201-3122-2
First Printing: January 2014

eISBN-13: 978-1-4201-3123-9
eISBN-10: 1-4201-3123-0
First Electronic Edition: January 2014

10 9 8 7 6 5 4 3 2 1

Printed in the United States of America

Acknowledgments

Releasing books into the wild takes a combined effort, and I'd like to acknowledge all the folks who helped me get *Secrets* out into the world. First, my editor John Scognamiglio, who has been so supportive of my work and of this new series; my sane and wonderful agent, Evan Marshall; the art department at Kensington, who give me the most beautiful covers; Vida Engstrand and Alexandra Nicolajsen and all the folks in publicity who help get the book into the hands of readers; and the patient Ross Plotkin from the production department. I'd also like to thank my assistant and Facebook wrangler, Kim Castillo, and my critique partner Debbie Mason, who always knows how to plug up the nasty plot holes. Thank you all for your kindness and support.

Finally, I want to thank my husband and writing partner, Randy Sykes. Not only is he a talented writer, he's an awesome husband who never complains about doing housework or laundry.

Chapter One

Smuggling tunnels near the Kentish Coast
October 1814

Aden St. George managed to avoid having to kill the guard stationed outside his quarry's cryptlike cell, although the thug outside the caves hadn't been so lucky. Still, that bastard had tried to knife him in the gut so Aden could hardly be faulted for returning the favor. And knowing what he did about the men who'd kidnapped Lady Vivien Shaw, he wouldn't waste his fitful conscience on that brutal but necessary act. Killing was not a favorite pastime, but only rarely did it disturb his sleep.

Tonight's rescue mission carried no inconvenient opportunities for remorse since a woman's life and innocence hung in the balance. True, the gossips whispered that Lady Vivien's innocence was an open question, but what would happen to her if Aden failed wasn't. Without his intervention she would disappear into a nightmarish life, forever beyond the protection of her family and friends.

Even if she'd simply been the victim of a kidnapping for ransom, as her wealthy brother suspected, her reputation at the very least was at stake—especially if rumors of her disappearance started to circulate throughout the *ton*. More importantly, Aden hoped he wasn't already too late to ensure she continued her easy, privileged life, and that her brutish guards hadn't already used her as their plaything.

As he eased the guard's beefy, foul-smelling form to the floor, Aden cast a swift glance down the dimly lit corridor. All was silent, as it should be if he'd done his job correctly. He normally felt little pride in his abilities, but he could at least acknowledge a grim satisfaction that his last disastrous mission in France hadn't affected his instincts or his lethally honed skills.

Shrugging away any residual tension, he extracted his picklocks from the inner pocket of his coat and went to work on the sturdy oak door separating him from his objective. Although no sound emanated from behind the rough-hewn panels, he was certain Lady Vivien was there. Three other tunnels ran up from the coast into the smuggler's lair, but only this corridor boasted a table, lamp, and chair for the guard by the door. An assessing glance down the other tunnels had convinced him the majority of the gang was elsewhere, probably in a room with a fireplace and more creature comforts than those in this dank corner. But clearly the bastards thought one of the rooms obviously used for storing contraband was quite good enough for a gently bred lady.

Aden forced down the flare of rage that a woman like Lady Vivien—or *any* woman—would be stowed like a cask of brandy in a moldering hole carved from dirt and rock. But he could hardly spare to indulge in that kind of emotion. Emotion was an insidious enemy that clouded the judgment, as it had only a few weeks ago in Paris. He couldn't afford it, not when the lady's life was at stake.

The lock snicked and the tumblers slid open. Aden slipped quietly past the door, ignoring the choking miasma of mold and dust that assailed his nostrils. It took a few seconds for his eyes to adjust to the murky depths of the room, illuminated by a single candle standing on a crate, burned down to a nub. Ghosting forward, he made out a pallet shoved against the sloping, roughly carved wall of the room.

A slight form lay motionless under a dark cloak.

Silent, he gazed down at Lady Vivien, sister to the Earl of Blake and one of the most acclaimed young women of the *ton* though she was a dab little thing to be the recipient of so much admiration and gossip. But even in the dim light cast by the candle, though disheveled and dirty her beauty shone clear to Aden in the cast of her elegant features. Hair the color of golden honey wound down from her ruined coiffure and tumbled around her shoulders. Her velvet evening cloak, woefully inadequate to ward off the chill from the room's moisture-slicked walls, had slipped from her shoulders to puddle about her waist, revealing creamy skin and gently sloping breasts that rose and fell in the rapid, shallow breathing of her disturbed sleep. A ridiculously delicate dress, all white lace and yellow silk, had silly little sleeves that exposed most of her arms and shoulders, and her pale breasts gently swelled from the wispy bodice of her gown.

Aden crouched beside her pallet, noting the dirt smudges on her pale arms and shoulders, and grimy marks of filthy hands streaking mud across the bodice of her gown. She'd clearly been manhandled, and anger again lanced through his gut like a poison-tipped blade. He feared he was too late to save her from a lifetime of remembered horror and degradation, just as he'd been too late to save John Williamson from a pointless death in a French inn not two weeks ago.

He throttled back his frustration, because he could at least save her from death or more abuse. For now, that was all he had. Any personal vengeance he chose to exact against her captors would come later, when he had extracted Lady Vivien from danger. The unconscious guard outside her room wouldn't stay down forever, and other members of the gang could wander along at any time, either to relieve the guard or check on the other man, now crumpled dead in the bushes outside the entrance to the tunnels.

Leaning over, Aden inhaled, taking in her sickly sweet, heavily scented breath along with the pallor of her winsome features. She'd been drugged, likely a blessing given what had happened to her in this disgusting hole.

He flicked the cloak up over her chest and gently slid his arms under her slender body. As he started to lift, she suddenly came to life in his arms, thrashing madly. Startled, he instinctively tightened his grip. But preoccupied with keeping a hold on her twisting body, he failed to notice her arm snake out from under the cloak until her fist smashed into his cheekbone.

Shock more than pain lanced through him as she wrenched herself free. She landed on the pallet with a startled *oof* and then exploded up again, her slender body a furious tangle of kicking, thrusting limbs. Her eyes blazed with rage, wide and full of desperation. She fought with the instinct and fear-generated strength of a cornered animal, one who preferred death to submission.

Recovering from his momentary paralysis, Aden pressed her back down onto the pallet, capturing her flailing arms and legs beneath him. She sucked in a sobbing, terrified breath but surprised him again when she lunged up, trying to smash the top of her head into his face. He jerked back just in time, then whipped a hand up, grasped the back of her skull, and held it firmly against the scratchy burlap cloth beneath her.

For a few infernally long seconds they glared at each other, their rasping breaths shattering the clammy closeness of the room. She shook beneath him, her body slim and lithe beneath the fragile silk of her ball gown. A heated tendril of scent reached his nostrils, an elusive whisper of roses and summer warmth. Her chest rose and fell in a pattern of fractured breaths, plumping the fullness of her breasts over the top of her low-cut bodice.

The candle on the crate beside them sputtered and flared, throwing light on her face. A hectic flush rose in her cheeks, driving a wash of pink across her pale skin. Her lips, plush and bow-shaped, trembled open in a travesty of invitation, and for one demented instant Aden fought the urgent need to taste them, to plumb the sweet temptation they offered.

And then she drew in a breath, preparing to scream. He whipped up a hand and covered her mouth, disgusted with his lapse in discipline and what it must have revealed to her. She might be the kind of spoiled beauty he disdained, but he'd consign himself to the darkest hell before he frightened her or harmed a hair on her head.

"Hush, Lady Vivien." He lifted slightly, giving her more room although he kept his hand clamped over her mouth. "Sir Dominic Hunter sent me. I'm going to get you out of here, but you can't scream or keep fighting or your captors will hear."

Her gaze darted to the door and the corridor beyond, then flashed back to his face.

"The guards won't trouble us," he murmured in response to her unspoken question. The terror that glazed her eyes dimmed a notch. She blinked rapidly as if to chase away her drug-induced confusion.

He held her gaze, willing her to trust him. "If I take my hand away, you must not cry out. You will endanger us both if you do. Understand?"

She stared up at him, eyes rounded with fear. He could practically hear the turning of the cogs and wheels in her brain and feel her body go still as she weighed her decision.

Blast. If she continued to fight him, a sharp tap to the jaw to knock her senseless might be the only safe way to handle her. But then he saw the clearing in her eyes and sensed the beginning of a wary acceptance of him.

"Yes?" he whispered.

The flush leached from her face. She gave one sharp, economical nod and then settled under him, as if waiting for him to respond. Cautiously, he removed his hand from her mouth, straining an ear for any noises. He deliberately pulled his awareness away from her, focusing his instincts, trying to sense traps that might await them in the corridor beyond.

"Who are you?" Her voice was a throaty croak. "You know Sir Dominic?"

"Yes. I'm a friend." Right now she didn't need to know more than the basics.

He rolled off the pallet, bringing her slight body with him as he rose. She gave a little gasp and staggered, sinking against him. Steadying her, he wrapped the velvet cloak tightly around her and lifted, settling her easily against his chest, a fragile package in his arms. The fact that she'd tried to fight him and struggled so desperately to defend herself spoke of a reckless courage that filled him with dismay. If she had struggled thus with her abductors, God only knows what they'd done to her. They would have relished the sport of breaking her in unimaginably brutal ways.

Once more, a thirst for vengeance settled low in his gut. His mind began to reshape itself into the cold, ruthless pattern that automatically formed whenever he planned a kill. Emotions began to fall away. He felt the man inside him—the creature of blood, bone, muscle, and morality—giving way to something akin to iron wheels and gears, defined by a single, deadly purpose that swept everything before it.

The girl stiffened in his arms. She peered at him, caution pulling her features tight as if she'd sensed the change in him. How the hell was that possible?

When she wriggled, clearly wanting down, he knew she

had sensed it. Swiftly, he refocused. Vengeance would change nothing. In this moment, the only thing that counted was saving Lady Vivien Shaw.

He tried a reassuring smile. Her eyes widened and she shrank into herself, her expression screaming distrust. Very well. She'd *have* to trust him, or he just might be forced to tap her under the chin after all. So far she'd surprised him with her lack of hysterics, but would that last much longer?

Her tongue swiped out to wet her full lips—a distraction he didn't need—then she spoke in that croaking whisper. "How will we—"

He shook his head in warning as they reached the door. A fine tremor flowed through her limbs before she fell silent and still against him.

Shifting her in his arms, he moved, keeping the door between them and the open corridor. He glanced down at the burly form of the guard crumpled against the wall. Aden gave him a hard nudge with his boot.

"Is he dead?" Lady Vivien whispered.

He shook his head. After what the guard had likely done to her, he'd assumed she'd want to see him dead. Yet she seemed relieved more than anything.

As he moved down the corridor, she stretched up again to murmur in his ear, "I can walk." Her warm breath slid over his skin like a caress, her soft lips brushing his ear. Aden had to repress an instinctive shiver of pleasure.

Scowling at his undisciplined reaction, he bit out a low reply. "We're almost out." He thought she rolled her eyes at him, but his mind rejected the absurd notion.

"I would nonetheless prefer to walk," she hissed.

Apparently she *had* rolled her eyes at him.

When they came to a branching intersection he stopped, hugging the wall as he listened while grasping her even more securely against his chest. She grumbled something under her breath, which he ignored. They *were* almost out. The fools who had snatched her had failed to avail themselves of the opportunity offered by the extensive network of tunnels. They could have stashed their captive in the deepest recesses of the smugglers' lair, making it hard to find her and harder to get her out. Instead, they'd dumped her in an easily accessible room in one of the first tunnels off the main corridor, topping off their stupidity by leaving her inadequately guarded. Those mistakes told Aden a great deal about her captors. He prayed their ineptitude would hold true for the rest of the night.

Not that he couldn't handle whatever problems arose. Dominic had wanted to send more men, but Aden had vetoed the idea. Time had not been on their side, and he preferred to work alone in any event. This type of mission suited his skills and temperament perfectly—in and out quickly using whatever amount of lethal force was required.

He glanced down at the bundle of femininity in his arms. If he had to kill someone else, he surely did not want a hysterical woman complicating matters. Not that Lady Vivien seemed predisposed to hysterics, but she was likely in shock and a good agent never took chances.

Or shouldn't, as he'd been so recently and harshly reminded.

Resting against the wall, vaguely aware of Lady Vivien's soft, rose-petal scent, Aden thought about his options. After a moment, he ducked his head to find her ear, blowing aside the fine strands of golden hair that had snagged in the collar of his coat. She jerked in his arms then looked at him, blue eyes wide and startled.

"Are you certain you can walk?" he murmured.

She blew out a relieved breath and nodded. For some reason, it annoyed him that she was so intent on freeing herself from his grasp. He felt better with the girl secure in his arms. Obviously she didn't feel the same way, and it did make sense to have his hands free, knives at the ready, when they reached the entrance to the tunnels. So far all had gone according to plan, which was usually the best evidence that matters were about to blow up in his face.

He eased her down until her feet touched the floor, the top of her head barely level with his chin. When she inhaled sharply, he glanced down at her feet and quietly cursed. They'd taken away her shoes and now she stood on the cold, dirt-packed floor in stocking-clad feet.

When he slid an arm around her waist to lift her again, she slapped a hand on his chest to stop him.

"It's fine," she whispered. "I can still walk." A wry little smile shaped the corners of her pretty mouth. "Besides, my feet are so cold I can hardly feel a thing."

Slightly bemused by her stoic attitude, he raised his brows. She simply shrugged. Aden cast an assessing glance at the tunnel floor. Though dirty and assuredly cold, it seemed relatively free of debris. The exit was close, and they should make it with little trouble if no one had yet discovered the dead guard in the bushes.

That, however, was a big *if*.

Aden bent to whisper, "Stay behind me. If there's any trouble, run for the woods. There's a horse tied up in a small clearing about four hundred yards straight ahead. If that's not possible, double back and hide down that corridor." He jerked his head to indicate a shadowed, low-ceilinged tunnel branching off to the right. "Wait there until I come for you."

She stared at him, and that glazed look of terror seeped back into her eyes as he sensed panic freezing her limbs. Ignoring his growing sense of urgency, Aden took her face between his gloved hands, stooping until their gazes were level. Her breath sawed in and out in shallow pants, as he stared into her eyes until the pupils contracted and focused on him.

"You are safe with me," he said quietly. "I will not let anyone harm you again. Do you understand?"

Her slender hands came up in a fluttering motion, touching his wrists. An elusive sense of connection shimmered in the air between them, slowing time to a crawl. Tension flowed from his limbs and evaporated in a gust of cool air blowing from the mouth of the tunnel. The outside world faded away and there was only her—her wounded, sapphire gaze, her slowly quieting breath, her beautiful, anxious face between his hands. Her needs became paramount, along with his need that she trust him. In that suspended moment, their mutual needs encompassed the entire world.

Finally, she blinked several times, breaking the ephemeral thread of the connection. She dropped her hands from his wrists and nodded her understanding.

"Good." His heart throbbed with a strange, pulsing ache as he brushed a stray lock of hair from her brow. Clamping down hard on the unfamiliar sensation, Aden gathered himself and turned to face whatever awaited them outside the tunnels.

Chapter Two

Vivien had no intention of lapsing into hysterics, not after everything she'd endured over these last hours. But when the dangerous-looking man who was rescuing her— at least she *thought* he was rescuing her—led her past the guard who now had a knife protruding from under his ribs, she realized her good intentions might be for naught. Bubbles of hysteria rose in her throat and her legs turned the consistency of porridge.

"Don't look," said her rescuer. He reached behind him and drew her to his side, gently turning her face until it rested against his chest. His big hand, encased in a black leather glove, cradled her skull and forced her to avert her gaze. She couldn't have looked if she wanted to, and she certainly didn't want to. All she could do was huddle into her would-be savior's muscled body and absorb the warmth and security of his enveloping embrace.

Against her expectations—and his, she suspected—it had proven amazingly easy to escape from the tunnels. Her rescuer had taken care of both guards—one lethally—and they had met no resistance so far. Now he was guiding her swiftly away from the gap in the rocks, heading into the sheltering cover of the forest. It was the blackest of nights, with clouds obscuring the moon and stars. Vivien could only make out murky shapes—the trees directly in front of her, and the man by her side. And he towered over her, a dominating presence even darker than the night. A disconcerting awareness of him prickled along her nerves, instinctively drawing her to him even as her mind sent out frantic warnings to mistrust everyone.

When jolted out of her drug-induced sleep, she'd thought she'd finally been released from her nightmare. Then the cold and the stench of her dreary prison had assailed her, and the nightmare twisted back into reality. She'd almost bolted upright from her moldy-smelling pallet when she sensed someone in the room with her—not one of the guards stationed outside her door, although she couldn't explain her certainty. No, this man was different. Silent, but with a powerful presence Vivien had somehow comprehended even in her dazed state. She had reacted by freezing, but when those big, leather-encased hands had slipped under her, panic had exploded in her chest. The rest of her body had followed suit and she'd fought as hard as she could. He'd subdued her with a ridiculous ease.

Though not before she'd left a mark on his handsome face, high up on his cheekbone.

Vivien winced, feeling guilty, and wondering why it should make a difference that he was handsome. He was certainly that, with a high, strong brow, a slashing jaw, and riveting eyes that almost defied description. Those raven-colored eyes had transfixed her, both when he'd held her captive on the pallet and then again when he'd been preparing her for the dangers that might await them at the cave's entrance.

Back in her cell, he'd terrified her. But in the tunnels, just the opposite had occurred. His penetrating gaze had sliced through her panic, triggering a strangely intimate moment, as if he'd seen deep inside her soul and captured everything there was to know about her. It should have sent her emotions skittering, but instead she'd sensed something akin to sanctuary, a safe harbor after years at sea. What she saw in his eyes had settled her frantic heartbeat and invested her with a fugitive confidence that kept her moving forward.

She stumbled a bit over a tangle of roots, causing his grip to tighten on her elbow. Exhaling a frustrated breath and peering ahead into the smothering darkness, she mentally scolded herself for indulging in fanciful notions. She'd always had a heightened imagination, but now was hardly the time to indulge it. They were far from any kind of safe haven and she needed to concentrate on her feet as they moved stealthily over the thin cover of dead leaves on the forest floor. Thank God she had so little feeling—

"Ouch!" She bit back a curse, hopping on one foot. Unfortunately, her feet were not as frozen as she'd thought.

The man stopped and dipped his head to look down at her feet. "What's wrong?" he asked in that deep rumble of his.

Vivien clenched her teeth, leaning into his muscular frame as she balanced and rubbed her unhappy toes. "What do you think happened? I walked into a blasted great rock, which has no business being in the middle of a path. If there is such a thing as a path through this benighted forest, that is."

Her eyes must have adjusted to the dark because she could clearly see him shaking his head. Not that she could blame him since she did tend to fall into a snit when in stressful or trying circumstances. And getting kidnapped, drugged, and locked away in a dank, smelly cave struck her as very stressful circumstances, indeed.

He reached for her, swinging her back into his arms. She thought about protesting—she *should* protest the fact that a stranger was handling her so intimately—but then decided against it. For a few moments back in her cell, the look on his face had frightened her half to death. She'd been desperate to get out of his arms. Much to her surprise, he seemed to understand her reaction. Since then, he'd treated her very gently, gaining her trust when her courage had failed and removing her swiftly and efficiently from captivity. She no doubt owed him her life, and she had every intention of properly thanking him once she was no longer in danger of succumbing to an epic bout of the vapors.

Of course, things could have been so much worse. She hadn't been raped or beaten or even manhandled too severely, at least not after the kidnappers had hauled her, kicking and screaming, out of her carriage in the middle of Mayfair. That particular moment had been wretched, and she would never forget her mother's terrified shrieks. The next awful moment had come when they'd forced the laudanum down her throat. But it hadn't entirely knocked her out. Certainly not enough that she hadn't felt one of the brutes pawing at her breasts. That memory brought the bile rushing up into her throat. Fortunately, one of her other abductors had lashed out at the man, telling him to keep his bloody hands to himself. Hours later, she'd tried to fight when they lifted her from the carriage and carried her into the caves, but they'd only laughed, hauling her along like a sack of coal before finally dropping her onto a disgusting pallet.

Thankfully, after they'd dumped her in that cold cell they'd left her alone. After fruitlessly searching every inch of the room for a means of escape, she'd finally dozed off, too weary to fight the effects of the drug any longer. She'd only awakened when her rescuer—really, she *must* press him for his name—had entered the room and miraculously swept her away. Even now as they tromped through the forest—well, he was doing all the tromping—she could still hardly believe they'd managed the escape.

The eerie hoot of an owl echoed through the night, and Vivien shivered. Strong arms closed tightly around her, cradling her into a rock-hard chest. She had to resist the urge to snuggle up, close her eyes, and go to sleep. It was a natural impulse because she felt entirely safe in this man's arms, his strength and heat seeping through her velvet cloak to warm her. In his arms she felt almost cherished, which showed how thoroughly off-kilter her thinking had become under the strains of her ordeal.

"Not much farther," he said, clearly sensing her fatigue. Strange that after so short a time he was already attuned to her state of mind.

She huffed out an impatient breath at such a demented notion. Her exhaustion and frayed nerves would be obvious to the average village idiot. Everything was finally catching up to her—not only the fear and the frustration, but the why of it, too.

Who could possibly have wanted to kidnap her? An idea— more an image—had floated through her mind when she'd first drifted off to sleep in her cell, but one she rejected now. The man her drug-addled brain had seized on as a villain was a prince, but princes most decidedly did not go around kidnapping gently born ladies. Well, perhaps in fairy tales they might, but certainly not in true life. Besides, Prince Ivan was more likely to be mistaken for a frog than a dream come true, and Vivien was very certain she would *not* be kissing him any time in the near or distant future.

"We're here," her companion said quietly a short time later.

Vivien jerked in his arms, realizing she'd drifted off. She clutched at the heavy wool lapels of the odd coat he wore, one that seemed suited to a fisherman or laborer. Still, the fabric under her fingers felt dense and rich, woven from the finest of materials. Everything about the man was a mystery, and it was one that pricked her curiosity with a persistent needle.

"Where?" she asked stupidly as he set her back on her feet. No matter how hard she tried, her brain didn't seem to want to fully wake up.

"In the clearing, where my horse is," he explained patiently.

"Oh, yes. I'd forgotten about the horse."

"You didn't think we'd be walking back to London, did you?"

The mild amusement in his tone had her shuffling her feet in the leaves. "Of course not. I simply forgot, that's all."

"It's perfectly understandable." He set her against a tree and stepped away, heading across the small open expanse. She could see rather more clearly now, and watched him move away from her. And even though she could follow him with her gaze, a spurt of anxiety welled within her now that he no longer held her. She clamped down hard, concentrating instead on the interesting fact that such a big man could move with such stealth.

Vivien heard the jingle of a horse's bridle before she saw her rescuer lead the creature toward her. Despite its intimidating size, the massive, dark-coated animal followed behind him like a docile lap dog, gently puffing out its breath and stepping softly in his wake. When they reached the edge of the clearing, her rescuer let the reins drop to the ground, not bothering to tie the horse to tree or branch. He mounted with a swift, practiced smoothness. The beast danced a few steps, prompting Vivien to scuttle back, but the man easily mastered him.

"Come, my lady. Up you go," he said, reaching down a hand.

Vivien stood rooted to the spot, wariness rushing back. "Didn't you bring another horse? How can we ride together all the way back to London?"

"We're not riding. It's too far and it would expose us to prying eyes. I have a carriage waiting for us in a nearby village. The sooner you mount, the sooner we'll get there."

The astringent note in his voice automatically raised her hackles. "I can't possibly ride on the same horse with you. It wouldn't be proper." She winced at how silly that sounded, given the circumstances. But the idea of being mounted in front of him on that great beast, with only her velvet cloak and two thin layers of delicate fabric between their bodies, made her feel much too exposed and vulnerable in a way she'd been fighting against since her kidnapping.

"Since there's no one here to see you, perhaps you could set decorum aside for now," he responded dryly. "And if you think riding on a horse with me constitutes a scandal, imagine what the polite world would say if they discovered that you'd been held captive by a band of thugs."

Her cheeks flamed with heat. "Well, put that way, I do see your point." She took a deep breath, mystified at her reluctance to ride with him. She'd let him hold her, lugging her for several hundred yards through the woods, so why did this particular activity make her squirm with discomfort? Somehow it seemed so very intimate, and she didn't even know his name.

Perhaps that was it.

"You still haven't told me your name. I should think I deserve to know that, at least."

His gloved hand tightened on the reins, and again the horse danced. He swiftly brought the beast under control. Silence fell again over the clearing, broken only by the nocturnal rustlings of some small creature.

"Aden St. George," he said a moment later, his reluctance to share apparent.

Vivien brightened. "St. George? Would that be from the Earl of Thornbury's family? My mother knows Lady Thornbury quite well."

She had the distinct impression her reply had him grinding his teeth.

"I'm aware of that. And now that we've been properly introduced, would her ladyship please deign to get the hell up on my horse? We're running out of time."

Though it was surely too dark for him to make out her expression, she scowled anyway. "There's no need to get huffy. I've had to endure quite enough tonight without rude remarks from the man who is rescuing me."

He expelled a sigh. "Forgive me. I would simply like to *proceed* with that rescue, if you don't mind. It won't be long before you're discovered missing, if it hasn't happened already."

Vivien cast a nervous glance over her shoulder. She strained to see something, anything, in the encompassing darkness. "Oh, yes. Quite right, Mr. St. George. No time for lingering." Wonderful. Now her nerves had set her to babbling. He must think her a perfect fool.

He stretched out his arm, gesturing her forward. "I'll pull you up in front of me. Step on my boot if you need to, but let me do the rest."

She swallowed hard and reached up, watched his hand swallow hers, and let out a startled squeak when he pulled her straight up into the air as if she were a cloth doll. Her feet scrambled for purchase on his boot, and she had a moment's panic when she thought she was about to tumble back to the ground. But he swept her up in a dizzying rush, and a breathless moment later she sat before him, her bottom enclosed by his muscled thighs and his arm wrapped around her waist in a solid embrace.

With her heart thumping wildly she clutched at the horse's mane, her skittish response to him blending with her fears about the danger that might lurk ahead. As she took a deep breath, trying to calm her jangling nerves, he pressed his knees against the side of the horse, and they moved into the dark reaches of the forest.

Chapter Three

Tremors shivered through Lady Vivien's slight frame as she held herself rigidly upright in front of him. It was a wonder she could still tolerate a man's touch at all, much less the close embrace they shared on Ranger's back. Though Aden had been surprised by her reluctance to mount up, her emotions were obviously seesawing from one extreme to the other. If only he could ascertain how badly she'd been hurt and the price her foul captors had extracted from her lovely body.

Not as much as he'd originally thought, he hoped and suspected. She had panicked a few times, which was perfectly understandable. But she'd also reacted to the challenges thrown at her with a wit and vigor inconceivable in a woman who'd just been raped. In fact, she'd almost made him laugh when she snapped at him after stubbing her toe. But only a few minutes later she was back to acting like a skittish foal, reinforcing his concern that something truly ugly had happened to her in those caves.

But how did one go about asking a gently bred lady such a question? Though Aden hadn't a clue how to broach the topic, knowing how badly she'd been treated would help him gauge how much more she could take. So far, they'd been lucky, but he couldn't depend on that luck continuing. They still had to get clear of these woods and make it safely to the hamlet where he'd stowed his coach and left his men waiting for them.

Ranger stepped carefully along the trail, as quiet and precise as always. Aden had taken the horse on a swift reconnoiter at dusk, looking for obstacles and imprinting the way through the woods in his mind. Ranger needed little guidance but Aden kept a firm hand on the reins even as he attempted to keep an equally firm grip on his growing awareness of the woman in his arms.

It didn't help one jot that the sweetly scented, intensely feminine Lady Vivien was so powerful a distraction. The bruised, vulnerable look in her blue eyes still haunted him, and he finally acknowledged it was partly for his own sake that he needed to know if she'd been raped. If she had, there wasn't a force on earth that could stop him from hunting down whoever had instigated her abduction.

He was still searching for the correct words to ask so appalling a question when he felt her body start to relax. Up until now, she'd held herself stiff as a hitching post, leaning as far forward as she could. All that did, of course, was push her sweetly rounded arse into his groin. Every motion of his horse's limbs jostled that lovely piece of her anatomy against him, and his groin naturally approved. Aden had been grinding his teeth for the last twenty minutes, telling himself to ignore the alluring sensations. But Lady Vivien served as a heady inducement to sin. Even dirty and disheveled, sharp-tongued and skittish, she was a dainty beauty whose scent reminded him of long summer days and soft, warm nights and a life he'd forgotten long ago.

Another few hundred yards and she slumped back into his chest, her soft, even breathing signalling she'd dropped into a doze. Her small change in position generated another set of challenges. Her upright stance had collapsed, bringing her breasts into contact with his forearm. When he pulled her up onto the horse he'd managed to get his arm inside her cloak as he wrapped it around her waist. Thank God he was wearing gloves because her silk gown and nearly nonexistent undergarments would have been no barrier against the touch of his hands. But with the change in her position her breasts now jiggled merrily on his sleeve, as if his arm was a nicely placed shelf for those tempting mounds to rest upon.

Aden had gotten a taste of her lushness earlier when he'd captured her body under his to prevent her from exploding off that blasted pallet. He'd been vaguely aware at the time that her slim frame held some enticing curves, but had been too busy keeping her quiet to pay much attention. Now he had all the time in the world to feel her breasts keeping her hips company as they drove his temperature up several degrees.

And wasn't he the right bastard to be thinking that way? The last thing the poor girl needed was his cockstand poking her in the back as they tried to escape danger and death. Yes, he was a hell of a hero. He didn't need tonight's escapade to confirm how far from the truth that notion had become.

A loud crack sounded off to the right, jerking both his and Ranger's heads in that direction. With a slight pressure on the reins he pulled the horse to a standstill. Lady Vivien startled awake and he had to clamp her against him to keep her from sliding sideways.

"Why are we stopping?" Her breasts rose and fell with a nervous breath. "What's wrong?"

Aden's chest pulled tight at the quaver in her voice. Lady Vivien did not strike him as a woman who easily succumbed to fear, but her voice told him she was skating on the edge of it now. He gave her a gentle warning squeeze and listened, peering into the endless gloom and shadows. To her credit, she held herself silent and still although he could feel the effort it cost as she shivered in his arms.

Then again, the shivering could signify she was taking a chill. The night air was mild, but she must have lain in that dank room for hours. A sense of urgency pricked at him. The need to get her warm and safe as quickly as possible challenged his discipline and his need to remain motionless and watchful.

That had never been a challenge before, and it baffled him. Dominic had drummed it into his head that a good agent never let emotion throw him off his course. And when civilians were involved, the agent must think of them as little more than an inanimate package. Lady Vivien was surely a package, but how could he begin to think of her as inanimate when she was the most tempting bundle of femininity he'd come across in a long time? No wonder he avoided women like her. The blasted things played havoc with a man's good sense. Aden relished a good tumble as much as the next man, but he kept his nocturnal adventures confined to the demimonde, and only to those few women whose discretion he entirely trusted.

Ranger's ears were still pricked forward, but he evinced no other sign of alarm. After another moment of listening, Aden nudged the horse forward. Every sound out there in the darkness belonged, he felt certain. But he reminded himself that he'd been equally certain in France, and he'd been disastrously wrong.

"Is someone following us?" Lady Vivien asked in a small voice.

Again, anger clawed through him that she could be reduced to a bundle of nerves by a single sound. He tucked her against his chest, murmuring quietly in her ear, "It's all right, sweetheart. It was only an animal in the underbrush."

Immediately, her muscles stiffened. She slowly eased herself forward, clutching his forearm to keep steady.

Christ. Had he really just called her sweetheart? What the hell was wrong with him? His control was slipping. No, in fact his control, for which he was justly famous in the Intelligence Service, had gone straight to perdition. And if all it took was a woman to send it there—no matter *how* delectable the woman—he either needed a long rest or some punishing rounds in the practice ring with his fellow agents. The sooner he got Lady Vivien back to London and out of his arms, the better.

For both their sakes.

Sweetheart? The impact of that little word shot through Vivien like a cannonball.

The only man who'd ever used that endearment had been Papa when he was ruffling her hair after she'd shown him one of her childish drawings, or when he was sending her off to look after her brother, Kit. But St. George had just called her that, and she had the distinct impression that what he felt for her was far from paternal. It wasn't merely the way he'd looked at her during that moment in the tunnels when she had almost lost her nerve, or the way he carefully cradled her body on top of his massive horse. No, she might be gently bred and a virgin, but she was far from naïve. On top of the endearment that now hung in the air between them, the bulge poking into her backside was ample proof St. George most decidedly thought of her in a way that left her thoroughly shaken.

Vivien stared ahead into the darkness, clutching the horse's silky mane and trying her best to ignore the brawny thighs that surrounded her and the muscled arm wrapped around her waist. Not that she was frightened of him, precisely, since she was confident St. George had no intention of acting on his . . . impulses. After all, he was related to the late Lord Thornbury, one of the most rigidly correct peers in the *ton*.

Still, it was hard to ignore her rescuer's obvious physical reaction. Idiot that she was, she couldn't help wondering if it meant something about *her*. Probably not, since she understood most men had little control over their baser impulses. That was the reason Mamma constantly lectured her about appropriate conduct, except, of course, when Vivien pitted her skill and knowledge against the most hardened rakes to win the money that kept the bill collectors at bay. Mamma never lectured her about *that*.

Kit, however, had explained all about men's animal impulses years ago when she was seventeen. Vivien had come across a rather alarming book tucked away on a top shelf in her father's library. She had no business looking up there, but once having seen the outrageous illustrations in the book she'd been too horrified and intrigued to let the matter drop.

And the only person she could question was Kit. Cyrus would have smacked her or run tattling to their father, but Kit was never shocked. He'd said men couldn't help the way their bodies reacted to women, and that a lady was best served by ignoring it. Only if she found herself in tricky circumstances that forced her to defend herself did a lady take action. Kit had recommended whacking a pencil or even a stout twig sharply down on the offending appendage. He claimed that to be an extremely effective deterrent to over-enthusiastic behavior.

Vivien had spent much of the last twenty-four hours vowing to never leave the house again without a stout pencil in her reticule.

Her rescuer's deep voice interrupted her ruminations. "Forgive my impertinence, but I must ask you a rather painful question." He hesitated a moment before continuing. "And please know that I ask this question because I must."

Vivien blinked. She heard the reluctance in St. George's voice and wondered if he was embarrassed by his rather forward behavior. Perhaps he wanted to make his apologies, poor man. "Mr. St. George, you may ask me anything you like. I will try my best to assist you in any way possible."

His hand tightened briefly around her waist. "Very well. Did any of the men who abducted you visit indignities upon your person?" he asked in a tight voice.

Confused, she twisted around to look at him. His features seemed carved from the hardest of stone, and his eyes were but shadows in the night. A muscle in his jaw ticked once, then once again.

"Surely the very act of kidnapping is an indignity, is it not?" she asked. "What exactly do you . . . oh!" She jerked back around, too embarrassed to face him. Humiliation sent blood rushing to her cheeks.

He wanted to know if she'd been raped.

She'd spent hours living with that fear, and hoped she would never have to think on it again. But his serious manner and the entire way he asked the question implied that her answer was of significant import to him.

Vivien swallowed against the sensation of ants crawling up her neck. "No, sir. I was not r . . . raped." She stumbled over the word, her throat closing around it. A moment later, she sensed a slight easing in the body that enveloped her.

"I am indeed happy to hear that, my lady, and I apologize for the discomfort the question caused you. That was not my intent."

Vivien nodded cautiously. "What was your intent, if I may ask?"

He paused. She got the impression he was weighing his answer carefully.

"I've not allowed you a moment's pause since we escaped the caves," he replied. "I needed to assess your degree of injury."

She frowned. What odd phrasing. "I have a notion you're not being completely truthful with me, Mr. St. George. What, exactly, worries you?"

He exhaled a quick puff of breath. Not a laugh, really, but something close to it. "Why Lady Vivien, what in the world could we possibly have to worry about?"

She couldn't help starching up. "As happy as I am to serve as a source of amusement to you, sir, I would appreciate an answer to my question."

He pulled her an inch closer. His mouth skimmed the crown of her head, and she shivered again, swearing he'd just brushed his lips against her hair. But that couldn't be right. Perhaps he was simply adjusting his seat, which would not be unlikely given the size of his—

Don't think about that.

"Forgive me," he said, all trace of amusement now absent from his voice. "Thus far we've been extremely fortunate to escape without raising the alarm. With a little luck, we'll reach my carriage and be on the road back to London before your abductors track us down. But if something should occur—"

She must have made some kind of noise, because he gave her a reassuring squeeze.

"—if something should occur," he carried on in a calm voice, "I need to know what more you can tolerate. You've been through a grave ordeal already, after all."

Vivien's throat grew tight once more, but this time with gratitude. It had been so long since anyone, especially a man, had worried about her. That this stranger's brave kindness should affect her so deeply surely said something about the quality of her relationships, and not in a way that could mean anything good.

"I'm quite well, sir," she managed to reply. "Whatever is required of me to complete our escape, I will gladly do it."

"I have no doubt of it, my lady," he said.

The approval in his voice brought warmth flooding to her limbs and her heart lifted. On the heels of those lovely sensations, however, came caution. St. George had made it clear they were still in peril and more might be asked of her.

A quiet voice in her mind issued an additional warning, too. If she wasn't careful, she was in danger of elevating her rescuer to some exalted, almost godlike status. That would be a mistake. He was clearly composed of flesh and blood and could be injured or shot, even killed, as easily as she could. And there hadn't yet been a man she could depend on since her father died, not even her beloved Kit. As much as she loved her little brother, he had a tendency to make life both complicated and difficult, and to fail her when she needed him most. As for Cyrus, her elder brother, the less said the better.

No, St. George had taken her this far, and she had no doubt he would do his best to see them safely the rest of the way home. True, he was formidable, resourceful, and handsome—not that handsome figured into the equation, of course—but she'd learned long ago not to put all her eggs in one basket. It was best to have some kind of plan to fall back upon, in case something bad did happen to them . . . to him.

She drew in a shaky breath, trying to think. But after pondering a few moments, she decided that more information was required to formulate a workable plan. She had questions, and perhaps St. George had some of the answers.

"Mr. St. George," she began, "do you have any idea who—"

"Hush," he murmured against her hair. "We're nearly there, but let's make sure we arrive in one piece. We're not out of danger yet."

Vivien froze. She hadn't noticed, but the trees had thinned out. A moment later, they broke from the forest and the shadowy outlines of a hamlet came into view. Only a field and a few hedgerows stood between them and civilization. Two days ago she would have laughed to call such a place civilization, but right now the teacup town might be the most beautiful sight she had ever seen.

The big horse lifted its noble head, scenting the breeze. St. George tightened his grip on her and urged the animal into a canter.

Vivien clutched the arm of steel wrapped around her waist. Relief that they had cleared the woods rushed through her, but she still hadn't forgotten the question she'd been about to ask, and she had a vague, vexing sense that her savior had deliberately cut her off. She had no idea why but she had every intention of finding out.

If they didn't get killed or recaptured first.

Chapter Four

The canter across the fields had been free of danger—although Vivian's bottom had not taken kindly to the jouncing—and they rode to the edge of the tiny hamlet. There, beneath a massive oak, waited a travelling coach and four horses, almost hidden in the deep shadows cast by the arching branches of the mighty tree.

As St. George brought them to a gentle stop, a form detached itself from the obscured outlines of the carriage and moved forward to greet them. It resolved into the shape of a man, one of average height but with an impressive breadth of shoulder. He wore a slouchy hat pulled low over his brow and a greatcoat that swept down past the top of his boots. Drifting silently forward, he took the bridle of St. George's horse, holding the beast steady for their dismount.

Vivien was pondering how best to maintain her dignity while scrambling from her immodest perch when St. George tightened his hold on her, swept his leg over the animal's neck, and smoothly carried them both to the ground in a flowing drop. She gulped down a startled shriek—though Vivien made a point of *never* shrieking—as St. George set her carefully on her feet.

Her abused toes curled into the frigid dirt and she staggered. His big hands wrapped around her waist. "Have a care, my lady. We don't want you taking a nasty tumble."

Her flaring temper served as a welcome respite from the fear that constantly hovered on the edge of reason. She was cold, exhausted, still fighting remnants of the laudanum, and heartily sick of being afraid.

Shoving the pathetic remains of her once-stylish coiffure out of her eyes, she glared up into his handsome, impassive features. "Perhaps if you gave me warning before flinging me about like a sack of potatoes I wouldn't need to be so careful."

For a few moments he stared at her with the same bemused look as when she'd snapped at him after stubbing her toes. As suddenly as it had flared up, her irrational anger faded, and Vivien began to feel rather foolish.

After several seconds of uncomfortable silence, St. George's mouth twitched as he tried and failed to repress a smile. "Forgive me, Lady Vivien. It was not my intention to discomfort you."

In the dim glow of the carriage lamps, his eyes gleamed. He was laughing at her, when there was nothing even slightly amusing about their situation.

Not that she could entirely blame him. She was acting like a ninny and she knew it. Yes, she'd been kidnapped, mauled by thugs, and dumped in a smuggler's cave, but that hardly excused her demented behavior. Events were certainly looking up, but her rescue wasn't over. Until she had reached the safety of her bedroom in the family mansion in Berkeley Square, with the brawniest footman in her brother's household standing guard, Vivien couldn't afford to succumb to the vapors.

Besides, nothing excused her rudeness to the man who had saved her life.

She forced herself to meet his still-amused gaze. "Forgive

me, sir. I had no cause to scold you. I cannot think what led me to do so."

His smile was warm and unexpected, and so charming that Vivien's breath caught in her throat.

"No apology is necessary, my lady. It's a wonder you're still standing on your own two feet, given what you've been through."

"Yes," she replied faintly, staring up at him.

She couldn't move, couldn't formulate a sensible response. She had the oddest feeling she could spend the rest of the night staring at him and be quite content. If not for the fact that her feet had been transformed into blocks of ice and danger still threatened, Vivien just might have done so. She could only hope she'd have the opportunity to stare at St. George at some later date when someone wasn't trying to kill them.

"Beggin' your pardon, Cap'n," said a rumbling voice from behind her. "But time's a'wasting. Beacon's men are probably already on your trail."

Vivien had forgotten the fellow patiently holding the horse's bridle. Whipping around, she peered across the field at the woods, straining to see but barely able to make out the line of trees against the midnight sky.

St. George settled a comforting hand on the small of her back, gently steering her toward the coach.

"Probably," he answered. "Although they struck me as the most inept bunch of criminals one could imagine. Still, it won't do to underestimate them."

He sounded not the least bit worried. Annoyed, more than anything else, as if the men who pursued them were little more than an inconvenience.

As St. George nudged her toward the coach, the other man moved ahead to let down the steps. He gave her a deferential nod, following it up with a kindly smile. By his ease of movement and his general air of stealth, she'd thought him to be a younger man. But in the light of the carriage lamps she could see his grizzled whiskers and the deep lines etched around his mouth. Despite the smile, he had a grim, hard cast to his features, as if life had thrown too many challenges in his path.

She gave him a tentative smile back, rather at a loss for words. A casual word of thanks and a nod, as if he were simply a footman escorting her on a round of errands, hardly seemed appropriate to the occasion.

An unexpected tremor wracked her body. The men who'd kidnapped her *were* dangerous, no matter what St. George might think. She'd sensed it in their handling of her, had seen it in their cold, lustful gazes. They would have raped her if they could, and killed her without a second thought. Only the threat of reprisals from the man who'd ordered her kidnapping had held them back. Of that, Vivien was certain.

As if he sensed her growing anxiety, St. George gave her back a slow, reassuring stroke. Sensation rippled up her spine and heat flowed from his gloved hand into her rigid muscles.

"My lady, I'd like you to meet Tom, my batman." St. George said. His calm tone wrapped around her like the warmest of cashmere shawls, settling her flustered pulses. "Neither of us will let anyone hurt you."

Tom touched the brim of his hat. "That's right, my lady. You'll be home and safe and sound before you know it. The cap'n and I will see to that."

Blinking back a sudden sting of gratful tears, Vivien hesitantly touched Tom's sleeve. "Thank you for helping me, Tom. I'm so very grateful."

He made an embarrassed, clucking noise with his tongue. "No thanks necessary, my lady. What's the world coming to when a young lady can be snatched right from her carriage in the middle of Mayfair? It ain't right, and I told the cap'n so in no uncertain terms, too." He looked mightily aggrieved.

She let out a watery laugh. "It's a pleasure to meet you, even if the circumstances are less than ideal."

While she and Tom were exchanging bizarre pleasantries, St. George stepped away to have a quiet word with the coachman. Vivien could see only the outline of a large, greatcoated man holding the reins of the restive horses, but she could hear him speaking in a low, urgent voice to his master.

"Is something wrong?" she asked anxiously as St. George returned to her side.

"Not in the least. I was simply conferring with my coachman on the best place to change horses. We'll be on our way this very moment, Lady Vivien."

She breathed a sigh of relief and took his outstretched hand. As she put a foot on the step of the travelling chaise, the coachman uttered a curse. St. George cast a glance over his shoulder at the field behind them.

"Aye, that tears it, Cap'n," barked Tom. "They're onto us."

Vivien froze, awkwardly poised on the carriage step. She craned her neck to see around St. George's broad shoulders. Unfortunately, the thick, obscuring clouds chose that moment to inconveniently part, and a half moon cast its rays across the shorn field they had crossed only a few minutes ago. Four horsemen broke free from the trees and pounded toward them, crouched low over their animals and bearing down on her party with reckless speed.

St. George's hand tightened on hers. "Get into the carriage," he said in a voice of icy calm.

Her body gripped with a strange paralysis, Vivien could only stare at the horrifying vision of her captors closing in on them. One of them raised his arm, pointing right at them. The sound of a pistol shot rang out, and a second later the branch above her head cracked, raining bark down onto the roof of the coach.

St. George let out a low curse. He yanked his hand free

from her clutching fingers, seized her about the waist, and dumped her onto the floor of the carriage. She went down in a heap, tangled up in her frothing skirts and her velvet cloak.

"Stay down," he snapped.

Flailing, Vivien struggled to right herself, fighting the material twisting about her legs. She finally managed to get up on her knees, gaping up at St. George. Braced against the door frame, his body shielded her from the danger racing toward them with a thundering beat.

Heart thudding painfully in her chest, she peeked around his legs, straining to see something—anything. But the vision of her kidnappers bearing down on them made her want to scramble into the corner of the coach, cover her ears, close her eyes, and pray for deliverance with every shred of piety in her soul.

The villains were already halfway across the field and closing fast. Vivien made a silent, desperate vow that she would go to church every Sunday without fail, even if their pastor gave the most boring sermons in London. It would be a small price to pay if she could escape this unending nightmare.

Pistol fire exploded once more, dangerously close and spooking the horses. The carriage jerked forward, slamming her into the seat. St. George slipped one foot off the step as he struggled to keep his balance. The coachman yelled, obviously attempting to wrestle his horses under control, but the carriage continued to lurch as the animals tried to bolt.

Righting herself, Vivien wrapped her arms around St. George's knees and pulled back with all her might. He steadied himself, then snapped instructions to the coachman who finally managed to bring his charges under control. Tom, now mounted on St. George's horse, flashed by the door of the carriage and sailed over the low hedge separating the laneway from the field. He headed directly toward the advancing horsemen.

St. George spared her a quick glance. "Thank you for your assistance, Lady Vivien. You can let go now."

Stunned, she ignored him. She gazed in horror after Tom, who was charging in a foolhardy manner across the open field.

Vivien yanked on the hem of St. George's coat. "Why are you letting him do that? He'll be killed!"

"He'll be fine," he replied in a maddeningly calm voice. "Now, let go of me, Vivien. And this time you *will* stay down on the floor."

Startled by the use of her name, she did as he ordered. He produced a large pistol from somewhere inside his coat, took swift aim, and discharged it. At almost the same time another shot from somewhere just above her head roared out. The coachman, obviously as well armed as his master.

Vivien crouched on the floor, covering her ears against the deafening reports and silently commanding her stomach to stay put. The laudanum had already made her feel queasy, and finding herself in the middle of a pitched battle didn't help.

St. George gave a satisfied grunt. "Two down, two to go." He pounded his fist on the top of the carriage. "Spring them, John. It's time to go."

He pivoted as the carriage lurched forward, pulling himself in and slamming the door shut in one swift, economical motion. Somehow he managed to avoid stepping on her although his booted legs crowded her against the rise of the seat. He reached for her, lifting her up and depositing her gently on the opposite seat, where she collapsed against the cushions, a breathless wreck.

For a long moment they stared at each other. Vivien sucked in huge breaths, convinced her heart would race up her throat to plop out onto her lap any moment. Every part of her body shook and she knew she must look like a wild-eyed escapee from Bedlam. St. George, however, was practically lounging in his seat, watching her with an expression that managed to convey both an absence of alarm and a readiness to spring into action. Considering what they had just experienced, she found it disorienting.

He cocked his head, studying her. "Were you injured when I lifted you into the carriage, Lady Vivien? You look unsettled."

Her jaw sagged. Vivien began to wonder if the man was mentally unbalanced. Not at *all* a comforting thought under the circumstances.

"You didn't lift me into the carriage, Mr. St. George," she croaked. "You *threw* me into the carriage. I assure you, there is a decided difference."

His mouth twitched. "I apologize for that, but events dictated swift action."

Blast the man for looking like he wanted to laugh.

"As for why I am unsettled, I can think of a dozen reasons," she said. "However, at the moment, I am most concerned about your man, Tom. Why in heaven's name did you leave him behind to confront those villains? Surely he will be killed!"

As she voiced the awful words, her chest pulled tight and she could barely breathe. She pressed a fist to her mouth, trying to hold back tears. As grateful as she was to be free of the monsters who'd taken her, she couldn't bear the idea that Tom—or anyone else—might have died while saving her.

St. George stripped off his gloves and leaned forward, taking her cold fingers between his blessedly warm hands. That brought them only inches apart, and she stared helplessly into the dark depths of his raven eyes. She felt trapped in his gaze, exposed, but not in any way that frightened her. Rather, it commanded all her attention so that no fear and no other emotion could be allowed to intrude. She bit her lip, holding back a fierce need to melt across the narrow space between them, into his arms and strength.

He gently smoothed a finger across her pursed mouth. His

eyes narrowed, his glittering gaze catching on her lips and remaining there.

Vivian jerked out of his hold, unnerved by the intimate touch. A prickling flush crept up her neck, stinging her skin.

St. George jerked a bit too, looking startled. Frowning, he sat back.

"Forgive me," he said in a tight voice. "You've been through a wrenching ordeal, and I've not been as careful with you as I should have been. As for Tom, you needn't worry. I shot one man and my coachman managed to wing another, knocking him off his horse. Tom will handle the other two."

She blinked at him, her heart still thrumming with the intensity of their silent exchange, but she decided to ignore that for now. Best to keep her attention on present circumstances. "I'm fine," she said. "But that leaves two men against Tom. Those are hardly even odds."

"In Tom's case, those are *very* good odds."

She eyed him doubtfully. She wanted to trust him, but after the last awful hours trust seemed very hard to come by.

"But what if one of them gets past him." A horrible thought struck her. "What if there are more? What if they come after us?"

In truth, she had no idea how many men had been involved in her kidnapping. But when they'd carried her into that cave, she'd gained the distinct impression there were at least half a dozen, if not more. What if they were in pursuit this very moment?

Despite her best efforts to remain calm, her heart began to race again. She swallowed the sensation that her stomach was crawling up into her throat. The feeble light of the single carriage lamp was hardly enough to push back the threatening night, and dark spots began to swarm across her vision.

"Lady Vivien, look at me." St. George's level voice slashed through her panic. She forced herself to focus on him. His black gaze captured hers again, although this time he maintained a respectable distance between them.

"Yes?" She winced, hating the quaver in her voice. She cleared her throat and straightened her spine, determined to bring her wayward emotions under control. Surely they weren't out of danger, even though the carriage had slowed to a steady trot from the initial mad dash of their escape. Logically, she understood the road would be treacherous at night, but every fiber of her being shrieked for them to hurry.

"I promise you, my lady, you are safe. I will not let anything happen to you."

She pondered his statement for a few moments. "I thank you, sir. And I'm sure you *think* so, but I will not feel out of harm's way until I have arrived home safely."

He crossed his arms across his brawny chest, frowning at her. For the first time, she noticed the hollows under his cheekbones and the drawn look around his eyes, as if he'd not slept well for quite some time.

"I gave you my word," he said. "Is that not enough?"

She almost raised her brows at his easy, masculine arrogance. "I'm sure it is, but you see . . ." she trailed off, not wanting to offend him. After all, the man *had* rescued her. Still . . .

"What?"

She grimaced. "What if there were more of them in pursuit? What if they got past Tom?"

He let out a weary sigh. Shifting in his seat, he drew back the curtain over the window and let down the glass. After a quick glance behind them, he called forward to the coachman.

"Any sign of trouble, John?"

The coachman's reply, muffled by the sound of horses' hooves and creaking wheels, drifted back, too indistinct to catch. But it satisfied St. George for he pulled his head inside, pushed up the window, and settled back in his seat. He extended his long legs, his boots pushing up against her skirts, his body seeming to take up every spare inch of space. He lifted one eyebrow, giving her a self-satisfied, challenging stare. Clearly, this was a man little used to being questioned and, she suspected, little used to failure. If he said he would do something, Vivien would bet one hundred guineas on his success.

She took in the muscular physique and the strong, determined face with its hard, deep-set gaze. An almost overwhelming sense of power emanated from him—carefully leashed, she thought, but still barely disguised by his relaxed pose. She also noted his plain but clearly expensive clothing and the well-made boots that encased his muscled calves. Then she glanced around the dimly lit interior of the coach, finally registering its details. The fixtures were handsome, highly polished brass, the wood framework richly dark and fine-grained, and the benches and cushions were covered in plush black velvet. Everything she saw spoke of wealth and power, and of a quiet confidence—one that had no desire or need to draw notice.

She snapped her attention back to the man sitting across from her, still and watchful and entirely in command. Vivien realized something then that her terror had not yet allowed her to fully grasp. From the moment he had walked into her dreary cell, St. George had controlled events with a calm yet lethal intent that swept everything before it.

Including her.

She froze, barely breathing as she met his gaze. He studied her, his eyes as dark, cold, and glittering as a winter's eve. She prised open her reluctant lips.

"Mr. St. George, who *are* you?"

Chapter Five

Given the look on Lady Vivien's face, Aden knew her question was not rhetorical. She stared at him, her blue eyes wide, her pretty mouth pursed with anxiety and doubt.

Doubt about him. He'd never thought of himself in heroic terms, but given the night's events he would have thought her ladyship would have been a tad more grateful. Such was obviously not the case.

When he didn't immediately answer, she shifted, trying to tuck her pale little feet under her mantle and away from his boots.

Her naked feet, the same feet that had been exposed to the elements for the last hour.

Idiot. If he didn't get her warm, she'd likely freeze to death before he returned her to the arms of her not-so-loving family.

He reached under the seat and pulled out a woolen blanket, then moved across to sit beside her. A little gasp escaped her and she shrank farther into her corner. Aden frowned. Her behavior made no sense. He expected some degree of skittishness, but her reaction was more than that.

"There's no need to be alarmed, my lady," he soothed. "If I don't get you warmed up, Sir Dominic will have my head on a platter as will your mamma, I expect."

Mentioning Dominic and her mother did the trick. Her shoulders, which had travelled up around her ears, dropped, and she gave him a tentative smile. He draped the blanket over her, tucking it around her waist. He hesitated a moment, but then common sense overcame social prohibitions. He bent forward, brushed aside the blanket, and grasped her ankles.

She gasped, trying to jerk away from him. "Sir, what are you doing?"

"Your feet are frozen," he said, grasping at his fraying patience. She needed his care, but it had become manifestly clear the lady had a strong will and an equally strong need to remain in control of her circumstances. He could respect that and would, at a more convenient time. Right now, she had to stop questioning him and start obeying.

Peering down at her feet, she wriggled her toes against his palms. She frowned. "I can't feel them at all."

"Exactly. If we don't get them warm, you might lose one or two toes to frostbite."

She squeaked with dismay. It was a funny, high-pitched little sound, and for some reason he found it adorable.

His brain stuttered. *Adorable?* When the hell did he start using a word like that?

"Turn sideways, my lady," he said in a brusque voice, shaking off the odd impulse to cuddle her.

She cast him an uncertain look but then complied, shifting along the padded bench. He drew her feet into his lap and settled the blanket over their bodies. The cold didn't bother him but it made sense to share body heat, particularly since it would be another hour before reaching the inn where they would change horses. While the ostlers took care of that, he'd procure heated bricks and something hot for her to drink.

He reached under the blanket to gently wrap his hands around her feet. *Blast.* He'd been right to be concerned. They felt like little blocks of ice under his fingers.

She jumped a bit, then settled. Shyly, she pushed back a bedraggled lock of hair and gave him a tentative smile. "If I could survive this incident with all limbs intact, I would be very grateful. I don't know what Mamma would say if I came home without my toes." She gave a little snort. "Actually, I do. She would find that more horrifying than anything else."

He studied her face in the flickering light of the carriage lamps. Her bow-shaped mouth had flattened into a cynical line. *Interesting.*

And disturbing. One so young and lovely should have no call to wear an expression like that. But from the little Dominic had told him about her family, Aden wasn't completely surprised.

"And you'd have the devil of a time finding dancing slippers to fit," he said as he began to carefully knead her feet. "You'd have to stuff the toes with rags to keep the slippers from falling off."

She snickered, and the muscles in the back of his neck loosened. Why the hell he should care about her relationship with her family was a mystery. In his experience, families were more trouble than they were worth. The only relevant question about Lady Vivian's mother and brothers was whether they'd had anything to do with her abduction. Given the fact that her older brother, Lord Blake, had flat-out refused to pay any kind of ransom—even before one had been demanded—certainly put him in a category of suspicion.

Glancing up, he was pleased to see she had finally relaxed, snuggling into her corner and closing her eyes. Much of the tension had drained from her face, although her delicate features were still devoid of color and she carried bruise-like smudges under her eyes. Those should quickly fade once she had food and proper rest.

Allowing a rare feeling of satisfaction to slip through him—a genuine sense that his actions tonight *had* made a difference—Aden concentrated on massaging her feet. At some point, he needed to question her and extract as much information about her kidnappers as she could recall. And he needed to know why *she* thought she'd been abducted. Lady Vivien was clearly an intelligent woman, more so than the average flighty *ton* female. She might very well have observed something—even unconsciously—that would help narrow his search for the villain who'd planned this.

For now, though, he would let her rest.

And he would allow himself the oddly pleasing task of taking care of her. As he rubbed her feet, stroking warmth and life back into them, his senses opened to her. Her feet were slender and high-arched, delicate like the rest of her, with skin like living silk under his touch. Carefully, he stroked a bit higher, moving over her ankles. He glanced up, checking for her reaction, but she was quiet and still. Slowly, he inched farther up to her calves. The soft skin chilled his fingertips, and he almost convinced himself that he touched her only to bring the warmth back to her limbs.

Liar.

It had been months since he'd been with a woman—too long, given how simply touching her ankles primed him for more. The last woman he'd taken had been a pampered beauty, a plump, sophisticated confection he'd thoroughly enjoyed. Compared to her, Lady Vivien was too slender, bordering on unfashionably thin. But she had gentle curves and a supple strength to her body that he found disturbingly attractive.

Aden frowned. Disturbing was unacceptable. Women offered a respite and a release, an interlude of charming companionship. Nothing more. Not by preference, but by necessity. His work dictated he suspend that part of his life, perhaps forever. Emotional entanglements always complicated an agent's life. Hell, they complicated life, period, and since he'd found out the dirty secret of his birth, he'd done everything he could to separate himself from the overwrought passions that too often came with close relationships.

Of course, his own family had been only too willing to assist him in establishing that distance. But there was something about Lady Vivien that tested the high barriers he'd wrought around his emotions. At this point, it was merely a light tapping on the wall, but it—

"You haven't answered my question, Mr. St. George."

He jerked, coming back to himself. Damn, stroking her like that, like she was a sleepy, purring cat, had tipped him into a mental lull. He'd practically forgotten they'd just escaped one of the most notorious gangs in the West End. Not that he had any doubts Tom had eliminated their two remaining pursuers, but Aden had played the fool to let his guard so thoroughly drop.

The fact that he'd done so—despite the incident in France only a few weeks ago—told him just how dangerous a distraction Lady Vivien posed. Little wonder she'd garnered the reputation as one of the most fascinating women—and gamesters—in the *ton*. Yes, she was lovely and intelligent, but that didn't explain it. Still, he'd have to spend more time with her to decipher that puzzle, and he had no intention of doing so. He couldn't afford to like her, for either of their sakes.

Briskly, he wrapped her feet into the folds of the blanket. When he finally met her gaze, she looked heavy-lidded and sated, and some of the color had returned to her cheeks. She looked like she'd just come from a man's bed after a night of thorough shagging.

Christ Almighty.

He lifted her legs and shifted off the seat, tucking the blanket around her limbs. Moving to the opposite bench, he pulled his coat around him. Now she looked puzzled, her luscious lower lip thrust out in a little pout that begged for a response. That did nothing for his self-control, but it certainly had a marked effect on his burgeoning erection.

He forced himself to give her an impassive stare. "What question would that be, my lady?"

When she rolled her eyes he had to repress a smile. He hadn't forgotten her question and she knew it.

"Who *are* you?" she repeated with a decisive tilt of her chin. Her tone brooked no attempt at evasion.

He gave her a lazy smile. "As I recall, we did exchange introductions. I am Aden St. George, at your service."

Now her lovely eyes narrowed with irritation. "Yes, of the Thornbury St. Georges. But that tells me next to nothing. You obviously know a fair amount about me—from Sir Dominic, I assume. But I still know very little about you."

He shrugged, holding his silence. After all, there was very little he could tell her.

A frown creased her brow and she glanced toward the window of the coach. And just like that, damned if she didn't begin to look nervous again, her gaze flickering back to him and then once more to the window.

Mentally, he sighed. The less she knew about him the better, but he didn't want her stewing all the way back to London. The last thing he wanted was for her to fret herself into a state of hysteria.

Not that she hadn't conducted herself with a great deal of aplomb so far. In fact, when he'd almost fallen off the step of the coach, she'd had the presence of mind to grab onto him. But now she had nothing to do but think, and worry over her abduction like a kitten with a toy. She had no control over events—even over her own person. She'd been mauled and terrified, and had lived for hours with the threat of rape. Aden had more than a passing acquaintance with helplessness, and if answering a few questions restored a measure of her dignity then he would do what he could.

Within limits, of course.

"What is it you wish to know, my lady?"

"Are you in the military? Tom called you *captain*, after all." She waved a vague hand. "And other things, too. Few men of the *ton* would be comfortable sneaking about damp tunnels and subduing dangerous criminals." She frowned. "In fact, that sounds more like—"

He cut her off. "Yes, I'm with the Royal Horse Guards." Partly true, since he'd served for six months in The Blues when he'd finished university. But it hadn't taken Dominic long to recruit him into the Service. His "commission" with the Guards was nothing more than a convenient cover, used only when necessary.

She raised her eyebrows. "Then why aren't you with your regiment?"

"I'm on leave, temporarily attached to the Home Office."

"So that's how you know Sir Dominic."

He gave her a slight smile, not answering. To the world at large, Dominic worked for the Home Office. Only a select few knew he was one of the most powerful spymasters in England, with extensive connections in both the highest and lowest circles of English society. On any given day Dominic could be whispering in the ear of the Duke of York or enjoying a pint of heavy wet with some of the more disreputable denizens of Whitechapel. He was equally at home in both settings, which made him invaluable to the Crown.

Lady Vivien chewed on her plump lower lip, sending a powerful flash of heat to his groin. He wished like hell she'd stop doing that.

"Why did Sir Dominic send you to my rescue, instead of alerting Bow Street and hiring Runners?"

"My lady, we're trying to stifle gossip, not generate it."

She grimaced. "Of course. How foolish of me. I don't know why that didn't occur to me before."

"You're doing very well, all things considered."

The carriage bumped through a rut, jolting her slight figure and sending the blanket sliding off her shoulders. Her mantle gaped open over her throat and chest, showing off the pale perfection of her skin. His hand itched to stroke her. Having already experienced the feel of that skin with his naked hand, he knew how soft she would be.

Staring at him with a thoughtful air, Vivien readjusted the blanket around her shoulders, shrouding herself with the heavy fabric. Aden told himself that was a good thing.

"How did Sir Dominic know where to find me?"

He forced back a stab of impatience. Normally, he was on the giving and not the receiving end of an interrogation. But he couldn't blame her curiosity.

"Let's just say that Sir Dominic has friends in low places. When your mother came to him with the news of your abduction, he made discreet enquiries. It didn't take long for information to filter back. Kidnapping gently born ladies off the street is not a regular occurrence."

"I should hope kidnapping any kind of woman off the streets is not a regular occurrence," she huffed.

He had to repress a smile at her tone. "I share your hope, my lady."

She eyed him narrowly, as if she sensed he found her amusing. He didn't, but he did find her . . . damn, the word that kept springing to mind was *adorable*.

"Of course you do." Her voice was dry as toast, which also made him want to laugh. He could well imagine her ability to hold her own with the sharp-toothed vipers of the *ton*. It would appear Lady Vivien did not back down from anyone.

"Why you?" she asked, abruptly changing course.

He raised his eyebrows, feigning ignorance. She was beginning to sail a bit too close to the wind.

She flapped a hand under the blanket. "I understand why Sir Dominic would not use Runners, but why did he not come himself, with more men? Surely he would wish to apprehend the villains responsible for this outrage."

"Which was exactly *why* he didn't show up in force. It would have tipped his hand to the man who arranged for your abduction. We still don't know his identity, but *he* will also not know who rescued you, either."

She stilled, staring at him with dawning apprehension. He must make it clear to her that she was not yet safe.

"I know it's an unpleasant thought," he said gently. "But we must discover who was behind this plot and apprehend him. You will not be safe until we do."

Her eyes grew wide and he could swear her pupils dilated with a stunning realization. What had she just remembered?

"Lady Vivien?" he prompted.

Her sapphire gaze refocused and she gave a slight shake of the head. The movement was tiny, but he sensed a barrier go up between them. She was hiding something from him, obviously something he needed to know.

"Why did Sir Dominic send you, a soldier, to find me?" She ran a swift, assessing gaze over his face and body. It swept over him, almost as real as the heated touch of her hand.

"Officers are not an unknown commodity in the *ton*," she added. "You're not like any soldier I've ever met."

Lady Vivien possessed a sharp sense of discernment. There were capable men amongst the aristocratic corps of officers, but she was correct. Very few were like him. She'd surprised him once again, and Aden had to admit he was beginning to enjoy playing this game with her.

He affected an incredulous smile. "Why, Lady Vivien, whatever do you mean?"

Her pretty mouth thinned. Apparently, she wasn't enjoying this as much as he was. "As I've already mentioned, most officers I know would make a point of *not* skulking around in dirty tunnels and acting with so much stealth. They would consider it . . ."

"Common?" he intoned in a haughty tone.

His amusement vanished with her words. She was right. Most aristocrats would curl their lips at his profession. God knows his stepfather had. That Aden had left his career in the military to be a spy had been the final degradation as far as Lord Thornbury was concerned. After all these years, he shouldn't let it bother him, but it did. The pampered members of the *ton* would never know the risks and the filthy jobs he and his colleagues took on to keep them safe in their useless, spendthrift lives.

She seemed to consider the word. "Perhaps, but it's more than that. Many of them are simply so . . . pampered. They couldn't do what you did, especially with that man outside the tunnels. I think of my own brothers, and I cannot imagine them having the fortitude to take on such a desperate villain. In fact, Cyrus would faint dead-away if faced with so dire a necessity."

Lady Vivien was beginning to look pale again, and rather queasy herself at the reminder of her ordeal. Aden's flare of temper faded in the need to draw her mind away from that ugly scene.

He reached across the small space and found her hand under the blanket, giving it a reassuring squeeze. Startled, her eyes flew up to meet his, but then she gave him a tremor of a smile. A muscle constricted somewhere in the vicinity of his heart.

"I saw a good deal of fighting in the Peninsula," he said. "That experience allowed me to do what was necessary. I don't enjoy killing, but Sir Dominic and I promised your mother we would return you safely home. I simply did what was necessary."

She stared at him, her eyes big and round and vulnerable.

The fear was gone, and in its place was something that looked disturbingly like hero worship.

Damn. He hated that look. It always led to trouble. A good agent did his job because he had to do it. Glory and admiration didn't enter into it. If it did, that man was a fool and was in the wrong profession.

"I'm very glad you did," she whispered. "And I will never forget it."

He nodded, giving her hand what he hoped was a fatherly pat before drawing it away. A few seconds later, he felt the horses beginning to slow.

"Mr. St. George, how was it that you—"

"Forgive me, my lady. We're at the coaching inn. I must ask you to keep any further questions or comments to yourself. We'll only be stopping for a few minutes, but I'd prefer we not draw any more attention to ourselves than necessary."

She pressed her lips firmly shut, looking slightly put out. He knew she had more questions, but he was done answering. In fact, as soon as they got back on the road, he had every intention of subjecting her to a little interrogation of his own. He was loath to upset her, but every one of his instincts was telling him that Lady Vivien knew something about her kidnapping that she had chosen not to share with him.

He'd let her get away with that a few minutes ago, allowing her to distract him, but there would be no more distractions. Very soon, the lady would be telling him everything he wanted to know.

Chapter Six

Vivien stumbled over the brick paving of the inn's courtyard, heavy-footed with exhaustion. If not for St. George's firm grip on her arm, she would have pitched face-first onto the muddy stones. The clogs the innkeeper had found for her, excavated from some dusty cubbyhole, weren't helping much either. They were at least two sizes too big and crudely made.

Still, she was grateful to have properly if clumsily shod feet. Not having shoes had been one of the worst parts of her ordeal. Her bare feet had made her feel intensely vulnerable, unable to fend for herself or attempt any kind of escape.

"Do you want me to carry you, my lady?" St. George asked as she righted herself.

She shook her head, barely able to make out his stern features in the flickering light of the torches in the inn's courtyard. He returned his attention to their surroundings, his gaze sweeping the courtyard, looking for danger in every shadowed corner. In her addled state, he reminded her of the gigantic mastiff that used to roam the lands of her father's estate, guarding her and Kit with a fierce, steadfast loyalty. St. George seemed invested with similar qualities—quiet but with hackles raised, ready to attack at the first sign of trouble.

Of course, he was the furthest thing from a drooling hound she could imagine, but that didn't prevent a semi-hysterical giggle from bubbling past her lips.

St. George glanced down at her with a questioning, wary countenance.

"It's nothing," she managed, waving her hand. "I just thought of something very silly."

"Oh, indeed," he replied politely, looking even more mystified.

That struck her as funny, too, although this time she managed to hold back her inappropriate mirth. The poor man had enough problems to worry about without having to care for a woman who acted like a half-wit.

Vivien grasped the door frame of the coach, gathering the energy to pull herself in. Even that simple movement seemed beyond her as her weary limbs sought to drag her down. Without a word, St. George tucked one arm under her knees, the other behind her back, and lifted, carefully depositing her on the cushioned bench. His strength and stamina continued to astonish her. St. George had lugged her about for the better part of the night, killed one man, disabled another, effected her rescue with competence and skill, and still showed no signs of flagging.

She'd never met anyone like him.

And he unsettled her to a degree she'd never thought possible. He was so intensely *masculine*. Everything about him heightened her feminine awareness, and that wasn't something that happened very often. Well, almost never, if she were truthful. Vivien liked men. She liked looking at the handsome ones and talking to the intelligent ones. But they did little to spark her romantic sensibilities, and she'd always found that rather depressing. As her friends had married,

Vivien had wondered if something was wrong with her. She'd encountered many men over the years whom she'd quite liked, but she'd never known one whose bed she wanted to share. On the few occasions when a man had kissed her, she'd either found it only mildly enjoyable or downright unpleasant.

Tongues being thrust into one's mouth was the worst thing of all. When Prince Ivan had done that just a few weeks ago, she'd almost retched, pushing him away with all her might. Actually sleeping with a man was beyond her imagination, since there would be a great deal more involved in that activity than just thrusting tongues. The very idea made her go weak behind the knees, and not in a good way.

But St. George had crashed into her life and was changing all that. Given that she'd been manhandled by the most disgusting villains, it seemed a bizarre and certainly unexpected reaction. And yet, when he'd been massaging her feet, her mind had drifted into a voluptuous lull. In that state it had been quite easy to imagine kissing St. George. That notion had presented such an attractive image she hadn't even objected when his powerful hands slid over her ankles to massage her calves.

Ridiculous.

Proper conduct aside, it would be foolish beyond measure to grow attached to him. He was a soldier—or something rather more than that—and quite obviously avoided *ton* circles. After tonight, she doubted she would rarely see him again, if at all.

That being the case, it behooved her to focus on her problems and not on handsome rescuers. Now that her head had cleared, her thinking process had also. Vivien now had her suspicions about who had ordered her kidnapping and why, and it wouldn't do for *anyone* to discover the real culprit.

St. George rearranged the blanket around her and settled onto the opposite seat as the carriage rattled out of the courtyard and onto the road. Vivien sighed with relief. As grateful as she was for the stop—it had been a *very* long time since a visit to the necessary—she couldn't wait to get back to London. The sooner she could put this entire experience behind her, the better.

Except, of course, that she couldn't. Not until she eliminated the threat to herself and to her family.

St. George stirred across from her. "I wish you could have been allowed more time for a proper meal, but I couldn't take the risk."

An odd little ache pulled tight in her chest. Vivien wasn't used to anyone taking care of her, besides her brother's servants, that is. St. George, however, went out of his way to attend to her comfort despite the trying circumstances. And when he looked at her as he did now, his handsome face somber with concern, she felt almost . . . cherished.

"Actually, being able to stretch my legs and have a bit to eat felt like heaven," she confessed. In her famished state, the hastily assembled plate of bread and cheese and the pot of tea had tasted like ambrosia.

St. George nodded, his eyes fixed on her face. He studied her with a steady intensity, as if he wanted something. That look made her wary and embarrassed—wary because of the questions she sensed hovering on his tongue, and embarrassed because she looked a positive wreck. That she should worry about her appearance told her something, and it was something she'd better stop thinking about immediately.

"My lady," he finally said, "I must ask you a few questions while your memory of events is fresh."

Blast.

His face remained impassive, his demeanor calm and watchful. She, on the other hand, was vibrating with nerves, and had to resist the impulse to fidget. Answering what were likely to be very intrusive questions—especially when her defenses were down—was dangerous, indeed.

"You're very tired, I know," he said gently. "But it's necessary. You must trust that I wouldn't ask if that wasn't so."

Mentally, she sighed. Might as well get it over with. If he strayed too close to what she suspected was the truth, she could always burst into tears and hope that put him off. Not that Vivien found it easy to turn on the waterworks, but she thought she might be able to make a credible job of it tonight, and without much prompting.

"Of course, sir. I am entirely at your disposal," she said in a hollow voice.

His brows slanted up in an incredulous lift, and she heaved another mental sigh. She'd always been adept at hiding her emotions—a lesson learned at the card table—but St. George had a way of seeing past that. She didn't like it one bit.

"Very well. Let's begin with the abduction itself."

He led her through the sequence of events. Although he encouraged her to describe everything in as much detail as she could recall, he treated her gently, never pushing her too far and always sensing the levels of her anxiety. It struck her once again that he was very good at what he did, and she found it hard to believe that the average army officer was anything like Aden St. George.

Eventually, they reached her rescue itself. Nothing she'd recalled so far would lead St. George in any way back to her family or what she suspected were the true reasons for her abduction.

He gave her an encouraging smile. "You've done very well, my lady. I have only a few more questions and then you can rest for the remainder of our journey."

She nodded, giving him permission to continue. Not that he needed it.

"From what I've been told, you have many admirers and suitors in the *ton*."

Vivien fancied she heard a note of disapproval in his voice.

Heat prickled at the back of her neck, and she couldn't help feeling defensive. "I'm sure you exaggerate, sir. I'm no more or less admired than dozens of other women in our circles."

Since her coming-out, she'd grown used to hearing herself described as one of the most eligible young ladies in society. But at age twenty-four she was perilously close to sitting firmly on the shelf. Add to that her decidedly unfeminine prowess at the card tables and the rumors that dogged her family, and Vivien found it safe to say that her star had long since started to fade.

"I commend your modesty, Lady Vivien, but it's neither necessary nor helpful. I need truth from you, not missish protestations we both know aren't true."

She flinched at the dry, almost scornful note in his voice. It didn't make sense given his careful consideration of her up to this point. But he'd obviously heard something about her that had given him a bad impression, and that stung her more than it should.

Crossing her arms over her chest, she stared back at him. "What do you wish to know, sir?" she said in a clipped tone.

He held her gaze, his hard-cut jaw darkened by masculine stubble that made him look dangerous and rather wild. The look suited him, she was sorry to say.

"Who are your most persistent suitors?" he asked. "Are there any whose conduct unsettles you, or gives you pause for any reason?"

She was about to return an automatic denial when she paused. The suspicions that had floated through her mind while still a captive resurfaced. She'd discarded them almost immediately, simply because they didn't make any sense.

St. George leaned forward, coming to alert. Vivien could practically sense the change in the atmosphere, and it made her shiver.

"What is it?" he asked.

"It's nothing. I thought perhaps—"

"Someone made you nervous," he said in a milder voice. "Who was it?"

This time she did fidget with the ruffle on her mantle. "It's nothing, really. In fact, it would be ridiculous to suspect him of anything."

"I understand, but it's necessary that you tell me. For your own safety," he finished on a warning note.

He was obviously trying to scare her into revealing something useful. Blast him, it just might work.

Unexpectedly, he smiled. She had to admit it was a *very* charming smile.

"Yes, I am trying to scare you, my lady. Just a little. I don't enjoy doing so, in case you were wondering."

She nervously licked her lips, once more discomposed by his ability to see past her defenses. Vivien had spent years perfecting an impervious façade, but he took it apart with uncanny ease. Nor did it help her equanimity to see his gaze go suddenly dark and smoky, drifting down to study her mouth.

"Yes, well, I'm sure," she said, struggling to regain her composure. Easier said than done, since her temples were starting to pound from exhaustion and her ears were ringing.

"You can trust me, you know." His warm, easy tone wrapped around her like a comfy blanket. "I will only share what you tell me with Sir Dominic." A slight smile lifted the corners of his hard, handsome mouth. "I will not break the seal of the confessional, I promise."

She blushed. He'd risked his life for her. Of *course* she trusted him.

Up to a point.

"Very well. I did think of someone, but it's too ridiculous. He's very rich and very important, and I can't imagine him behaving in so outrageous a fashion."

"You'd be surprised at the acts carried out by rich, important men."

His cynical tone sounded a warning bell in her weary brain.

"You're right of course, Mr. St. George," she replied cautiously.

He again flashed that unexpected grin. "There's no need to keep calling me *Mister* St. George will do nicely. Now, why don't you tell me who ruffled your nerves?"

She grimaced. "I thought at first that Prince Ivan Khovansky might have been behind my abduction. But of course that's ridiculous." She sat back, waiting for him to scoff at her suspicions.

He didn't. Instead, he sat back, stroking his beard-shadowed jaw.

"Really," she insisted, "it's ridiculous. He's a Russian prince, for heaven's sake. Besides, the Russian ambassador and his wife are his friends, and are seen with him everywhere."

In fact, it had been Countess Lieven who introduced them in the first place. The prince had begun courting Vivien immediately, much to her dismay, and it wasn't because he looked like a squat toad. She liked a handsome man as much as any girl, but it was his oily, arrogant demeanor and his aggressive pursuit that made her bristle. She'd turned him down three times already in the past six weeks, but the man wouldn't take no for an answer.

"What has he done to offend you?"

"Have you met Prince Ivan?"

"I know of him, but I've never met him."

"If you had, you'd know exactly what I'm talking about," she replied dryly.

He gave her a faint smile. "Tell me anyway."

"He's arrogant and extremely forward, and quite certain that any woman who is the object of his attentions should be bowing down before him with gratitude." It would be a frosty day in hell before she bowed to any man, much less Khovansky.

"Go on."

"He refuses to take no for an answer. In fact, he—" She stopped, too embarrassed and angry to recount the last episode when he'd backed her up behind a column at the DeLancey ball and forced his tongue halfway down her throat.

"I understand," he replied gently. "He's asked for your hand?"

"Three times, and each time I refused him in no uncertain terms."

"And what does your brother, Lord Blake, have to say about all this? Surely he cannot wish to see his sister the recipient of unwelcome advances."

She scowled. "He thinks I'm a fool for saying no."

That earned another lift of his eyebrows, and Vivien silently cursed. Too late, she realized their discussion touched too close to home.

She waved a dismissive hand. "Truthfully, I don't think Cyrus cares one way or the other about my suitors. I suppose he'd like to get me off his hands, but he doesn't favor the prince over any other man."

"And do you have many suitors?"

Vivien hunched her shoulders. Not only was this discussion veering into dangerous territory, it was downright mortifying. She had no desire to talk about her suitors with anyone, especially not St. George.

"No more than the usual," she said stiffly. "And lately, none of any note. Besides Prince Ivan, that is."

"And how does your—"

She cut him off. "It's ridiculous to think Prince Ivan might have a role in my abduction. I don't like the man, but he's a *prince* and a guest of the Crown. Princes don't go around acting the part of the villain, now do they?"

His lips parted in a smile that looked more like a snarl. "Have you met any of the king's sons, my lady?"

He had a point. King George's sons were an appalling group, which anyone with half a brain understood.

Vivien pondered that fact, then finally let out a sigh. It wasn't Khovansky—she'd stake her life on it. She had a fairly good idea who was behind her kidnapping, but she had no intention of sharing that bit of news with St. George or anyone else.

"Truly, my dear sir, I don't like Prince Ivan but nor do I think he had anything to do with my abduction. I wouldn't be at all surprised if he's already given up on me. In fact, I hadn't seen him for several days before I was attacked in Mayfair." She'd ended their last encounter by kicking him in the shins. The prince hadn't appreciated that move one bit.

St. George inclined his head. "I'll take your word for it. I do have a few more questions, though, about your brother, Lord Blake."

Vivien's heart skipped a few beats. "Please, no more. My head is spinning and I can barely stitch together a coherent sentence. You must forgive me, but I cannot answer any more questions tonight."

Her voice quavered, which she made no attempt to hide. In fact, she hoped she looked as frazzled as she felt.

His gaze was dark with suspicion, but finally he relented. "Very well." He brushed aside the window drape with one finger and studied the sky. "We should be reaching the outskirts of London by dawn's break, in about an hour. We can talk later."

Swallowing a sigh of relief, Vivien gave him a grateful smile as she settled back in her seat, closing her eyes and willing herself into a doze.

She'd managed to put him off for now but she'd have to be on her guard. The situation was much more appalling than St. George even suspected, and only she could fix it. Because it wasn't a Russian prince who'd been the catalyst for her abduction. No. The culprit was much, much closer to home.

Chapter Seven

The carriage turned into Upper Wimpole Street just as faint tendrils of light cut through the smoky darkness of the city. Aden stretched his cramped limbs, more than ready to see this night to a close. He'd been awake for over thirty hours and even he had his limits. But Lady Vivien's situation threatened to deny him much-needed rest. His brain restlessly searched for patterns and explanations that made sense, but there were none. The fact that the lady was withholding information only added to the mystery.

He didn't like mysteries. In his line of work, he'd grown used to them. But the best thing about any mystery was solving it, and the one he currently found himself embroiled in seemed far from reaching its conclusion.

As light filtered into the carriage, he studied the heart of the conundrum, curled up on the opposite seat. Once she'd fallen asleep, she'd fallen hard, barely stirring when he'd eased her down onto the bench and covered her with the blanket. Even when he'd smoothed her pale golden hair away from her face she hadn't moved. Her vulnerability touched him, as did the trust she obviously felt in his presence. Knowing now the strength of her character, he recognized that Lady Vivien would never have allowed herself to fall asleep if she didn't think he could see to her safety.

Too bad she didn't trust him enough to tell him the truth about what she knew. She clearly had suspicions as to the culprit behind her abduction, and equally clearly had no intention of sharing them. That probably meant what Aden had suspected all along. Namely, that her brother Lord Blake was involved. The reason was yet obscured, but Dominic would get to the bottom of it.

Cases involving families or friends always ended badly. Whenever emotions clouded judgment, as they were bound to do, mistakes were made. Aden hated those cases, and he had every intention of handing the whole damn thing over to Dominic. That included Lady Vivien, too.

The carriage jerked to a halt in front of Dominic's town house. Even then, Lady Vivien did not stir, although she drew in a shuddering breath and curled her hand up under her chin. She looked so young and innocent, her smooth cheeks flushed from sleep, her mouth soft and vulnerable. Something twisted in Aden's chest and he had to resist the impulse to go down on his knees beside her and kiss her awake.

His hand clenched into a fist with the effort to resist the demented impulse. Yes, it was definitely time to hand Lady Vivien over into Dominic's safekeeping.

Reaching for her shoulder, he gently shook her. "My lady, it's time to wake up."

Another one of those shuddering breaths and her eyelids fluttered open. She gazed at him with drowsy, sapphire-colored eyes and gave him a sleepy smile. For a second, a very long second, that smile robbed him of breath.

He shook it off. "We've arrived at Sir Dominic's town house, Lady Vivien." Deliberately, he looked out the window, thankful to break the unnerving connection between them.

She yawned and pushed herself upright. The blanket slid

down to her waist, revealing the white skin of her shoulders and gently curving breasts. As she stretched like a kitten, those pretty breasts plumped up over her bodice. With her tousled hair and heavy eyelids she looked like she'd just recovered from a good romp between the sheets.

His body approved of that look, reacting with inconvenient dispatch.

He repressed a frustrated sigh and reached across to re-arrange her mantle around her shoulders. Their gazes met and held. Her eyes widened and her pupils seemed to dilate as her cheeks flushed a brighter pink. Then she seemed to retreat, giving him a cool smile as she brushed his hands aside to tie the velvet tasselled cords of her mantle firmly shut.

Irrationally irritated that she was putting distance between them, he brusquely flipped up her hood and pulled it close around her face.

Startled, she frowned. "Are you quite finished with ar-ranging my clothing to your satisfaction, sir?" she asked in a frosty voice.

Aden stared at her with disbelief, biting back his instinctive response. He could think of many ways to rearrange her cloth-ing, but all of them involved removing them from her body.

A second later, she blushed scarlet as she realized the im-plication behind her words. A better man would ignore her flustered reaction. Clearly, he was not a better man.

"Satisfaction? Hardly," he drawled. "And as much as I enjoy a good debate on semantics, we need to get you inside."

She rolled her eyes and muttered something unflattering about men under her breath. Perversely, that lightened his mood. She had an uncanny knack for amusing him in the most bizarre circumstances, and Aden had to admit he'd miss that.

Signalling her to be quiet—which earned him another eye roll—he opened the door and let down the steps. He carefully scanned the street. No activity, no one watching.

The first carts would soon be rumbling along the streets, but for now Upper Wimpole Street still slept.

Aden lifted Lady Vivien to the pavement. She clutched at him, stumbling a bit in her damned oversized clogs, and he wrapped an arm around her waist to hold her steady. He steered her down the steps to the basement entrance while John Stevens set the horses to a brisk trot. A few moments later, the carriage disappeared around a corner and silence fell like a shroud.

Shielding her with his body, Aden tapped out the signal on the basement door. Only then did the latches pull back. He urged her across the threshold as he cast one last glance over his shoulder.

Nothing suspicious, he was certain of it. He shoved the door closed and slid the bolts. He leaned against the door and closed his eyes, letting some of the tension flow from his body.

He'd done it. He'd transported her safely home.

"Mr. St. George, are you unwell?"

He opened his eyes to meet her concerned gaze as she hovered just a few feet away. She was almost dead on her feet from fatigue and still she apparently worried about him. That touched him more than he cared to admit.

Dredging up a smile, he shook his head. "I'm fine, but let's get you upstairs where it's warm."

He glanced at Wilkinson, one of Dominic's servants, who stood quietly awaiting instructions.

"Is Sir Dominic awake?" Aden asked as he took Lady Vivien's arm and nudged her along the basement passage that ran the length of the house.

"He is, sir, as is Lady Thornbury. Sir Dominic sent Lady Blake home last night, but Lady Thornbury refused to leave until the young miss was returned safely home."

Aden cursed under his breath. Why the hell had his mother decided to hang about? Besides the fact that she would likely complicate matters, she would want something from him. She always did these days, although he couldn't figure out why. She'd spent a great many years doing her best to ignore him, but ever since his stepfather died she'd been relentlessly doing her best to interfere in his life.

"Thank God," exclaimed Lady Vivien. "I was terrified she and Mamma might have been injured in the abduction." She glanced up at Aden. "My mother could do nothing but scream, but Lady Thornbury fought back. I have the distinct impression she even broke somebody's nose."

Aden could well believe it since his mother had an iron will. The only person she'd never stood up to had been his bastard of a stepfather.

"No need to worry about her ladyship," Wilkinson said cheerfully, looking over his shoulder. "Lady Thornbury is as tough a nut as a body could ever be."

Aden smiled as Vivien stared up at Dominic's genial giant. Wilkinson was always a sight at the best of times—well over six feet tall and broad as a barn, with an old scar down the left side of his face, and a heavy, bristle-covered jaw. The man looked like something out of a nightmare, but had an incurable soft spot for children, puppies, or any innocent thing that stumbled into harm's way.

He was also the deadliest of assassins, one who could kill a man with his bare hands in ten different ways and not blink an eyelash.

"Ah, I'm glad to hear that, um . . ." Lady Vivien stuttered.

"Wilkinson, my lady," he said.

Wilkinson led them past the kitchen, occupied at this early hour only by Peter, the scullery boy. Even Peter could handle a pistol, and like all the servants he possessed one key attribute—fanatical loyalty to Dominic.

When they reached the steps leading up to the main house, Wilkinson stepped aside to let them pass. After starting Lady

Vivien up, Aden turned around. "I don't think anyone saw us. But make another check and have Peter stay on alert," he said quietly.

The big man nodded and slipped back down the passage.

Aden took the stairs two a time, catching up with Lady Vivien as she hesitated at the top.

"This way," he said, taking her hand.

They crossed the short entrance hall to a closed door. Aden tapped once and ushered her into Dominic's study. He placed his back against the door, standing guard, as she rushed across the room and threw herself into his mother's arms.

Not that Aden really had to stand guard. Not here in Dominic's inner sanctum. But it gave him a task and allowed him to maintain a safe distance from his mother.

"I'm so happy to see you safe," Vivien choked out as the older woman held her in a fierce embrace.

They clung together. His mother stroked Vivien's pale hair, holding her close with obvious affection. As much as he tried, Aden couldn't squash a flash of resentment. He couldn't remember the last time his mother had hugged him like that, or shown much concern. And yet, with Vivien, she did it easily.

Then again, Vivien wasn't the bastard child whose very existence had blighted the famous Lady Thornbury's life, particularly since that child was the result of an affair with the Prince of Wales, now England's Regent. Aden's mother had subsequently spent years trying to erase the damage caused by her reckless indiscretion, which seemed to include keeping her ill-gotten son at a polite distance in an attempt to regain her cuckolded husband's trust. The logical man in Aden couldn't blame her, but the boy inside the man obviously still did.

As for his relationship with his natural father, Aden had made a point of keeping the Prince Regent at a coolly polite distance for years, so he supposed he took after his mother, in that respect. But it was the only way the Thornbury household—his stepfather and half siblings included—had been able to maintain a united front against the scandal that had once rocked the family at its very foundations.

While the two women hugged, talking to each other in low, emotion-laden voices, Dominic unfolded his lanky frame from behind his desk and strolled over to greet Aden. One of Dominic's rare smiles lit up his usually impassive façade as he extended his hand.

"Well done, Aden," he said. "Lady Vivien seems to be in remarkably good shape, all things considered."

"Yes, we were fortunate in that respect."

His chief cocked an eyebrow. "Ah. Then she wasn't—"

"No, she was spared that degradation, thank God. They drugged her, but they obviously had instructions not to do her grievous harm. But she wasn't well treated, which tells me something."

Dominic frowned, the harsh angles of his face looking grimmer than usual. And since he almost always looked grim, that said something to Aden too.

"Was she able to tell you anything useful?" Dominic asked.

Aden started to answer but then glanced at Lady Vivien, still nestled in his mother's embrace. She had not cried once during her entire ordeal this night, but now she was sniffing like a heartbroken child, tears trickling down her face. What the devil had his mother said to upset her?

Dominic glanced over at the women, then back at Aden. "She's fine," he said. "It's just relief, now that she's safe." A mocking smile lifted the corners of his mouth. "Of course, you could always go over and give her a hug."

"With all due respect, sod off," Aden growled.

Dominic simply snorted in reply.

His chief could frequently be annoying as hell, but Aden was also irritated that he actually *did* want to hug Lady Vivien.

Fortunately, his mother prevented the need for him to act in so idiotic a fashion by murmuring something that brought a watery smile to the girl's face. She settled Lady Vivien onto the settee in front of the fireplace, before finally deigning to acknowledge his existence.

Aden braced himself against the rush of emotions that swept through him whenever he met his mother.

As always, reluctant admiration warred with bitterness. His mother stood barely five feet tall and was as slender as a reed, but she packed a formidable will in her petite frame. Few could stand against that will when she chose to exert it, and Aden remained convinced she could have exercised it to protect him from his stepfather's resentment—hatred, even, toward the child who was living proof that his wife had betrayed him, and with a prince, no less. Only once had his mother intervened, when Lord Thornbury had raised a hand to him when he was thirteen, striking Aden across the face. Then, she had stepped between them, telling her husband in a quietly lethal voice to never again lay a hand on her son.

Thornbury had turned on her with a snarl, but his mother had simply placed a restraining hand on her husband's chest and stared back at him. To Aden's everlasting amazement, the old bastard had retreated. Aden's mother subsequently never mentioned the incident, and although his stepfather didn't stint on the tongue-lashings, Thornbury never struck him again.

"Good morning, Aden," his mother said. "Why are you skulking by the door? Can you not give your mamma a proper greeting?" She finished with her most charming smile, clearly wishing to take the sting from her words.

Too bad it didn't work.

Not bothering to repress a sigh, he trod wearily across the library to pay his respects to the one person who still had the ability to make him feel like an awkward schoolboy. He also couldn't help glancing at Lady Vivien, whose sleepy eyes had just popped open with astonishment. She stared at him for several long seconds, her lips thinned into an irritated line. "You are Lady Thornbury's son?" she asked.

His mother threw her a startled glance. "Aden didn't tell you?"

"No. Apparently he did not find that detail to be of any importance." Lady Vivien glowered at him.

Wonderful. Just what he needed after a long and trying night.

His mother looked at him and he shrugged, expecting her to make one of her typical sarcastic responses. She didn't. In fact, she looked wounded, as if he'd insulted her somehow.

"I didn't do it on purpose, Mother," he said. That wasn't quite true, but he had no intention of admitting that. "We *were* rather busy, what with the escape from dangerous armed criminals."

The pain faded from her gaze as one eyebrow slowly lifted in a sardonic arch. No one could do that better than she and he couldn't help giving her a sheepish grin.

Her mouth twitched. "Very well, but I still suppose you could give your mamma a kiss. It's been ages since I've seen you."

As he bent to kiss her, the familiar scent of rosewater teased his nostrils. An indefinable emotion ticked through his chest, as it always did when she showed him affection. If he was forced to identify it, he might call it . . . regret.

When he straightened, she ran an assessing gaze over him. "I take it you suffered no harm?"

"I'm fine. Just tired."

Dominic crossed to the bell pull. "I'll ring for tea."

Aden cast him a startled glance. "Shouldn't we get Lady Vivien back home as soon as possible? It won't be long before there's activity on the streets." Already the gray light of dawn was filtering through the shutters across the long casement windows.

"Be that as it may, I would very much like a cup of tea," snapped the object in question. "Surely fifteen minutes one way or the other won't make a difference. And I'm parched."

Grumpy, more like it, Aden thought as he studied her pinched brow. He smiled at her, but that simply made her pretty mouth turn down in an irritated curve.

He gave up and looked at Dominic. "What's the plan, then? Bring her home in broad daylight and pretend nothing happened? I can't imagine that'll work."

"Don't fuss, Aden," his mother said. "Of course Vivien may have a cup of tea, and a nice wash and change of clothes, too."

"Well, that's putting me in my place," he replied.

His mother narrowed her eyes at him as if she might put him over her knee and paddle him. Aden rubbed the spot between his brows, wondering if the day could grow any more bizarre.

Fortunately, there was a tap on the door and Smithwell, Dominic's butler, came into the room. He acknowledged Aden with a respectful bow and then crossed to the women.

"Lady Thornbury, your maid has arrived with Lady Vivien's things. She's waiting to help her ladyship upstairs, in the guest bedroom."

"Why not my maid?" Lady Vivien asked, looking puzzled. "And why isn't my mother here?"

"We sent her home last night," Dominic answered as he moved to his desk. "There was no reason for her to remain all night, keeping vigil."

Lady Vivien pressed her lips together, as if struggling to maintain her composure. "And yet Lady Thornbury elected to stay," she finally said.

Aden's gut twisted with sympathy at the quiet pain in her voice. Obviously, he wasn't the only one with family problems.

His mother smoothly intervened. "Your dear mamma was hysterical, Vivien. Both Sir Dominic and I thought it best she go home and rest. She hasn't left her bedroom, and we've put it about that she has a cold. Since she couldn't control her distress, it was for the best."

"Yes, I can imagine," Lady Vivien replied in a colorless voice.

The way the life had drained from her made Aden want to smash something.

"Come, my dear," said his mother, helping her to her feet. "My girl will help you get changed and Smithwell will bring you a nice cup of tea. By the time you're finished, we'll be ready to take you home."

Lady Vivien nodded, letting Aden's mother guide her toward the door. As she passed Aden, she looked up at him, her gaze shadowed with a weary sadness.

"Will you still be here when I come back?" she asked with the tiniest quaver.

Unable to resist the impulse, he touched her kitten-soft cheek, momentarily forgetting everyone else in the room. There was only Vivien and what she needed from him. "Yes, I'll be here. There's nothing to worry you. I promise all will be well."

She gave him a trembling smile, then let Smithwell usher her out of the room.

Once the door closed behind her, a heavy silence fell. Reluctantly, Aden turned to face Dominic and his mother. As he could have predicted, they were both staring at him with avid curiosity.

He spread his hands. "What?"

Dominic appeared to be smirking, and as for his mother . . . her hands went to her hips and she started tapping her daintily shod foot.

"Well, my son," she began. "Given the fact that we haven't a clue who abducted Vivien, perhaps you'll tell us exactly how you intend to keep that promise?"

Chapter Eight

Aden grappled with his mother's question. Why had he made that damn promise? His responsibility for Vivien's safety had ended as soon as they crossed the threshold of Dominic's town house, and any further involvement was a very bad idea. He'd learned the hard way how women and emotion complicated things, and so had his friend, John Williamson. John had also been Aden's responsibility, but he had failed him, missing the signs that had led to a fatal disaster.

"Aden?" His mother's voice held a questioning note.

"It was a figure of speech, Mother. I'm certain Dominic will have the situation well in hand. Surely you don't need me."

Her nose twitched, a sure sign of her displeasure.

He switched his attention to his superior, knowing Dominic would support him. Unfortunately, Dominic remained silent, stroking his chin and regarding him with a thoughtful air.

Bloody hell.

That look boded ill.

"You do not need me to look after the girl now that we're back in London, do you?" Aden snapped.

Dominic's only answer was a slight, maddening smile.

Thrusting his hands through his already disordered hair, Aden stalked to the fireplace. He rested one hand on the marble mantel and the other on his hip, staring down into the flames as he struggled to keep his frustration under control. After a minute of silence, he turned around.

Dominic and his mother waited patiently, but their brand of patience resembled nothing so much as a wolf pack waiting to spring on its prey.

"Dominic, I've just come off that bloody hellacious mission in France," he said. "I think I deserve a rest."

His mother looked startled, although not about his reference to a mission, he knew. She'd spent much of her life close to the highest powers in the land, and there was little she didn't know about the Crown's dealings. She'd known for years he was a spy, as had his stepfather. But Aden had never gotten the sense that his mother disapproved of his work.

No, she was surprised because Aden had actually *referred* to his work. It was something he never did.

"Were you injured on this mission, son?" she asked in a tight voice.

"I wasn't," he replied tersely, not in the mood to explain.

His mother accepted that without comment, looking relieved.

With a few words, Dominic invited them to take seats. His mother perched on one of the leather club chairs in front of the desk, while Aden decided he preferred to remain standing—more to be contrary than anything else.

"You've earned a rest," Dominic said. "But I'm not sure it's the wisest course of action. If you don't stay busy you'll keep brooding over what happened in France."

Aden scoffed. "That's ridiculous. I never brood."

His mother tut-tutted him. "That's not true, dear. You were quite melancholic as a child. I'd hate to see you fall into those habits again."

Dominic nodded wisely and Aden could do nothing but give them an incredulous stare. He must be the only spy in history forced to put up with a damned lecture from his mother while reporting to his superior.

"I can assure you," he growled, "I will not sit at home and brood."

Except they were correct. He *had* planned to lock himself in his rooms and drink himself into a stupor for at least a week. Until just a moment ago, brooding had been a major part of his plan.

Dominic waved a negligent hand. "What matters most is Lady Vivien's safety. I've thought a great deal about how to handle this situation, and I've decided we need you. Because of your standing, you'll be able to move freely within the *ton* and keep an eye on her. No one will think to question your presence, which should make it easy for you to gather information regarding those closest to her ladyship."

He almost groaned. The *ton*. His worst nightmare.

His mother perked up. "I can assist you, Aden. I know all Vivien's friends and acquaintances, and her family, of course."

This time he couldn't keep his mouth shut. "You must bloody well be joking, Mother."

Her eyebrows arched up in admonishment. "Aden, your language."

He glared at Dominic, determined to refuse. He would not be coerced into babysitting a spoiled society miss—no matter how enticing that miss might be—and he would certainly not work on a case with his mother. It was the most demented idea he'd ever heard in his life.

But the words died on his tongue when he took in his chief's face. The craggy, lean features looked carved from granite, the severity more than matched by the cold expression in his flinty green eyes. Dominic allowed his agents a great deal of latitude when it came to speaking their minds, but there always came a point when the discussion ended. Usually when he looked like that.

Sighing, Aden dropped into the other club chair in front of the massive desk. A great weariness tugged at his limbs and he wanted nothing more than to fall into bed and sleep for a month. He didn't want to take responsibility for Vivien. For anyone. Not after the botch he'd made of things in France.

"It's been ages since I've been in London," he said, not yet ready to give in. "I'm completely out of touch with that nonsense."

"Lady Thornbury will assist you," Dominic said with an evil grin.

"Yes, since my mourning period is now over," his mother added. "It makes perfect sense that I would be out and about again, and no one would think twice if you escorted me." She levelled her most winning smile at him. "It will be delightful for us to spend time with each other."

Aden wanted to shoot himself. His mother had been avoiding him for years, and *now* she wanted to spend time with him?

"Is there no one else?" he asked in a resigned voice.

Dominic shook his head. "All my other men are out in the field. Naturally, I will continue to investigate the abduction, and I have contacts who will be useful in that regard." His eyes turned coldly furious. "I will be doing everything I can to run down the villain behind this outrage. Lady Vivien will not be put in harm's way again."

Aden barely kept surprise from registering on his face. Rarely did his superior display such emotion or become so directly involved in cases—especially one of this nature. Clearly, something about Vivien's situation had struck Dominic in a very personal way.

Then Dominic seemed to shrug it off. "But I need someone on the inside. A man who can move everywhere throughout the *ton* and also remain close to Lady Vivien." He paused and exchanged a veiled glance with Aden's mother.

Aden sighed. "Now what?"

His mother gave him a placating smile. "It's just that Vivien seems to trust you, and that's unusual for her. Since her dear papa died several years ago, she's been quite reserved when it comes to men. I know she has a reputation as something of a flirt, but it's entirely undeserved."

Christ. That was the last thing Aden wanted to hear. He did *not* want to get emotionally involved with Vivien, and he did *not* want her developing some misplaced sense of hero worship.

"She would feel that way toward any man who'd effected her rescue," he replied in a cool voice.

"Perhaps," said Dominic. "But do you really want to entrust her safety to just anyone? Whoever did this *will* try again, and we all know it."

Aden clenched his fist, scowling at his chief. Between the two of them, they'd very neatly backed him into a corner, and now they sat like a bloody pair of sphinxes, waiting for his answer.

He'd already made his decision. All he had to do was think of Vivien when he'd found her—drugged, terrified, and achingly vulnerable. The idea of that happening again was unacceptable.

Of course, he'd have to figure out some way to maintain a reasonable distance from the girl, since she'd already displayed an uncanny ability to unsettle him. That being the case, he'd do everything he could to protect her, but from an emotionally safe distance.

But let her stumble into harm's way, when he might be able to prevent it? *Hell and damnation, no.*

He glanced at the clock on the mantelpiece.

"We don't have much time before Lady Vivien returns," he said, addressing Dominic. "I doubt you've been idle these last twenty-four hours, so tell me what I need to know and who I might have to kill to protect her."

Chapter Nine

Vivien clutched the polished oak banister, carefully coming down the stairs. She finally felt human again, her numerous aches and pains soothed by the absolute luxury of a hot, rosewater-scented bath. In truth, the long soak meant more to her than simply washing away the dirt of her grim adventure. It also helped cleanse the gruesome memory of filthy hands groping her body and of the terror of anticipating the worst.

She stifled a yawn as she reached the bottom of the staircase. Almost drunk with exhaustion, she was more than tempted to sink into the comfy-looking chair tucked by the door to the study and close her eyes to drift off to sleep. What she did not want to do was talk about what had happened to her, or what might confront her in the days to come—especially with Sir Dominic. He possessed a knack for penetrating one's deepest thoughts.

Not that St. George was much better. Vivien feared he knew she was holding something back, so the sooner she got away from their well-meaning but unsettling questions, the better.

Smithwell smiled at her and opened the study door. She composed her face, knowing she must now calmly confront the problems looming before her without tipping her hand.

Lying to those who had so faithfully secured her safety had her mentally wincing, but she had no choice.

But she checked on the threshold a moment later, surprised to find Sir Dominic, Lady Thornbury, and St. George sharing a cup of coffee, lounging about as if they had nothing more pressing to attend to than a cozy little chat.

Actually, only St. George could be accused of lounging. He relaxed in an elegant sprawl in one of the big club chairs, his long, muscular legs thrust out before him, a coffee cup held negligently in one hand. But as she stood in the doorway, his dark gaze fixed on her. Her stomach jumped and she had the oddest feeling he'd instantly come to alert even though he hadn't moved a muscle.

Vivien gave him a tentative smile, deciding to ignore—for now—her irritation with him for withholding the specifics of his relationship with Lady Thornbury.

Her rescuer came to his feet with smooth, economical grace. He reached out and placed his cup on the edge of Sir Dominic's desk, never taking his eyes from her face. It amazed her that so big a man could move with such precision and quiet elegance. That grace, combined with his handsome features and his hard-edged masculinity, left her blushing like an inexperienced chit. Without the press of immediate danger to distract her, she felt tongue-tied before him.

Don't be a fool, Vivien.

She'd been courted by men so handsome they were prettier than she was, but they'd never caused her to feel the slightest bit discomforted. It was only her fatigue and stress that had her reacting in such a silly fashion now. And despite the foolish way she'd clutched at him earlier, Vivien had no intention of developing a schoolgirl crush on St. George. Despite his impeccable background, he was no idle bachelor. She had developed some sharp instincts at the card tables and those instincts were shrieking that he was dangerous. For one, she found it very difficult to lie to him. For another, she sensed he would break her heart if she were foolish enough to develop feelings for him.

"Lady Vivien." With a warm smile, Sir Dominic rose from behind his desk and crossed to meet her. "You're looking rather more the thing, my dear," he said as he drew her to the chair St. George had just vacated. "Come have a cup of coffee."

St. George stepped back as she passed him, but her shoulder brushed his chest. Their brief contact shivered through her body with surprising force. She forced herself not to look at him to gauge his reaction to that simple touch.

"I would adore a cup of coffee, sir," she replied, affecting a brightness she didn't feel. "But is it not time to return to Blake House?" She cast a nervous glance toward the window. It approached full daylight, and the costermongers and everyone else who rose at first light would now be out on the streets.

"There's no rush," Sir Dominic replied. "We'll be having breakfast in just a few minutes. You need proper nourishment, or you'll fall ill. We mustn't allow that to happen, now that we've finally got you back safely."

"But I've been gone two days!" She cast a worried glance at St. George. "I have to get home before anyone sees me, don't I? That's what you said last night."

St. George moved closer and gently pressed her shoulder, apparently seeking to reassure her. "You needn't worry, Vivien. Sir Dominic has everything in hand."

She blinked at the use of her Christian name, but everyone else seemed to ignore his slip. In that case, she supposed she'd better do the same.

"I don't understand," she said to Sir Dominic. "Are we not risking exposure by acting in so cavalier a fashion?" Vivien never paid much attention to what gossips prattled about her, but she had no desire to be ruined, either.

"St. George was correct," Sir Dominic replied with a smile. "We have a plan already in place to explain your disappearance."

Vivien shook her head, unable to rid herself of the knot in her stomach—the one that told her she wouldn't be safe until she returned home. On top of that, she needed to speak with Kit, and very soon. Her suspicions about her little brother's role in this affair had mushroomed into horrible certainty, and she could barely restrain herself from shrieking with impatience.

Sir Dominic cocked his head, studying her. "You trust me, don't you?"

A flash of guilt stabbed through her. Of course she trusted him. He'd been one of her father's oldest friends, and after Papa had died Sir Dominic had often stepped in to support Mamma and Cyrus in any way he could.

Not that they'd ever expressed any real gratitude to him, but their negligence had never prevented Sir Dominic from treating Vivien and Kit with a great deal of kindness. It hadn't surprised her to learn he had organized her rescue, especially with his political connections and the resources available to him through the Home Office.

And she supposed it made sense that Mamma had gone to him for help instead of Cyrus, who was always useless in a crisis, but . . .

She frowned at Sir Dominic, silently taking a coffee cup as questions swarmed in her mind. Why had she been brought here and not to Blake House? And why was Cyrus seemingly not involved in this? As her older brother and head of the family, he should have led the effort to find her. So far, no one had even mentioned his name.

"My dear, what's the matter?" Lady Thornbury's voice pulled her out of her ruminations.

Vivien glanced at her friend, vaguely registering that Lady Thornbury and her son shared the same dark, mysterious gaze, one that seemed to hold a myriad of secrets. She had known the older woman for most of her life and yet she'd never met her youngest son, and had rarely heard Lady Thornbury even mention his name. No wonder Vivien hadn't made the connection.

"Why isn't Cyrus here?" she asked bluntly. "Did he not play a role in my rescue?"

St. George went straight as a poker, and a wary glance passed between Sir Dominic and Lady Thornbury.

And then it hit her. Groaning, she slumped back in her chair. Hot coffee sloshed over the rim of her cup into the saucer, threatening to drip onto the carpet. Deftly, St. George plucked it from her hand and placed it on the desk.

"Cyrus refused to pay the ransom, didn't he?" she said, forcing the words past her tight vocal chords. "That's why you had to rescue me."

Something flashed in St. George's gaze—pity, she thought. But a moment later that look vanished, replaced by his usual impassive expression.

Cyrus had refused to come to my aid.

The, the . . . bastard. She might have known. He would never lift a finger to help anyone. Not if it involved money.

"No ransom demands were made, nor did we hear anything from your kidnappers at any time," Sir Dominic replied.

Vivien narrowed her eyes, not quite believing him. "Then why isn't Cyrus here? He *does* realize I was kidnapped, doesn't he?"

"Of course. He knows what we know," Sir Dominic replied. "Lady Thornbury and I simply thought it best that he remain home with your mother."

"Good heavens, yes," exclaimed Lady Thornbury. "Your poor mamma was such a wreck that we felt it better that Lord Blake be at hand to, ah, comfort her."

Vivien couldn't hold back a disparaging snort. "I can just

imagine." Cyrus had no patience for their mother's frequent bouts of hysterics, and she doubted that even his sister's kidnapping would make a difference.

A tap on the door interrupted them, and Smithwell poked his head in to inform them that breakfast was served. Vivien scowled. She had no desire to eat. What she wanted to do was go home and talk to Kit. And to Cyrus. She would find out her brothers' involvement in her abduction, or lack thereof, if she had to kill them both to extract the information.

St. George gently grasped her hand and drew her to her feet. Her head swam as she rose, forcing her to clutch his arm. He steadied her, and it took all her willpower not to sink into his warmth and strength, instinctively asking once more for his protection. She shivered, cold and exhausted, and overwhelmed by the futility of trying to make sense of it all.

"Come, Vivien. You must have something to eat," St. George said in a coaxing voice. Those deep tones stroked her nerves, soothing her. She had the feeling she would do anything he asked, if he asked it in that voice.

"You must stop worrying and trust us." He nudged her toward the door.

She stared up at him, taking in his determined, bristled jaw. "I do trust you, but I don't understand what's happening. I don't understand any of this," she said.

Well, she thought she understood a little, but it didn't make things any better. Especially since she couldn't tell anyone. And right now, she longed to spill it all out to St. George. Her suspicions, her fears, even her rage.

And that told her once again how dangerous he was to her.

"I know it's frustrating," he said, leading her across the hall to the dining room. "Have something to eat, then we can discuss arrangements to get you back home. All will be well, I promise."

She stifled a sigh. All was far from well, and they all knew it.

* * *

In the end, her return to Blake House was easily accomplished. In fact, ridiculously easy might be the best way to describe it. Lady Thornbury had set it about already that Vivien had come to stay with her a few days ago in preparation for a visit to the country. But prior to setting out for Thornbury Hall in Essex, Vivien had fallen ill with a terrible cold and been confined to bed, cared for by Lady Thornbury and her maid. Since Lady Thornbury's servants were well paid and devoted to the family, there was only a slight chance the lie might be discovered.

"Your brothers, thank God, both had the sense to keep quiet," Lady Thornbury had added. "So, with a little luck, we should brush through very nicely. Your mother, of course, also retreated to her bedroom, again under the pretense of illness."

The trick, as Sir Dominic had explained, was to carry it off in broad daylight. "No one will think twice if Lady Thornbury brings you home as soon as you've recovered enough to leave her house. Of course, since you're still unwell, you'll have to take to your bed for a few days to maintain the fiction."

And to bolster that fiction, Lady Thornbury would immediately depart to Essex for a few days, accompanied by her youngest son, Aden. Under those circumstances, it made perfect sense to return the ailing Vivien to her brother's mansion.

It was nearly nine o'clock by the time the Thornburys' travelling coach pulled up to Blake House in Grosvenor Square. Lady Thornbury took Vivien in her arms and hugged her. "Now, you're not to worry," the older woman scolded in affectionate terms. "Sir Dominic will get to the root of everything, and Aden will be keeping an eye on you."

Vivien's stomach flopped over on itself, but she forced a weak smile as she drew back. The last thing she needed was either man continuing to dig into her affairs.

"I promise I won't worry," she replied. "Frankly, the only thing I want to do right now is sleep. For a week, I hope."

"Yes, keep to your bedroom for as long as you want. Don't forget that you *do* have a miserable cold." Lady Thornbury's eyes twinkled at her.

Vivien was sure she looked the part. With her pale complexion and horribly bloodshot eyes, she certainly could pass for an invalid.

"Thank you for everything," she whispered, giving her friend another quick hug. It touched her more than she could say to know that Lady Thornbury had stood by her. It was too much to expect that her own mother could act like, well, a mother. Vivien loved her remaining parent, but she'd realized long ago that her role in the family was to take care of Mamma, not the other way around.

She placed her hand in St. George's gloved palm, her fingers disappearing in his encompassing grip. He handed her down to the pavement, steadying her until she found her footing, and handling her as carefully as Venetian glass.

"Thank you, but I have no intention of pitching over onto my face," she said wryly as he assisted her up the broad marble steps to the house. "I'm twenty-four, not ninety-four."

He gave her a genuine, charming smile, one that quite took her breath away. "I'm not so sure about that," he answered in a grave tone, even though his eyes gleamed with amusement. "It's a wonder you can even stand on your own. Perhaps I should carry you into the house." He slid a hand around her waist, as if preparing to do just that. "It wouldn't be the first time I did so," he finished in a low, teasing voice.

Vivien scowled, more at her body's shivery response than to his gentle ribbing. She simply could not allow him to affect her this way.

She was preparing a scold when the door to the house flew

open. Darnell, their butler, stood at the threshold, his eyes shining with a suspicious brightness.

"My lady," he exclaimed. "Thank God you're home."

St. George cast him a warning glance as Vivien mentally sighed. Clearly, poor Darnell knew of her abduction. She could only hope the tale had not spread beyond the butler and Mrs. Hammond, the housekeeper, both of whom had been forced to deal with Mamma's hysterics.

"Thank you, Darnell," she said. "My *cold* is much better, although I'm not yet up to snuff."

"Indeed, my lady," he replied, striving to recapture his professional demeanor. He stepped aside, allowing St. George to hand her over the threshold. "Your brothers are waiting for you in the library," he added. "Along with—"

The doors to the library banged open and Kit came charging out.

"Is that Vivi? Is she home?"

Her little brother—who topped her by a good six inches—dashed across the cavernous entrance hall and swept her into a fierce embrace. She squeaked, losing her breath, but hugged him back. She had little doubt Kit was up to no good. But he was her brother and she loved him, even if he could never manage to keep himself from tumbling from one mess to another.

He eased back, staring down at her, his blue eyes drenched with emotion. She saw relief in them but also stark guilt, and her heart sank. At twenty-two Kit was only two years younger, but since the death of their father Vivien had watched out for him like a mother hen. She loved him more than anything on the earth, and despaired he would ever grow out of his slap-dash reckless ways.

"I'm sorry, Vivi," he whispered in a choked voice. "I had no idea—"

"Hush, Kit," she interrupted, casting a nervous glance at St. George, who studied them both with narrow intensity.

Blast. She *had* to get rid of him before he started asking Kit questions.

She forced a smile at her brother, hoping her eyes conveyed a warning. "My dear, I'm feeling much better. There's really no need for such a fuss."

Reckless was Kit's middle name, but thank God he was as sharp as a pin. He flinched but then gave her a boyish grin. "Glad to hear it, sis. Although I must say, you look a regular quiz. That nose of yours is as red as a sailor's on shore leave."

She gave him a playful slap on the arm and then turned to introduce him to St. George, who stood with his arms crossed, eyebrows raised. He clearly wasn't fooled a bit.

Vivien repressed the impulse to glare at him. Instead, she drew Kit forward. "Kit, I'd like you to meet Captain St. George, Lady Thornbury's son. St. George, my brother, the Honorable Christopher Shaw."

After they exchanged formal bows, Kit grabbed the other man's hand and practically wrung it off. "My dear sir, it's a pleasure," he enthused. "I can't thank you enough for bringing my sister safely home."

"Your thanks aren't necessary," St. George replied in a warning voice. "I was happy to escort my mother and Lady Vivien to Blake House."

Kit grinned and tapped the side of his nose in understanding. Vivien gave St. George a rueful smile, shrugging her shoulders in apology.

St. George opened his mouth, but whatever he intended to say died on his tongue as he stared past her. What she had begun to think of as his warrior's face settled over his features, rending them wary and grim.

"Vivien, you have returned home," said her brother Cyrus

from behind her. She turned with a composed smile, only to feel her jaw drop open.

Her older brother paced steadily across the marble floor of the entrance hall looking his usual pompous self. But what transfixed her was the rather squat, cold-eyed figure walking by his side, although at the moment that man's eyes seemed to be anything but cold. In fact, if she didn't know better, she'd think he was enraged and barely repressing the emotion behind his correct Russian demeanor.

She snapped her mouth shut as Cyrus brushed a barely-there kiss across her cheek.

"I'm happy to see you safely home, my dear," he said in a flat voice. "And look who's come to call, especially to enquire after your health."

The cold-eyed Russian took her boneless fingers in his hand. Before she could stop him, he raised it to his froglike lips and pressed a damp kiss upon it. Vivien's stomach lurched as she suddenly regretted her large breakfast.

"Lady Vivien, I am overjoyed to see you. But you are looking most unwell. I insist you repair to your bed before you suffer a relapse," he said in his heavy-accented but fluent English.

Still struggling for words, she stared into Prince Ivan Khovanksy's flat, mud-colored gaze.

Chapter Ten

Vivien stifled a shudder as Khovansky's greedy gaze swept over her figure and came to rest on her face. She must have only imagined his anger a few moments ago, because right now he looked supremely self-satisfied, as if he'd just been proven right about something. He squeezed her hand, adopting a solicitous attitude.

"Truly, my dear lady," he said. "You look most unwell. I insist you retire this very minute."

He finished off his impertinent demand with an oily, intimate smile that had her palms itching to slap him. Unfortunately, it appeared that even a firmly delivered kick to the shin had failed to deter her most ardent and unwanted suitor.

She tried withdrawing her hand from his grasp but he refused to release her. When a barely audible growl sounded from behind her, she glanced over her shoulder to find St. George standing close, inspecting the prince through eyes dark with suspicion. She turned back, dismayed to see Khovansky glaring back at St. George, his lips parted in a contemptuous sneer.

Wonderful. Two hostile males squaring off in the entrance hall, in front of the servants, no less.

She yanked her hand away from the prince. "Your Highness, how kind of you to call and enquire after my health. Kind, but unnecessary. As you can see, I'm merely suffering from a bad head cold."

He astonished her by waving a playful finger in front of her face. "Ah, but colds can turn dangerous if not properly attended to. I would be heartbroken if you were to suffer a relapse. My lady, for my sake, you must not take any risk."

Baffled, Vivien peered at him. Khovansky was acting like a man who had a claim on her. Where in God's name did he get the idea he could treat her with such an inappropriate degree of intimacy?

"You needn't worry my sister will fall sick again, sir," Kit interrupted in an ugly voice. "We are well able to take care of her."

"Christopher, that is no way to speak to the prince," Cyrus snapped. "If you can't behave with a modicum of decorum, you will excuse yourself."

Kit bristled, ready to fire up. Vivien stepped in between her two brothers, facing Cyrus. "Kit is merely being protective, Cyrus. As it so happens, I *am* feeling rather unwell, and the last thing I wish to listen to is an argument."

Cyrus, although not as tall as Kit, still topped her by several inches. He frowned down at her, his sharp face pinched with his habitual expression of disapproval. His mouth worked as he struggled not to snap back at her, but he finally regained control of himself.

"Of course, Vivien. I have no desire to distress you." But he cast another resentful glance in Kit's direction. "There was, however, no need to be rude to Prince Ivan. I, for one, was most glad to receive so gracious a visit from His Highness this morning, and exceedingly grateful to accept his solicitous generosity on your behalf."

Vivien's eyes almost crossed as she waded through her brother's verbosity. He only spoke like that when he was upset or done something she would disapprove of. Cyrus could care less about Kit or Mamma, or what they thought about anything. But he could never force Vivien to accede to his will and he knew it. Even though he'd been head of the family for years, he'd learned to step carefully if he wanted something from her.

Then, like a crackling ember, understanding exploded in her tired brain. Khovansky was here because Cyrus had *asked* him to be here. Her brother had never made it a secret he wanted her to encourage the prince's suit. Vivien had warned him just last week that she would never do so, but apparently he'd chosen to ignore her warning.

Another idea bolted through her, one that had her stomach lurching once more into her throat. Had Cyrus been idiotic enough to tell Khovansky what had really happened to her? If the prince had access to that information he could use it to ruin her, chasing away any future suitors. Though she would rather dwindle into a poor old maid than marry Ivan the Terrible, as he'd been deemed by some of the more outrageous *ton* wags, Khovansky would never understand that. He seemed incapable of understanding anything about her, including her refusal to marry him.

Unnerved, her gaze jumped back to the prince. Again he reached for her hand, adopting an expression of soulful solicitude. It only made him look even more like a toad with dyspepsia.

Vivien hastily stepped back, evading his pudgy hand. She collided with a hard and very familiar chest. A pair of black-gloved hands steadied her, and then St. George released her and stepped forward, casually inserting himself between her and Khovansky. A moment ago, she'd been wishing her savior gone. Now, she was beginning to wonder what she would do without him once he walked away.

A disturbing and lonely thought.

"Perhaps someone would be so kind as to formally introduce me to the prince," he said in a deceptively mild tone.

"I'm afraid, sir, that I have no idea who you are," huffed Cyrus, obviously annoyed. "For all I know, you might be Lady Thornbury's footman, come to escort my sister home."

Vivien practically choked. "Try not to be more of an idiot than you already are, Cyrus." She ignored her brother's outraged spluttering. "Prince Ivan, may I introduce you to the Countess of Thornbury's son, Captain Aden St. George. Captain St. George, Prince Ivan Khovansky, member of the Russian ambassadorial delegation."

St. George executed a faultlessly correct bow, while the prince responded with an imperious inclination of his head.

"Captain, you are out of uniform," the prince said, his voice heavy with disapproval. "What is your regiment?"

"The Royal Horse Guards," St. George responded politely. "I am currently on leave, recovering from a bad fall from my horse."

Vivien frowned. He'd not mentioned that before, and he'd certainly not acted like he was recovering from an injury. Just the opposite, in fact. Once again, she couldn't help wondering what it was, exactly, that St. George really did.

"Well, now that you've done your duty, Captain, and delivered my sister home, I'm sure you'd much rather be about your business," Cyrus intoned. "Don't let us keep you."

Vivien anger's spiked, but before she could say anything, Kit jumped into the fray. "I was just about to ask the captain if he'd like some tea. No need to run right off, is there?" Kit turned to Vivien with an eager smile. "Surely you could do with a cup of tea, couldn't you, Vivi? Just the thing for a head cold, don't you think?"

"I hardly think that's wise," Khovansky interjected. "Lady Vivien needs to be resting, not entertaining bachelors with nothing better to do than flirt with young ladies and carouse around town."

Even Cyrus looked put out by that remark. But St. George simply adopted an expression that managed to look vaguely annoyed and yet slightly bored at the same time. Kit, however, flushed red, looking ready to pick a fight right there in the hallway before Vivien had even had a chance to divest herself of her pelisse. She had half a mind to go into the library, pull down her father's old duelling pistols from above the fireplace, and shoot the whole lot of them.

She wrapped a hand around Kit's wrist. "I don't care what the rest of you do but I'm going upstairs to see Mamma," she said in a voice that brooked no opposition. Keeping hold of Kit, she dipped a curtsy to St. George. "Sir, thank you for bringing me home, and please extend my gratitude and affection to Lady Thornbury."

With a grave expression on his face, although his gaze held amusement, St. George accepted his dismissal with a polite bow. "It was my pleasure, my lady. I make every wish for your speedy recovery."

He made a slight inclination of the head to Cyrus and Khovansky and gave Kit a warm, parting smile. Turning on his heel, he strode across the entrance hall, not checking his stride as Darnell scrambled to pull open the door. When it closed behind him, the echo of his absence seemed to reverberate through the high-ceilinged space. A fraught silence settled around them, one that seemed invested with a volatile, dangerous quality.

As she turned back to her older brother and his unwelcome guest, Vivien told herself that she wouldn't miss St. George in the least. In fact, the very idea of Kit volunteering them to spend time with St. George made her break into a cold lather. She needed to get her scapegrace brother alone so she could get to the bottom of whatever trouble he had gotten himself into. And she needed to keep that trouble between Kit and herself—at least until she understood all the particulars.

"Is Mamma awake yet?" she asked. She truly wished she could avoid that meeting, since Mamma's usual response to any major event, happy or ill, was a bout of hysterics. But she couldn't allow her mother to suffer a moment longer than she needed to.

Kit shook his head. "No. Dr. Patterson gave her something to help her rest, because she, ah, is also under the weather. Her maid is to look for me as soon as she's awake. I'll tell her you've returned home."

She gave Kit a grateful smile, then flicked a glance at Cyrus and his guest. "I'm going to my room and I would ask that I not be disturbed for the rest of the day. Kit will help me up, so there's no need for you to abandon the prince to see to my comfort."

She barely managed to temper the cynical tone in her voice. Cyrus wouldn't give a tinker's damn for her comfort, or dream of helping her up to her room. More likely, he wanted to drag her into his study and demand a full accounting of what had happened to her over the last few days. The only thing Cyrus truly cared about was his infernally stolid, pristine reputation and how the antics of his family affected it. Her older brother nursed rather extravagant political ambitions, and he would no doubt be terrified that her kidnapping would have a negative impact on those ambitions.

But Cyrus, ever sensitive to the nuances of insult, caught the implied criticism in her voice. He bristled, ready to defend himself, but the prince intervened.

"Of course you should retire to your bed, my dear lady," he said, adopting a solicitous tone. "You are not to give a moment's thought to me or to your brother. The only thing that matters is your health. I would never forgive myself if my visit this morning were to cause you any distress." He pressed a hand to his barrel chest, looking affected in the extreme.

It was all nonsense, but if the prince prevented Cyrus from pestering her, so much the better. Feeling more charitable toward him than she normally would, she gave him a curtsy and a slight smile. "Your Highness, thank you for your kind wishes. I bid you good day."

She spun on her heel, almost toppling over with exhaustion, and headed for the stairs. Kit kept a firm hand on her arm, the click of their shoes echoing through the silence of the entrance hall. Vivien forced herself not to look back to see what the prince and Cyrus were doing. She couldn't shake the sense her brother had told Khovansky everything, but that was a problem she would deal with after she'd had some rest.

In her current state of weariness, the imposing central staircase of Blake House seemed an obstacle as forbidding as a snow-capped alp. If Kit had offered any resistance to accompanying her, she might have collapsed in a heap on the floor. Her leg muscles had adopted the consistency of runny blancmange, and she had to clutch Kit's arm to remain upright.

As they mounted the stairs, her little brother tugged loose from her grasp and wrapped an arm protectively around her waist. "Hang on, sis," he murmured. "Only a few more steps and you'll be there."

He glanced over his shoulder, a scowl descending on his boyish features. "Why doesn't Cyrus take Ivan the Terrible back to his study? What the devil does the man think he's doing, standing in the hall and staring after you like that? It's bloody indecent."

Prickles shivered up the back of Vivien's neck, and she again resisted the temptation to look behind her. Obviously, the prince had decided not to relinquish his courtship, and it appeared Cyrus fully intended to support him. She would stand firm against him, of course, but it would make life more difficult at Blake House. And they were hardly a happy family to begin with.

First things first.

And that first thing was Kit. "Just ignore him, Kit. It's not important right now."

He grumbled, but gave it up. "You're right. But why the hell Cyrus agreed to see him this morning, what with—"

"Hush, Kit. Not here," she warned as they reached the floor where the family's private chambers were located. She smiled at an upstairs maid, who bobbed a curtsy and gave her a welcoming nod as they passed.

They turned right into the short corridor to her bedroom. Blowing out a heartfelt sigh of relief, Vivien opened the door and stepped inside, Kit following behind. She dragged herself across the room to the fireplace and collapsed onto the infinitely soft silk chaise, letting the heat and cheerful crackle of the flames wash over her.

Her gaze wandered gratefully about the cheerful space. More than once during her ordeal, she'd feared she'd never see her favorite retreat again. Finished in calming shades of white and pale blue and accented with cushions, drapes, and bedcovers of buttery yellow, Vivien's bedroom had always been her one safe haven from chaos and trouble. Reading on her chaise, writing to friends at her elegant Sheridan desk, escaping the travails imposed on her by her family. Of course she loved them—even Cyrus, in a way—but they tried her patience to the breaking point.

Sometimes, the Blake mansion had even seemed more like a prison than a home. But in that horrible cave in Kent she'd sorely regretted her ingratitude and her careless acceptance of her privileged life. Over and over she had prayed to safely return home, vowing to shoulder any burden necessary. Now, by God's grace and St. George's, she'd been delivered. It was time once again to take up her responsibilities to her family.

"Mamma must have been terrified by all this," she said, unbuttoning her pelisse. "God knows she screamed loud enough when they dragged me out of the carriage."

Kit's eyebrows flew up, and she winced.

"I'm sorry. I'm so tired I don't know what I'm saying," she apologized. Of course her mother had been terrified. But a tiny part of Vivien couldn't help remembering her mother shriveled up into a wailing ball in the corner of the carriage, not even trying to help her.

Unlike Lady Thornbury.

She shook off the uncharitable comparison, focusing on her brother. Kit gave her a lopsided grin and shrugged. "Well, old girl, it ain't like you're exaggerating. According to Lady Thornbury, she had an epic fit of the vapors and didn't come down until Lady T.'s doctor shoved a mighty dose of laudanum down her throat."

Vivien draped her pelisse over the end of the chaise, drew her legs up, and nestled against the plump cushions. "How in heaven's name did Cyrus prevent all the servants from finding out what happened to me, especially with Mamma in such a state?"

"Lady T. again. She had the presence of mind to send the carriage straight to Sir Dominic's house after your abduction." He gave a low whistle. "Thank God for her and Sir Dominic. Don't know what would have happened if they hadn't come to the rescue."

"Indeed," Vivien replied dryly.

Looking like he'd been caught putting frogs in his big sister's shoes, Kit warily sat down on the padded stool before Vivien's dressing table.

Yes, my lad, it's time to own up to your sins.

"Anyway, once they calmed Mamma down," Kit hastily continued, "they brought her home and put her right to bed. She's stayed there ever since, supposedly with the same cold that felled you. Only Darnell and Mrs. Hammond know what really happened."

"Good God," she sighed. "What a disaster."

It would be a miracle if they managed to squeak through this without a scandal. Fortunately, the senior servants had been with the family forever and were very loyal. Vivien who'd been managing the household for years—had always made sure they were paid well enough to ensure that loyalty, even if she had to scrimp and save to do it.

Kit nodded sympathetically. "I know. But so far, we haven't heard a stitch of gossip. Sir Dominic was quite forceful in impressing on the staff just how dire the situation could become."

Vivien's anxiety eased a fraction. "We've obviously been very lucky, thanks to Lady Thornbury and Sir Dominic."

And St. George, of course, but she had no intention of sharing the intimate details of her rescue with anyone, including Kit.

"And speaking of luck," she continued in a severe voice. "It's time for you—"

She broke off as a tap sounded on the door panels. "Enter," she called in a resigned voice.

Susan, her maid, edged into the room, wreathed in a welcoming smile and bearing a tray laden with enough cakes, scones, and tea to supply half of Wellington's army. They did look awfully tempting despite the generous breakfast she'd consumed a short time ago. It was a consequence, she supposed, of having nothing to eat for two days but some dried bread and a piece of moldy—and not in a good way—cheese.

"My lady, welcome home," Susan exclaimed as she placed the tray on Vivien's writing desk. The maid turned and inspected her, a frown marking her pleasant features. "Oh, you do look peaked." She turned her frown on Kit. "Now, Master Kit, I think it best if you let her ladyship get some rest. She needs to be in bed asleep, not chatting with you."

Vivien tamped down her impatience. Susan had been with the family for years and had been a true support during some very trying times. "I'm fine, Susan. You may pour the tea, and then I'll ring for you when I want to get undressed."

Susan looked ready to disagree, but instead poured out the tea and heaped two plates with cakes and scones, grumbling all the while. After gathering up Vivien's pelisse, she stalked back to the door. "Fifteen minutes, Master Kit," she said sternly. "And then I'll be back to put her ladyship to bed."

Kit answered with an engaging grin, his mouth already stuffed with scones. At any other time Vivien would have laughed, but right now it felt like everyone and everything was out of her control. If only she could have confided in St. George. *He* would have known what to do, and how to handle Kit. *He* would have—

Stop.

She couldn't allow her thoughts to drift in so perilous a direction. Besides, he would no doubt soon return to his regiment— or whatever it was he really did—and she must handle this latest crisis by herself. After all, she had promised Papa on his deathbed that she would look out for Kit and Mamma, and that vow had become the underpinning of her life. It often weighed heavily on her, but Papa had been the best father in the world. He had depended on her, and she wouldn't let him down.

Vivien and Kit sat facing each other, with no more interruptions to prevent them from confronting the truth. Her brother knew it, too. He carefully set down his plate, brushed the crumbs from his hands, and faced her with the same apologetic, guilty expression she'd seen on his face countless times.

Setting aside her teacup, Vivien looked her brother in the eye and asked the question that had been rabbiting about in her brain for hours.

"Kit, exactly how involved *were* you in my abduction?"

Chapter Eleven

The blood drained from Kit's face, leaving him the color of curdled milk. His gaze darted about, seeking escape before settling back on her. His bright blue eyes, so like her own, pleaded for understanding.

Vivien's stomach twisted into a painful knot with his unspoken confirmation of guilt. Even though her brain had assembled the facts with an almost mathematical precision, her heart had still foolishly hoped her conclusion wasn't true. She should have known better. If there were two things Kit excelled at, they were running up debt and getting into trouble.

Just like his mother, the reason why Mamma and Kit were usually thick as thieves.

"Oh, Kit," she exhaled in a despairing breath. "How could you?"

He rushed over to flop to his knees before her, grabbing her hands. "It wasn't like that, Vivi. I had no idea you'd be kidnapped. I didn't think for a moment that blasted scoundrel would actually carry out his threats." He clutched her hands in a convulsive grip. "I'd die before I let anything bad happen to you. You know that."

His eyes grew wet, and for an awful moment Vivien was thrown back into a well of bitter memories. Kit hadn't cried since Papa's death. He'd shed many tears on that horrible day, heartbroken by his beloved father's death, and it had almost destroyed her own heart. She'd vowed that Kit would never have reason to cry again, not if she could help it.

This time, though, Vivien had no idea if she could fix whatever disaster he'd stumbled into.

Letting her anger bleed away—it never paid to be angry with Kit—she drew him up from the floor to sit beside her. She patted his broad back while he composed himself, as she'd so often done when he was a boy. Then she placed her hands on his shoulders and turned him to face her.

"It was that moneylender, wasn't it?" she asked. "The one we talked about last week."

He averted his eyes. "I . . . I think so."

"Kit," she warned.

Grimacing, he met her gaze. "Yes, I'm almost positive. I've spent the time since you were taken trying to run him to ground. Couldn't find him, so I can't be perfectly certain, but it makes sense. Sorry, old girl," he said, despondent. "They didn't hurt you, did they? I mean, not really." His eyes glistened again. "Please tell me they didn't hurt you."

"I'm fine," she said, absently patting his hand while she puzzled over what she already knew.

Vivien had sensed something was wrong with Kit over a week ago. She'd always been able to do that, and with Mamma, too. Not that it posed much of a challenge. They were both inveterate gamblers *and* terrible liars. Still, she'd been forced to resort to an unpleasant subterfuge when Kit refused to tell her what was wrong. She'd searched his room until she'd found the vowels that revealed debts of over ten thousand pounds owing from losses at the tables.

The size of the sum had staggered her, and the moment he'd returned home Vivien had confronted him. Kit had reluctantly confessed he'd gone to a moneylender in order to pay off his debts and that choice news had led to a blazing row. But before he'd stormed out of the room, he'd demanded she stop treating him like a little boy and told her that he'd fix the problem on his own. And instead of insisting that he let *her* deal with the moneylender, Vivien had decided he was right. She'd spoiled Kit for his entire life, and it was past time he accepted responsibility for his own mistakes.

She'd woefully underestimated the depth of his mistakes, and the criminal inclinations of the man holding Kit's vowels.

"Did you speak to this moneylender after our fight last week?" she asked.

"The next day. I told him that he'd have his money within three days. He said he would give me the time but if I didn't pay up by then, my family would pay the price." Kit raked a hand through his tumbled blond hair, looking ill with anxiety. "I suppose I could have gone to Cyrus, but you know how he reacts. If he's not threatening to exile me to the countryside, he's vowing to force me into an infantry regiment and ship me off to India or some godforsaken place. I think he'd do it this time, too. Not that I don't deserve it," he finished bitterly.

"No one is going anywhere," she responded sharply. The idea of her darling, feckless little brother facing danger and disease in foreign lands was intolerable. "You're not to worry about Cyrus or his threats, especially that one."

"I don't know. Maybe it's time I—"

"No, Kit. You are not running away from this and you are not going off to join the army," she said firmly. "And don't distract me. Why three days?"

"What? Oh, three days to repay the money, you mean. Well, there was a horse race at—"

She rested her forehead on her fists. "You didn't."

The heavy silence told the tale. If there was one thing Kit liked more than gaming hells, it was the track. That was to be expected, since her father had owned a string of thoroughbreds, but Cyrus had sold them off within weeks of Papa's death. As a child, Kit had loved hanging about the stables and he'd inherited his father's love of horses. Unfortunately, he had not inherited Papa's discipline and self-control.

Vivien rubbed her temples, wishing she could crawl into bed and not speak or even see anyone for a week. But that wouldn't protect her or Kit, and it wouldn't make the problem go away. She'd learned long ago that problems must be managed directly or they would mushroom out of control.

She dropped her hands to her lap and sat up straight. If she *looked* calm and in control, dealing only with facts and not emotion, perhaps she would *feel* calm and in control.

"How much did you drop on the horse, Kit?"

He seemed to shrink into himself, and Vivien had the oddest impression that his formfitting coat was suddenly two sizes too large. Under her eyes, Kit transformed from a strapping young man into a frightened boy.

Her heart seized in her chest when he didn't answer. "How much? Tell me," she demanded through lips gone stiff and cold.

He swallowed again. "Twenty thousand."

For a moment, the words couldn't penetrate the haze of weariness that had apparently taken up permanent residence in her brain.

"Twenty thousand?" she repeated, her voice sounding dim and far away. Then she drew in a gasping breath. "Do you mean an additional twenty thousand pounds on top of the ten thousand you already owe?"

When he nodded miserably, Vivien's last, lingering hope crumbled into dust. Since Papa's death, life hadn't always been easy, but for the last several years she'd been able to keep her mother and Kit more or less out of dun territory by consistently winning respectable and even substantial sums of money at the card tables. She even enjoyed the challenge, the pitting of her brain and skills against some of the finest gamblers of the *ton*. When she sat down to play, she could forget the rest of the world, all her willpower and wit focused on that square of green baize cloth. In taking on her opponents, in using all her skills, she could exert some degree of control over the chaos of her family and partly overcome her own financial circumstance.

Of course, she exerted great care not to let arrogance sweep away her native caution. When she began to lose significant amounts—which occurred quite rarely—she always walked away. She enjoyed the game and enjoyed the control it gave her, but she had vowed long ago never to let it control *her*.

But thirty thousand pounds? Even she couldn't win that much, not in the period of time required. Vivien felt completely and utterly helpless, sunk by the selfish disregard for consequences too often displayed by her mother and Kit.

She stared into the fire, her emotions blanked out under a smothering weight that seeped into her mind and spirit. Her vision narrowed to a pinprick of concentration, all focused on one penetrating question.

How in God's name could she fix this? Even as a last resort, she could not go to Cyrus for help. Although the Blake family fortune was entirely respectable, they didn't have *that* kind of money lying about, especially since Mamma had substantial debts as well. Mamma had an allowance, of course, but she always exceeded it. Only Vivien's winnings at the tables allowed them to hide the extent of the problem from Cyrus.

Besides, Cyrus despised the way Kit and Mamma gambled and he'd balk at even paying a farthing to help them. He'd rather see Mamma exiled to the country and Kit sent off to the battlefield than see any of the estate's hard-earned money reward their folly.

And right in this moment, Vivien was halfway to agreeing with him.

"Vivi, wh . . . what's wrong with you? Why aren't you talking?" Kit's voice held a frightened, quavering note.

She tried to marshal her thoughts, tried to care that her beloved younger brother so desperately needed her. But that smothering emotional fog refused to give way. It was as if someone had again forced laudanum down her throat. Aware and surrounded by danger but with every sense blunted, unable to think or act to save herself or anyone else.

Her brother convulsively gripped her shoulder and shook. "Vivien! What's the matter with you?"

With a great, shuddering effort, as if she rolled a tombstone from her chest, Vivien came back to herself. Anger and frustration rushed up with a cleansing blast, forcing past the leaden weight in her head.

"Yes, Kit. I hear you," she snapped. "There's no need to shout at me. I'm simply trying to think."

He jerked back, startled by her reaction. She ruthlessly shoved aside her natural instinct to comfort him. If anything, she should box his ears, though Kit deserved a good deal more than that.

Still, his panic faded and color returned to his cheeks. He got up and began pacing the room, his long legs carrying him quickly to the far window and back again. She let him work off the energy, happy for the silence while the vague outlines of a plan began to take shape in her mind's eye.

After a few minutes of wearing a path on the weave of her Axeminster carpet, Kit came to a halt in front of her, looking despondent yet resigned. Vivien cocked an eyebrow in silent question.

"You're right, Vivi. I've made a complete muddle of things, and it's time I owned up to it. This is all my fault and I'm going to fix it."

She could barely repress a shudder at the idea of Kit trying to fix anything. "And how do you intend to do that?" she asked, curious despite herself.

He thrust up his chin, like a defiant boy owning up to a silly prank. "I'll leave for the Continent immediately. Tonight, if possible. If I'm gone, there's no chance of recovering the money, so the bastard will leave you and the family alone. Yes," he said, growing more enamored of the idea by the second. "That's the ticket. If I just disappear, there's nothing anyone can do. I won't tell you where I'm going, and that way no one can hold you or Cyrus at fault."

He thrust his hand into his waistcoat, trying to look tragic. He likely saw himself as romantically heroic in his willingness to sacrifice himself for his family.

"I see," she replied, nodding pensively. "You do realize the Continent is still in turmoil. I wonder where you will go and how you will get there."

Kit's mouth twisted as he tried to puzzle that out. After a few moments, his eyes lit up. "I'll go to Egypt! I've always wanted to see the pyramids and go up the Nile."

Vivien sighed. Kit was nothing if not predictable. Even as a child he'd loved to indulge in fantasies of grand Oriental adventures.

"And how will you support yourself?"

After several moments of frowning silence, he cast her a doubting look. "Well, perhaps I could work on one of those archeological expeditions that some fellow is always putting together. I'll just trot down to the Royal Society and ask around. I'd make a jolly good secretary and assistant to an expedition, don't you think?" He finished with a hopeful smile.

Vivien rubbed her temples. Given the outrageous nature of his flights of fancy, she would hardly be surprised if a garden fairy flew through the window and alighted upon the mantelpiece. "Kit, that's hardly in keeping with your plan to escape from England undetected, is it?"

Disappointment darkened his eyes, but only for a second. "I know," he started, perking up again.

"No!" Vivien chopped down her hand. "Running away is a ridiculous idea and you know it. Nor would your disappearance solve our problem. Your moneylender would eventually begin pestering Cyrus, who would refuse to pay. The scandal would be enormous. Besides, you would never be able to return to England. Is that what you really want?"

He looked stricken again, but for once Vivien didn't care. She pushed to her feet, the restless need to do something driving her past exhaustion. Kit watched in wary silence as she traced his path, pacing from one end of the room to another.

After a few minutes the vague outlines of her plan solidified. It was risky, even foolhardy, and each step would have to be carefully worked out before she took action. The consequences of discovery could be dire, but what choice did she have? Even without the fodder of her recent disappearance, Vivien's reputation had come under increasing scrutiny. Some considered her card playing *fast,* and it wouldn't take much to tip her over the line. She needed to be very careful if she were to preserve her reputation and her safety, *and* save Kit from debtors' prison.

She came to a halt in front of her brother. "Kit, how much will you need to pay this man to prevent any more punitive actions on his part?"

He rubbed his chin. "I suppose four or five thousand pounds would do it."

She sighed. "That's rather a substantial difference. Which is it? Four or five?"

He grimaced. "Four should do it. He's not exactly in the mood to trust me, but anything is better than nothing."

"And if we can get that to him within the week, will that prevent him from going to Cyrus?"

"Yes," he answered, looking more certain by the second. "I'm sure it will. But how are we going to find that large a sum?" His eyes suddenly rounded. "You're not going to put it on a horse, are you Vivi?"

"Don't be an idiot," she said, sitting next to him on the chaise.

He gave her a lopsided grin. Her anger faded away, pointless given the fact that in so many ways this wasn't entirely Kit's fault. He'd been terribly spoiled his entire life, and being such a handsome, sweet-natured boy hadn't helped. Only Cyrus had ever demanded more of his brother, but his open contempt had only prompted Vivien and her mother to spoil Kit even more. Now, of course, they suffered the consequences, but there was little to be gained by lamenting it.

"You've always had the brains in the family, sis. But I still don't see how we're going to wrestle up even that amount of blunt."

"As it so happens, I do have a plan. The annual Darlington ball is on Friday. You know how deep the play is at that particular gathering. With a little luck, I can win what we need to keep your moneylender at bay."

On top of that, Vivien could dip into the tidy sum of money she'd managed to put away from her winnings. Two thousand pounds wasn't that much, but if she could manage to win at least another two at the tables, they should be safe for the time being. It killed her to think of throwing away her carefully earned money on a stupid, reckless debt, but their safety and reputation took precedence.

Kit frowned. "Then what? That barely puts a dent in what I owe."

"We'll worry about the next step after the ball." Vivien wasn't yet ready to discuss the next part of her plan. It was so risky, she had little doubt that even Kit would object. Better to coach him along by degrees.

"If you say so, Vivi," he said doubtfully.

"And you are not to play cards or bet on the horses, or

anything else for that matter. I mean it, Kit," she said, adopting a threatening tone.

He put a hand over his heart, looking solemn. "I won't, Vivi. That's done. If you really want to know, I'm sick and tired of that life. It feels so . . ." he trailed off, lifting his palms up in a helpless gesture.

"Useless?" she asked softly.

"Yes."

She took his hand. "I know, dear. It's time for you to grow up."

He nodded, shamefaced. "I just don't know how to go about it."

Her heart seemed to scrunch up in her chest. "We'll figure it out later. But I do need you to do something."

He nodded eagerly.

"You must go to this moneylender," she said, "and tell him that you will pay him at least four thousand pounds by Saturday, and that the rest of the money will follow within the month."

"Yes, I will. I don't know if he'll believe me, though."

"Tell him that Lady Vivien Shaw gives her word the money will be repaid. I have never reneged on debt, and I have no intention of doing so now." If necessary, she'd sell her jewelry, too.

Kit nodded. "What about Mamma? Cyrus has been complaining about her debts, too. He was railing on about it after you were kidnapped. Mamma got hysterical and told him everything was his fault. That if he'd only pay off her debts everything would be fine."

Vivien rubbed her throbbing temples, certain her headache had, indeed, taken up permanent residence in her skull. Not for the first time, she wondered if Mamma, Cyrus, or even Kit really spared a thought for her.

She didn't think so.

"I didn't realize that," she answered wearily. "I cautioned

her last week against spending so much money, but it's like trying to convince a toddler not to cry when she's skinned a knee."

"I'll speak with her," Kit offered. "You shouldn't have to do it. Not with everything else you have to worry about."

Vivien stood, eager now to be rid of Kit. To be rid of all the troubles in her life. She passed a hand over her eyes and, for a second, the image of Aden St. George emerged from the darkness. For a fugitive moment her heart cried out for the strength and protection she'd found in his arms.

"Vivien? Are you all right?"

She dropped her hand and forced a smile. "I'm fine. Just tired. I'll speak to Mamma this afternoon, after I get some sleep." She wrinkled her nose at him. "I can't bear the thought of dealing with her right now, which I suppose makes me a terrible daughter."

Kit gave her a fierce hug. "You're the best daughter and sister anyone could ask for. None of us are the least bit worthy of you."

She let out a thin laugh. "Right now, I'm inclined to agree with you. Now, off with you, Kit. I'll see you this evening at dinner."

Her brother walked to the door, then paused and looked at her. "Everything will be all right, won't it, Vivi?"

She heard it then, the plea she'd heard a thousand times since the death of her father. A thousand times Mamma or Kit had come to her, asking her to make things right.

"Yes, Kit," she said, as she always did. "Everything will be fine."

But this time, she couldn't be so confident. This time, if she wasn't very careful and very adept, they could lose everything she'd struggled so hard these long years to protect.

Chapter Twelve

Aden scowled at his mother's butler, refusing the fellow's repeated attempts to move him from the hallway into the drawing room. He had no intention of getting comfortable, and he had no intention of letting his mother *think* he was getting comfortable visiting her in Duke Street. There was only one reason for his presence here—Lady Vivien. She would be attending the Darlington ball, which meant *he* would be attending as well. It had been years since he'd graced such an event, and having made his disdain for the *ton* abundantly clear, Aden needed an excuse for overcoming his aversion to society.

That excuse was serving as his widowed mother's escort, the prodigal son returning home to attend to his filial duties.

And as much as it galled him to admit it, he needed his mother's help. Aden could recite from memory shipping schedules, French troop movements, and the likely boltholes of every spy in Europe, but he'd be damned if he could keep straight the arcane social relationships of the British aristocracy. He'd walked away from that world long ago, and only his work could make him walk back in. With any luck, his stay would be mercifully short and free of opportunities to stumble into embarrassing social situations.

Like seeing his natural father. On the occasions when they

had encountered each other before Aden had joined the army and then the Intelligence Service, the Prince Regent had greeted him with bluff cordiality, seemingly unaware of the avid and mean-spirited gossip whispered behind fluttering fans and in the card rooms. Aden, however, remembered each humiliating incident all too well. It hadn't been much better for his mother, who'd had to suffer both the gossip of her peers and the smoldering anger of her affronted husband. To give her credit, she'd endured it all with a dignity and grace that Aden could only admire, however reluctantly.

He pulled out his watch to check the time. Again. His gaze flickered to the butler who sighed in sympathy, obviously commiserating on the inevitable delays that accompanied the arrival of the fairer sex.

Holding back an unexpected snort of laughter, Aden leaned against the bottom post of the staircase, letting his gloved hand absently trace the barley twist pattern of the carved baluster. He relaxed his shoulders and let tension flow from his body. It would be a long and trying evening. There would no doubt be many long and trying evenings over the next few weeks, so he'd better get used to it.

Growing bored, he let his gaze wander. The discreet elegance of his mother's small but well-appointed town house had surprised him, used as he was to the smothering opulence of the family mansion in Berkeley Square. He'd been forced to visit the huge pile last year, paying his respects after Thornbury's sudden demise. The experience had made his skin crawl. Fortunately, Aden's mother had soon moved out, leaving the Berkeley Square mansion to Edmund, oldest son and heir, and Aden's half brother.

Edmund wasn't a bad sort. He had always treated Aden with a sort of distant kindness, inviting him to stay at the mansion whenever Aden was in London. But Edmund could also be insufferably pompous and could never seem to forget that his half brother was not truly a Thornbury. The less the family saw of the proverbial black sheep, the better, as far as the new earl was concerned.

Aden couldn't agree more.

"Aden, why are you waiting in the hall? Surely Patterson hasn't been neglecting you?" His mother's cultured voice floated down from the first-floor landing.

Glancing up, he studied her as she descended the staircase. Although no longer young, no one could doubt the beauty she had once been. She carried herself with a grace and elegance that put many a younger woman to shame. Only up close, when one could see the lines around her eyes and mouth, and the gray streaks threading her raven-colored hair, did her age reveal itself.

And when a perceptive observer gazed into her dark eyes, he might observe sorrow and a certain kind of weariness, one that came of too many mistakes made early in life. Mistakes that could never be forgotten or forgiven, at least by the person who had mattered most—her husband.

"Good evening, Mother," Aden responded, leaving her questions unanswered. He'd fallen into the habit long ago of holding his counsel from her, even over trivial matters. That had subsequently formed the pattern of their relationship—a polite distance neither seemed inclined to break. Lately, though, he suspected she chafed against their mutually agreed boundaries, which left him uncomfortably bemused.

She reached the bottom step and stopped, meeting him eye to eye. The slight frown on her refined features, combined with her assessing gaze, still had the power to discomfort him.

Resisting the urge to tug at his too-tight cravat—God, he hated wearing them—he returned her gaze, finally lifting an ironic eyebrow. She gave up, but not before she rolled her eyes.

"Would you like a brandy before we leave?" she asked, letting him hear the note of exasperation in her voice.

"Thank you, but no," he answered. Then he relented, dropping his shield just a bit. "And, yes, Patterson fussed about me in the most entirely correct way. You may rest easy on that account."

Her mouth quirked up as she took his arm. "You have ever been the most stubborn of my children, you know. I have always wondered where you acquired that particular trait."

"No doubt passed on to me by my dear father."

She cut him a sharp glance, a faint blush coloring her cheeks. That startled him and a throb of guilt beat in his chest. Over time, his mother had armored herself against insult and gossip, especially when it involved references to her affair with the Prince Regent. But she'd undergone a gradual change during this year of widowhood, as if something had breached her ironic detachment. Aden didn't know what to make of this woman, so like the mother he knew, and yet not.

"Mother," he began, starting a sentence he didn't know how to finish.

She pressed her hand against the inside of his elbow. "Never mind, dear. I understand."

At least someone did, but it wasn't him.

Patterson bowed them out, and a moment later Aden had them settled in his town coach. An uncomfortable silence thickened the air, one that his mother obviously wasn't inclined to break. Although only to Park Lane, he suspected the trip to the Darlington mansion would seem endless unless he did something to break the brittle tension.

No wonder he avoided his family.

He capitulated, at least for now. "I'm grateful for your help this evening. I'm sure you have better things to do than play nursemaid to me and Lady Vivien."

Her eyebrows arched, then her lips parted in a generous smile, lighting up her handsome features. With that smile came a rush of memories—happy ones, when he was a little boy and she still loved him. Before she came to see him as a source of shame rather than of pride and affection.

"Indeed, I'm quite delighted to be able to assist you," she said. "I can only devote so many hours in the day to visiting, shopping, and my correspondence. Since your brother has taken over the estates, I have little meaningful work to keep me occupied."

He could well imagine. His mother had managed the Thornbury households and staff to perfection, including the London house, two large manors in the country, and a hunting box in Kent.

"Why did you move out of Thornbury House?" he asked, curiosity drawing him in. "I'm certain Edmund and Elizabeth would have made you welcome. And I know you must miss the children."

Unlike many women of the *ton,* his mother doted on Edmund's two little boys and Aden's half sister's children as well. Given her cool relationships with her own children, his mother's open devotion to her grandchildren had come as something of a surprise.

"I do," she said with a sigh. "But one's children and grandchildren cannot become the center of one's life. Besides, although she would never say it, your sister-in-law could never be comfortable while I was there. Elizabeth is something of a shrinking violet, and does not need me looking over her shoulder."

Aden contemplated her words—and what lay underneath—for a few moments.

"I'm sorry, Mamma," he said.

Her eyes rounded. He hadn't called her *mamma* in years, nor was he in the habit of expressing sympathy toward her. Aden had surprised her, and himself.

"Thank you, my son," she whispered, her voice husky with emotion.

"Yes, er . . . you're welcome," he said, feeling awkward. God, he hated emotional entanglements.

Her gaze sharpened and her manner changed in the blink of an eye. "You'd better tell me everything," she said in a brisk voice. "What have you been doing to protect Vivien, and what do you wish to gain from this evening?"

Grateful for the change in subject—and for his mother's astute perceptions— Aden was more forthcoming than usual. Not that his mother didn't know exactly what he did for a living. He just wasn't used to discussing it with anyone outside the Service.

Especially his mother.

"I've had her watched, from a distance, of course. We don't want to tip anyone off. With a little luck, the kidnappers might show themselves sooner rather than later. Then we'll be able to track them back to the source of the plot."

She looked worried, but he waved a reassuring hand. "You needn't be concerned. If anyone tried to snatch Lady Vivien, my men would be close enough to prevent it."

Dominic had given him carte blanche to pick whichever men Aden wanted to assist him. Aden had kept the number small in order to minimize detection—two agents that Dominic agreed to recall to London, along with two others from Dominic's personal staff. The other agents had made it possible for Aden to devote his time to tracking the villains responsible for her kidnapping, and had the added benefit of keeping him well away from Vivien's path.

But despite long days and longer nights trolling through London's underbelly, he'd only managed to gather a few bits of useful information. Nothing close to what he needed to discover who had actually planned the abduction, and why.

And that had forced Aden to come out of the shadows and into the bright, overheated ballrooms of the *ton,* placing himself directly in Vivien's orbit. Down deep, a growling satisfaction with that notion rustled within him, which served as more than ample warning.

"Does she seem well?" his mother asked. "I just returned to London this morning, so I've not yet seen her."

"She appears to be fine, and she's displayed a satisfactory degree of caution, I'm happy to say. Lady Vivien has only left the house twice in the last two days. Once to visit Hatchard's and once to Bruton Street to see her modiste. Both times she was accompanied by a very large footman and her maid."

"Vivien has always been a very sensible girl."

Sensible was not a word others had used to describe her. Aden had made it his business to find out how others perceived her, especially men. *A prime article*, *a charming piece*, *a reckless flirt*, and *fast* had been descriptions crossing the lips of more than one gentleman in London's most expensive gaming hells or in the coffeehouses. Anger had tightened every muscle when hearing those insulting descriptions, but he'd forced himself not to react. Her reputation didn't match his experience with her, but he couldn't afford to let that cloud his judgment.

How she'd acquired that reputation was something of a mystery, although he suspected it had to do with her success at the card table. No man appreciated losing to a woman, especially a beautiful and young woman.

"What do you think of her brothers?" he asked.

His mother blinked at the abrupt change in direction. "Well, Kit—Christopher—is a lovely boy, but too reckless by far. He is forever in his brother's bad books, and I fear he causes Vivien much heartache. Both she and Lady Blake are afraid that Cyrus will soon lose his patience with Kit and force him to take a commission."

Aden frowned. "What would be wrong with that?"

"Kit is much too young. Barely more than a boy."

"He's more than twenty, from what I understand. And if it's maturity Lord Blake seeks for his brother, then the military will provide it."

His mother sighed. "You wouldn't understand."

"You're right. No, don't bother to explain," Aden said, waving a hand. "We're almost to Darlington House. Tell me about Cyrus, Lord Blake, instead."

His mother's lips thinned with displeasure. "You've met him. He's a prig. Unbearably pompous and solely devoted to the political career he hopes to achieve."

"Ah. That would likely explain why Khovansky was hanging about Blake House the other day." The friendship of a wealthy and influential Russian prince would be of great advantage to a man with political ambitions.

His mother looked startled. "Was that dreadful man there when you brought Vivien home? You didn't tell me."

"Didn't I?"

"Aden, if you wish me to help you, you must tell me everything."

He raised his brows. "Hardly everything, Mother."

She scowled. "Aden," she began in a threatening voice.

"Yes, I understand. Forgive me. I wasn't sure what the prince's presence meant at such a delicate time in the Blake household. It struck me as odd."

"What *was* he doing there?" she demanded.

"He'd come out of concern for Vivien, having heard she was unwell."

But Aden didn't believe that. In fact, he'd be willing to bet a hundred guineas Lord Blake had told Khovansky about Vivien's abduction. Why he would do that was a mystery, but Aden didn't trust the barrel-chested, sneering Russian, and didn't want him anywhere near Vivien.

"Good God," exclaimed his mother. "Vivien can't stand Khovansky. He's the last man she'd want hanging about."

Aden's gut unclenched a bit with that news. "She told you that?"

"Well, not in so many words. Vivien is a lively, charming

girl, but she's also surprisingly self-contained. She doesn't share her thoughts and feelings lightly, and never in public. But I've watched her with the prince. Her manners are always faultless—Vivien could never be rude—but I can tell he discomforts her. She avoids him whenever possible."

Aden tensed. "Has he made improper advances?"

She frowned down at her lap, obviously thinking it through. "I don't think so," she finally said, "but he's very persistent. Princes can be that way, you know," she finished on a bitter note.

Aden fought back a flare of anger, whether on his mother's behalf or Vivien's, he couldn't tell. "I understand. I've not yet had time to investigate the prince, but I will."

Her eyes gleamed with curiosity. "Who exactly have you been investigating?"

He gave her a sardonic smile. "Lady Vivien's family. It's almost always the family."

"Really, Aden, I doubt—"

"Mother, enough," he warned, as the coach came to a halt. "We've arrived. I suggest we save further discussion for a more private setting."

He heard her mutter *dreadful boy* as he handed her down to the street, and couldn't hold back a grin. Ignoring him, she sailed up the steps and into the Darlington mansion. Aden had forgotten how entertaining his mother could be. She was an intelligent, quick-witted woman who never failed to challenge him on those rare occasions when he found himself in her company. He could almost regret all the lost opportunities between them, the missed chances to truly become friends.

Almost.

He caught up to her just inside the door, handing over his hat and cloak to the waiting footman. She slipped her hand through his arm.

"Ready to face the lion's den?" she murmured.

He bent down to whisper in her ear. "Mother, I'm a spy. Really, how bad could this be?"

She gave a strangled laugh. "My son, you have no idea. Why do you think Dominic rarely ventures out into polite company? These people are truly terrifying."

"You have me quaking in my boots. Or, should I say, my blasted dancing shoes."

She laughed outright as she led him through the imposing marbled entrance hall to meet their host and hostess. Aden had only a hazy recollection of Lord and Lady Darlington from the short period he'd spent in London before joining the army, but Lady Darlington certainly seemed to remember him. She fussed over him like a hen-wit, exclaiming how thrilled she was to be the first hostess to welcome Aden back into the fold. He fought not grind his back teeth, especially when she promised—or threatened—to introduce her unmarried daughters.

"Clarissa and Eunice are quite the loveliest, most biddable girls in the *ton*," she said, inspecting him with an avaricious gleam. "I know you will be quite taken with them. And such splendid dancers, too. I'll be sure to tell them to save at least two dances for you, Captain St. George. You will be delighted with my girls, I assure you."

Lord Darlington was only slightly less alarming than his wife, wringing Aden's hand and loudly inviting him to his hunting box in Lincoln for a week of shooting.

"It's quite the snuggest little box you've ever seen," Lord Darlington boomed in a genial voice. "Your father, Lord Blake, that is," he said, carefully making the distinction, "used to visit every season, along with mutual friends. Every year, without fail. Practically a ritual, don't you know. We love the ladies, but every once in a while a man needs a respite from all that domesticity, eh, my dear?" he finished, with a broad wink at his wife.

Lady Darlington, who looked fifty if she was a day, slapped

her husband's arm with her fan and giggled like an untried maiden. Darlington roared with laughter and passed Aden along, but not before Lady Darlington added an invitation of her own for Lady Thornbury and Aden to spend Christmas with them in Somerset.

"Capital idea, my dear." Darlington looked much struck at the notion. "The girls will be pleased as punch to spend the holiday with St. George, I'm sure. They're such merry little pusses, you'll have a grand time."

"And mind," he called as Aden and his mother escaped, "I'll be expecting you for a week of shooting, too. Asked that brother of yours time and again, and he always refuses. But someone has to follow in his father's footsteps, my boy, and it might as well be you."

For once, Aden found himself in agreement with his brother. Clearly, he hadn't been giving Edmund nearly enough credit.

"I told you these people were dangerous," his mother murmured as they made their way down the crowded passage to the ballroom.

"If anything, you underestimated the situation. I feel positively faint with horror."

She smirked. "It gets worse."

He snorted. He'd actually forgotten how competitive and cutthroat the marriage mart could be. Boney's most lethal spies would have nothing on Lady Darlington.

It took forever to reach the ballroom since every person they brushed against seemed to be on intimate terms with his mother. Adroitly, she managed introductions, moving Aden along before he could be trapped by any more matchmaking mammas, or old gentlemen who wanted to gossip about France and the meetings in Vienna. Her touch was light and, with only a word or two, she managed forward motion while never giving offense.

With reluctant admiration, Aden watched his mother exercise her considerable talents. No wonder Dominic had insisted she help him. No one was more practiced in the social arts of the *ton* than Lady Thornbury. Without her, he'd be blundering about like a half-wit in a dark cave.

They finally pressed through the chattering throng to reach the massive ballroom. The air hung heavy with the scent of a thousand hothouse blooms, while hundreds of candles imparted light and an already oppressive heat.

"Gad, Mother," he muttered as they pushed their way up to the head of the room, "how do you stand it?"

She shrugged. "I'm used to it."

Aden had almost forgotten what these gatherings were like. With the noise and crowds, it would be difficult if not impossible to protect Vivien, much less have the opportunity to observe her suitors. In fact, this might be the perfect opportunity for someone to make another abduction attempt. There was so much chaotic motion, both on the dance floor and the perimeter, an invading army of Turks could kidnap half the dancers and no one would ever notice.

His instincts prickled to full alert, pushing him hard.

"Mother, I need to find Lady Vivien," he said, letting his gaze roam over the crowd.

She started scanning the room as well. "It's a little early for her to be in the card room. I would think . . . Ah, yes, there she is. Up at the top of the room by the orchestra." She went up on tiptoe, looking startled. "Goodness, she's with—"

"I see," Aden responded grimly. Leaving her, he pushed his way through a knot of lounging young bucks, ignoring their outraged objections.

Yes, he saw Vivien. With her back against a marble column, her beautiful face a carefully blank mask as she stared into the greedy gaze of Prince Ivan Khovansky.

Chapter Thirteen

Vivien's shoulder blades made contact with the column, the cool marble sending a shiver down her spine. That, or Khovansky's ugly leer, triggered the sensation of ants crawling under her skin. Why wouldn't he leave her alone? She was beginning to suspect he saw her as a challenge to his manhood, an obstacle to be overcome rather than a woman to be wooed and won.

"My dear lady," the prince drawled in his heavy accent. "You look flushed. The heat is too much for you, especially in your weakened state. You must allow me to escort you to a quiet alcove, or even Lady Darlington's drawing room. Then you may rest and we can have a pleasant chat."

The tone of his voice signalled it as an order, not a request. But she calmly met his gaze, refusing to flinch under a bold perusal that managed to be both lascivious and imperious.

They stood almost eye to eye. The prince wasn't tall, although he was broad across the shoulders and upper body. With his elaborate Russian uniform, his chest beribboned and pinned, he resembled nothing so much as a colorful rooster. His red hair and whiskers only added to the effect, as did his rather florid complexion.

He was as arrogant as a rooster too, despite the smooth superficiality and elegance of manner that charmed more than a few members of the *ton*. But that polish was as thin as a sheeting of frost on a windowpane. The prince knew his standing and woe betide any man—or woman—who crossed him. Then, those muddy green eyes would grow icy with rage, promising a painful retribution for the unfortunate object of his anger.

Vivien sent up a prayer of thanks that she would never be in his power. "I thank you, Your Highness, but I am quite recovered. Your concern is appreciated but unnecessary."

As much as she couldn't stand the man, he *was* a prince. She didn't dare treat him in the same cavalier manner as she had during their unfortunate encounter at Lady Templeton's musical, when he'd trapped her in an alcove. She simply could *not* kick him again, especially in public, no matter how much he deserved it.

A quick glance over his shoulder told her they were already attracting more than a few curious looks. There was already enough gossip about them, and rumors had already begun circulating about an impending engagement. Vivien knew whom to thank for that lovely little tidbit. Cyrus, who would like nothing better than to marry her off to a powerful and wealthy Russian prince.

The very idea of marriage to the man made her gorge rise.

He stepped closer, crowding her against the column. Vivien's polite expression began to slip. Her palm itched to slap him, and she wondered if it might not be a good idea to cause a scene after all. At least that way everyone would know how much she loathed him. The gain would almost be worth the scandal.

"Ah, sweet Lady Vivien," he crooned affectionately, even though his eyes had acquired a menacing cast. "So beautiful, so delicate, so sweetly foolish. You are like a little dove in need of shelter and protection. You must allow Prince Ivan to take care of you. In fact, I insist upon it."

She almost bit her tongue in shock. *Little dove?* Had he lost his mind?

"Sir, your remarks are most inappropriate," she said sternly. "I insist you let me by. Now."

She started moving before she finished talking, sliding along the column in an effort to get around him. He tracked her movements. Frustrated, she stopped, glaring at him.

"Prince Ivan, I repeat. Please step aside."

His charmless smile transformed itself into a contemptuous one. "Or what, Lady Vivien? You will kick me? I do not counsel you to make that mistake twice."

Vivien's heart thumped at the threatening tone in his voice. She'd always thought the prince an arrogant pig, but now she wondered if he was actually insane. There could be no other explanation for his truly demented behavior, especially in so public a venue.

Unless he thought himself so powerful he simply didn't care. But scandalous scene or no, it was time to get rid of him, once and for all. Just as she lifted a hand to shove him, a figure loomed behind the prince. Towered over him, actually. Vivien sagged back against the column in relief.

St. George, impeccably attired in evening garb, arriving once again to rescue her.

"Lady Vivien," he said, shouldering the prince aside and ignoring the outraged hiss from the other man. "My mother has been looking all over for you. Imagine my surprise to find you hiding behind a pillar. Are you avoiding someone?" A casual smile curved up the corners of his hard mouth, but his eyes probed her, acutely watchful.

"Captain, how lovely to see you again," Vivien replied, surprised her voice wasn't shaking. "I was just, ah, saying goodbye to Prince Ivan."

St. George peered down at the prince from his considerable

height, looking faintly surprised. "Indeed. Is that what you were doing? I wondered about that."

Vivien didn't know whether to laugh or wince at the blatant insult. But then she saw the deadly look on the prince's face and decided wincing was the more appropriate response.

Not that St. George looked the least bit intimidated. He regarded the prince with an aristocratic disdain that could not have been topped by any member of the British royal family.

Khovansky flushed a brick red, and Vivien had little doubt he'd be happy to run St. George through with his ceremonial sword. If she didn't want the evening dissolving into a complete nightmare, she'd better take matters in hand.

"Captain, I'm sure you remember Prince Ivan Khovansky. You met him the other morning at Blake House."

St. George gave a slight bow, as if he could barely be bothered to acknowledge the other man's existence. "Of course. How could I forget?" he said in a bored voice.

Khovansky surprised her by tilting his head, looking more curious than anything else. "Ah, Lady Thornbury's son. Your mother is a charming woman, a trait which you do not share."

Vivien couldn't quite smother a gasp. She cast a desperate glance around their immediate vicinity, praying no one overheard the snarling exchange. Fortunately, the drunken frolics of the *beau monde* swirled about them, unabated and uncaring of the little drama in the corner.

St. George replied to the prince's insult by smiling. "My mother would share your opinion, Your Highness. In fact, why don't you go ask her? Lady Vivien and I will be happy to excuse you."

This time Khovansky's jaw worked, as if the words were trapped on his tongue. "As delighted as I would be to speak with Lady Thornbury, I must decline. I was about to escort Lady Vivien to an anteroom. She is greatly in need of some rest and quiet as she recovers from her illness."

He turned, trying to grasp her hand. "Come with me, my dear. You can speak with Lady Thornbury later."

Vivien snatched her hand away, speechless with frustration and disbelief. When the prince reached for her again, St. George stepped between them.

"I don't think so, Your Highness," he said. He tilted his head, listening to the first strains of the waltz. "Ah. Our dance, I believe, Lady Vivien."

His charming smile didn't fool her, despite its outrageously attractive appeal. She'd already begun to learn how to read the expression in his dark eyes, and those eyes were commanding her to comply. Fortunately, this was one order she was happy to obey.

"Dear me," she said. "How could I have forgotten?" She pressed a hand to her chest, trying to look regretful. "Please forgive me, Prince Ivan, but I mustn't disappoint the captain." She finished on a firm note, hoping he would finally comprehend the message in her voice.

The prince stared at her for a few seconds, his features pulled tight with disbelief and rage. Then he blinked slowly, twice, and the rage disappeared, leaving in its wake a flat, expressionless mask she found more disturbing than the rage.

"Of course, my dear," he said in a precise and chilly tone. "Young ladies must be allowed their little diversions and entertainments before taking up the responsibilities of marriage. I shall leave you to it." He gave a slight inclination of the head and then was swallowed up in the throng—but not before casting a menacing, promise-filled glance at St. George.

St. George watched him go with a thoughtful expression, then glanced down at her. "You certainly have some interesting suitors, Lady Vivien, I'll give you that much."

She scoffed. "Don't be an idiot. Of course he's not one of my suitors."

He gave her a faintly skeptical smile.

"Well," she amended, "he is, but not because I want him to be. It's not as if I have any control over the situation. What am I to do?"

He reached out then and took her into his arms, sweeping her onto the crowded floor and into the first turns of the waltz. The heat and strength of him, the clean masculine smell of soap and starched linen enveloped her as she melted into his embrace. Her emotions took flight in a startling leap, matching her racing heart. Although they'd never danced, it felt wonderfully familiar to be in his arms again.

Her breath left her in a whoosh as clarity struck. She'd spent the last five days and nights secretly wishing to be exactly where she was—in his arms, cradled against him.

That understanding stunned her into silence as she stared up into his darkly intense gaze. Thank God her arms and legs knew what to do as she followed him in the graceful motions of the waltz. Or perhaps that was all him, guiding her down the room in flowing revolutions that swirled the rose-colored silk of her skirts around his legs as their bodies touched, separated, and touched again in the seductive figures of the dance.

"He is a prince," he replied in answer to her last question. "I doubt anyone would blame you if you did entertain his suit. In fact, I suspect there are any number of young ladies in this room who would trample you into the dance floor to capture even one iota of the attention Prince Ivan directs your way."

His words brought her thumping back to earth, as did the cool look on his face. If she didn't miss her guess, he studied her with dispassionate interest, as if she were an interesting specimen to be observed or an equation to be solved.

"They can have him," she groused. "And I'm not sure, Captain St. George, what you expect me to do to rid myself of his attentions. Pistols at dawn, perhaps?"

He laughed, a deep, husky sound that rippled along her nerves. But the laugh failed to reach his eyes. Instead, he watched with that disturbingly perceptive gaze, all while skillfully guiding them through a mass of jostling dancers. As annoyed as she was, she couldn't help but admire his strength and control. Oh, yes, and the muscles in his shoulder that flexed beneath her fingers. They were most admirable too.

"That might be one approach, but I suggest a simple *no* might do the trick," he said.

"Thank you," she said sarcastically. "That had not yet occurred to me. Of *course* I told him no, but the blasted thickhead won't listen to a word I say. Even a kick to the shins didn't do the trick."

She could have bitten her tongue as soon as the words slipped past her lips. How humiliating to reveal that embarrassing incident, especially to him.

He looked startled, then his hand flexed on her waist and he pulled her closer into his embrace. Vivien couldn't repress a shiver as the tops of his muscled thighs brushed against her pelvis. She pulled in a deep breath, suddenly feeling a constriction around her ribs.

His gaze flickered down to her bodice, then back up to her face. His eyes darkened with a raw heat.

Oh, she recognized *that* look. She'd seen it before in more than one man's eyes, but never had it affected her like this. Excitement and apprehension danced along her skin and she had to drop her gaze, biting her lip like a nervous child. All the while the dancers spun around them in a jewel-like whirl, the strings of the orchestra swelling to a crescendo. But she felt apart from all of that, every particle of her being aware only of him.

When she finally worked up the courage to look past his white satin waistcoat, he had shifted his gaze over her shoulder. With a few deft turns, he moved her down to one of the corners of the room and to a door leading out to a side hallway. Quickly and efficiently he guided her out of the room and to a quiet window alcove, one that afforded them some privacy but was still well within view of anyone strolling in the hall.

"What are you doing?" she asked, forcing the words out.

"It's all right," he said in a soothing tone. "You needed to catch your breath. I was twirling you about in a rather vigorous fashion, wasn't it?"

She nodded, pretending to agree. But it wasn't the dance that had robbed her of breath. It was St. George, and those looks had swept through her like a summer storm. He seemed to have a lethal effect on her emotions, turning her into a blithering idiot, and it was time she remembered that.

He waited patiently while she took a few moments to steady herself. When a waiter passed by carrying a tray of crystalline goblets, St. George snagged one and handed it over. She sipped the icy punch, studying him surreptitiously over the rim of the glass.

Heavens, he was a gorgeous man, especially in evening dress. The stark black coat and trousers set off his muscular build to perfection, and his white cravat and silk waistcoat enhanced his tanned features. He radiated masculine vitality and power, and a raw sensuality that set off an odd pinging sensation low in her belly.

But there were other things that went along with all that power and masculinity, like the ability to knife someone to death without turning a hair. Generally speaking, not a talent one looked for in a suitor, although her recent experience suggested that having a man like St. George as an escort was actually rather desirable.

He waited patiently while she finished her punch, then took the glass and set it on a little side table. "Better?" he asked.

"Yes, thank you."

"Good. Now, why don't you tell me what happened with Prince Ivan. I believe you said you kicked him in the shins?"

She should have known he wouldn't let it go. "It was nothing. Really."

He leaned a broad shoulder against the curved wall of the alcove, as if ready to settle in for the evening. "He must have done something to elicit so forceful a reaction from a well-bred young lady."

She eyed him suspiciously but decided he wasn't mocking her. Still, she loathed having to explain it to him. She still felt like a complete fool for allowing the prince to trap her like that in the first place.

He sighed. "Vivien, you might as well tell me everything. I'll just keep pestering you until you do."

She blinked, startled that he used her given name so easily. She supposed it made sense given what they'd been through together, but it made her feel shy. They barely knew each other, and yet their shared experience had created a level of intimacy she found both reassuring and disconcerting.

It also seemed to tangle her tongue in knots.

"Vivien?" he gently prompted.

"Oh, very well. It happened a few weeks ago at Lady Templeton's musicale. Prince Ivan managed to trap me in a secluded alcove, and he grew quite . . . quite amorous."

His gaze sharpened. "What exactly does that mean?"

"What do you think it means? He tried to kiss me." As hard as she tried, she couldn't help blushing. The rude curse St. George muttered didn't help either.

"And that's when you kicked him in the shins."

She rolled her eyes. "Obviously."

"Then what did he do?"

Vivien eyed him uneasily. The polished aristocrat seemed to have disappeared, and in his place was the cold-eyed killer she'd glimpsed back in the smugglers' cave. A chill skated up her spine, and she couldn't help edging back an inch.

Something like guilt flashed across his features, and then

was gone. But so was the other man—the killer who unsettled her so deeply.

He rubbed a hand across his forehead. "Vivien, you do realize I would never hurt you?"

She nodded.

"Good. I apologize if I frightened you, but I can't stand the idea of that toad putting his hands on you."

She bit back a startled laugh at his description. That's exactly how she'd always thought of Khovansky too. "I don't like it very much, either, which is why I kicked him."

He gave her a faint smile. "Good girl. Then what happened?"

She shrugged. "I got away from him and left the ball almost immediately. I didn't see him after that. Not until the other day when you brought me home."

"Interesting. Khovansky made no attempt to call on you to make an apology? He didn't send you a note?"

"Nothing." She frowned. "That is rather odd, now that I think about it. At the time, I simply thought he'd finally gotten the message."

"You'd rebuffed him before?"

"More than once. He's very persistent, even though I clearly told him I had no intention of accepting his suit."

"So, he actually did ask you to marry him."

"Yes."

"And then gave up, just like that?"

"Y-yes," she answered slowly, wondering what he was getting at. She studied him, but he'd adopted his impassive face. From the little she'd seen of him in action, it meant he was thinking.

"What's Khovansky's relationship to your brother?" he finally asked.

Blast and double blast.

"Which one?" she hedged.

"Lord Blake."

Relief weakened her legs. "They're friendly," she said with a vague wave of her hand. "Cyrus moves in political and diplomatic circles, like the prince."

He fell silent again, rubbing his jaw. Vivien tried not to fidget but her nerves got the better of her. She started tapping her toe, a habit she usually managed to keep under control. St. George had a remarkable ability to fluster her.

"What are you thinking?" she finally blurted out. For a moment, she thought he didn't intend to answer.

"I'm wondering just how far the prince will go in order to win your hand," he mused, half to himself. Or all to himself, since he wasn't even looking at her. He stared down at his feet, as if some message were scrolled in the patterns of the marbled floor.

She shook her head, more for her own benefit than his. "If you're thinking he was behind the abduction, I think that highly unlikely." No matter how much she loathed him, she simply couldn't believe he'd go about kidnapping innocent women. The scandal around that sort of escapade coming to light would be earth-shaking.

St. George cut his gaze up to her face. "And what does your younger brother think about the prince? Does he travel in his circles as well?"

Vivien's heart skipped a beat. The discussion was coming much too close to home, but she couldn't let him see that. "He barely knows him," she said with a dismissive shrug of her shoulders.

"Really? I got the impression the other day that your younger brother knew him quite well."

She tried to force down her escalating panic, knowing she had to get away from him before she blurted out something that might further draw his focus to Kit.

A handsome longcase clock behind them bonged out the

approaching supper hour. She seized on the excuse to escape. "Goodness, look at the time," she exclaimed. "I promised Mamma I would meet her for supper."

His gaze flicked down the hall and then returned to her. "Very well. I'll be happy to escort you up to the supper room. I'd like very much to meet your mother."

The grim tone of his voice told her he wouldn't like it at all, but wanted to add her mother to his list of suspects. And if there was one thing Vivien could count on, it was that Mamma would fold like a house of cards as soon as St. George began to question her. Her mother had *no* sense of discretion, nor could she ever resist the attentions of a handsome man.

Well, any man, for that matter. But she'd surely dissolve into a compliant puddle once St. George turned his seductively dangerous eyes upon her.

"That won't be necessary," she exclaimed in a dementedly cheery voice. "But thank you for helping me with the prince. I'm most grateful."

Ignoring his objections, she slipped past him and down the hall. Only when she fell in with a stream of guests heading toward the front of the house did she relax.

She glanced over her shoulder. St. George stood where she had left him, fists propped on his lean hips and attention still fixed on her. His gaze bored into her, alert and perceptive, and far too suspicious. When he started toward her, a hunter intent on his prey, her courage failed.

Vivien turned and fled as if a pack of baying hell hounds snapped at her heels.

Chapter Fourteen

"Vivien, please stop twisting about like a top," Mamma ordered. "I vow I'm getting dizzy simply watching you."

Flashing a guilty smile, Vivien faced her mother across the table in the elegant supper room. In all fairness, she'd been restless since she and Mamma settled in to enjoy a plate of sweets and a glass of champagne. But that wasn't her fault, was it? She'd been forced to keep an eye out for St. George, praying that he and Lady Thornbury would find themselves too busy to visit with them.

Apparently, they were. St. George was part of a noisy group ensconced by the fireplace, with his mother seated on one side of him and the over-endowed Judith Compton on the other. Judith—the *worst* flirt—appeared to be making a concerted effort to claim his undivided attention. She batted her eyelashes, trilled with laughter at his every word, and leaned forward in the most obvious way to give him an ample view of her impressive bosom. He didn't seem to mind in the slightest, not even when Judith let her hand *accidentally* brush his thigh. He'd simply bowed his head even closer, all the better to hear her social inanities.

Yes, St. George seemed quite taken with her, which struck Vivien as odd since Judith was not only blowsy and obvious but nasty-tempered as well. It represented the mystery of the male mind, although Vivien had the lowering feeling that the generous décolletage factored into the equation.

She gave a disdainful sniff as she pushed a piece of iced pound cake around her plate. Not that she cared one way or the other where St. George bestowed his attentions. The more time he spent in Judith's company, the less he could study her with those penetrating eyes or pry information out of Mamma. That had clearly been his intention when he offered to escort her up to supper, not the pleasure of her company.

"Vivien, you mustn't frown," Mamma said with a gentle scold. "It wrinkles your brow, and nothing is more fatal to a woman's beauty." She peered across the small, linen-covered table. "In fact, you're already getting a wrinkle between your eyebrows. You simply must start using that Denmark Lotion I gave you last month. You are no longer in the first blush of youth, my love. You cannot afford to neglect your complexion so dreadfully."

Vivien wanted to grind her tooth, but that would probably give her wrinkles, too. According to Mamma, just about everything did.

"I shall be sure to use it before I go to bed," she replied, trying to sound dutiful.

Her mother rewarded her with a beatific smile, her blue eyes—so like Vivien's—shining with maternal pride. "Thank you, darling. You are still quite the most beautiful and charming girl in London, and a great matrimonial prize. Everyone knows it, too."

Vivien didn't bother denying the fallacy of that particular observation, since she knew it sprang from genuine affection on her mother's part. There were any number of girls in the *ton* both younger and prettier, and Vivien's dowry was merely respectable. She often wondered if she'd ever find a man she truly wanted to marry. As comfortable as she was in her brother's house, she still longed for a home and a husband of her own. A husband who would actually care about *her* needs, and who would help relieve her burdens instead of adding to them.

"Will you be visiting the card room tonight, my love?" Mamma asked in a carefully matter-of-fact voice. Though she flashed a lighthearted smile, Vivien wasn't fooled. Her mother's eyes looked haunted, and she held her delicate lace fan in a convulsive grip as she tapped it on the base of her champagne goblet.

But even looking so anxious, Vivien's mother remained one of the most beautiful women in the room. In her fifties, she was slender and graceful of form with golden hair only just threaded with a few errant strands of silver. And when she cast aside her troubles, she sparkled with a youthful vibrancy that could charm any man under the age of eighty.

Unfortunately, that youthful nature also extended to her temperament. In fact, the older Vivien got, the more her mother depended on her for everything, from running the household, to playing hostess, to paying off her and Kit's foolish debts. There were days when Vivien felt crushed by the burden of familial responsibility, and more than once she'd been tempted to accept one of the proposals of marriage that had been made to her. But she'd never been able to do it. Her mother and Kit often drove her insane but she couldn't abandon them, especially for a man she didn't love. Her family truly needed her, and that had to count for something.

Vivien nodded. "I was just about to go up. Given how deep the play always is at Lady Darlington's affairs, I think I should do quite well."

Her mother exhaled with relief. "Splendid. Perhaps I'll join you."

Vivien almost dropped her champagne glass. "You will do no such thing."

Lady Pilkington, seated next to her, glanced over from her conversation with the Dowager Duchess of Rothering, her bushy brown eyebrows raised in disapproval. Vivien gave her a weak smile, murmuring an apology. Lady Pilkington looked her over with a supercilious sneer, gave a disgusted little sniff, and turned back to the duchess.

Mamma whispered loudly across the table. "Dreadful woman. No wonder Lord Pilkington spends all his time in brothels. I would, too, if I had to face her in my bed every night."

Vivien swallowed a laugh. "Thank you for that image, Mamma. But as I was saying, I think it best if you not visit the tables tonight."

She gave her mother *the look,* the one that said she would brook no argument. On their way to the ball, Vivien had finally pried out of her the total of her latest round of excesses, at the gaming tables and the shops. The amount had staggered her. Three thousand pounds, added on to what Kit already owed. Vivien had her work cut out for her and she did not need her mother racking up yet more debt at the loo or whist tables.

Mamma thrust out her lower lip, like a pouting child denied a treat.

"No," Vivien reiterated in a firm voice. "If you play tonight, you'll distract me. I must be able to concentrate if I am to win."

She rarely had trouble concentrating. From hardened gamesters to seductive rakes seeking to flirt with her over the cards, none had the ability to break her singular focus. Only when Kit or her mother was playing, and invariably losing, did Vivien mentally blink. Whenever that happened, she had the devil of a time getting her concentration back.

Her mother sighed. "Oh, very well, but I do think—"

She broke off as she looked past Vivien's shoulder, a delighted smile warming her face. "Rebecca! I've been longing to speak with you but I couldn't find you in this mad crush. How lovely to see you here tonight, and with your son, too. I declare, I cannot remember when last I saw you, you naughty boy. You've been neglecting your family and friends in the worst possible manner."

Vivien didn't require her mother's flirtatious behavior to tell her who was standing behind her. Slowly, she twisted in her seat and looked up—way up—to meet the gaze of the man who was quickly becoming both the bane of her existence and her savior. From the sardonic expression on his face as he studied her, bane was more like it at this particular moment.

Ignoring the ripple of nerves in her belly, Vivien warmly greeted Lady Thornbury. Her friend leaned down and pressed a soft, perfumed kiss on her cheek.

"How are you, my dear? Have you recovered from your cold?" Lady Thornbury's eyes, as all-seeing as her son's, gave her a thorough inspection.

"I am well, my lady, thank you," Vivien replied, rising to her feet. "And I'm very glad to see you. I was intending to go up to the card room, and I was hoping you could sit with Mamma."

"Of course," Lady Thornbury said instantly, taking her seat. "I'd like nothing better than to have a comfortable coze with your mother." She glanced up at her son. "Aden, you were thinking of playing some cards as well, weren't you? You children should run along and enjoy yourselves."

Mamma, who had been looking disgruntled, perked up. "Yes, darling. Go along with Aden. I'm sure he'll take splendid care of you."

Vivien could have cursed. The two mothers had virtually thrown them together, albeit for different reasons. Lady Thornbury obviously wanted St. George to keep a watch on her, while Mamma was no different from any of the matchmaking mothers in the *ton*. Unfortunately, her target had designs on Vivien of a different sort, ones that could be dangerous for the Blake family.

"No, really, Captain St. George, that's not necessary," she protested, starting to back away from the table. "I'm sure you'd much rather be dancing. Miss Compton, for instance. I'm certain she's eagerly waiting for you to claim her for the next waltz."

Oh, dear. That *had* sounded rather snippy. Whatever was the matter with her?

With a hint of a smug grin, St. George reached out and snagged her by the wrist. "As it so happens, I was intending to visit the card room."

Experimentally, she tugged her arm. Of course the stubborn man wouldn't let go, and she couldn't possibly get away from him without causing a scene. This was all she needed—him shadowing her every move like a watchdog. Given how the evening was going, Vivien might as well decamp right now and go home.

For a moment, she contemplated doing just that. But she desperately needed to dip into the deep pockets of Lady Darlington's guests. She simply couldn't afford to waste the night's opportunity, St. George or no. "Very well. If you insist," she replied in a grumpy tone. "It doesn't really look like I have much of choice in the matter."

"Vivien!" Her mother's eyes rounded with shock although Lady Thornbury appeared on the verge of laughter.

"I should be honored to escort you, my lady," St. George said, as if she hadn't insulted him.

He slipped her hand in the crook of his elbow and Vivien had no choice but follow his lead. As annoyed as she was, she couldn't repress a little spurt of triumph when they passed the party by the fireplace. Judith Compton was still holding court, tittering at the sly remarks of an aging, rouged dandy, but she found the time to break off and direct a glare Vivien's way.

When Vivien gave her a polite nod, Judith sneered and tossed her curls as she turned back to her companion.

"A friend of yours?" St. George asked dryly.

"Why, Captain," she said, feigning an innocent look, "I thought she was a friend of yours!"

He grinned. "Touché. If you want to know the truth, the woman terrified me. It was cruel of you to abandon me, throwing me to the wolves like that."

"Yes. I noticed you seemed paralyzed with fear, especially when Miss Compton put her hand on your thigh."

His grin went charmingly lopsided as they passed into the hall. "So, you noticed that, did you?"

"The entire room probably noticed."

St. George laughed outright as he ushered her toward the front central staircase. She pulled on his elbow, bringing him to a halt.

"The card room is in the rear of the house," she said.

He stood his ground. "I was hoping I could solicit your hand for another dance. Perhaps a waltz?"

She frowned. "I thought you wanted to go to the card room."

He shrugged, and for a moment she was fascinated by the way his muscles, well defined under the close-fitting fabric of his dark coat, rippled and moved. "I would prefer to dance. With you." His voice dropped to a deep note, husky with an intent she couldn't miss. And the sensual gleam in his eyes sparked a ripple of sensation along her nerves.

It was matched by irritation as he tried to divert her from her purpose.

"I thank you, but no," she answered.

His eyebrows arched as if he were offended. That bothered her more than she cared to admit. He was the last person on earth she wished to offend, since not only had he saved her life, she actually liked him.

Too much, unfortunately.

"Well," she amended, "perhaps later. But right now I truly

would like to visit the card tables." She tugged his arm and he finally relented, although he didn't look happy about it.

They joined the stream of guests making their way to the gaming tables. When Vivien was jostled by two lads no older than Kit and eager to get to the tables, St. George gently moved her to his other side, protectively sheltering her. She had to resist the temptation to snuggle into him, much as she had done the night of her rescue when he had swept her into his arms.

That memory—and his nearness—triggered another image. A sensation, really, of what his rampant masculinity had felt like pressed against her backside. It had made her nervous but it had intrigued her, too. *Everything* about him intrigued her, and she couldn't help wondering what it would be like if he were her suitor and not some kind of bodyguard commissioned to protect her. What it would feel like if he kissed her, taking her in his arms and pressing her up against—

"Lady Vivien, are you well?" he interrupted her thoughts.

Her face burned with heat. Lord, what an idiot she was. Having fantasies about the man when he was standing right next to her!

"Ah, I'm fine. Why?"

"You're very flushed." He eyed her, then glanced at the small mob trying to crowd through to the drawing room set aside for the card players. "It's much too warm in here for you. We should return to the supper room for a cool drink."

She sighed, wishing he would stop treating her like a baby. Or an invalid. "I said I was fine. And I intend to play cards. If you do not wish to play, there is no need to accompany me."

His mobile, well-shaped mouth thinned into a hard line. "You like playing cards, don't you?"

"Yes. Is there anything wrong with that?" She tried not to sound defensive.

He didn't immediately answer. They reached the entrance to the spacious drawing room and he steered her just inside the door and to the side, out of the flow of traffic. His gaze was hooded as he seemed to weigh his reply.

"You are known for playing deep and often, and for winning," he finally said. "Very consistently, I might add. Gambling to such a degree is a rather unusual avocation for a gently bred, unmarried young woman."

Normally, it didn't bother her that some members of the *ton* disapproved of her behavior. Almost everyone gambled and played cards, even young ladies like her. Of course, most young ladies didn't bet the kind of sums she did, or play at tables with experienced gamblers, most of them men. But Vivien wouldn't apologize for that. She'd learned long ago to take pride in her skills and to leave shame behind. Yes, some might find her conduct bordering on the disgraceful, but she'd far rather face a little gossip and the occasional snub than have her mother reduced to impecunious dependence on Cyrus. Or see Kit land in debtors' prison or the army.

But for the first time in a long time, her cheeks heated with shame, both for herself and for her family. She didn't like that one bit.

"Do you disapprove?" she challenged, lacing her fingers together in front of her as she waited for him to answer. She would *not* apologize for what she did, nor stoop to defend it. If he didn't understand, so be it.

He studied her, part of his face cast in shadow by the flickering light of the wall sconce behind him. His gaze was veiled, unknowable, and Vivien suddenly realized how little she understood him. Their enforced intimacy of a few nights ago had been nothing more than a trick of the emotions, generated by the bizarre and dangerous situation. She might have fooled herself into thinking she knew him but, in truth, he remained a stranger.

But a stranger whose approval, for some reason, she craved.

Just when she began to think he wouldn't answer, his lips

parted. "It is not my position to approve or disapprove, my lady. Only you can be the true judge of your own behavior."

Which clearly meant he *did* disapprove, putting him in the camp of those who judged, and found her behavior wanting. She stared at him for a few seconds before she found a way past the irrational disappointment to answer him.

"Well, I shall leave you to your own devices then, Captain. I wouldn't want my scandalous behavior to shock you more than it already has. Good night."

Impatience flashed across his face, breaking his iron control. "That's not what I meant," he said, reaching for her.

Somehow, she evaded his grasp, slipping away into the crowd. As she moved between the tables, she resisted the temptation to look back. But her chest squeezed with a horrible combination of resentment toward him and dissatisfaction with herself. Even worse, she missed him by her side, an emotion that surely qualified her for the madhouse. How could she long for the company of a man who disapproved of her, and probably saw her as no more than a troublesome obligation foisted on him by Sir Dominic?

No. The sooner she forgot about Captain Aden St. George, the better. She had business to attend to this night, and she needed to have all her concentration focused on that business.

But as Vivien slipped into an open place at the loo table, she couldn't help one glance back at the door. St. George was gone, thank goodness, but her concentration had probably departed with him. Fighting a headache from the noise and heat, and from her own tangled feelings, she put her markers down on the table.

When she lost three tricks in a row, she knew her luck had vanished with St. George.

Chapter Fifteen

Susan beamed as she finished curling Vivien's hair. "You look a picture, my lady, God's truth. Those Russian lords and princes will be falling all over themselves to sit next to you."

Vivien managed to give her maid a sickly smile. That was her exact fear, and from one Russian prince in particular. Lord knows she'd made every excuse to avoid her brother's dinner party to honor the Russian ambassador once she'd confirmed that Khovansky would be attending. But Cyrus wouldn't hear of it, thundering that she must attend or face any number of vaguely uttered threats. Even when their mother had offered to play hostess in her stead, Cyrus had still carried on, reducing Mamma to a quivering bundle of nerves. Finally, Vivien had relented in the certain knowledge that Cyrus would make everyone in the house miserable if she didn't.

Susan moved about the bedroom, tidying up and putting away discarded clothing. Vivien rummaged around in the drawers of her dressing table until she found the gold fan that matched her dress. It wouldn't be just an accessory, not tonight. Between the roaring fires in the overheated rooms Cyrus insisted upon and her anxiety over Khovansky, she'd be in a nervous lather all night. Truthfully, she already was.

She'd done what she could to minimize contact with Ivan

the Terrible, like sneaking down earlier and switching the place cards at the dinner table. Khovansky would now spend dinner between the Dowager Countess of Markwith, the deafest woman in the *ton,* and Lady Peaksworth, the most talkative. The fact that Vivien had been reduced to such a childish subterfuge was a sad indication of how desperate she'd become.

Gathering up her fan and gloves, she did a last check of her shimmering gold silk dress and headed for the door. She couldn't wait for the evening to be over since she had better things to do—like winning enough money to pay off Kit's debt. Thanks to St. George and his uncanny ability to fluster her, Vivien's winnings at the Darlington ball had been meager. The man was a menace to her peace of mind and she needed to stay well away from him, especially given the next step in her plan.

Before she could reach the door a brief knock sounded. Cyrus let himself in, looking pompous and harried.

"What is it, Cyrus?" Vivien asked as she pulled on her gloves. "The guests will be here any minute and I don't want to be late."

Her brother scowled at her from under his thick, dark brows. Of the three Blake children, only he took after their father. Tall and rather heavyset, he carried himself with the same innate dignity. Cyrus, unfortunately, had not inherited their father's kind nature. Her brother combined the worst of their parents' dispositions—Papa's ponderous dignity combined with Mamma's selfish nature did not make for a happy combination of traits.

"This will take but a minute," he said, giving Susan a brusque nod of dismissal.

When Vivien let out an audible sigh, he cast a dark glance her way then stalked over to the fireplace. He turned around and lifted his coattails to warm his backside.

"As you know, Vivien, Prince Ivan will be attending our party this evening."

She barely managed to keep from rolling her eyes. Trust Cyrus to state the obvious. Repeatedly.

"What you might not know," he continued, "is that the prince has asked my permission to court you. Naturally, I assured him that his suit would be most welcome, both to you and to the family."

A haze of anger clouded her vision. Fists clenching, Vivien charged forward a few steps and then came to an abrupt halt at the startled look on her brother's face. She sucked in a deep breath, struggling to contain her fury. Blustering at him would only make matters worse.

"You had no right to make any such claim, brother. I have already made it clear to His Highness that I am not interested in his suit."

Cyrus looked offended. "I never took you for a fool, Vivien. Unlike Mother and Kit, you actually have some brains. But in this matter, I do believe your wits have gone begging."

"You are entitled to your opinion, but I cannot agree," she snapped. "In any event, I reached my majority long ago, and I need neither your approval nor disapproval in this matter. And since I have no intention of marrying Prince Ivan, this discussion is officially over."

She turned her back on him and headed for the door.

"It is not, Vivien. You are dependent on me for your financial support, and I will certainly withdraw it if you defy me. And Mamma's and Kit's as well."

She stumbled to a halt, almost tripping over her pretty, gold-embroidered slippers. She *did* drop her fan, and she used the few seconds needed to pick it up to recover her countenance. When she turned to face him, her stomach fell at the shocking and unrelenting contempt in his gaze. Had her brother always disliked her so much, or had it gotten worse over the last few years? She could no longer tell.

"You would do that?" she asked, incredulous. "Do you loathe us all that much?"

He snorted. "Don't be such a dramatic little fool. I'm doing this for *you*. For all of us. The Blake family teeters on the verge of ruin, Vivien."

Her breathing stalled in her throat. Had he found out about Kit's debt? "What in heaven's name are you talking about?"

"You know very well what I'm talking about. Mamma's extravagance is ruinous, and Kit's not much better. Not a day goes by that I don't receive some outrageous bill from one tradesman or another." He scowled, thrusting his hands behind him and puffing up his chest. "If I didn't keep such a close eye on things, the pair of them would have bankrupted us long ago. And there's no knowing how much they've lost at the gambling tables and are hiding from us."

Vivien finally let out her breath. At least he hadn't discovered that horrible secret.

"That is indeed unfortunate, but how does Mamma's or Kit's spending habits affect my decision?" she asked, trying to sound like she didn't already know the answer.

He scoffed. "You're not a green girl, Vivien. You know very well. Prince Ivan is willing to pay off *all* of the family's accumulated debts, and also make you a very handsome settlement with very generous provisions for pin money."

Cyrus paused, then let out a ghost of a laugh. "In fact, I can't believe how much the man is willing to spend on you. A fortune, in fact. It's quite remarkable."

An icy thread of apprehension curled through her. She could practically hear the wheels turning in his head, calculating how the marriage—and the money—could benefit his political career. This was bad. Catastrophic, in fact. With a settlement like that, even Mamma and Kit might press her to accept.

"I don't care if it's enough money to pay off the Prince Regent's debts," she said, her voice tight with impending panic. "I have no intention of accepting the offer."

"Christ, Vivien, what's the matter with you? Not only will you be marrying a man as rich as Midas, you'll be a princess! What girl doesn't want that?"

"I don't," she flared back, waving her arm. "Whatever you might think of me, I'm not that shallow. Nor do I care to be forced into the position to say good-bye to my family and friends—possibly forever—and move to Russia. Lord, Cyrus. I don't even speak the man's bloody language!"

A quiet fury seemed to settle over him and his gaze turned flat and hollow. He took a menacing step forward and it took all her discipline to hold her ground. Cyrus loved to bluster and storm about, but he'd never intimidated her. This reaction to her refusal was different. She found it almost frightening.

"Then I suggest you start learning Russian because my mind is made up," he answered in a voice as harsh as rocks grinding under a wheel. "If you do not marry him, I will send you and our mother north to the estate in Yorkshire. You will both stay there until you come to your senses."

She stared at him in horror. The Yorkshire estate was nothing more than a small manor house on the edge of the moors, a legacy from a paternal uncle who'd died without issue. It was barely habitable, and miles from anything that resembled a town. Mamma would have a complete break-down, and Vivien would go insane having to deal with her.

Her face felt numb. "You wouldn't dare," she hissed.

He curled an imperious lip. "Need I remind you that I control the purse strings in this family? And if you do refuse, not only will I exile you to the north, I will cut Kit's allowance, as well. That will leave him with two choices—join the army, or go to debtors' prison. And I will *not* be buying him a commission."

She flinched, as if he had slapped her. Without the funds to buy a commission into an elite regiment Kit's only choice would be to join the infantry. And then where would he be sent? Some horrible battlefield? Or India, to die of disease?

"Cyrus, you mustn't do this," she pleaded. "The prince . . . he's . . . I don't like him. He's not a good man."

A strange expression flitted across her brother's face. Was it guilt? She couldn't tell because it disappeared so quickly.

"Well, he's not an Englishman," Cyrus admitted grudgingly. "But if you give him a chance, I'm sure he'll grow on you."

"It's got nothing to do with his nationality," she gritted out. "And I'm certain he will not grow on me."

Cyrus shook his head. "Then I have nothing more to say to you. On the morrow, you and Mamma will begin packing for your trip to Yorkshire." He turned on his heel and headed for the door.

Vivien clutched her forehead, trying to think. "Wait," she cried as his hand wrapped around the doorknob.

He slowly turned back, not bothering to hide the triumph on his broad, fleshy features. In that moment, any lingering remnants of affection Vivien harbored for her brother died a swift death.

"What is it, my dear?" he asked in a falsely affectionate voice.

Repressing the impulse to fly at him, Vivien gave him what she hoped was an apologetic smile. "Perhaps I was too hasty. Cyrus, surely we can talk about this."

"We've talked enough," he said impatiently. "Our guests will be arriving momentarily. Make your decision, Vivien. One way or the other."

"Yes, well, I might have been a little too hasty in my judgment of the prince. Perhaps we should spend more time together, get to know each other. I'm sure you're correct that Prince Ivan will improve on further acquaintance."

Cyrus barked out an ugly laugh. "You think I'm a fool, don't you? You cannot charm your way out of this dilemma, Vivien. Not with me."

She stared at him, truly sick and tired of being treated by men as a mere pawn to move around the chessboard of their ambitions and desires. But she couldn't afford to let him see the depth of her disgust.

"For God's sake, I'm not saying no. I'm saying I need a little time to get used to the idea, before you force me into an engagement by making an announcement without my agreement. Have you forgotten that little more than a week ago I was abducted and brutalized? Must I be put in the position of thinking my own brother is little better than the villains who kidnapped me?"

His eyes widened and his fleshy features paled. When she continued to glare at him, he shifted his gaze off into the corner. "Forgive me," he muttered. "You seemed fully recovered or I would not have broached the subject."

"Well, I'm not. And forcing me into an engagement before I'm ready is *not* the act of a loving brother," she said in a severe voice.

He stiffened, and Vivien realized she'd overplayed her hand. She opened her mouth, intending to placate him, but he waved an irritable hand.

"Whether you find me a loving brother or not is beside the point. You have a duty to your family, as do I. I will tell Prince Ivan that you are willing to entertain his courtship, although no formal announcement will be made at this point in time. That should satisfy His Highness."

Vivien nodded weakly in relief. She had no intention of ever accepting the prince's proposal, but at least she'd bought some time to put her plan into effect. With a little luck, within a few weeks she should have most of the money she needed to reduce Kit's and Mamma's debts to a manageable level, and enough to set the three of them up in a small town house, if necessary. A very small town house, but it would at least gain them their freedom.

"Very well," she said. "I will agree to your terms."

He nodded and his color returned its normal, ruddy hue. "It's time to go down," he said, opening the door. "Come, Vivien."

She was hard-pressed not to refuse, but there was little to be gained by provoking his temper.

Repressing the urge to bash Cyrus over the head with a heavy object—the fireplace poker would do nicely—Vivien took his arm.

"I'm sorry, darling, but I don't know what else we can do," Vivien's mother said in a dramatic whisper. "Cyrus can be the most stubborn man in the world when he gets an idea in his head." Her bright blue eyes, so pretty and youthful-looking, rounded with dismay. "I don't want you to marry Prince Ivan either, not if you don't want to. But I simply cannot bear the thought of being exiled to Yorkshire. I will die, I know it!"

Vivien cast a glance around the crowded drawing room. Her mother's dramatic tones had attracted some attention, including that of Countess Lieven, the wife of the Russian ambassador. Her sharp eyes, alive with curiosity, settled on Vivien and her mother.

She gave the countess a gracious smile before turning back to her mother. "Careful, Mamma," she said in a low voice. "We cannot speak of this without attracting attention, and we don't want that."

"But what are we to do?" her mother moaned. "Cyrus swore he would—"

"I know what he said," she said firmly. "I will take care of this."

Mamma eyed her with doubt. "If you say so." She glanced across the room to one of the big bow windows where Prince Ivan stood talking with Cyrus. "Perhaps it wouldn't be so bad," she said in a musing tone. "After all, he *is* a prince and frightfully rich."

Vivien could barely refrain from clutching her carefully styled ringlets in frustration. "Don't even speak of it, Mamma. The man is a toad, and you know it. In fact, I'd rather marry a toad. At least then I'd have a chance of kissing him and turning him into a different prince than that horrid specimen."

When confronted with Prince Ivan in the flesh, Vivien had no trouble believing that the wilds of Yorkshire were a far preferable option than marriage.

Her mother giggled. "I'd never quite thought of him in those terms, but you're right. It must be the bulging eyes and that rather wet mouth. I must agree, my love. You can't possibly marry that man."

"I'm glad someone agrees with me," Vivien responded dryly.

"Yes, but . . . ah, Mrs. Canning-Smith. Yes, it is a delightful gathering, isn't it?"

Her mother was forced to turn away to chat with one of their guests, and Vivien took the brief respite to flick her glance around the room. Thanks to her gruesome conversation with her brother, she had not had the chance to attend to the usual last-minute details before dinner. Darnell and his footmen, however, seemed to have everything in hand, wending their way through the scattered groups dispensing chilled goblets of champagne. A few of the guests were late, but once they arrived Vivien would signal to the butler to ring the dinner bell.

She had to wonder why she even cared about her brother's blasted dinner. Cyrus and his guests—all from the political and diplomatic set—could go hang as far as she was concerned. But old habits die hard, and Vivien had always derived a great deal of satisfaction from running her brother's household, even if they all maintained the fiction that Mamma was still his hostess. As difficult as her family could be, Vivien loved Blake House and she enjoyed running the household as much as she enjoyed her life in London. Everything had fallen to pieces after her father had died, but she'd eventually managed to build it back up, creating a home for all of them, even Cyrus. It wasn't perfect, but it gave her a purpose in life and it suited her.

But that life was now sorely in danger, thanks to that same blasted, ungrateful family. If her plan failed, she would be the one to suffer most, she would be—

"My dear Lady Vivien," a guttural voice purred at her shoulder. "You appear to have fallen into a brown study. You must allow me to coax you out of it."

Speak of the devil.

Vivien turned to meet Khovansky's greedy gaze moving over her in a possessive sweep. She had to resist the impulse to shrink back—or slap him—when it lingered on her chest.

"Prince Ivan," she said, dredging up a weak smile, "How delightful to see you again."

"And you are looking most radiant, Lady Vivien. Like a ray of sunshine piercing November's gloom."

When his eyes remained fixed on the high slope of her breasts, Vivien decided she would have her dressmaker add at least three inches of lace trim to *all* her bodices.

Irritated by his impertinence, she loudly cleared her throat. His gaze snapped up to meet hers, and she had to swallow hard. His pale green eyes seemed to shine with an unholy light, cruel and avaricious, inspecting her as if she were chattel and not a human being composed of flesh and blood.

Yorkshire was looking more attractive by the minute.

"Oh, how kind. I do hope you're having a pleasant time tonight, my dear sir," she said, sounding like an idiot. But how could she carry on a conversation with a man whose very presence made her skin crawl? The idea of actually sleeping with him made her nauseous.

"I am having a delightful time, thank you, especially after having just spoken to your brother. I was most encouraged by what he had to tell me."

One thick-fingered hand landed on her waist, hidden from the rest of the guests by the fact that she stood with her back to the fireplace. When his fingertips dug into the thin silk of her dress, she almost jumped out of her shoes.

Hastily, she jerked back, almost stumbling over her feet. She was normally not clumsy but the prince truly unnerved her.

Fortunately, her awkward movement forced him to drop his hand, but his eyes had gone flat with displeasure. She groaned inside. She couldn't afford to anger him or he would surely go tattling to Cyrus about her lack of cooperation. For her plan to work she needed time, which meant placating the odious toad until she had enough money to thumb her nose at the whole lot of them.

"Do forgive me, Your Highness. I'm not usually so clumsy, but I'm perhaps a bit nervous tonight. With such distinguished company, Cyrus is most eager for our guests to enjoy themselves. Especially you," she added with a treacly smile.

"You are likely still recovering from your . . . illness," he said, his manner clearly indicating he knew she hadn't been ill.

Vivien stared at him, not sure how to respond, but he seemed more than content to carry on the conversation by himself.

"You overextend yourself," he added. "I feared as much the other night. If you will recall, I begged you to allow me to take care of you, but you refused. Obviously, you preferred to dance with Captain St. George rather than enjoy a quiet chat with me. That was a mistake and you now suffer the consequences of your poor judgment."

Her jaw sagged open in disbelief, and she no longer had to wonder why he made her skin crawl. The man was arrogant beyond belief. No wonder she'd kicked him in the shins.

"Yes, well, I do like to dance," she said, too stunned to make much sense.

He gave her a tight-lipped smile. "Fortunately, after my conversation with your brother, I find myself in a magnanimous mood. I am willing to forgive your past contretemps, if we can avoid any more unfortunate incidents in the future."

He leaned forward, so close she could see pores on his wide, flat nose. "Are we clear, my lady?"

She swallowed past the lump in her throat. Clearly, he had not forgotten the shin-kicking episode. Now she knew how a fly felt in the instant before the toad flicked its tongue out to swallow it.

Behind her, someone delicately cleared her throat. She spun around, grateful for the excuse to turn away from her gruesome little scene with the prince.

Vivien stared, trying to gather her wits. She'd been expecting Lady Thornbury, but not St. George. But there her protector stood, his mother on his arm.

And he didn't look happy at all.

Chapter Sixteen

St. George's sternly handsome features were pulled tight with disdain, initially taking Vivien aback. Fortunately, the target of his ire was Prince Ivan, not her. In fact, both men appeared to be taking each other's measure, as if ready to face off across a battlefield instead of exchanging *bon mots* over dinner.

With a sharp look, Lady Thornbury took the matter in hand. "Good evening, Prince Ivan. How delightful to meet you in so convivial a setting. I was so happy to be invited to such a distinguished gathering, and knowing you were amongst the guests has made it a particular treat."

As usual, Lady Thornbury's instincts were bang-on because the prince returned her smile, bowing over her hand with a great deal of condescension. St. George, however, looked anything but thrilled. With his narrowed gaze, he appeared ready to throttle Khovansky, which would certainly be Vivien's preferred outcome.

"Lady Thornbury, I'm very happy you could join us tonight," Vivien said, giving her friend a grateful smile. "And you, too, Captain St. George. I did not expect to see you, but your presence is most welcome." In fact, his appearance was rather a puzzle since Vivien had gone over the invitation list and St. George had not been included.

"Thank you, my dear," replied Lady Thornbury. "I do hope we didn't hold you up for dinner." She cast a mocking glance at her son. "I was waiting for Aden, who can never seem to be precisely on time. Such a shocking habit for a military man."

St. George rolled his eyes but didn't bother refuting his mother's teasing.

"Indeed," interjected the prince. "Most lamentable. One would think the captain could treat both his mother and his hostess with greater respect. I believe a man's attention to the smaller niceties of life is a great indicator of his character. After all, the devil is in the details." He punctuated his insult with a supercilious sneer.

St. George's only response was to level a cold, infinitely calculating smile at the prince, one that chilled Vivien right to the bone.

"Better late than never, and it's very nice to see you regardless, Captain," she said with demented cheerfulness. "One mustn't be too much of a stickler over these things or one risks turning into a pedant, don't you think? Why, I'm sure I'm late for dinner on a regular basis. No one ever seems to mind in the least."

Thankfully, St. George switched his attention to her. His raven gaze, so lethally black just a few seconds ago, now simply looked wary. But at least he no longer seemed inclined to disembowel the prince right there on her brother's best Wilton carpet.

"Thank you, my lady. It's a pleasure to be here," he finally responded in a polite tone.

She didn't think so. St. George wore the same, long-suffering expression on his face that Kit did when Mamma forced him to accompany her to some boring dinner party or musicale. Lady Thornbury must have forced him to come.

She also wouldn't be surprised if he still resented her conduct at the Darlington ball, preferring the card tables to his company. She should be used to that response by now though. Most men either disapproved of her card playing, or thought it *fast*. St. George obviously fell into the first category, which she found rather depressing. That's what came of saving a woman's life, she supposed. A woman couldn't help liking her rescuer, and wishing that said rescuer might come to like her in return.

Why had he even bothered to come tonight? The last thing she needed was an irritated, erstwhile protector, snarling at the one man she needed to keep in a good temper. And St. George had gone back to staring at the prince again, that disemboweling expression once more gleaming in his eyes.

The prince, his frog lips drawn back in a vicious smile, looked equally hostile and just as inclined to shed blood. If this kept up, Vivien was certain she'd have to have the carpets cleaned first thing in the morning.

Lady Thornbury carried on cheerfully, ignoring the men. "I'm sorry you weren't aware of the last-minute change to the guest list, Vivien. Your mother dashed off a note to me only a few hours ago asking me to bring Aden. Apparently you were short a man at the dinner table, so my son happily agreed."

"It's encouraging to know the captain serves at least one useful purpose," the prince said, the insult sounding even worse in his heavy Russian accent.

Vivien pressed her tongue against the roof of her mouth, holding back a blighting retort. She knew Prince Ivan to be a haughty, sharp-tongued man, but she'd never seen him react with such blatant rudeness. The prince had always ignored her other suitors—probably thinking them unworthy of his notice—but St. George evoked an altogether different response.

Fortunately, before the situation could deteriorate any further, Vivien's mother came floating over, a softly sparkling vision in her sapphire-blue silk dress. Frowning, Vivien peered at her. She'd been too upset a few minutes ago to remark on Mamma's attire, but now she realized she'd never seen this gown before. Which meant it was new.

Which also meant that Vivien had yet to see the bill.

Out of habit, she started calculating the likely cost, totalling the already horrific list of numbers that made up their mountain of debt. The imaginary mountain stretched up a few more feet now, and it took all her willpower not to gulp back her glass of champagne in one burning swallow.

That, or flee on the first boat she could book passage on to the Americas. With her family, who could blame her?

"Captain, I'm so pleased you could replace my naughty boy at the table tonight," her mother exclaimed. "Vivien, I hope you don't mind that I didn't consult you."

When Mamma flirtatiously batted her eyelashes at St. George, Vivien prayed for a sudden earthquake to swallow up Mayfair so she could escape this absolute nightmare of a dinner party.

The other four were all staring at her, waiting for her to answer.

"Of course, I don't mind," she managed. "I'm just a bit surprised. I didn't realize we were short."

Her mother fluttered her fan. "Kit told me this afternoon he had other plans. Something about attending a party with Mr. Tucker and Lord Heyworth."

Vivien almost groaned out loud. Bertram Tucker and Viscount Heyworth were reckless gamblers who didn't share an ounce of sense between them, and were the last people Kit should spend time with.

Mamma cast the prince a deprecating smile. "You must forgive my son, Your Highness. He's the sweetest boy, if just a tad strong-headed. But he meant no insult."

Khovansky smiled. "My dear lady, I am charmed by your entire family, as you must know." He reached over and grasped Vivien's hand, raising it to his lips and pressing a kiss moist enough to leave a mark on her glove. She tried to discreetly tug her hand away but he refused to let go.

"I understand you made your first visit to Oatlands recently," Lady Thornbury said, tapping her fan on the prince's arm. "You must tell me all about it."

Khovansky's eyes flashed with displeasure, but he finally let Vivien go.

As he and Lady Thornbury discussed the eccentricities of the Duchess of York, Vivien forced herself to meet St. George's gaze. It remained dark, and this time she understood his displeasure was directed straight at her. Clearly, he thought she was engaged in some sort of flirtation with the prince. As much as she wished to deny the charge, she couldn't take the risk of alienating Khovansky, not before she'd had a chance to dig her way out of her current predicament. But she hated the way St. George's disapproval made her feel, and it took a good deal of discipline not to scowl back at him.

The doors to the drawing room opened and Darnell *finally* announced dinner.

"Goodness!" her mother exclaimed. "I must see to the ambassador and his wife."

As she bustled off, the prince turned back to Vivien with a gracious smile, offering her an arm. "Lady Vivien, please give me the honor of escorting you into dinner," he said, taking her hand.

The prince had very neatly backed her into a corner, and

there was little Vivien could do without insulting him. So, she smiled and let him lead her from the room, feeling St. George's angry stare scorching the spot right between her shoulder blades.

Dinner had been horrific. When Khovansky escorted her to the dining room, Vivien had been stunned to see that the little gilt place card bearing his name had been moved back to its original setting—next to hers.

Dumbfounded, she'd stared at it for several seconds, finally lifting her eyes to meet Cyrus's triumphant gaze as he took his place at the head of the table. Mastering her temper, she simply raised an ironic brow and then turned her smiling attention to the prince. Cyrus might fancy himself a master at some chessboard game of politics, but Vivien had learned to fight in a much less civilized venue—at the card tables, where hardened gamesters battled over fortunes and even their lives. She still had a few tricks up her sleeve and she intended to play them.

But by the end of the second remove, her smile had frozen into a grimace as Ivan the Terrible engaged in a continuous, skin-crawling flirtation. By the dessert course, the prince became so emboldened he placed his hand on her thigh just as she put a spoonful of strawberry trifle into her mouth. Only with the greatest discipline did she manage not to spit the entire mouthful onto her plate.

Aghast, Vivien had slipped her hand under the table and firmly plopped his hand back in his lap. Prince Ivan hadn't liked that, but fortunately, she'd had the presence of mind to borrow a trick from her mother's book, batting her eyelashes at him in shy flirtation. The prince had eyed her suspiciously but finally chuckled, whispering that he would spare her maidenly blushes. Vivien had given him a vague smile, doggedly returning her attention to her plate.

But not before glancing down the table to see St. George watching her with an ironic eye, obviously thinking the worst of her. Their gazes had locked for a moment, searing her with the intensity of their shared glance. But then he'd turned back to his neighbor, the lovely young wife of a member of the Russian delegation who had done her best throughout dinner to keep his attention. St. George had seemed happy to comply.

Vivien gloomily inspected the elaborately detailed basket of candied flowers that served as one of the centerpieces on the long table. She'd spent the last ten minutes ignoring Prince Ivan—and couldn't she just feel his ire burgeoning over that— and was wishing Mamma would rise from the table and escort the ladies to the drawing room. Vivien would give her another two minutes, and then she would do it herself, rudeness be hanged.

A rustle of silk called her attention to the head of the table. "Come, ladies," Mamma said, rising to her feet. "We'll repair to the drawing room and hope the gentlemen don't linger too long over their horrid political discussions."

The prince, like all the men, rose with the ladies. He seized Vivien's hand and again pressed a kiss to her glove, leaving another moist smudge. At this rate, he would ruin every pair of her gloves before the week was out.

"Be sure to save a seat for me, Lady Vivien," he murmured in a throaty tone. He sounded like a frog croaking and not the seductive cavalier he imagined himself to be.

"I'll do my best, but I can't make any promises," she said in a bright tone, wagging a finger at him.

His rolled his broad lips in on themselves, as if displeased at her clumsy attempt at flirtation. Not that she could blame him. She sounded a complete imbecile.

She fled the room, but not before she saw St. George's dinner companion stretch up on tiptoe and whisper something in his ear, something that made him smile. Well, at least *someone* was having a good time.

Vivien followed her mother out into the hall, taking her arm and holding her back for a moment. Her mother peered at her with concern. "What's wrong, my love? You're looking flushed."

"You'd be flushed, too, if you had an awful toad pawing at your leg all through dinner."

"He didn't!"

"I'm sorry to say he did."

"I will speak to Cyrus as soon as the guests leave," her mother huffed. "I know you have to be polite to the man, but I will not tolerate that kind of conduct at my dinner table."

Oh, and wouldn't *that* conversation go over splendidly.

"Don't bother, Mamma," she said with an artificial laugh. "I can handle Prince Ivan. I just need a few moments to myself. I'll join you and the ladies shortly."

Her mother chewed on her lower lip, then shrugged. "Perhaps you're right. I suppose we can't expect a Russian—even if he is a prince—to act with the same sense of decorum as an Englishman."

Vivien refrained from pointing out how badly the average English aristocrat behaved on a regular basis, starting with the Prince Regent and moving down through the ranks.

Lady Thornbury came out of the drawing room to look for her. "Vivien, my love, are you well?"

"I'm just a little overheated. The dining room was rather stuffy tonight."

Her friend gave her an understanding wink. "I quite agree, especially at your end of the table. Perhaps you should take a few minutes to gather yourself. I'll help your mother pour the tea."

Vivien smiled her thanks, trying for the thousandth time *not* to wish that Lady Thornbury was her mother, and headed toward her brother's library. She was sorely in need of a brandy and she intended to have a generous one, no matter how indecorous that might be.

Even though it was now Cyrus's domain, Vivien loved the quietly elegant room, little changed since the days of her childhood when she immersed herself in her father's poetry collection and read the novels of Defoe and Fielding. Decorated in the simpler lines of the Queen Anne style, its pale green walls and inset shelves, crammed with books, reminded her of a happier time.

She poured herself a brandy from the drinks trolley and wandered over to the fireplace, gazing at her father's portrait over the mantel. Superficially, neither she nor Kit resembled him, although when her little brother smiled Vivien could see traces in the curve of the lips and the dimple to one side of his mouth. Cyrus most resembled Papa, although her brother could not have been further in spirit from her father's loving and generous nature.

Sighing, she let her fingers brush affectionately along the oak frame of the portrait. Nothing had been the same since Papa died. It was almost as if a light had been extinguished in her family, taking most of the joy with it. Sometimes she imagined that Mamma's and Kit's frantic gaiety was a desperate attempt to make up for his absence. As much as she sympathized with that impulse, it irked her, too. Her father would not have been pleased with the way their selfish behavior affected the rest of them.

She turned her back on the portrait. There was little point indulging in maudlin memories or wishing for things to be different. Life had dealt her a hand to play, and she would see it through to the best of her ability. The sooner she could begin her plan to do that, the better.

Discarding her drink, she started for the door. But when it swung open, she came to a surprised halt.

Surprise turned to dismay when Prince Ivan Khovansky walked into the room and shut the door behind him.

Chapter Seventeen

Khovansky leaned back against the door panels, his greedy eyes inspecting her. He didn't really seem toadlike anymore. Now he seemed like a snake spotting a tasty little rabbit, wanting to swallow it whole.

Vivien refused to be the rabbit.

"Prince Ivan, you surprise me," she said in a firm voice. "Have you lost your way?"

Peeling back his lips in a smile that was more leer, he advanced toward her. She took a hasty step back, tangling her heel in the ruffle that hemmed her dress and almost losing her footing.

So much for not being the rabbit.

In the few seconds it took to recover her balance, Khovansky rushed across the room to her side. He took her elbow in a hard grip, trying to pull her against him. Stepping back, her legs collided with her brother's desk and Vivien smacked her free hand down on its polished surface to keep from falling.

"My dear lady, your delicate constitution has been overtaxed this evening," the prince exclaimed. "You are most unsteady on your feet."

"I'm perfectly fine, sir," she responded, struggling to pull her arm away from him. "And I'm not the least bit delicate. You may let me go."

She finally yanked her elbow free, although the movement tipped her back against the desk, offsetting her balance again. Smothering a curse, she slapped both hands behind her, gripping the edge of the polished walnut to hold steady.

The prince refused to back away. He crowded her against the desk, his barrel chest mere inches from her bodice. If she took a deep breath she would scratch herself against the display of unearned medals so ostentatiously pinned to his uniform.

He inched closer, forcing her to arch away from him. The lascivious gleam in his heavy-lidded eyes combined with the smell of creamed onions on his breath to make her stomach lurch.

Vivien wished she could hold her breath and talk at the same time. "Prince Ivan, I must insist that you step back. You are making it impossible for me to catch my breath."

"But if I do, I'm quite terrified you will tumble to the floor."

"I told you," she said through clenched teeth, "that I'm perfectly fine."

His gaze flickered over to the drink trolley, with her half-empty glass of brandy. "Then perhaps there's another reason you're so unsteady on your feet, my sweet lady. You appear to have gotten into your brother's brandy."

He leaned forward and sniffed her breath, so close that Vivien could see the black hairs in his nostrils. Her outrage was overborne by the smell of the onions, now mingling with the odor of his heavily scented snuff. She had to swallow hard against the impulse to gag.

The prince chuckled. "What a naughty young lady you are, but I'm devastated you didn't invite me to join you. We could have enjoyed a brandy together, along with other more pleasurable activities."

Khovansky finished off his insult by skimming his blunt-tipped fingers along her exposed clavicle. The touch of his clammy flesh on her overheated skin made her shudder.

Seething, Vivien placed her palms against his chest and gave a hard shove. He staggered back a bit, but as she tried to slip past him he grabbed her by the upper arms and wheeled her to face him. With surprising strength, he crushed her against his chest.

She gasped. "Unhand me, sir!" His fingers crushed the delicate silk of her sleeves, digging into her arms. "Your Highness, you're hurting me!"

The pressure eased fractionally, but then he shoved her backward, slamming the back of her thighs against the desk. She grimaced. That bit of violence would certainly leave a set of bruises in its wake.

"It is not my desire to hurt you, Lady Vivien," replied the prince in a strange, rasping voice. "But if you continue to defy me, you will give me little choice."

Actually, she had the disturbing notion he would very much like to hurt her. His lips curled up with sadistic delight and his fingers squeezed and released in an odd pumping action he seemed to enjoy. Nor could she ignore the thrust of his pelvis against her belly or mistake the hard ridge of flesh pressing into her.

But it was the look in his eyes that truly unnerved her. They glittered with an unholy passion, staring at her with menacing promise, as if he would flay the very flesh from her bones if she challenged him. For the first time since she'd met him, she was terrified.

"You need a lesson in appropriate conduct toward those of higher station," he continued, sounding eager to school her. "I told your brother that would be so, but he seemed reluctant to believe me. And now we see that I am correct."

What? Cyrus and the prince had discussed teaching her a lesson?

She glared back at him. "I fail to see why my conduct should be any business of yours, Prince Ivan. Nor did my brother have any right to discuss it with you."

He let out a harsh laugh. "We had every right, my lady, since I intend to marry you. It is a husband's duty to school his wife in proper behavior. You will soon be a princess of Russia, and you must learn to conduct yourself obediently, and with proper decorum at all times."

"I'd sooner marry a bloody chimney sweep than agree to be your wife," she responded, unthinkingly snapping out the words.

His gaze went blank for a few seconds, then blazed with a demented-looking rage. In that moment, Vivien truly believed he might very well throttle her if she didn't comply.

Her heart crashed against her ribs as she started back at him. "Prince Ivan," she said, struggling to contain her fear. "I insist you let me return to my mother. This unfortunate interlude has gone on too long."

He barked out a laugh. "Or you'll do what, dear lady? Threaten me?"

"I'll scream as loud as I can," she said, already raising her voice.

To show him she meant business, she sucked in a huge breath and opened her mouth.

The prince moved with astonishing speed for such a bulky man. He lunged forward, crushing his body against hers, his fleshy lips smashing into her mouth. This time Vivien did gag and her legs started to slide out from under her.

The top of the desk arrested her downward fall and she crashed, half-on and half-off the edge. As the prince, using the weight of his body, tried to squash her flat, Vivien thrashed wildly, trying to pull free of his sucking, voracious kiss. Her knee connected with something soft, and he jerked. The motion gave her just enough space to break free and let out a strangled shriek.

With a guttural snarl, he redoubled his efforts, trying to hold her still as he assaulted her mouth. Frantic, Vivien whipped her head back and forth as he bobbed at her, like some huge awful bird intent on pecking her to death.

Suddenly, she heard the door open and the tread of a hard footfall, then Khovansky cried out and let go, flying back through the air as if jerked away by an irresistible force. Vivien crashed back onto the desk, her bottom making contact with a force that jarred her spine.

Dazed, she pushed her hair out of her eyes and peered at Khovansky, thrashing about on the carpet in an undignified sprawl. She lifted her eyes to the apparent irresistible force— St. George, come to her rescue once again.

He stood over the prince, his hands balled into fists as he glowered down at him. Vivien was willing to bet that St. George would be delighted to continue the business he'd started. But he must have thought better of it because his eyes flicked up to her, and his murderous expression abated a notch.

Ignoring the outraged spluttering from the prince, St. George stepped around him and came to her.

"Did he hurt you, my lady?" he asked in a low, quiet voice, as if he were soothing a frightened child.

She pushed herself upright, trying to quell the trembling in her legs.

"I'm fine," she quavered. "It was all just a stupid misunderstanding."

Even so, she couldn't help glaring at the prince as he struggled up onto his knees.

St. George ran a gentle finger along the bare skin of her

arms. Several red marks stood out on her pale flesh, lingering evidence of Prince Ivan's punishing grip.

"That doesn't look like a misunderstanding to me," he murmured.

She shivered—a soft, breathless shifting as her body responded naturally to his touch. St. George stroked over the marks, as if he wished to erase all trace of harm.

This close to him, Vivien had to tilt her head to look into his face. The remnants of a savage anger rode in the harshly set angles of his features, but his eyes held a grave sympathy that had her blinking back tears.

His hand came up to her chin, tilting it as he gave her a brief but thorough inspection.

"You're safe now," he murmured. "I won't let him near you."

She gave him a trembling smile. "Thank you, but I— "

"How dare you touch me, you peasant?" growled the prince from behind them. "I will kill you for that."

Vivien sighed and peeked around St. George's broad shoulders. Ivan the Terrible had finally hauled himself up and now stood in the middle of the library, feet planted wide, glaring at them with black rage in his eyes.

Leisurely, St. George turned to face him. "Oh? How do you intend to accomplish that?" He sounded only mildly interested, as if asking how long it might take to travel from Moscow to St. Petersburg.

The prince started yanking one of his gloves off, obviously intending to slap St. George in the face with it.

Not bloody likely, Vivien thought with a spurt of panic. Not only didn't she trust the prince to fight like a gentleman, the last thing she needed was the gossip that came along with a duel.

She scampered around St. George and planted herself between the men, bracing her hands on her hips as she faced the prince. Several of his medals had been knocked askew in his tumble, which struck her as bizarrely comical.

Struggling against the impulse to laugh, Vivien stared haughtily down her nose at him. "Your Highness, you will *not* insult the captain, nor will you challenge him to a duel. For one thing, duels are illegal in England. For another, you have treated me in the shabbiest fashion, and you may consider yourself extremely fortunate I do not wish to make a scene. I would ask that you return to the drawing room and refrain from speaking to me for the rest of the night."

He hissed at her reprimand, but with St. George at her back Vivien had nothing to fear. "And if you are indeed a gentleman, then I ask that you *never* mention this incident again, or importune me with any more advances."

The prince pulled himself up to his full height, which was only slightly taller than Vivien. "You will do well to remember who I am, my lady," he said in a voice heavy with menace. "It would not be wise to threaten me." He glanced past her to St. George. "And I suggest the captain remember that too because I assure you both I will not forget tonight's insult."

St. George moved up right behind her, letting his big hand span the width of her lower back. Her anxiety dissipated under his touch, as if he had simply plucked it from her body.

"Really?" he drawled. "What do you intend to do?" Again, simply a mild note of curiosity in his voice.

The prince looked remarkably like a bull about to charge. Vivien wondered if he would soon begin pawing the carpet in rage.

She was working up the nerve to ask Khovansky to leave when the half-ajar door flew open. This time Cyrus came charging through.

"Vivien! What the devil—"

Her brother stumbled to a halt, his mouth dropping open as he stared at them. From the look on his face, Vivien had the feeling he'd expected to find an entirely different scene than the one playing out before him.

She drew in a huge gasp, finally understanding. Cyrus and the prince had likely seen her escape to the library as a fortuitous opportunity to place her in a compromising position, one where her brother could have raised a huge and very public fuss. Her reputation would have been blighted by the incident, thus forcing her one step closer to marriage.

Right then and there, Vivien decided she didn't care if she had to spend the rest of her life in Yorkshire living in a shack on the moors. It would be far preferable to having to spend another minute under her brother's roof, much less marry a brute like the prince.

But there was still Kit and Mamma to consider, so she needed to tread carefully. "Goodness, your library certainly is a busy place tonight, isn't it, Cyrus? I merely slipped away for a few minutes to rest and it would appear the entire party decided to join me."

St. George gave her an approving pat just above the swell of her bottom, and then dropped his hand and stepped up beside her. She gave a tiny sigh, already missing his warmth.

Cyrus glanced uneasily at the prince. "Your Highness. I . . . I was wondering where you were. I . . . I wanted to see if you needed anything."

Vivien frowned. It wasn't like her brother to babble. Was he afraid of his unpleasant accomplice?

The prince didn't even look at him, keeping his glare fastened on St. George. "You might suggest to your sister that she not stain her reputation by consorting with so coarse a man as St. George. After, of course, you have him removed from the premises for insulting me."

Cyrus recovered himself enough to look outraged. "Is this true, Vivien? Did the captain insult the prince?"

"Don't be such a fool," she snapped. "If you really want to know what happened—"

"Dear me, what a great deal of fuss and bother," interjected Lady Thornbury from the doorway. She smiled, looking as gracious and composed as always, but she looked straight at Vivien, a clear warning in her gaze.

"Ah, Mother. There you are," Aden responded in a gently mocking tone. "I wondered when you would show up."

She glided into the room, the epitome of a grande dame. Not by the bat of one eyelash did she acknowledge the volatile atmosphere, despite the presence of a clearly furious Cyrus and an outraged Russian prince.

"Silly boy," she said to her son, patting him on the cheek.

His only response was a sardonic smile.

"Vivien, my love," she continued. "Your mother is wondering where you are. I told her I would come fetch you."

She took Vivien by the arm and led her to the door, nodding genially to Cyrus and the prince. St. George followed right behind, forming their rear guard. Vivien, having had *more* than enough of her brother and Khovansky, refused to even look at them.

But she did hold her breath until they reached the safety of the hall.

St. George closed the door quietly behind them. He glanced at his mother, contemplating her with a slight smile lifting the edges of his handsome mouth. "Well done, my lady. I was wondering how we were going to escape without bloodshed."

Lady Thornbury gave him an affectionate smile. "My dear boy, who do you think you inherited your prodigious talents from in the first place?"

He let out an amused snort. "Certainly not from my father."

"Very true," replied his mother with a dramatic sigh.

Vivien stared from one to the other, mystified by their odd conversation as they led her back to the drawing room.

Chapter Eighteen

Aden climbed into his mother's town coach, grateful the hellacious evening had finally come to an end. Thirty minutes after he escorted Vivien back to the drawing room, she quietly excused herself, pleading a headache. Coming so soon after Khovansky's precipitous departure from the party—the bastard hadn't made any effort to disguise his foul temper—Vivien's exit had caused more than a few raised eyebrows.

Fortunately, his mother had jumped up to escort Vivien to her bedroom, exclaiming all the while that she shouldn't tire herself out so soon after recovering from her illness. Her act might not quell all the gossip, but when the influential Lady Thornbury behaved as if nothing were amiss, then everyone else was obliged to follow suit.

He couldn't hold back a quiet laugh at the image of the petite and elegant Countess of Thornbury standing up to the infuriated Russian. She pulled her gaze away from the carriage window, where she'd been perusing the night-shrouded streets of Mayfair, and gave him a puzzled smile.

"What amuses you, Aden?"

"I'd forgotten how much fun these evenings were," he replied with gentle sarcasm. "What a fool I've been to stay away all these years."

She gave an exaggerated shudder. "It was horrid, wasn't it? Although certainly a great deal more lively than the parties Lord Blake usually gives, I'll say that much for it."

"I would happily be spared that kind of excitement."

She grimaced in sympathy. "I'm sorry you had to be dragged into this mess. But you handled it very well. Eventually."

He frowned. "What the hell does that mean?"

"Language, dear boy, and you know very well what it means. You behaved like an irrational, jealous male before dinner. Not that you acted much better *during* dinner. Really, Madame Bezrodny was extremely forward and you did nothing to discourage her."

Aden scratched his cheek. Thank God the carriage was only dimly lit by one lamp because he could swear the skin felt hot under his fingers. He hadn't blushed in years, but apparently his mother still possessed the ability to embarrass him with only a few words.

"I have no idea what you're talking about," he said, more for form's sake than anything else.

"Ha. I'm amazed you and the prince didn't come to blows in the drawing room. Fortunately, Vivien managed Prince Ivan very adroitly. She really is the most remarkable girl."

Aden crossed his arms over his chest, feeling more disgruntled by the second. "For someone who supposedly doesn't like the man, she seemed quite chummy with Khovansky to me. She was hanging all over the man during dinner."

His mother studied him with pity. It was the look she generally reserved for idiots and small children about to be paddled by their nannies.

"What?" he asked defensively. He was a trained spy, for Christ's sake. He knew how to observe people, and his observations of Lady Vivien had told him she welcomed Khovansky's attentions. That had made him want to throttle someone, except he couldn't tell whether he wanted to throttle Khovansky or Vivien, or himself for being stupid enough to care.

"Vivien was clearly trying to placate the prince," his mother explained, "although I'm not sure why. She loathes the man, I'm certain of it."

"She has a strange way of showing it, and the prince was more than happy to capitalize on her generous behavior."

His mother stiffened. "Are you implying that Vivien was responsible for Prince Ivan's outrageous behavior in the library?"

"Of course not, but he's not the sort of man a girl can lead around by the nose. Lady Vivien should have realized that before she tried to manage him. If I hadn't intervened, God knows what would have happened."

His anger spiked when he thought of how she might have been harmed. When he came through the door of Blake's library to see Vivien struggling in Khovansky's foul embrace, a red-hot fury had seized him. He'd lost all control, pulling the prince away from her and hurling him to the floor. Only Vivien's presence had kept him from giving the pig the thorough beating he deserved.

"She wasn't flirting with him for the fun of it," his mother retorted. "That's not the kind of person she is."

Aden decided to let that comment pass. Despite his mother's insistence, Vivien did have that reputation, whether she deserved it or not. And tonight, for the first time, he'd started to understand why some thought she merited it.

"Then what could her purpose be in encouraging the attentions of a man she supposedly dislikes?"

"I suspect Cyrus is forcing her to entertain Prince Ivan's suit," his mother replied. "It's the only explanation that makes sense."

Aden shifted sideways, trying to ease his cramped legs. He wasn't used to so much inactivity, being cooped up in carriages or kicking up his heels at balls and boring dinner parties, waiting for something to happen. Tomorrow, he'd take Ranger out for a long ride on Hampstead Heath, shaking the fidgets out of both of them.

"Lady Vivien isn't a green girl, Mother. Nor is she under her brother's guardianship. And she doesn't strike me as the sort of woman who has trouble saying no to a man."

"True, but I believe that Cyrus is holding something over her head, probably something to do with money. Perhaps Kit has fallen into debt again, or her mother. Lady Blake let slip some weeks ago that Cyrus refused to increase her pin money. She made some alarmed references to being forced to rusticate in the country."

Aden cocked his head. Now, that was interesting. "And the younger brother? How does he figure in?"

"He's a dear boy, but quite feckless and a terrible gambler. Cyrus has been forced to pull him out of the River Tick on more than one occasion."

"And what does any of this have to do with Lady Vivien? As far as I can deduce, she has no outstanding debts despite the fact that she plays rather deeply at the tables."

"Because, Aden, she feels responsible for her mamma and little brother," his mother said, her tone indicating the answer was obvious. "Ever since her father died, Vivien has taken it upon herself to keep them out of trouble as best she can."

He scowled. "That should be Lord Blake's responsibility." The outlines of Vivien's life were finally starting to take shape. He couldn't say he liked it very much.

His mother shrugged.

Aden rubbed a hand over his face. "So, it's entirely possible that Lady Vivien's kidnapper was connected in some way to her family. If one of them owes a large amount of money that could certainly be a motive for kidnapping and holding her to ransom."

His mother nodded. "Yes, especially since Cyrus made such a point of refusing to pay, despite the fact that no demands even came forward."

Aden grunted, lost in thought. He'd already spent several days rooting around in the stews, seeking information and attempting to ascertain who'd hired the smugglers in the first place. Frustratingly, that line of investigation had yielded little fruit, so it obviously called for him to look closer to home. The Blake finances deserved investigation.

"And don't forget Prince Ivan," his mother added. "You should add him to your list of suspects."

"I already have."

In fact, the bastard was moving to the top of the list, if for no other reason than he'd tried to force himself on the girl. Aden would never forget the panicked look on Vivien's deathly pale face when he pulled Khovansky away, or the way she'd trembled in his arms. Despite her strength of character and remarkable resilience, she was alarmingly delicate. That brought out all his protective instincts, and something more. He'd meant it when he said he wouldn't let Khovansky hurt her again. He'd kill the man if he had to, or anyone else who tried to lay a finger on Vivien.

His mother drew in a breath, as if about to say something, but then she clamped her lips shut.

"What now?" he asked in a resigned voice.

She grimaced. "You know Vivien is hiding something, don't you? There's something she doesn't want us to know about all this."

He sighed, hating that she'd confirmed what he'd been trying to deny all along. "Do you think she suspects who was behind the kidnapping?"

His mother nodded reluctantly, and Aden couldn't hold back a curse. This time she didn't reprimand him.

"To protect someone? A family member?" he asked.

"I'm afraid that seems the most likely explanation."

Aden yanked his hat off and threw it on the opposite seat. "How the devil am I to protect the blasted girl if she won't cooperate on even the most basic level?"

His mother patted his knee, as if soothing him. "Vivien is very loyal, especially to her family. She's always been that way, but that sense of loyalty has only grown since her father died. He made her swear to take care of Kit and her mother since he knew Cyrus couldn't be trusted to do that. Vivien takes that promise very seriously, I assure you."

"She'd even risk her own life to honor it?" he asked, incredulous.

"I'm sure of it."

"How old was she when her father died?"

"Seventeen."

Something went tight in the vicinity of Aden's heart. "That's a hell of a burden for a girl that young to bear."

His mother nodded. "You, of course, would understand about that."

That startled him into silence. Neither he nor his mother ever acknowledged how difficult his youth had been, and how his stepfather's animus had made him grow up hard and fast. Aden sure as hell hoped she didn't want to start discussing it now since he hadn't a clue how to respond on that subject.

"I'll never get to the bottom of this if the very person I'm meant to protect keeps throwing obstacles in my path," he said, ignoring his mother's previous comment.

Before she could answer, the carriage came to a halt in front of her town house. She waited for Aden to hand her down before she answered him.

"You must get Vivien to trust you," she said, as they waited at the door. "And that means you must spend time with her."

Hell, no. That was the *last* thing he needed to do. He was already too involved in this case, and had already let his emotions run away with him. His reaction to the prince tonight had shown him that as clear as lightning streaking across a pitch-black sky.

The door opened and Aden followed her into the entrance hall. "Why can't you do that, Mother? You've known the girl for years. Surely she must trust you."

She cast him an impatient glance. "Obviously not enough. But she does trust you, which is not surprising under the circumstances. After all, you're her knight in shining armor."

"What are you talking about?" he asked through clenched teeth.

"Darling, don't be so obtuse," she said as she handed the butler her wrap. "It doesn't become you. Come into the morning room and let's discuss what you need to do next."

Aden wanted to bang his head against the wall. Where was a nice little nest of French spies when you needed it? People who were clearly the enemy, and who didn't require any sort of mollycoddling or hand-holding?

Then again, he hadn't done very well with that last batch of spies he encountered. This situation, however, was shaping up to be just as difficult.

Bracing himself for the worst, he followed her into the morning room. "All right, Mother," he said, watching her settle into an overstuffed chair by the fire. "Tell me what it is you think I should do."

She gave him a mischievous smile. "It's very simple, my son. You have to make Vivien fall in love with you."

Chapter Nineteen

Vivien hurried down to the morning room, fastening the last few buttons at her wrist on her way. She'd barely had time to finish dressing before one of the maids tapped on her bedroom door, relaying her mother's request to join her *immediately*. It surprised her that Mamma was actually up and about given the commotion of last night's party. Vivien prayed there wasn't more trouble awaiting her, and before breakfast, too.

She knew a showdown with Cyrus was imminent, but there wasn't one thing he could say to change her mind. By this time next week, she hoped to have enough money to pay off Kit's most immediate debts and alleviate the most pressing of the tradesmen's bills. That should be enough to keep the worst of her troubles at bay.

If not, then a drafty manor house in Yorkshire figured prominently in her future.

She waved the footman back to his front-door post and slid open the pocket doors to the morning room. Expecting only her mother, she froze on the threshold, gaping at Lady Thornbury and St. George. They were seated with Mamma at the small breakfast table, sharing coffee and a plate of pastries.

As St. George rose to his feet, Vivien resisted the impulse

to smooth back her hair and straighten her skirts. She'd donned a very plain gown, intending to spend most of the morning in the small conservatory at the back of the house. Digging about in the dirt and repotting plants always calmed her, and helped her mind to focus and work through problems.

But between the faded blue of her oldest muslin dress and the circles under her eyes from lack of sleep, she must look a veritable hag. She could kill Mamma for not giving her some warning that guests would be present, especially *him*.

Telling herself she didn't really care, Vivien crossed to the table with a smile, dipping a shallow curtsy in response to St. George's greeting and then dropping a quick kiss on Lady Thornbury's cheek.

"There you are, Vivien," her mother exclaimed, looking rattled. "Lady T. and Aden have stopped by for an unexpected visit. So kind to enquire after your health, and so early in the morning, too!"

Vivien glanced over her shoulder to thank St. George as he held her chair. Their gazes caught and the breath snagged in her throat. His obsidian dark eyes mapped her face with careful intent. And from the frown gathering between his brows, he apparently didn't like what he saw.

Hag. That would be the word he was searching for.

"My love," said her mother, peering at her. "Are you quite well? You're looking rather peaked." As she handed over a coffee cup, her gaze fastened on Vivien's gown. "And why are you dressed like that?"

Humiliation crawled up Vivien's spine. "I was intending to repot some of the rose bushes this morning, Mamma. There's no point in dressing up for that since I'll end up covered with dirt."

Her mother made a clucking sound with her tongue. "I don't understand why you insist on grubbing around in the soil like a tenant farmer. After all, that's what servants are for."

Vivien stared down into her cup. The morning was off to a splendid start, thanks to her mother's unerring ability to embarrass her.

"I can't agree with you there, Delia," Lady Thornbury said. "I like nothing better than puttering about in my garden. Very soothing for the nerves." She smiled at Vivien. "I wish more young ladies would take up the hobby instead of languishing about drawing rooms or wasting their time in the shops, as they so often do these days."

Mamma couldn't resist rising to that bait, and she and Lady Thornbury embarked on a lively discussion of appropriate hobbies for young women. Vivien finally brought herself to look at St. George. Lady Thornbury was used to her mother's flighty behavior, but he certainly wasn't.

He watched her from the opposite side of the table. When their eyes met, he gave her a charming smile before lifting his cup to his lips. When he winked at her, she almost dropped her cup in her lap.

She'd never seen him in a playful mood or been on the receiving end when he unleashed a truly devastating smile. Her heart tripped over itself, and she had to carefully place her cup back in its saucer to avoid slopping coffee into the dish. But his smile had done the trick. Her tension eased and a glow of pleasure warmed her limbs.

"And how *are* you this morning, my love?" Lady Thornbury asked her. "I trust you slept well last night despite the evening's merry excesses."

Vivien didn't miss the dry note in her voice, or the real question in her enquiry.

"I'm fine," she said, although she wrinkled her nose a bit. "Perhaps a little tired. The evening went on quite late, didn't it?"

"I hope you're not feeling too knocked about," St. George said casually. "I intend to persuade you to stroll in the park with me this morning, and I won't take no for an answer. It's a fine day and the air is quite mild."

For the second time that morning, Vivien blinked with surprise. She glanced past him to the window, noting the gloomy, overcast skies and the gusts of wind skittering leaves around the square. Not that she minded a little bluster and fresh air. She'd been intending to go out for a walk later, regardless.

"Really?" her mother opined in a doubtful voice. "It looks quite dreary out to me. Besides, it's much too early to promenade."

"Nonsense," said Lady Thornbury. "It's very mild out and it would do Vivien a world of good to get some fresh air. Besides, we must let the children have their fun, mustn't we?" She finished the question by giving Vivien's mother an arch smile.

Puzzled, Mamma peered at St. George and then at Vivien. Then her eyes went wide with understanding.

"Oh," she breathed. "Of course! Vivien, that's a splendid idea. Go up and change right now so you can go walking with Aden."

Vivien let out a tiny sigh at her mother's predictable response. St. George wasn't the sort of man who spent his time strolling about parks with young women, so the only possible explanation for this odd little scenario was that he wished to speak to her about her abduction, without Mamma overhearing it. Unfortunately, an intimate chat with him was the last thing she wanted for a number of reasons, some of which she had no intention of admitting to herself. But if she made too big a fuss she might make him wonder why she wished to avoid him. She'd done that the other night at the ball and she'd sensed his suspicion even then.

And since everyone had lined up against her—her mother so easily manipulated by his mother—it appeared Vivien had no choice.

"Oh, very well," she replied in a grumpy voice. She ignored her mother's shocked expression and rose to her feet. "I'll be down in twenty minutes," she said in a waspish voice to St. George. "I hope you don't mind waiting."

A teasing smile shaped his mouth. "I'm sure it will be worth it."

She glared at him as she left, and she could swear he laughed softly. How delightful that he found her so amusing.

"Don't forget to dress warmly," he called as she swept out of the room.

As she stomped upstairs muttering to herself, she tried to prepare for whatever questions he might ask. And ask her he would, no matter what her mother thought was going to happen. Mamma now clearly expected Vivien to throw herself in St. George's path. He might be a younger son, but his family was old, distinguished, and, even more important, disgustingly rich. Vivien might have a wealthy prince dangling after her, but Mamma would clearly prefer that her only daughter not be whisked off to Russia.

Too bad St. George's ulterior motive was investigating her abduction. Rather than promoting a match between them, letting him get closer to *her* meant letting him get closer to the family, Kit in particular. From there, it probably wouldn't take long for St. George to sniff out what had really happened. After that, it would be a short step to Cyrus finding out, and . . . well, Vivien could not allow that to happen.

After fifteen minutes spent running over vague, innocuous answers to potential questions, she returned downstairs garbed in a stylish wool pelisse in plush, hunter green. She paired it with a dashing hat in the same color and an elegant, dreadfully expensive fur muff. The muff might be overdoing it since it wasn't that cold out, but it gave her an excuse to keep her hands to herself. The thought of strolling with St. George, her hand tucked cozily in his arm, unnerved her. Under the circumstances—which would no doubt include the necessity of telling him several whopping lies—the less physical contact between them, the better.

St. George waited for her at the bottom of the steps, shrugging into his greatcoat while the footman stood by with gloves and hat. He glanced up as she descended the stairs. His eyes narrowed, but then a seductive and very appreciative smile curled the corners of his mouth. A silly, girlish pleasure had her heart fluttering in response.

That delightful sensation was quickly followed by dismay, because she needed to be careful with him or she might find herself in deep waters. In so many ways he posed a danger to her family's security and reputation. In his presence, she must never forget that. It would be best to treat him with the wary caution of a potential enemy rather than as a friend.

Her foolish, skipping heart disagreed. After all, the man had saved her life and preserved her reputation. On top of that, he was ridiculously handsome. A girl would have to be dead—or at least apoplectic—not to react to a man like St. George.

He took her by the elbow and gently steered her to the door. "I would say that you look very sensibly dressed for the weather, but no one could call so dashing an outfit *sensible,* nor apply that to the lady who graces such an ensemble so beautifully."

She darted him a startled look. He was obviously quite adept at flirtation—another talent in a long list of impressive skills. Unexpectedly, she felt rather shy, so she simply responded to the compliment with a smile. Not that he meant anything by those words. He was likely just maintaining the fiction that he was . . . what? Courting her?

He kept his hand under her elbow until they made the sidewalk, then he released her. She once again found herself missing his touch, which only confirmed her wisdom in bringing the muff. Vivien had no intention of developing a *tendre* for him since she had no doubt he would disappear from her life as soon as her problem was resolved.

She actually hated the idea of never seeing him again, and couldn't hold back a tiny sigh. Naturally, he picked up on it.

"Are you unwell, my lady?" he asked in a solicitous tone.

She realized she loved hearing his voice. It reminded her of something both rough and yet incredibly soft, like rich, chocolate-colored velvet that had been rubbed the wrong way.

"You don't have to keep asking me that," she said with a wry smile. "I'm actually much sturdier than I look."

He kept his attention on the bustle of the street, steering her around a few carts and a lumbering hackney as they headed toward Green Park.

"I do realize that about you, but you had a shock last night." His mouth pulled into a grim line. "Any woman would be upset by such an ugly incident. I hope the prince didn't hurt you in any lasting way."

At the reminder, she had to resist the impulse to slip one hand out of her muff and curl it around his arm. "It was revolting, I'll grant you that, but he didn't do anything worse than give me a few bruises."

At the sharp intake of his breath, she glanced up at him. The harsh cast to his features told her the prince had made a fortunate escape last night, and he might not be so lucky in the future. Not if St. George had anything to say about it.

His anger on her behalf sparked a warm glow in her chest, and she decided to drop her defenses. On this issue, at least, there seemed no reason not to speak frankly. "You'll think me silly, Captain, but I'm worried for your sake. Your mother provided an excellent diversion last night, but Prince Ivan is not a man who brushes off slights or insults. What you did to him was rather more than an insult. Not that he didn't deserve it," she added hastily. "I would have very much liked to throw him to the floor myself."

They stopped at the corner to wait for a break in the steady stream of vehicles. When a curricle and pair stopped, its driver gallantly waving them to pass, St. George guided her across the street. He hadn't responded to her last comment, save to give her a questioning look.

"Is there something you want to ask me about Prince Ivan?" she asked.

He looked a little startled. "Am I so obvious?"

"You forget that I play cards. I've grown quite adept at reading people."

He slowly nodded, as if suddenly realizing something. "I'll have to remember that," he said.

It seemed an odd response, but he'd already made it clear he disapproved of her activities at the table. Mentally, she tried to shrug it off, but she couldn't deny that his disapproval stung.

"Your question, Captain?" she prompted.

"Please, call me Aden," he said as he placed a light hand on her back, guiding her onto the gravel path cutting through Green Park.

She cast him a wary glance. His somber expression of a moment ago had been replaced by another one of his teasing smiles, which he seemed to be employing a great deal this morning. His ability to switch so readily from one mood to the next unsettled her. He was either a very changeable man— which was doubtful—or he possessed the ability to adopt a charming social mask with disconcerting ease. Vivien reminded herself that she was engaged in a battle of wits and, for Kit's sake, it was a battle she must win.

"That would hardly be proper, my dear sir," she protested in a polite voice. "I hardly know you."

There. *That* put him in his proper place.

He grinned at her, and in one moment to the next that smile bowled past her prim defenses, blasting them sideways like a ball knocking down pins. It was a rogue's smile, a pirate's smile, transforming his hard, handsome features with a masculine amusement that scrambled her brains.

A pair of elderly women, swaddled in layers of taffeta, approached them from the opposite direction. The one closest to them glanced up at St. George as they passed. Her mouth dropped open, and then she flushed an extraordinary shade of pink, letting out a girlish giggle as she elbowed her companion in the side.

Vivien couldn't blame her in the least. She'd almost gotten used to his brand of good looks, but that particular smile was positively lethal. If he kept that up, she very likely wouldn't have much of a brain left to deal with him.

St. George, however, didn't seem to notice anything amiss. "Considering our brief but eventful history together, I'd say we know each other rather well. It's ridiculous for you to keep referring to me as *Captain,* or *St. George,* like I'm a barely met acquaintance. We faced death together, or have you forgotten?" His voice held a regretful reprimand.

"No," she muttered. "I haven't forgotten."

"Besides, our mothers have known each other forever and are even distant cousins, as I understand," he said in a coaxing voice that slid along her skin like warm honey. "That practically makes us family, doesn't it?"

At some point during his speech, they'd slowed to a stop. Vivien gazed up at him, trying to think. This man was certainly not family, nor was he trying to be. He was flirting with her and very expertly too, although for what purpose she couldn't fathom. Even worse, she had to fight against an odd feeling of breathlessness.

But St. George didn't strike her as a man who dealt very often in charm—especially with such an extravagant display— which meant he must want something. Had he sensed she was hiding something from him? That seemed likely. After all, this was the man who'd found her hidden away in a smuggler's cave. Ferreting out her secrets would be child's play for him.

Still, it seemed foolish to resist him on so minor a point and, charm aside, it made a certain amount of sense. St. George knew more about her in some respects than most of her friends. It was rather silly to continue to treat each other so formally.

"As you wish." She forced her feet moving again after she realized she was staring at him like an addlepated twit. "But only in private," she added. "It wouldn't be appropriate to employ our Christian names in company. People might get the wrong idea."

He affected a wounded look as he placed one gray-gloved hand over his chest. "My intentions are only of the purest nature."

She scoffed. "You may cease acting like a buffoon any time now, *Aden*. And I do believe you had a question for me, although I can barely remember what we were discussing."

"Very well," he said, turning serious once more. "I need the truth regarding your relationship with Prince Ivan. Do you have, or did you have an understanding with him?"

She pulled up short. He kept on a few paces before he realized she no longer walked at his side. When he turned back to look at her, he let out a resigned sigh. "I knew you would be offended."

She stalked up to him, resisting the impulse to whack him with her muff. "How could you possibly think I would have an understanding with that beastly toad? The very idea is ridiculous."

"Not so ridiculous, according to the rumor mill."

Lovely. He'd donned his inscrutable face again. No sign of the charming flirt now, either. He might as well be a marble statue of a Greek warrior for all his expression conveyed. But as she told him already, she was good at reading people, and her reading of him indicated he didn't wholly believe her indignant protestations.

"There's even a wager in the book at White's on your impending engagement. The betting runs quite heavily in the prince's favor," he added in a voice that amounted to a sardonic shrug.

Fuming, Vivien glared at him, all but oblivious to the gaggle of children and their nursemaids forced to go around them on the path. St. George, however, was not oblivious. After intercepting several curious stares from the nursemaids, he took her by the arm and steered her to a bench under the trees but well in sight of the main path.

By the time they reached the bench, her temper had already started to cool. She hated the idea that her name would ever be coupled with Ivan the Terrible's, but it made sense. The man wouldn't leave her alone, and she had little doubt Cyrus encouraged the rumors as well.

She perched on the edge of the bench, staring warily up at her silent companion who remained standing.

"I suppose I'm not surprised I've been the subject of that kind of *on-dit,*" she said grudgingly. "The blasted man won't take no for an answer. You've seen what he's been like, even before last night," she said, waving her muff with frustration. "But why would you assume I formed an attachment with him? The prince makes my skin crawl, which should be evident to anyone who sees us two together."

"As loath as I am to disagree with you, before dinner last night you seemed quite, ah, chummy with him. And he certainly viewed you with a proprietorial eye the entire evening."

"Circumstances can be deceiving. For instance, by all outward appearances you were quite proprietorial with Madame Bezrodny too."

As soon as the words escaped her mouth, she wanted to smack herself for revealing her childish jealousy.

He'd turned half away from her to idly watch a few strollers making their way to the ornamental dairy in the center of the park. But her snippy comment pulled his attention back around. He studied her for a few moments, no doubt taking in the fiery blush climbing up her neck.

"Ah, yes," he said with a smile that hinted at pleasant memories. "Madame Bezrodny. Quite a lovely woman, and very friendly too."

"Well, she certainly seemed very friendly with you," she said, giving Aden her own version of an ironic shrug.

Uttering a soft laugh, he sat beside her. "I take your point, my lady. Forgive me for making what was obviously an erroneous assumption."

He said that in such a contrite voice she couldn't help feeling a twinge of guilt. It wasn't entirely his fault he'd misunderstood. To even the most casual observer, it must have seemed that she was encouraging Khovansky's attentions.

She finally relented. "Thank you. And if I'm to call you Aden, then you must call me Vivien," she said, making a peace offering. "I do believe you'd done that before, so it's silly not to continue, at least in private."

"I'm honored," he said in a grave voice.

She wasn't fooled, since his eyes were dancing with laughter. For a man who gave the impression that he rarely smiled, he seemed to be doing rather a lot of it. At least with her.

"But to return to Prince Ivan," he started.

"Must we? It's such a dreary subject."

"I agree, but I wouldn't pester you about it if I didn't think it was necessary. Given that you do not have an understanding with him, what could have encouraged him to molest you last night? The man is obviously a poltroon and completely lacking in manners—even for a prince—but I still find it hard to believe he would feel comfortable enough to impose such liberties on the sister of his host unless he felt he had the freedom to do so.''

Inside her muff, Vivien anxiously twisted her fingers together. How much could she afford to tell him before he guessed the truth?

They sat for a few moments watching little boys play at soldier, waving sturdy twigs at each other in mock swordplay. St. George—Aden—casually stretched his arm along the back of the bench as he waited patiently for her reply. He didn't touch her, but Vivien swore she could feel the heat from his body radiating against her shoulders and neck. She had a crazy urge to snuggle up under his arm and lean her head on his chest, seeking his steadfast strength.

"You can trust me, you know," he said. "Whatever you tell me will remain between us."

He still didn't look at her, and she had the notion he was allowing her to make the decision to confide in him with as little pressure as possible.

Trust.

Such a rare commodity, and yet Aden offered it as easily as he would a pinch of snuff or a glass of wine. Despite that, she believed his word was gospel. But she'd also spent years defending herself and her family from the malicious gossip and mischief-making of life in the *beau monde*. After so much time, she found it difficult to allow anyone to breach her carefully constructed battlements.

When she hesitated, his gaze flicked over her, head to toe, like a soft stroke from a peacock's feather. "I have proved you can trust me, haven't I? I will not allow anything or anyone to harm you. You know my word is good." His deep voice held a note of challenge—and of obligation.

She shook free of her muff and crossed her arms over her chest. "Well, that's certainly not playing fair, is it? How the devil am I to respond to that?"

He slid his arm from the back of the bench and turned sideways to face her. One booted leg stretched in front of her, the lean, tensile strength of his muscles clearly defined by the cling of his breeches.

"It's anything but fair, and I'm not above using whatever means I have to encourage you to confide in me. If that means making you feel guilty because I saved you, so be it."

His baldly stated honesty startled a laugh out of her. As much as she disliked his attempt to manipulate her—the men in her life were always trying to manipulate her—she knew he did it with the best of intentions.

"Well, that's putting me in my place," she said dryly. "Very well, I will give you my trust, at least in this matter."

He smiled, clearly having the sense not to push for more. In that respect, he was decidedly *not* like the other men in her life.

"Prince Ivan has been persistent in his attentions despite my repeated rejections of his suit," she said. "But I was convinced until last night that I had persuaded him to leave me alone."

"A good kick to the shins can often do that," he replied with a slight smile. "So, what happened to change that?"

"My brother, Cyrus. He's determined I accept the prince's offer of marriage. Unfortunately, Cyrus is almost as bad as the prince, refusing to take no for an answer. And believe me," she said, laying a hand over her heart, "I've tried."

"But last night you seemed rather more, ah, amenable to the prince's attentions, at least earlier in the evening." He held his hands up, palms out. "I'm not trying to pick a fight. I'm simply telling you what I observed. Was I wrong?"

Vivien resisted the impulse to hunch her shoulders around her ears. This had to count as one of the more embarrassing conversations of her life, and she had yet to truly shake the family skeletons out of the closet.

"No, you're not wrong. Cyrus came to my room and insisted I entertain the prince's suit," she confessed.

He frowned. "And you acquiesced to his demands? Just like that?"

"Let's just say he applied pressure that was difficult for me to resist."

Aden bowed his head, and for several seconds he seemed to be pondering the flawless shine of his boots. Vivien prayed her vague answers would satisfy him.

"I presume Lord Blake used some kind of threat of financial retribution to gain your cooperation," he finally said.

When she grumbled under her breath, his dark eyes lit up once more with amusement. "It's the obvious answer according to my mother," he said, trying to sound contrite.

Failing at it, too. Vivien suspected contrite wasn't a word in his vocabulary.

"Your mother is correct," she said, unable to keep a note of chagrin from creeping into her voice. "And *my* mother obviously cannot keep what should be a private family matter, private."

"Mothers can be an exceeding trial, especially in their inability to keep their noses out of their children's lives. That being the case, you might as well tell me the rest of it, since your mother will no doubt tell my mother everything, anyway."

He gave her an encouraging smile, but Vivien suspected that when she finally told him the truth, he wouldn't be smiling at all.

Chapter Twenty

As Vivien pondered where to begin, a gust of wind shivered through the branches of the large oak that sheltered their bench, shaking free dead leaves. One drifted down into her lap, a lifeless reminder of the passing season. She couldn't help shivering, both with a sense of impending trouble and with the chill seeping through the wool of her pelisse.

"Come," Aden said, pulling her to her feet. "You've been sitting too long. My mother would have my head on a platter if you caught a chill."

"I told you," she said, automatically, "I'm much—"

"Sturdier than you appear. Yes, I remember. But I suggest we stroll up the Queen's Walk to Piccadilly. We can stop in at Hatchard's to warm up, if you like."

She slanted him a sideways glance. For a man who only pretended to want to spend time in her company, he seemed content to maintain the fiction.

Then again, he was in the middle of grilling her. Once he extracted the information he wanted, he'd no doubt whisk her home and that would be the end of it.

Taking her exposed hand in a gentle grip, he nudged it back into her muff. "Now, you were just about to tell me everything."

She ignored the heated tingle where his gloved fingers had

brushed her palm. "As you surmised, it does have to do with money. Or lack of it."

"Lord Blake's lack of money?" he asked.

"No. Cyrus is actually a good steward of the family finances, if rather tightfisted."

"Are your finances a problem?"

"No. I abhor debt, which I know must surprise you given my habit of spending time in the gaming rooms."

"You do more than spend time. From what I understand, you frequently best the most accomplished gamesters in the *ton*. Quite a feat for a sheltered young miss."

She wrinkled her nose at him. "Not so young to realize the perils of falling into debt. I know the limits of my skill, and I never allow desperation or emotion to rule my play. I also invest a portion of my winnings and I've had some modest success with that as well, thanks to my banker."

His brows lifted and he looked genuinely impressed. Vivien couldn't help preening a little, at least on the inside.

"I congratulate you," he said. "But since neither you nor Lord Blake is a reckless spendthrift or gambling wastrel, I assume the problem lies with your mother or your younger brother."

"With both," she replied with a touch of bitterness. She cleared her throat. Her mother and Kit would probably never change, so it fell to Vivien to manage them as best she could, regardless of her resentment.

"Mamma has no notion of economy and she is too fond of deep play. Not as much as Kit, though. He's dreadfully reckless, and not just at the card tables. He'll put a wager on anything, and he has a *fatal* attraction to betting on the turf."

Aden shrugged. "He sounds much like any other young buck."

"Except for the fact that he has almost no income of his

own to subsidize his folly," she sighed. "Which is where Cyrus comes in."

"Lord Blake is refusing to honor your younger brother's debts, I assume?"

She nodded.

"How much does Kit owe?"

Vivien had to swallow twice before she could get it out. "Almost thirty thousand pounds."

She felt the pause in his step, then he smoothly guided her into the path that cut diagonally up to Hyde Park Corner.

"A considerable sum," he responded. "That being the case, I would hazard a guess your younger brother has paid at least one visit to the cent per cents."

"Yes," she replied tersely, dreading the conclusions he might draw. She hadn't yet decided if she could confide everything in Aden. Though he'd promised to hold what she told him in confidence, Kit's stupidity was on an order of magnitude that might defy all attempts to keep it hidden.

"And then there's Mamma," she hurried on, hoping to divert his attention away from Kit's failings. "Her debts are substantial as well, although nothing like Kit's. Between the two of them it's a crushing amount. And Cyrus doesn't even know the half of it, especially about Kit," she added bleakly. "If he did, he'd throw Kit out on the street or force him to join the army, and then exile Mamma and me to a ghastly little manor house in Yorkshire."

He cocked his head. "I can certainly understand your desire to avoid exile in Yorkshire, but how would it harm your brother to take up a commission in the army? That can be the making of a man."

Vivien started to bristle before recalling that he was an army officer. And given the kind of man he was, she could hardly argue with the conclusion that Kit might do worse than a stint in the military.

"Yes, but Cyrus is not willing to buy him a commission in one of the better regiments. In fact, he said he wouldn't buy him a commission at all, instead forcing him to join the infantry. If he did, who knows what would happen? Kit might have to go to the Americas, or even India. And he is such a boy at heart. He'd never be able to . . ."

She broke off, biting her lip against the panic that rose at the idea of Kit facing such dreadful circumstances.

Aden gave her arm a gentle squeeze. "Vivien, Lord Blake is making an idle threat. He can't force your brother to join the army. Besides, that would hardly shelter him from his obligations to pay Kit's debts. It seems to me the more likely threat is debtors' prison."

She cast him an exasperated glance. "Oh, that's *so* much better."

He barked out a short laugh. "Yes, that was clumsy of me. My apologies. I take it, then, that Lord Blake is insisting you marry Prince Ivan, who will then settle a large sum on you and allow Lord Blake to clear the family debt. Do I have that right?"

"Exactly right," she said gloomily. "Prince Ivan is prepared to settle an obscene amount of money on me, and even offered to pay Kit's and Mamma's debts."

"So, under pressure from your brother, you agreed to entertain Prince Ivan's suit. That, in turn, led to his caddish behavior in the library last night—"

"And I threw his suit back in his face," she finished. "Now I'm no better off than when I started, except for the fact that I don't have to marry the wretched toad. That's an inestimable blessing, but we still face ruin."

"Were you ever intending to marry him?"

"Good Lord, no. I was just trying to buy myself some time."

He shot her a penetrating look. "And what did you hope to accomplish by delay?"

Drat. She'd certainly let him walk right into *that* pertinent question. That's what resulted from trusting someone. Inconvenient, dangerous questions.

"Come up with some sort of plan," she said, vaguely waving her muff in the air.

The soft fur ruffled up with a cold gust of wind. She shoved her other hand back into its warmth and pressed her lips tightly shut. Under no circumstances could she tell Aden—or anyone—of her carefully developed plans to drag Kit and Mamma out of debt. The results of such a slip could be explosive.

Aden grasped her elbow, bringing her to a halt. His gaze probed her, sharp and insistent. "What aren't you telling me, Vivien?"

"Nothing," she protested. Her heart stuttered, but she managed to adopt an expression of wounded innocence.

She hoped.

"You're not responsible for your family's behavior," he said in a kind but firm voice. "Your mother is in Lord Blake's safekeeping and Kit has reached his majority. I understand your worry, but his gambling debts are his and his alone. Regardless of what Lord Blake might say, no one should ask you to sacrifice yourself on their behalf. If you were wise, you would do well to steer clear of your family's troubles. You have enough of your own to contend with."

She didn't know whether to be angry or dumbfounded that he would take it upon himself to lecture her in so familiar a fashion.

"I mean it, Vivien," he said sternly. "You are not to get involved in either of your brothers' affairs. Lord Blake can't force you to do anything against your will if you simply mind your own business and let the other members of your family be responsible for theirs."

Anger. Definitely anger.

"I beg leave to say that you have absolutely no idea what you're talking about," she responded hotly. "I'm already in the middle of it, and so is Kit. If I don't take care of the problem, Kit will be in terrible—"

She broke off when she saw the gleam of understanding spark in his eyes.

Stupid, stupid, stupid. She'd walked right into that one, too.

Lanced by a sense of betrayal, she turned from him and stomped off in the direction of Piccadilly. But he caught up with her in two easy strides, clamping a gentle yet unshakeable hand on her elbow. Refusing to look at him, she yanked her arm, trying to break free.

"Stop struggling," he said. "You'll hurt yourself."

The faint note of amusement in his voice spiked her temper. "You tricked me," she hissed out through clenched teeth.

"It was necessary, sweetheart. You're putting yourself in danger and I can't allow that."

"I am very well able to conduct my own affairs," she said, refusing to be seduced by his masculine wiles. "And do not call me *sweetheart.*"

He glanced around the park, taking in the other strollers on the path and lawns. Fortunately, there was no one close enough to overhear them, although she supposed she looked mad enough to spit dragon's fire.

Not that she cared. She was ready to shriek with frustration—at him, but mostly at herself.

He inclined his head, looking arrogantly aristocratic and not the least bit put out by her flash of temper. "Very well, but we need to discuss this matter calmly." He slanted her an ironic glance. "Or I will discuss it calmly. You can listen, and simply nod when you agree with me."

She glared at him until he nudged her elbow, getting her moving again.

"Let me see if I can figure this out," he said. "Your brother

is in debt for a shocking amount of mor
moneylender, presumably one possessed of
character, even more than the norm of that
right, so far?"

She gave a grudging nod.

"Good. I suspect that your brother probably compounded the problem by borrowing even more in a foolish attempt to recoup his losses so he could pay off his debt." He arched an enquiring brow.

She let out a dramatic sigh and nodded again. Why had she ever bothered keeping it from him in the first place?

He smiled at her. "See, we're making excellent progress. Imagine what we could do if you actually cooperated with me."

Vivien narrowed her eyes at him. "It's impolite of you to tease me, sir. This is a very serious matter."

"Yes, I'm an insensitive brute, but I do wish you would learn to fully trust me. I've repeatedly told you that I will let nothing harm you. If you will allow me, I can probably aid Kit, as well."

She wavered, torn by conflicting impulses. She wanted to believe him—no, she *did* believe he would do his best to protect her. But when it came to Kit, why would he get involved? Only a few minutes ago, he'd been counseling her to abandon everyone in her family to his or her own fate. What were his motives? Why would he even care about her family?

Aden insisted that she share everything with him and yet he guarded his thoughts so carefully. Trust had to run both ways, as far as she was concerned.

"That's all very well," she hedged, "but it's very difficult to turn my life over to you when I know so little about you. You ask me to tell my darkest secrets, and yet you share so little of yourself."

A change passed over his features, like a ripple of wind

oss a still pond. She could almost feel him withdrawing from her.

That made her even more determined to find out everything she could about him.

"Vivien, I'm nothing that you haven't seen before," he replied in a cool voice.

She let out a small snort. "You'll have to do better than that."

A muscle ticked in his jaw, hinting at his irritation. Vivien allowed herself a moment of smug satisfaction that she'd finally penetrated his façade.

"If I tell you a little about myself, may we then return to the subject at hand?"

"Of course," she said magnanimously.

"Very well. What do you want to know?"

She could think of a hundred questions—most of them too personal to voice—so she stuck with the one that seemed most pertinent. "How is it that you can do the things that you do?"

He gave her a questioning glance.

"Your skills," she prompted. "Disarming desperate men, infiltrating smugglers' lairs, planning escapes . . . it hardly seems the sort of thing one learns at Oxford."

"Are you saying I'm not a gentleman?"

She'd obviously hit on a sore point. "Of course not. You're the son of Lord and Lady Thornbury. Still, you're not like any gentleman I've ever met."

He stared straight ahead, then took a deep breath and exhaled, as if letting go of some troubling thought. "I learned what you call *my skills* in the military. I was very young when I joined my regiment, and I've seen a great deal of action over the past eleven years."

"Really?" She counted a number of officers among her acquaintances and she doubted any of them could do what Aden did.

"Not all victories are won on the battlefield, Vivien. Sometimes stealth is called for, and sometimes a man is called to do things he might loathe. Things even more destructive than the thrust of the lance or the shot of a pistol. But if that man wishes to serve his king *and* survive, he learns the necessary skills and then puts them to use in whatever way he must in order to accomplish his task."

The angles of his face had gone sharp, as if cut with furious strokes from a piece of marble. "And come home in one piece. More or less."

She heard it then, a heavy bitterness lacing the words. She'd obviously disturbed some dark place in his soul.

"Oh, I see," she said lamely.

"No, you don't."

She had no answer to that.

"May we return to our previous conversation?" he asked after an uncomfortable silence.

She nodded, deciding she'd done enough probing for one day.

"Good," he said. "Then let me make plain what I think you're worried about. You believe that your brother's moneylender made threats against him and his loved ones. And when your brother did not make good on his debts, this nefarious character kidnapped you, hoping to hold you to ransom. Is that correct?"

Vivien stopped in the middle of the path and eyed him suspiciously.

He tapped his chest with an index finger. "Skills, remember?"

She couldn't help peering at him anxiously. Now that he knew, would he feel obligated to share his knowledge with Sir Dominic? Even Cyrus?

Dropping her muff to the ground, she grabbed his sleeve. "You won't tell Cyrus, will you?"

He swept up her muff, handing it back to her. "Let's keep walking. We're starting to attract some attention."

She glanced around her. They were indeed encountering some curious looks from other strollers, including Mrs. Baird and her two prissy daughters, incurable gossips all. She forced a friendly smile as she took Aden's arm and strolled past them.

"To answer your question," he said once they were out of earshot, "no, I will not tell Lord Blake. At least not now. That would simply confuse the issue and make my job more difficult. Besides, I'm not convinced Kit's situation is what prompted your abduction in the first place."

Her brain stuttered. "I don't understand," she said slowly.

They turned into Piccadilly, skirting the edge of the park.

"Khovansky comes to mind as another candidate," he said.

"But he's a *prince*," Vivien argued.

"Princes do all manner of ugly things, I assure you. And after witnessing that prime example of Khovansky's behavior last night, I believe him capable of anything."

Troubled, Vivien tried to sort through her jostling thoughts. "I grant you, the prince is adamant about marrying me—"

"Obsessive seems a more accurate description."

"But I just can't believe he'd do such a thing. It's demented to think he would take such a risk. Can you imagine the scandal if it was discovered? I'm hardly worth the trouble." She shook her head. "No, he's only persisted because I hurt his pride by refusing him in the first place. I'm sure he'll want nothing more to do with me now. Not after last night."

"You underestimate your charms, Vivien. I suspect the prince won't give up nearly so easily."

She flashed him an impatient look. "I'm sure he hates me by now."

He laughed, and his dark mood seemed to lift. "Very well. But I don't trust the man, and I insist you keep your distance."

"Thank you for stating the obvious. But I still think Kit's moneylender is the likely explanation for my abduction."

"I have my doubts, given that no ransom demand was ever made. With your permission, however, I will speak with Kit directly. It makes sense to explore every possibility."

"I suppose that makes sense," she said dubiously. "But let me explain the situation to Kit first. That way he'll be more amenable to your questions."

He nodded. "Fine, but the less detail you give him about my role in this affair, the better. You can simply say Sir Dominic asked me to look into it."

"Would it help if I was with you when you questioned him? Kit might be more forthcoming," she said, unable to repress her instincts to protect her brother.

That raised an eyebrow. "The opposite would be true, I fear. You'll just humiliate him."

She began to starch up, but he held up a forestalling hand.

"Vivien, you are not to worry or try to intervene in any way. Sir Dominic and I will deal with this. All we ask is that you exercise caution and not go anywhere without an appropriate escort. In fact, the best thing you can do for now is to stay safely at home as much as possible."

She had a number of objections to that confining course of action. None, however, that she could share with him.

"I'll do my best," she said. "But I've already accepted a number of invitations. It would look odd to decline at this late date, especially after last night."

Aden started to object, but she cut him off. "I will not spend my life in hiding. You must trust me to exercise the appropriate caution." She mentally winced a bit at that, considering what she had planned, but with any luck he'd never know about it.

A deep frown marked his brow but he finally nodded. "Then perhaps you would be so kind as to give me a list of your invitations when we return to Blake House."

She cut him a puzzled glance. "Why? Are you going to have someone follow me?"

"No. I'll be escorting you to those affairs."

Her heart gave a funny little skip. "I don't understand."

He glanced down at her. "Don't you? Then let me explain. From now on, until we find the man who planned your abduction, I'll be escorting you on every one of your social occasions. That will serve the dual purpose of allowing me to keep an eye on you and to observe those you come in contact with."

She slowed as they approached the first row of shops. "But that will appear very odd, won't it? How will we explain all this . . . togetherness?"

For the first time since she'd met him, he seemed a trifle embarrassed. "I will be seen to be courting you, of course. It's the obvious conclusion."

"Courting me?" she yelped.

"Just pretending," he hastily added. "And hopefully for only a short time." He reached up and tugged on his cravat, as if it was too tight around his neck. "It was my mother's idea," he finished in an apologetic tone.

"Oh. I see," she said in a faint voice. She didn't, actually. Her brain had been stunned into a daze at the idea of Aden courting her, pretend or not.

"It makes perfect sense when you think about it," he mused. "For one thing, it should keep Khovansky at a distance, which you must admit is a definite advantage."

"Yes, I suppose so," she managed.

He smiled his approval. As he ushered her into Hatchard's, he launched into a quiet recital of all the reasons why a fictional courtship would be just the thing. She listened in silent dismay, convinced that *his* plan would destroy *her* plan before she even had a chance to put it in motion.

Chapter Twenty-One

Yanking his collar up against the needling sleet, Aden turned into Jermyn Street at a pace barely short of a run. The streets bustled with activity—mostly young bucks and other men out for a convivial evening in the clubs and gaming hells populating the area around Pall Mall.

He was headed to one of the most notorious hells, although not by choice. A note from Griffin Steele had pulled him from the peace of his apartments only minutes after he'd settled in with a brandy and book for a quiet read.

Aden had spent the day chasing dead-end leads, and that was after a frustrating interview with Kit Shaw—whom he'd finally run to ground at White's—regarding his possible role in Vivien's abduction. Kit had been alternately guilt-ridden and defensive, insisting he could take care of the problem on his own. Only when Aden had outlined in detail what had happened to his sister and what *could* happen in the future had Kit relented. Then, white-faced, he'd confessed everything, in more detail than Aden had wanted to hear. But at least he'd offered up the necessary information—the name of the cent per cent who had Kit in his thrall.

Aden actually knew the man, a jeweller whose shop trafficked as much in foolish young men like Kit as it did in gold.

But although Ben Cribbens was an ugly customer, Aden was convinced the man's threats were more bluster than fact. Nonetheless, he had paid him a visit, making it clear that if he made any more threats against the Blake family—veiled or otherwise—hellfire would rain down on his head. Blanching the shade of curdled milk, Cribbens had agreed to give Kit extra time to meet his obligations.

That left Aden back where he'd started, with Lord Blake as a possible conspirator in the abduction scheme along with his newest and favorite suspect, Khovansky. The prince was clearly obsessed with Vivien. Naïvely, she seemed determined to ignore that pertinent fact, but Aden could not. Starting tomorrow, his investigation into the prince's background would begin in earnest.

But first he had another and more urgent chore to attend to—namely, pulling the blasted girl out of one of the worst gaming hells in the city. Already worn thin by the frustrations of the day, Aden's temper had shredded when he'd read the terse note delivered by one of Griffin's street urchins. A fast jog through the streets of Mayfair, quicker than catching a hackney, hadn't improved his mood, especially given the sodding November rain that fell in driving gusts.

Vivien, sadly for her, would be the recipient of his temper. The woman clearly hadn't an ounce of sense in that beautiful body. He should have known her quiet compliance this morning was a ruse. Well, he wouldn't make that mistake twice. It was time for her to learn that although she might be able to run circles around the other people in her life, she could not do so with him. He'd pull her over his knee and paddle her little bottom to make the point clear, if he had to. Vivien obviously needed a sharp reminder that she was still in danger, and he was the man to give it to her.

He reached the deceptively genteel-looking house on Jermyn Street, with its red brick façade and imposing marble porch. Griffin's establishment had the best whores, the finest food, and the deepest play in London. The surroundings were luxurious and the patrons hailed from amongst the wealthiest and most powerful men in the *ton,* men who came to the house to let slip the bounds of propriety.

But the real draw was Griffin, himself. Rumors had swirled about him almost from the day he appeared in London at the age of fourteen. The most persistent of those whispered rumors was that he was not simply the proprietor of wildly successful gaming houses, but was a crime lord as well.

That rumor wasn't true, but Aden did know that Griffin ran a growing financial empire that sometimes operated within the gray areas of the law. He might not be a criminal, but his tentacles of influence snaked in multiple directions—in the dank streets and rookeries, in the wealthiest drawing rooms of the *beau monde,* and even to the highest levels of government. There were many who owed Griffin Steele favors—or money— and who feared him in equal measure. No man in his right mind ever crossed him. His enemies had a way of quietly disappearing, or coming to ruin in so absolute a way they might have preferred a bullet in the back of the head.

But once a man stepped foot into Griffin's gaming hell, he felt his pulse race with excitement. Something forbidden and dangerous scented the air, like the perfume of the most expensive of courtesans, enhancing the thrill of pitting one's luck against the house.

Griffin was also Aden's cousin—another bastard with royal blood simmering in his veins.

He knocked on the door of Cormorant House and was received by a burly footman dressed in elaborate livery highly suggestive of the costumes worn by staff in service to the Prince Regent. Griffin did have a nicely twisted sense of humor, which Aden could certainly appreciate.

"Good evening, Captain." The footman took his greatcoat and hat. "Mr. Steele is waiting for you in his office."

Aden nodded, repressing the impulse to storm up to the gaming rooms to find Vivien and haul her out of the house. But Griffin surely had eyes on her, so she would be safe for now. Given that Griffin was in his office rather than up in the gaming rooms where he would normally be at this time of night, it meant there was something he needed to tell Aden in private.

He strode down the passage to the back off the house. Griffin's office was located in an annex behind the reception rooms, tucked between the main house and the pantry, kitchen, and mews. From there, he kept an all-seeing eye on the large establishment and everything in it, much like the mythical creature for which he was named.

Although not spacious, Griffin's office was richly ornamented, almost extravagantly so. The walls, covered in striped paper in rich shades of red, shimmered under the light of several branches of candles as well as gold-plated wall sconces. A highly polished cabinet, lavishly covered in gilt, stood against the wall, and two beautifully fashioned Hepplewhite-style chairs sat before the fireplace grate. Griffin had a passion for Hepplewhite furniture, a rather odd interest for a man of his ilk.

The master of Cormorant House sat behind a massive desk in the center of the room, his dark head bent over a pile of ledgers. He looked up when Aden shut the door and laid aside his pen.

"Ah, Cousin. How delightful to see you." Griffin had a cultured voice, but it also carried a hint of something ragged and rough, as if the smooth cadences of his aristocratic background had been dragged through the broken, garbage-strewn alleys of Covent Garden.

A fairly accurate description of the man's history, all told.

"Must you call me that?" Aden took a seat in front of the desk.

Griffin's dark eyes gleamed with malicious amusement. "You're the only member of the family who will acknowledge me. How can I resist?"

"Try," he responded in a dry voice. Aden, of course, shared some of that same problem, but that was the price paid by the bastard son of a prince.

"Speaking of our fathers—"

"Which we weren't," Aden said.

"Have you encountered yours, lately?" Griffin asked, ignoring Aden's interjection. "I've been wondering if you'd managed to overcome any of your antipathy for him."

Aden stared at him, refusing to dignify the absurd question with an answer.

Griffin gave a casual shrug. "Ah, well. One can hardly blame you. After all, Prinny has to be the most disgusting excuse for a prince one could imagine."

"Except for your esteemed parent."

Griffin's father was Ernest Augustus, the notorious Duke of Cumberland and one of the younger brothers of the Prince Regent. In public, Cumberland's conduct was entirely reticent compared to his brothers, but accusations of murder and even incest, although never proven, were whispered against him, and his cold temperament and sharp tongue earned him more than a few enemies.

But Griffin's hatred for his father stemmed from the fact that he'd ruined Chloe Steele, Griffin's mother. An innocent girl of fourteen, Chloe had fallen prey to a young Prince Ernest's seduction, which had left her pregnant, her reputation destroyed. Chloe had been sent away shortly after Griffin's birth, and she'd completely disappeared a few years later, seemingly abandoning her son. When Griffin had run away after the death of Bartholomew Steele, his great-uncle and the man who'd raised him, he'd first come to London, looking for his mother. But he'd never found her, and Aden suspected the loss still affected him. No matter what trials Aden had suffered as a result of his parentage, they'd been nothing compared to Griffin's many tribulations.

Not that they'd ever compared notes. Although Griffin had eventually adopted a cavalier attitude toward the circumstances of his birth, anyone who knew him well had learned to avoid the subject, or risk Griffin's wrath. What details Aden had acquired about his cousin's life had come from Dominic, who'd known Chloe as a child. It had been Dominic who'd finally tracked Griffin down in a London gaming hell, where he'd found employment running errands. And it had been Dominic who, years later, had introduced Aden to his cousin. As cousins they were not particularly close, but occasionally they came into each other's way. Griffin had access to information that Aden often found useful. And, for some strange reason, Griffin seemed to derive enjoyment from acknowledging his familial relationship with Aden.

Griffin let out a dramatic sigh. "I suppose one could quibble, but at least your father isn't a murderer."

"That we know of, anyway."

"Well, your dear pater *is* certainly guilty of murdering the canons of good taste," Griffin said in a contemplative tone. "He deserves the hangman's noose for that, if nothing else."

Aden laughed, and Griffin cracked a smile, his dark mood seeming to lift.

"Now that we've caught up on family," Aden said, "perhaps we can get to the matter at hand."

Griffin rose and strolled to the cabinet. As usual, he was dressed simply but expensively in black. Only the white linen of his shirt relieved his dark garb. With the thin scar that cut from his left temple down below his cheekbone and his black hair pulled back in an old-fashioned queue, he looked like a buccaneer. A refined one, but a buccaneer all the same.

He extracted a bottle from the cabinet and poured out two brandies, handing one to Aden.

"Your little problem," Griffin said, leaning against his desk, "is currently upstairs with her idiotic brother in one of the card rooms." He held up a hand. "And, yes, she is well guarded. My factotum is up there along with two of my men. No one will harm her."

"How bad is it? Tell me they just didn't waltz into the place, the Lady Vivien Shaw and her brother, the Honorable Kit Shaw." *Christ.* Did she have any idea what she was doing to her reputation?

"She's in disguise," Griffin said, trying to hold back a grin. Aden frowned. "As what?"

"I believe she's attempting to portray herself as a mysterious widow. She's swathed in enough veils and drapery to decorate half of Carlton House. It's a miracle she can even see what she's doing."

"Her disguise obviously didn't fool you," Aden pointed out.

"No, but I believe it's managed to trick everyone else, which should surprise me but doesn't. Most of the men who grace my establishment are fools, of course, all too ready to be parted from their ill-gotten gains."

"And what's the brother's role in this little charade?"

"He is attempting to portray himself as her cicisbeo. Failing miserably, I might add."

Aden hauled himself to his feet. "Which room?"

"The Green Room."

Aden cursed. The Green Room was infamous throughout the *ton.* Only the most hardened gamblers and degenerate rakes crossed its threshold. The stakes were astronomical, with entire fortunes won and lost in one night.

"A question, Cousin," Griffin said as he followed him to the door. "What is she doing here? Even for an accomplished gamester like Lady Vivien, this is rather reckless."

"She's attempting to tow Kit and her mother out of debt," he answered from between clenched teeth. It made perfect sense, now that he thought about it. For a lunatic, anyway, which he was beginning to think she might be.

Griffin nodded. "One has to admire her courage, if nothing else."

"How's she doing?"

"Bloody well, at last report," his cousin replied, cracking a smile. "She's holding her own against Barrymore and Castle, which is really quite extraordinary."

Aden spun on his heel and hurried toward the stairs, his cousin's mocking laugh echoing behind him.

Leave it to Vivien to sit down at a table with the most unrepentant rakes in the city. When he got her away from that table, she'd find herself in an even more difficult situation—explaining her actions to him.

For her first experience of a gaming hell, Vivien had been pleasantly surprised. The appointments were elegant, the rooms decorated with tasteful luxury, running heavily to the classical style with touches of French extravagance. The champagne was delicious and well chilled—she managed to sneak in a few sips under her veils—and she had no doubt the food laid on in the supper room would be fresh and well prepared. She'd been too anxious to eat earlier in the day, preoccupied with planning tonight's expedition with Kit, and she allowed herself a tiny sigh at the thought of having to forgo Griffin Steele's lovely food. But she couldn't manage to eat behind all these veils. Her stomach might grumble at her, but it was imperative she keep her identity unknown.

She and Kit had argued long and hard over her plan, and

he'd only agreed to her scheme when she told him she planned to go in disguise. After they considered and discarded a number of possibilities, the idea of a veiled widow had seemed most likely to fit their needs. Kit had also been insistent they play at the gaming hell where they stood the least chance of running into someone who knew Vivien well. She might be swathed in two layers of black veils and careful to keep her voice to a low murmur, but her disguise wouldn't fool a friend or close acquaintance.

They'd also sought a club catering to hardened gamesters and reckless, wealthy men, the kind who weren't averse to losing monstrous sums of money in one night. They also needed a house with a reputation for fair play and, according to Kit, The Cormorant fit the bill nicely. Its clientele was well heeled and its owner known for keeping the play honest while not asking inconvenient questions of his patrons.

This afternoon, she'd asked her banker to withdraw one thousand pounds from her account. Stuffing the wad of notes in her purse had made her sick with anxiety, but she had no choice. Her word as a newcomer would have meant nothing to Steele. Only by providing a stake would she be able to play the kind of game that suited her purpose.

Fortunately, her nerves had settled as soon as she started to play, and Vivien now glanced with satisfaction at the tidy pile of markers growing in front of her. She and Kit had done very well, especially against the likes of Barrymore and Castle. Kit was under strict instructions to play straight, leaving the brain-work and subtleties to her. So far, he'd been following her lead, playing a respectable if cautious game.

"Your play, Madam," Barrymore intoned in a bored voice.

She pretended to study her cards, and then trumped his ace. Barrymore pressed his lips into a thin line, once again displeased.

He and Castle had initially seemed quite keen to take her

on when she and Kit first entered the card room. Even through the layers of dark veiling masking her face, she had seen their gazes filling with an unholy mix of lustful curiosity and greed. To such jaded men, she must have presented an interesting challenge, and they'd made several bald innuendoes when they'd first started to play. Kit had turned beet red but he'd managed to keep himself under control, maintaining the fiction of her masquerade as a merry widow. Vivien had also blushed at their remarks, and had blessed the veils that covered her. As inconvenient as all the swaddling was, she was grateful for the protection.

But the crude remarks and her opponents' enthusiasm for the game had markedly decreased in the last hour as the points on her tally had added up and her pile of markers had grown. Vivien was hitting her stride and the cards were cooperating. The bets had been high and reckless from the start. With a little luck over the next few games the rubber would be hers, along with a very sizable increase in her winnings.

And she had to admit she'd be happy to take her winnings and exit. Despite the elegance of the surroundings, corruption whispered through the air like a dark symphony. Women, beautiful birds of paradise in the employ of the house, drifted in and out of the rooms, their expensive perfumes carrying the heavy scent of decadence. They wove their soft white arms around the men at the tables, whispering seductive lies, enticing them into their beds. Those men—men like Castle and Barrymore—had the coldest and the most calculating gazes Vivien had ever seen. Part of her relished the opportunity to best them, but they made her skin crawl, nonetheless.

Kit played the final trick of the current game, flashing a triumphant smile. Behind her veiling, she grinned. If they kept this up—

Her mind stuttered when a large, masculine form loomed

close over Kit's shoulder, blocking the light from the wall sconces.

"What the devil," Kit snapped, twisting around in his chair.

The words died on his lips at the same moment Vivien's stomach pitched upward into her throat. She stared at the man standing behind her brother, straining her eyes to confirm what couldn't possibly be true.

Except that it was.

"Why, Mr. Shaw," Aden drawled in a dangerously soft voice. "Imagine running into you at The Cormorant. Not your usual sort of haunt, is it?"

"I, ah, no . . . that is to say . . ." Kit stuttered.

Vivien gripped the edge of the table, silently begging her brother to button his lips. She tried stretching out a leg, hoping to give him a warning nudge with her foot, but couldn't reach him. Right now, her veils figured as the only barrier between her and certain destruction.

But when Aden's gaze fastened on her, she knew destruction had arrived. Even through the layers of net she could see the fury in his dark eyes, even though his features showed no sign of emotion. She reluctantly admired his discipline as panic roared through her veins.

For a few nauseating seconds, she thought she might faint. And for a few *more* seconds, that seemed the desirable option. Unfortunately, she'd never fainted in her life, and it didn't appear as if she was going to pick up the habit anytime soon.

"Mr. Shaw, you seem to have a mysterious companion. Perhaps you will be so kind as to introduce me," Aden said, resting a heavy hand on Kit's shoulder.

"Smith," her brother blurted out. "My friend goes by the name of Mrs. Smith. She's a widow, but she prefers to remain incognito. I'm sure you understand."

Vivien's chest squeezed so tight she could hardly breathe, but she had to give Kit credit for trying.

"A veiled widow. How very delightful." Aden gave her a graceful, mocking bow. "Mrs. Smith, it's a pleasure to meet you."

Vivien hardly knew how to respond. She'd never seen this side of Aden before, and it unnerved her to the point of idiocy. But as much as Aden's anger unsettled her, she knew he wouldn't expose her to damaging gossip. All she had to do was finish this game and make a graceful retreat. Yes, she would be subjected to a stinging lecture from her erstwhile suitor, but it would be a small price to pay for the tidy purse she'd won tonight. As long as he didn't tell Cyrus about tonight's escapade, she and Kit should escape fairly well.

Holding on to her nerve by the merest thread, she gave a dignified nod by way of greeting.

"As you can see," Lord Castle sneered, "the lady's words are few and far between. One would think she had something to hide. I, for one, would be delighted to discover her secrets."

Vivien froze at the malicious tone. Castle hadn't earned his name as the Vicious Viscount for nothing. She rarely encountered him since he usually shunned *ton* events, but she had little doubt he would relish destroying her reputation if he discovered her identity.

Aden's gaze flitted to Castle. "My lord, I see you are between hands. Perhaps you would be willing to relinquish your seat to me. I'm certain you must want to stretch your legs, or perhaps visit the supper room."

Alarmed, Vivien peered at Aden through her veiling. Castle looked as flummoxed as she felt.

"Why the hell would I want to do that? I'm in the middle of a game. You're mad if you think I'm going to give you my place."

Aden gave him a smile so cold Vivien half expected to see icicles form on Castle's long nose.

"Then you'd better reserve a cell in Bedlam," Aden said,

"because I intend to take your seat. It's up to you how easily I do so."

Castle leaned comfortably back in his chair. "Don't be a fool, St. George. I'm sure the lady will be happy to oblige you in whatever way you fancy once our game is finished."

Vivien's breath caught in her throat when Aden gave a negligent shrug. "Have it your way," he said, moving toward the viscount.

Castle came to his feet just as Aden reached him. Vivien also scrambled up, although she hadn't a clue what she could do to prevent the impending mayhem.

Fortunately, she didn't have to do anything. Griffin Steele suddenly appeared from nowhere, sliding gracefully into the small space still separating the two men.

"Gentlemen," he said in a soothing voice. "This is unnecessary. I'm sure we can find a satisfactory solution to this little problem."

He turned his back on Aden, which surprised Vivien. Aden was a quiet man and not given to dramatics—except for tonight, apparently—but no one in his right mind would underestimate him. But Steele didn't seem worried in the least.

"Get the hell out of my way, Steele," Castle snarled. "That bastard insulted me, and I'll not put up with it."

Steele chuckled indulgently. "In this establishment, my lord, bastards are always welcome. I suggest you remember that if you wish to continue taking advantage of my hospitality. Now, why don't you let the captain take your place? In exchange, I'll fetch a bottle from my private stock of champagne for you to enjoy at supper. Compliments of the house, naturally."

He raised a long, elegant hand and beckoned to a woman hovering over one of the other tables. She swiftly came to her employer's side, waiting to do his bidding.

"Eloise will be happy to escort you to the supper room, Lord Castle," he said, making it sound like an order.

Steele was neither as tall nor as broad as Lord Castle or Aden, but he possessed a lean, graceful physique that held whipcord strength. And at this moment, a lethal and focused sort of energy shimmered in the air around him. If there was danger in the air, it came from the proprietor of The Cormorant, not from Castle or even from Aden.

In fact, Aden had stepped back a few paces and crossed his arms over his chest, assuming a relaxed pose and looking positively amused. Vivien peered at him, amazed to see a small but genuine smile shaping his mouth.

Mystified, she sank back into her chair. What in heaven's name was going on?

Finally, Castle shuffled his feet and his gaze cut sideways to Eloise. "Oh, devil take it! Have it your way. But I have no doubt she'll fleece you too, St. George. She's a sharp, unless I miss my guess." He cast an angry glance at Steele. "Didn't expect that sort of thing at The Cormorant."

"Shocking, I know," Steele replied in a soothing voice. "I will take care of it immediately." He drew Eloise forward, and she took Castle's arm and began to lead him away. Steele followed, but not before he gave Aden an oddly conspiratorial wink.

As Aden took Castle's seat, Vivien let out a shaky breath. Although grateful one crisis had been averted, she did not look forward to the next.

"Well, that was amusing," drawled Barrymore. "But perhaps we could turn our attention back to the business at hand."

"Of course," said Aden, who began to deal the cards.

Across the table, Kit rolled his eyes at her, panicked. Since Vivien could do nothing about that, she picked up her cards and arranged them. Aden had adroitly backed her into a corner, and there was no choice but to gather her wits and play through the rest of the rubber.

The next hour turned into an epic nightmare as Aden's tally steadily increased. Even worse, her nerve deserted her as the evening wore on and Aden trumped her repeatedly. Kit made it worse, taking foolish risks in an effort to recoup their losses.

But it was more than simple mistakes and lost nerves. It was Aden. Vivien had played against the best, but she'd never encountered someone as skilled and intuitive as him. He never faltered, never made a bad move. Blast him, the cards had so far favored him too, giving him one strong hand after another.

Two hours later, Vivien found herself staring in horror at her tally. Not only had she lost all her winnings from earlier in the evening, she'd lost most of her stake, too. Rather than acquiring the means to rescue Kit, she'd made the situation infinitely worse.

"Well, St. George," Barrymore said with a laugh. "It was a lucky night for me when you walked in the door. So, Mrs. Smith. Another rubber? A chance to recoup your losses?"

Vivien swallowed with a throat as dry as cinders. Panic tightened her chest, making it impossible to speak. Disaster no longer simply waited at her door. It had moved in and taken up residence.

"I think not," Aden said. "Mrs. Smith is finished with games, at least for this portion of the evening." He rose to his feet and held out a hand. "In fact, I will be escorting her home."

Barrymore studied them for a moment and then guffawed. "So, you do know her. I thought this felt personal. Well, have at it, my friend. God knows you've earned the right to take your pleasure with the lady."

From the look on Aden's face, pleasure was the last thing on his mind.

"Thank you, sir," she managed in a low tone. "But Mr. Shaw will be escorting me home tonight."

As if waking from a trance, Kit lurched to his feet.

"No, he won't." Aden's tone brooked no opposition. "You will be leaving with me, immediately."

"See here, St. George," Kit spluttered. "You have no right to order us around."

Aden ignored him, instead gently grasping her hand and drawing her to her feet. Vivien felt like a puppet on a string, unable to resist.

Kit jerked forward. "I'm warning you, St. George. You have no right to touch my—"

"Be quiet," Vivien hissed. She cast a quick look about the room. As she feared, they were drawing attention. She took Aden's arm, shaking her head at Kit.

Aden tucked her against him and ushered her to the door. When they reached it, he moved behind her, keeping one hand upon her waist. His touch was light yet possessive, and a shivering sensation vibrated through every part of her body. She felt the heat of him along her back, a barely contained blaze. That was his anger, so carefully repressed during their game and now struggling to break free.

Vivien sighed as she made her way down the stairs to the front door. Her actions had tempted the devil, and now he would surely take his due.

Chapter Twenty-Two

Vivien, Aden, and Kit huddled under the porch of Cormorant House, avoiding the icy rain spattering down. Between the foul weather and the late hour, Jermyn Street stood quiet with only a few carriages waiting in front of the gaming hells and bawdy houses.

Expelling a tense breath, Vivien threw back her veils to let the air cool her overheated skin. She didn't relish explaining her behavior to Aden, but she was grateful to quit the stifling, nerve-wracking environment of the club.

It was a temporary respite, unfortunately. Aden might have a bone to pick with her, but she had a whole graveyard to pick with him. His meddling had cost her four thousand pounds. Not only would Kit be unable to make a down payment to the moneylender, but Vivien had also lost a significant portion of her own savings, making it that much harder to stake herself at the tables. And the fact that Aden was the man who'd fleeced her made it that much more difficult to bear.

He glanced down at her and let out a smothered curse. With a quick movement, he flipped her veils back down over the brim of her hat.

"What are you doing?" she snapped, grabbing the swaths

of fabric to pull them back up. "I'm about to expire from the heat of that dreadful place."

"We're not in the clear, in case you've failed to notice," he growled. "And if you found it so damn dreadful, I wonder why the hell you stayed."

She ignored the second part of his statement, instead making an exaggerated show of perusing the streetscape. "There isn't a person in sight. And I'll thank you to keep your hands to yourself."

"Yes, by God," Kit jumped in, flapping his arms in an agitated fashion. "You've truly rolled us up tonight, Captain. Vivi had Castle and Barrymore on the ropes until you came along and spoiled everything. What the devil are we to do now?"

Aden slowly turned and fastened a murderous gaze on Kit. Even in the flickering light of the door lamp, Vivien could read the frigid disbelief in his dark eyes.

She laid a hand on her brother's arm, pressing it in silent warning. Lord knows she shared his frustration and anger, but a brawl on the front steps of a gambling house would be a disaster.

Kit subsided with a grumble, satisfying himself with a seething stare. He'd been fighting his resentment even before tonight's disaster, the result of Aden's grilling this afternoon. According to Kit, Aden had thoroughly dressed him down and had ordered him to stay away from the cent per cents, the tables, and the racetrack. Vivien had supported Aden's view, at least until he'd shown up tonight and cleaned her out.

"Why are we standing here, anyway?" Kit demanded of Aden. "It's bloody freezing."

"I'm waiting for Mr. Steele's carriage so I can escort Lady Vivien home. You, however, are free to do as you bloody well choose. In fact, why don't you take yourself off immediately? I find I've had quite enough of your baffle-headed idiocy for one day," Aden said with brutal frankness.

Vivien resisted the urge to slap her hand to her forehead. Was she always to be surrounded by bad-tempered males who ordered people about?

She forestalled Kit's bristling response by stepping between the two men. The sooner she separated them, the better. "Kit, there's no need for you to stand around in this horrible weather, and it's not so late, after all. Weren't you going to join some of your friends later? Or perhaps you could drop in to your club for a brandy."

Her brother goggled at her. "Vivi, it's after three in the morning, and it's freezing out. After the hellish night we've had, all I want to do is go home to bed."

"Then you can walk to Blake House," Aden said. "The fresh air will do you good. I need to speak privately with *Mrs. Smith.*"

He took her arm and nudged her down the steps as an elegant landau rattled out from the mews behind Jermyn Street. When the coachman pulled up in front of them, Aden pulled her over to the street. He opened the door, wrapped his big hands around her waist, and tossed her up with ruthless efficiency onto the cushioned bench. Vivien let out a startled squawk and fell back on the squabs, her veils tangling up as her hat pitched forward over her eyes.

As she struggled to right herself, the carriage dipped with Aden's added weight.

"But why can't we all ride home together?" Kit called in a plaintive voice.

Muttering under his breath, Aden knocked on the roof of the carriage and the coachman set the horses bowling down the street, leaving poor Kit behind. Vivien finally managed to push back her hat and free herself from her entangling veils.

"That was incredibly rude," she said. "There was no reason Kit couldn't have come with us."

He leaned back on the opposite seat and slowly crossed his

arms across his brawny chest. Masculine ire shimmered in the air between them. "There was a very good reason. I was on the verge of killing him for being such an idiot, and for allowing you to act like an idiot, too."

The bubble of frustration building in her chest popped. "Everything was fine until you came along," she snapped, waving her hand. "I had the situation perfectly under control."

He stared in open disbelief. "You were gambling in the most notorious hell in London, challenging two degenerate rakes. Do you have any idea what would have happened if they discovered your identity? Besmirching your reputation would have been the least of it. Both would have had no compunction to try to blackmail you into their beds—probably at the same time, too. You rendered yourself completely vulnerable to their foul advances. By even stepping foot in such a place you acted the worst sort of jade. After what you've been through, I had not thought you so careless of your safety. It would appear I've been sadly mistaken."

Vivien flinched, stunned by the disdain on his features, so harsh in the dim light of the carriage lamp. His words slashed her pride into a thousand ribbons. She pressed a gloved hand over her breastbone as if to calm the sickening gyrations of her heart. Closing her eyes, she took slow, deep breaths.

She opened her eyes and their gazes tangled, his now displaying less anger but more frustration. As she shifted in her seat, her knees bumped against his long, booted legs. The small space enclosed them in claustrophobic intimacy, and a heightened sense of emotion swirled in the air between them, fracturing the air in Vivien's lungs into uneven breaths.

He sighed and pressed an index finger to the bridge of his nose. "Vivien—"

"I did what I needed to do," she snapped. "And if that forced me to act the jade, then so be it. But why did you challenge me in so callous a fashion? Now what am I to do? I could ill afford to lose even one pound of my savings, and now I have lost thousands. Both Kit and I will suffer for it."

"If you had stayed home as I requested," he growled, leaning forward, "you would not have been placed in so untenable a position." His broad shoulders seemed to fill up half the carriage.

She resisted the impulse to shrink into the squabs. Aden didn't frighten her, not really. She knew he would never harm her. But with that glowering expression on his stone-cut features and his air of primal, aggrieved masculinity, he cut an intimidating figure.

Well, she would not be intimidated. She adopted her haughtiest air, trying to stare down her nose at him. But even squashed into the carriage, he loomed over her.

"I have no intention of sitting home like a poor dab of a thing, unable to influence the course of my own life," she said. "I am more than capable of looking after myself."

He slapped his palm to his forehead. "Really? That didn't appear to be the case when I found you locked in a grotty cave just over a week ago."

Her dignity abandoned her in a rush. "Yes, really," she bit out. "And you are a brute to throw that ugly memory in my face, and no gentleman for fleecing me in that card game tonight. You have put me in an awful position when you promised to protect me, and I will *never* forgive you for that."

He responded with a truly foul curse, and she couldn't help uttering a gasp. He dug into the pocket of his greatcoat and drew out a thick wad of notes.

"The money is yours, Vivien. Did you really think I would keep it?" He flung the packet onto her lap. "I do not fleece women, and I especially do not fleece *you*."

Her mind blanked as she stared at the notes. When a few of them fluttered to the floor, Aden snatched them up with an impatient hand.

"Um, so does that mean you do fleece men?" she asked. It was a ridiculous thing to say, but Aden had a knack for stunning her into stupidity.

Her demented attempt at levity did nothing to lighten his grim visage. She swallowed nervously. Finally, the most pertinent question forced itself to the front of her brain.

"Why?" she asked. "Why would you do this?"

"Let me show you, Vivien."

He reached across and snatched her up in a hard grip, pulling her across the intimate space and into his lap. All the breath whooshed out of her lungs as she grabbed his shoulders. Her heart tripped over itself, racing to catch up with the excitement and anxiety zinging along her nerves.

Clutching the thick wool fabric of his coat, she gazed up at him. His raven eyes burned with heat, and he showed his white teeth in a smile that looked more like a wolf's snarl.

"Wha . . . what are you doing?" she stammered.

"I'm answering your question," he murmured, the dark rumble making her shiver.

Then he moved, tilting her back over his arm as he swooped in to kiss her. His mouth fastened over hers. Not gently, either. He plundered her lips, demanding entrance with a masculine arrogance that swept past her resistance in one skipped heartbeat.

Not that Vivien put up much of a fight. She stiffened momentarily, then collapsed in a swift rush of burgeoning pleasure, whimpering with an odd feeling of relief as his tongue swept boldly into her mouth.

When she softened beneath him, Aden's touch gentled. Even as he continued to kiss her, feeding the raw heat with sweeps of his tongue, he slipped a hand under her knees and corrected her inelegant sprawl. He brought her legs up, letting her feet rest on the bench as he settled her more comfortably onto his lap. Her bottom nestled into his groin and—

Her eyes flew open and she jerked back, breaking the contact of their lips. She'd felt *that* hardness before, the night of her rescue when he'd taken her before him on his horse. His, er, manly appendage had been nudging into her then, too. It felt even bigger tonight, and any doubts she'd been harboring about his interest died a quick death.

For several tense seconds they stared at each other. He didn't relinquish his grip, but nor did he attempt to return to her mouth. Instead, he studied her face, his dark eyes both acutely watchful and smoldering with desire. The combination made her head spin.

As if she were in a trance, her hand drifted up to touch her lips. They felt hot and swollen. His pupils seemed to dilate, flaring as he tracked her movement. Vivien let her hand drop to his chest, sliding her fingers past the lapels of his coat to clutch the fine linen of his cravat. Beneath her fingertips, his heart thrummed in a rapid, steady beat, his life and heat flowing into her hand

"Yes, well, I think I understand your explanation," she whispered. "But I might need further clarification."

He groaned, resting his chin on the top of her head. "Christ, woman, you drive me mad."

His arm tightened around her shoulders, snuggling her more closely against his broad chest. He felt so wonderful—so hot and so strong—that she couldn't help wriggling a bit with delight. His erection pressed against her bottom, and her pleasurable little ache of desire made her squirm even more.

Aden hissed out a breath and his head came up. A flush crept across his chiseled features and his eyes grew heavy-lidded, seductive, and hungry.

A second later and his mouth took hers again. He thrust past her lips, feeding her with intense, devouring kisses. Vivien could do nothing but surrender, opening herself in a way she'd never done before. Not for any man.

Shaking with longing, she struggled deeper into his embrace as she pressed upward into the kiss. She wanted everything from him, even though she hardly understood what *everything* was. But when Aden's other hand slipped under the hem of her skirts, trailing up her stocking-clad leg, she moaned and wrapped an arm around his neck. She wanted all of him, and even though it felt like he was kissing her with his entire body, it wasn't enough. When his long fingers, their calloused tips sending delicious shivers across her skin, trailed up past the tops of her garters, her body seemed to melt. Almost unconsciously she parted her thighs, silently urging him to take whatever he wanted.

The carriage clattered to a halt, jerking them both. Aden's hand froze on her thigh and he broke the kiss. With a muttered oath he hauled himself up, bringing her with him.

Vivien's head swam as she came upright. She clutched at him, struggling to gather her scattered wits. Aden continued to mutter imprecations under his breath even as he hurriedly pulled down her skirts and straightened her clothing.

"What's wrong?" she asked in a breathless voice. "You look angry."

He lifted her from his lap like a sack of feathers and deposited her on the other bench. Vivien stared at him, blinking at the sudden change in his demeanor. Only moments ago she could have sworn he'd been as swept away by passion as she. But now he vibrated with tension, and almost looked . . . flustered?

Aden St. George, flustered? Impossible.

"What's wrong?" he repeated her words with a fierce glower. "Bloody hell, Vivien. Another minute and you would have been half naked, with my hands all over you. Are you completely lacking in any sense of self-protection?"

Scowling, Vivien snatched her hat from the floor of the carriage—it must have fallen when he grabbed her—and jammed it back on her head. Cursing under her breath, she struggled to untangle the layers of netting twisted around the hat's brim. After tonight's escapade, she would *never* wear a veil again.

"There's no need to be rude about it," she snapped. "Up until a few moments ago you seemed quite enthusiastic yourself."

"And you should have boxed my ears for taking such liberties," he retorted as he tried to straighten his cravat. "The entire evening has been one disaster after another, and this little episode is the topper on the cake."

Vivien's heart twisted with a stab of pain. "I'm sorry you feel that way," she said with as much dignity as she could muster. "I thought it was very nice, actually. How foolish of me to think you would feel the same."

She hoped she didn't look as wounded as she felt, but the guilty expression that came over Aden's face suggested she did. He sighed and leaned forward, carefully taking her hands between his palms. His touch, both gentle and cautious, brought an unexpected rush of tears to her eyes.

"My sweet girl," he said in a voice that sounded strained, "after everything you've been through these past few weeks, you're much too vulnerable. It was entirely inappropriate of me to take advantage of you."

She yanked her hands away and crossed her arms over her chest. "I'm not a child, you know. You did not take advantage of me, because I'm quite capable of making my own decisions." If that sounded surly, so be it. His actions were beginning to feel very much like rejection rather than gentleman's remorse.

He straightened up, putting distance between them. Given the frown pulling his brows together in a disapproving line, it felt like leagues instead of inches. "Vivien, it would be a mistake for you to make assumptions about me based on our very brief history. I'm not some kind of hero out of a schoolgirl's fairy tale."

Now he thought she behaved like a schoolgirl? "If you think it was such a mistake, why did you kiss me in the first place?"

He turned his hands over and stared at them, as if expecting to read an answer in the lines that crisscrossed his palms. Then he looked up and she instantly knew he'd regained his control. Something that felt too much like sadness rustled around the vicinity of her heart.

"My lady, I say to you again, you know little about me. I fear you have painted a picture that is far from the truth. It is best for both of us if we understand that, and best if we forget this incident."

He moved as if to open the door, but Vivien placed a stilling hand on his arm.

"Then why don't you tell me who you are?" she asked. After what had just occurred between them, she had no intention of letting him simply walk away. No man's touch had ever affected her so greatly. She needed to understand why she felt that way, and know if he felt it too.

He gently placed her hand back in her lap and then stretched down an arm to fetch the bundle of pound notes that had fallen to the floor. Scooping up her reticule from the seat beside her, he tugged it open and began to stuff the bundle inside.

Vivien snatched the reticule away from him, and the notes fell to the floor. In how many ways would he insist on insulting her this night? "I don't need your charity, Captain. You bested me in fair play, so the winnings are yours."

His eyes opened wide with surprise. She answered his unspoken question with a haughty smile, a little smug that she'd broken through his impassive demeanor.

Then he narrowed his gaze. "Don't be a goosecap, Vivien. Take the money."

She clutched her reticule to her chest. "I will not. I must say, Captain, that your insults are most unwelcome. And I'm not referring to the fact that you kissed me."

"Then what the devil are you talking about?" he snapped.

"A person of honor pays her debts. As a man of honor," she said sarcastically, "you should understand that simple concept."

His nostrils flared, making him look like a bull about to charge anyone foolish enough to wander within his range.

"Do you really think I would take your money?" he demanded. "Damn it, Vivien. I was trying to teach you a lesson, not make your situation worse. Surely you know that."

She reached for the door handle, but he clamped a hand on her arm. Despite her anger, she couldn't deny the excitement rippling through her, just from that simple touch.

"I don't require any lessons from you, sir," she said. "Please let me go."

"Not until you take the blasted money," he said.

A nagging voice in her head urged her to capitulate, but pride wouldn't allow it. Aden obviously had very little respect for her, and if she gave in on this, he would ultimately think her without honor.

"No."

For several long moments, they stared at each other. Vivien struggled to hold his searing gaze, but with every passing second she descended further into misery over the night's work. She'd gambled away any chance to save Kit, and she'd made a fool of herself by exposing her feelings to Aden. And as much as she needed the money he kept trying to thrust upon her, taking it would leave her without a shred of dignity. He thought her little more than an impetuous jade. That was obviously why he kissed her, and why he subsequently rejected her.

She swallowed the sickening lump in her throat, hating the

self-pity that threatened to overwhelm her. Finally, she let her gaze drop, unable to stare him down.

He made a soft, scoffing noise. "Sweetheart, look up."

The gentleness she heard in that low rumble made the ball in her throat swell to twice its size. She shook her head, too humiliated to respond.

A gloved finger came to her chin, tilting it up. He studied her with a grave and yet tender expression. As she stared back at him, a slow heat began to build in his raven eyes.

"You speak of honor," he said, stroking her jaw. She couldn't repress a tiny shudder, and his eyes flared with interest.

Perhaps he didn't find her so repulsive, after all.

"But what about my honor?" he continued. "What kind of cad would I be if I treated you in so shabby a fashion?"

"Then why did you play me in the first place?" she whispered.

"I needed to protect you. Both Barrymore and Castle were practically slavering at your feet. In winning such large sums from them, you would have gained their undivided attention and that could have been very dangerous. I needed to get you out of there, and playing against you seemed like the fastest route to achieve my goal."

She thought about that, testing it against what she already knew about him. From Aden's point of view, it made sense.

"You didn't have to be so blasted good at it," she finally grumbled. "Where did you learn to play like that, anyway?"

"Oh, here and there. I seem to have some talent for it," he answered lightly, carefully prising her reticule from her fingers.

Like his talent for kissing, she supposed. But she didn't want to think about where he'd learned to do *that* so well.

When he began again to stuff the pound notes into her reticule, she stiffened. "Captain—"

"No, Vivien," he said firmly. "You need this money and I

intend for you to have it. I told you I would keep you from harm, and I keep my promises. Besides, I'm terrified at what other mad schemes you and your brother might otherwise hatch to raise money. This is the safer route, by far."

She started to weaken. He had a point, but she didn't much like the idea that she was nothing more than an obligation to him. Or a source of aggravation, which was even worse.

"But it's an awful lot of money," she protested, making one last attempt. "I couldn't possibly do that to you."

He laughed. "Trust me, I won't suffer. Now, please assuage *my* wounded pride and take the bloody money."

No, he wouldn't miss the money. That part was true, at least. The St. George family possessed one of the largest fortunes in England. Even though a younger son, Aden was surely much plumper in the pockets than she.

"Oh, very well. But I promise to make it up to you, and I will expect you to accept my payment when I do."

That hot gleam flared in his eyes again, and her stomach tilted with a funny little pitch. She was beginning to think Aden's most lethal skill was his ability to reduce her brain to a puddle of mush.

"I just might hold you to that promise," he said. He tightened the cords on her reticule and handed it back to her.

She glanced out the carriage window and sighed, noticing for the first time that they'd come to a stop a few houses up the square from Blake House. "I suppose I'd better go in now. Sooner or later, someone's going to come along and wonder why we're lounging about in the carriage."

And wouldn't that be the perfect end to the evening? Aden would no doubt be horrified to be discovered alone in a carriage with her. The last thing he would wish for was to be forced into a compromising position.

On that gloomy thought, she reached for the door handle. Aden's hand covered hers.

"Not yet. We still have one other matter to discuss."

"You must be joking," she said, sighing.

"Sadly, no. I'm assuming that you will use the funds from tonight's delightful adventure to pay off your brother's vowels?"

"Yes, but you know he owes a great deal more than this."

Aden was back to looking stern. "It's unfortunate, but you must refrain from any more outings like tonight. In fact, until I can determine the man responsible for your abduction, it's best that you remain as close to home as possible."

Drat. She eyed him, calculating just how far she could push him.

His eyes narrowed into warning slits. "Vivien, you are trying my patience."

Resisting the temptation to respond in kind, she strove for a reasonable tone. "I know, and I'm sorry for that. But you are well aware of how much Kit owes. I simply cannot stand by and allow mayhem to break loose in my family."

"I told you before that you are not responsible for either your mother or Kit."

"We will have to disagree on that point."

He looked disgruntled, but then he surprised her by leaning forward and tapping her lightly on the chin.

"You, madam, will drive me to Bedlam, which at this point sounds rather restful. I will concede the point—"

When she grinned at him, he held up a hand.

"—for now, but I insist you tell me everything you intend to do. I still need to protect you."

For the first time in hours, her anxiety eased. She might be a burr under his saddle and she still couldn't decipher how he really felt about their kiss, but it warmed her from the inside out to know he intended to hold fast to his vow to keep her safe. And now she no longer had to lie about her plans to help Kit, which made things much simpler.

"I do have a plan, as a matter of fact," she confided. "And I think it's a good one. I'm sure you're aware of Lady Bentley's masked ball tomorrow night. I know it's a rather risqué affair, but all the biggest gamesters will be there and I'm *certain* I can do quite well at the tables." She beamed at him. "And with you there to look after me, I won't have to worry about a thing."

Vivien had no choice but to ignore Aden's muttered string of curses as he handed her out of the carriage.

Chapter Twenty-Three

Aden propped a shoulder against one of the marble columns in Lady Bentley's ballroom, scowling at the cause of his foul mood. Not that Vivien noticed. When she'd caught sight of him, she'd given him a cheeky grin and a cheery little wave and then turned back to her slavering admirers. Right now the blasted girl was smiling at Reggie Devane, a harmless sort who trailed her around ballrooms and drawing rooms like a faithful hound. The others were not so harmless, and it took all of Aden's willpower not to storm across the room and spirit her away to complete safety.

When it came to a sense of self-preservation, Vivien sorely lacked some essential instincts.

It was enough to make his temples throb even if he didn't already have a headache. The overpowering scent from the bouquets of lilies on all the sideboards combined with the stifling heat and Lady Bentley's garishly gold decor into a sensory assault that had Aden longing for a nice little stint of real spy work—preferably somewhere outside in the freezing cold. And as far away from the British aristocracy as possible.

And far away from Vivien and the torture of watching her smile at other men. After that delicious but disastrous kiss in the carriage last night, the thought of her engaging in even the mildest flirtation made his gut pull tight.

Not that she was truly a flirt. As far as Aden could tell, Vivien attracted this sort of masculine attention wherever she went, whether she wished for it or not. Her ethereal beauty and engaging wit demanded attention, but she also had a way of looking at a man, directly and without artifice, that exerted an almost irresistible pull.

Unfortunately, he suspected it was her appearance tonight that served as the biggest draw, not her manner. In yet *another* astounding example of lack of a self-preservation instinct, she'd tricked herself out as Helen of Troy. She wore a Grecian-style robe with a gold clasp holding the bodice up over one shoulder, the other shoulder naked and gleaming white in the candlelight. Add in the soft, silky material of her white gown, caught under and around her pretty breasts with a gold cord, and the woman posed an insane temptation. One did not have to be obsessed with her to be shot through with a burning need to stalk across the ballroom, toss her over a shoulder, and carry her away for a thorough bout of ravishing.

And on that vibrant image, Aden shifted, all too aware he'd turned as hard as a pikestaff. Repressing a groan, he pulled the edges of his black domino around his body. He loathed masquerade balls with a passion, and the domino was his only concession to the idiocy of adults dressing up in costumes ill-fitted to either their personalities or their physiques. But right now he breathed a silent prayer of gratitude that his mother had insisted he wear the enveloping cape, since it saved him a world of embarrassment.

He glowered at Vivien's little court for a few more minutes, but came to full alert when Lord Castle drifted into her orbit. Had the bastard deduced who the mysterious Mrs. Smith was after all, or was he simply joining her merry band of idiots? Even more to the point, how would Vivien react when she saw him?

Castle slithered his way to the front of the pack and took Vivien's hand. When he bent low and pressed a lingering kiss, Aden pushed off the column, ready to head across the room. But a large restraining hand landed on his arm. He whipped around, his muscles automatically tensing with the need to fight, only to encounter his mentor's ironic gaze.

"Really, Aden," Dominic said. "I believe I taught you better than this. Firstly, you failed to notice me coming up behind you. Secondly, you are scowling at Lady Vivien like a husband about to be cuckolded. If you aren't more careful, you will draw attention both to yourself and to her."

Aden's temper spiked, but he managed to hold back a hasty retort by grinding the words to dust between his teeth. Dominic was right even though he had no intention of admitting it.

"I am merely concerned to see Lord Castle pay her such attention. As you know, he was one of the men she encountered at The Cormorant." He finished with a bland smile.

"Go ahead and tell yourself that if it makes you feel better," Dominic said. "I'm sure it will stand you in good stead for the rest of the evening."

"Don't you have anyone else you can bother? Lady Bentley, perhaps?" Aden nodded to the rattled-looking older woman at the head of the room, dressed unfortunately as Cleopatra. "Then I can do my job in peace."

"No need to worry, since Lady Vivien is dispatching Lord Castle with her usual panache."

Aden glanced at Vivien just in time to catch her direct a cold, cutting look at Castle before she turned her back to him.

"The girl has a great deal of sense," Dominic said. "Apparently more than you."

"What the hell does that mean?"

Dominic studied him with that calm, maddening way of his, the one that frequently made Aden feel like a callow youth. His mentor was a tall man, as tall as Aden, and still as fit as the day he entered the Service. They stared at each other, eye to eye, neither breaking contact.

"You may cease glaring at me in that murderous fashion, Aden," Dominic finally drawled. "You know it hardly intimidates me."

Aden couldn't help cracking a reluctant smile. "Yes, but I like to keep in practice for situations when I *do* need to intimidate someone."

A glimmer of amusement lightened Dominic's hard gaze. Then he switched his attention to Vivien. "And what about Lady Vivien? Do you intimidate her?"

"I can only wish. The woman is stubborn to the point of madness. If Griffin hadn't sent word last night, God knows what would have happened."

"Yes, it was a stroke of luck she chose his establishment."

Aden folded his arms across his chest. "If that's your idea of luck, I hate to think of your notion of ill fortune."

Dominic froze with the unnerving stillness that sometimes came over him in the strangest situations. Aden suspected it signalled some kind of retreat into memory, triggered by a seemingly innocent statement that yet held a deeper, mysterious meaning. Whatever the meaning, it seemed to weigh heavily on his chief's spirit. Aden had seen it happen more than once but he'd never asked why, knowing such questions would be unwelcome. Dominic was an exceedingly private man who rarely shared personal confidences.

"My idea of ill fortune is something I hope you never experience," he replied in a quiet voice. Then he shook himself free of whatever had gripped him and turned an assessing eye on Aden. "You're emotionally involved." He raised his hand, palm out. "No, don't bother to deny it."

Aden cursed under his breath. He'd never been able to hide anything from Dominic.

His chief smiled. "It's not *always* a bad thing, you know, especially in a case like this."

"No, it's always bad," Aden replied in a grim voice. "That situation in France . . . John's death. All that could have been avoided if I hadn't let our friendship muddle my vision. I cannot allow something like that to happen again."

His gut twisted as the lights and sounds of the ballroom faded, replaced by a grisly scene—John, his friend and fellow spy, his face lifeless and covered with blood as he lay sprawled in the bed of the woman who betrayed him.

"We all make mistakes, Aden. You make fewer than most."

"One was enough," he said with a bitter twist of the lips.

Dominic's face took on a familiar, imperious cast. His chief was once more England's great spymaster, not the surprisingly kind man Aden had come to know over the past ten years. "This is not a discussion for a ballroom," he said. "Simply ensure that Lady Vivien returns home safely, and then stop by Upper Wimpole Street later. We can talk then."

With a nod, the older man faded into the crowd.

Irritated with his gloomy turn of mind, Aden refocused his attention on Vivien. In the last few minutes she'd taken to the dance floor and was currently waltzing with a brash young cub who'd been trying to engage her favor for most of the night. He held her much too close, and Aden's hands twitched with the need to teach the idiot a lesson in propriety.

At this point, Aden much preferred that she spend her time at the gaming tables. At least there she was surrounded only by hardened gamesters instead of hardened rakes. But Vivien had spent but an hour in Lady Bentley's game room, playing hazard with a nerve and skill that had prompted his reluctant admiration. She'd tripled her stake in short order and then wisely excused herself from the table. Clearly, her gambling had little to do with any need for excitement, and everything to do with providing for her family. It was a novel approach and although he couldn't entirely approve he couldn't entirely fault her, either.

Besides, she was bloody good at it, and Aden could appreciate that, too.

After the conclusion of the dance, Vivien curtsied to her partner, who offered his arm. She was just refusing it when her gaze locked with alarm on something on the other side of the dance floor. Aden glanced over and let out a low curse.

Prince Ivan Khovansky, garbed like a Russian Cossack, making a late appearance and heading straight for Vivien.

Pushing away from the pillar, Aden started toward her when a commotion broke out to his right. A group of partygoers blocked his way to Vivien, and he lost several precious seconds. And a moment after that, a feminine hand clasped his forearm, stalling his progress.

"Aden," his mother hissed in a tense voice. "I've been looking for you everywhere. I need a moment of your time."

He peered at her, taking in her Grecian robe, the gilt spear in her hand, and the odd-looking helmet perched far back on her head. "Who in God's name are you supposed to be?"

Her lips twitched. "Athena, the Goddess of Wisdom."

Aden frowned. "It looks like you're wearing a bucket on your head."

She rolled her eyes. "Never mind that now. You must come with me. There's someone who wants to speak with you."

He took in her tight smile and saw the strain around her eyes. Something was making her anxious, but right now he didn't have time to deal with it.

"Not now, Mother." He cast a quick glance over to Vivien who had retreated with her swain to the other side of the room, getting as far from Khovansky as she could. The prince hadn't given up, though. He tracked her like a wolf after a hare.

He removed his mother's hand from his arm. "I need to keep an eye on Lady Vivien. This will have to wait."

"It can't wait," she said in a low tone.

"I'm sorry, but—"

"Well, well, who have we here?" boomed a loud voice behind him. "It's the charming Lady Thornbury, and her son, too. This is delightful, and very well met."

With a sinking heart, Aden pivoted on his heel. A few feet away stood the Prince Regent in all his corpulent glory, his entourage clustered behind. His father beamed at him, his round face shiny with perspiration and good cheer.

Aden stared back, his mind a blank. When his mother jabbed him between the shoulder blades, he broke free of his paralysis and managed to execute an awkward bow.

"Well, my boy," said the Regent, "it's been years since I last saw you in London. You've been neglecting your mamma and your friends. We can't have that!"

Aden heard the quiet titters from some of the bystanders as shame prickled up the back of his neck. And no wonder. What could be more amusing than the Prince Regent running into one of his by-blows, the child of his affair with the famous Lady Thornbury?

He stared into his father's expectant gaze, wishing the earth would crack open and swallow them whole.

Vivien flicked her gaze in horror between Khovansky, who was plowing toward her, and Aden trapped in conversation with the Prince Regent. And by the tense set of Aden's shoulders, he wasn't happy about it, although the Regent seemed to be distinguishing him with unusual attention.

Not that it mattered. What mattered was that Aden wouldn't be able to come to her rescue this time, and she simply refused to spend even one minute talking to Ivan the Terrible. Drastic measures were clearly called for.

Spinning on her heel, she encountered the ardent gaze of

Viscount Tumbler. The man had been pursuing her for months in his own ponderous fashion, refusing to take no for an answer. For a few seconds, Vivien indulged her irritation that all the men she wished to have nothing to do with *insisted* on pursuing her while the one man she longed to spend time with wouldn't. Despite that smoldering kiss in the carriage last night, Aden had gone out of his way to keep his distance.

She glanced back at Khovansky, now halfway down the room and closing fast.

"My dear Lord Tumbler," she said in a bright voice, "how lovely to see you."

Tumbler frowned. "But you saw me just a few minutes ago, before you went out on the dance floor with Mr. Perkins. Don't you recall?"

She gritted her teeth. Of *course* she did. Did the man have to be so blasted literal?

"Oh, la," she said with a witless giggle. "The heat in here must be addling my brain. I so long to escape this crush and get a little fresh air."

Lord Tumbler was a tall, plump, and rather fussy man who carried himself with an air of perpetual befuddlement. He stared at Vivien as if she were a puzzle to unravel.

"It's November, Lady Vivien." He eyed her floating garments. "In that rig you'll catch your death of cold."

She grabbed his arm and steered him to the arching doorway and out to a passage leading to the back of the house. "If I'm not mistaken, Lady Bentley has an enclosed orangery. I'm sure the air will be much fresher and it won't be nearly as crowded."

Tumbler looked confused but allowed her to tow him along. But by the time they reached the corridor, he'd figured it out— at least he thought he did.

"Oh, ho!" he crowed, understanding dawning on his heavy

brow. "You wish to be alone with me. What a capital idea, Lady Vivien. I approve entirely."

She gave him a weak smile. She hated using him so ruthlessly, but explaining the situation was impossible. Besides, although Lord Tumbler had fallen into the inconvenient habit of pestering her, he'd never displayed anything less than perfect manners. She could certainly stand to sit on a bench for a few minutes smiling at the poor man while he prattled at her, and then they could go back to the ball.

By then, she could only hope Aden had shaken himself free of the Prince Regent. He'd certainly looked disgruntled enough to wish to escape as quickly as he could. Vivien didn't blame him. She'd only talked to the Regent on two occasions. One time he'd winked at her, and the other time he'd pinched her bottom.

"Here we are, my lady," Lord Tumbler enthused as he swept her through a set of glass doors into the orangery.

Vivien snuck a peek over her shoulder and breathed a sigh of relief. No one had followed them. She was so relieved she rewarded his lordship with a grateful smile. He blinked rapidly several times and then puffed out his chest. In his vaguely Elizabethan-looking costume, he looked like a rooster. "This looks like a delightfully refreshing place to sit," he said.

He led her to a pretty scrolled bench next to a small fountain. Grateful to be off her feet, Vivien sank down. She wriggled her toes as she looked around the spacious room, enjoying the sound of splashing water in the marble bowl of the fountain. The orangery was a delightful space, floored with large paving stones and with one wall composed almost entirely of glass. Dozens of potted shrubs covered the floor in an artful display, and the air carried the soft scent of orange blossoms.

Lord Tumbler lowered his bulky physique, pressing against her. Vivien tried to shift away as far as possible but he was determined to squeeze her between his body and the metal arm of the bench.

He half turned, draping his arm across the back of the bench. "There, now," he said with an arch smile. "This is much better than being cooped up in that stuffy old ballroom. Now we can be quiet and comfortable, and no one will interrupt us."

A whisper of alarm rippled along her nerves. She peered up into his pink face and took in the ardent gleam in his pale blue eyes. Perhaps this hadn't been such a good idea, after all.

Vivien cast a nervous glance at the door, trying to decide what to do. Fortunately, Lord Tumbler launched into what he labeled a *cozy gossip,* mixing the latest *on-dits* with the usual fulsome compliments he liked to pay her. Gradually she relaxed, smiling vaguely and nodding in all the right places even as she kept a wary eye on the door—more to watch out for Khovansky than to escape her companion. Lord Tumbler might be encouraged by this little interlude but he was too much of a gentleman to cross the line.

As the minutes passed and Khovansky did not appear, she realized that disappearing with Lord Tumbler for any length of time carried its own set of problems. She was skating on the edge of scandal as it was, and she had no desire to be trapped in a compromising situation. It was time to take her chances and hope Ivan the Terrible had found other diversions for the evening.

"Lord Tumbler," she said, breaking into his chatter. "I think it time we return to the ball. I'm feeling much better and I know Mamma will be looking for me."

Tumbler halted in midstream, gazing at her with some confusion. But then his eyes glittered with an oddly cunning look and he grabbed her hand and clasped it over his breast.

"Dear Lady Vivien, you cannot be so cruel as to take me to the high reaches of heaven and then cast me so precipitously into the darkness," he exclaimed in a dramatic voice. "Allow me to take this golden opportunity to proclaim my feelings for you, once and for all."

She struggled to pull her hand from his grip. "I'd rather you didn't."

He adopted what he must have thought was a soulful expression, but which really made him look like an unhappy basset hound. "Lady Vivien, when you asked me to spirit you away from the ball, I was convinced you were finally going to make me the happiest of men. Why else would you suggest it?"

Vivien finally managed to yank her hand away. "Because I was trying to—oh, never mind. It would take too long to explain."

She struggled to stand, no easy feat since Tumbler was squishing her against the unforgiving metal arm of the bench. Before she could escape, he wrapped his pudgy fingers around her shoulders and leaned in, clearly intent on a kiss.

Startled, Vivien planted her palms on his chest and shoved with all her might. She managed to break his grip and stagger to her feet. When she tripped over the hem of her gown, she grabbed the back of the bench to keep herself upright. Unfortunately, in doing so she lost her small window of escape. Tumbler's face was now determined and set, and he heaved himself to his feet, grabbing her once more.

"My lady, you must know how ardently I love you," he cried. "How can you deny me when you have so clearly indicated you feel the same?"

"Oh, bother," she muttered. "I meant no such thing, Lord Tumbler. I merely wished to escape from the heat and the noise. Please accept my profound—"

She bit off her apology with a startled squeak as he pursed his lips and came in for the kill. Clearly, nothing she said would have the slightest impact on him.

Silently cursing herself as a fool, she dodged his kiss. She twisted in his grip, planted her shoulder against his chest, and rammed him with all her might. He let out a cry and fell backward, his legs fetching up on the rim of the small fountain. His fingers clutched at her, tangling in the small drape of the train over her shoulder. She heard a rip, and a piece of the silk tore free as he tumbled—bottom end first—into the gurgling fountain behind them.

For such a small amount of water it made a huge splash. Vivien scrambled back a few steps, barely managing to avoid a dousing as she stared at him in horror.

"Oh, dear, I'm so sorry!" She stepped around the puddles to the edge of the fountain. "Here, let me help you up." She extended a hand, giving him a weak smile.

He floundered about in the fountain, making noises remarkably like a snorting bull. "Don't touch me," he spluttered. "You've done quite enough for one evening."

Vivien was torn between guilt and a terrible impulse to burst into laughter. With an effort, she repressed the uncharitable reaction. "I understand, and I do apologize most sincerely, my lord. Truly, I do."

He managed to haul himself to his knees, and from there to his feet. Standing in the middle of the small pool, his clothes clinging in unforgiving drapes to his portly body, he glared at her. "I do not accept your apology, Lady Vivien. This is all your fault, you minx!"

Miffed, she glared back at him. "Well, I do feel rather bad about the way things turned out, but I believe I made it quite clear I wanted to return to the ballroom. And I certainly never asked you to kiss me!"

He waved an impatient hand, sending a small spray of water arcing in her direction. She jumped back, barely avoiding a wetting.

"Don't just stand there," he snapped. "Go fetch a footman."

She didn't much like his tone but she couldn't really blame

him. Besides, there was nothing to be gained by arguing over whose fault it was. The faster she could extract herself from this ridiculous situation, the better.

"Yes, of course," she said, backing away as he hauled himself out of the fountain. "I'll send a footman to help you immediately."

He shot her another furious look as he began wringing out the tails of his coat. Practically strangling on horrified laughter, she turned and fled for the door to the corridor. She paused there, craning her neck to peer through the glass down the hallway. All seemed quiet, so she opened the door, turned around, and shut it carefully behind her.

When she turned back, she almost jumped out of her shoes. Aden loomed before her, his black domino swirling around him. Like some kind of wizard, he seemed to have appeared from thin air.

Vivien clapped a hand over her thudding heart. How so big a man could move in such a stealthy manner defied understanding. "You startled me."

His dark gaze flitted over her shoulder to the glass doors. "What's going on? Where's Lord Tumbler?" he asked, his voice laden with suspicion.

She frowned. "How did you know? I was very careful to slip out with as little fuss as possible."

"You shouldn't have slipped out at all, and never out of my sight. We talked about this, Vivien."

Inspecting her with that disapproving glower, he should have intimidated her. But he didn't. She loved that he worried about her, and couldn't hold back the silly desire to be alone with him. That, of course, was very bad, since she would probably use such an opportunity to tempt him to kiss her again.

"Well, why did you disobey my orders?" he asked.

She shrugged. "I was trying to avoid Prince Ivan."

He started to answer, but then stopped and peered at her shoulder. "What happened to your dress?"

"What? Nothing—oh," she said, her cheeks burning with a guilty flush. "It's nothing. Just a little tear. I, er, think I caught it on one of my earrings."

"You'll have to do better than that. Where's Tumbler?" He reached past her to fling open the door to the orangery.

She slapped a hand to his chest—a chest decidedly harder than Lord Tumbler's, she couldn't help noting.

"Nothing happened," she said in a firm voice.

He gave her a disgusted shake of the head.

"Very well," she amended. "Something did happen but I took care of it. And, believe me. Lord Tumbler came out much worse for wear."

His eyes narrowed and he stared at the door, as if debating whether to go in or not.

"Can we please just go back to the ballroom?" she pleaded.

His glance flicked over her with sharp assessment. "You can't go back now. That little rip is rather obvious, and your hair is coming down from its chignon."

Grimacing, she touched a hand to the elaborate creation woven out of hair and gold-spangled ribbon. Several tresses had slipped down around her shoulders.

"Drat. I'll never get it back up by myself. Oh, very well."

He took her by the elbow and began to lead her toward the front of the mansion.

"Oh, wait," she exclaimed, stopping abruptly. "We have to find a footman and send him to the orangery. Lord Tumbler needs help."

Aden stared straight ahead, slowly shaking his head. "Do I even want to know?"

"Probably not."

He pulled her into a window alcove that was partially

hidden by a thick velvet drape. "Don't move. I'll be right back."

While he was gone, Vivien amused herself by doing math problems in her head. He returned in just a few minutes, her velvet cloak thrown over his arm.

He flung it around her shoulders, deftly tying the ribbons about her throat. She shivered when his calloused fingers brushed the sensitive skin under her jaw, but he didn't seem to notice.

"Did you find a footman?" she asked in a husky whisper.

He glanced up, their eyes meeting. He studied her for a moment, then nodded. "A footman has been dispatched, along with strict instructions to keep his counsel."

"How much did you have to pay him?" Vivien asked in an anxious voice.

"A guinea. Fortunately, no one seemed to notice you slip away with Lord Tumbler, as far as I can tell."

"Except for Prince Ivan," she mused. "But I imagine he won't say anything, and you can be assured Lord Tumbler will not."

"We're going to have a chat about that once I get you out of here," he answered in a grim voice as he led her to the entrance hall.

Fortunately, only Lady Bentley's servants were present since it was too early for most guests to leave the ball. As a liveried footman opened the door, Vivien halted, clapping a hand to her cheek.

"Mamma! I can't just leave without telling her."

"My mother took care of it," Aden said as he nudged her through the door.

"Really? What did she tell her?"

"That you felt unwell."

Vivien sighed. "Of course. I'm assuming Mamma did not

feel the need to find me to see how I was." Her mother's neglect shouldn't sting, not after all these years.

Aden gave her elbow a sympathetic squeeze as they waited on the pavement for his carriage. But his silence spoke volumes. Vivien fell into a brown study, staring at the tips of her toes. When a frigid gust of wind blew up the hem of her cloak, she shivered and glanced at Aden. She frowned, struck by his tense, watchful demeanor as he scanned the line of carriages and the street.

"What's wrong?" she asked.

"Nothing," he said in a flat voice.

She didn't believe that, but just then a carriage pulled up to the front of the house. A plainly garbed groom swung down to open the door. Aden handed her in, then stepped forward to murmur something to the coachman. Then he vaulted in, taking the opposite bench.

In the soft glow of the coach lamp, his face looked somber, even grim. Obviously he was still annoyed with her. A carriage ride alone with Aden had initially seemed a welcome opportunity to explore what they had begun last night, but from the irritated cast of his mouth he would be doing something else with those lips other than kissing her.

He crossed his arms over his chest and narrowed his eyes with an all-too-predictable severity. "Now, Lady Vivien, perhaps you will explain why you took it upon yourself to behave in such an idiotic and reckless fashion."

Chapter Twenty-Four

Vivien bristled. Perhaps she had been foolish to go off with Lord Tumbler, but how else was she to avoid Prince Ivan? "I don't see what else I could have done," she said in a grumpy tone.

"You could have stayed right where you were. I made it clear that you were not to wander off where I couldn't find you."

"Well, you did find me, despite your claim that no one saw me leave." That gave her pause. "How *did* you know where to look for me?"

"My blasted mother, of course. She sees everything. And don't change the subject, Vivien. Despite your abduction, you apparently do not have the wit to recognize you're still in danger. A great deal of danger," he added with unnecessary emphasis.

A chill of fear slithered up her spine. With effort, she pushed it aside, taking refuge in outraged dignity. "I do not appreciate your insults, sir. My actions were perfectly reasonable given the circumstances. You know very well why I tried to avoid Prince Ivan."

Aden's jaw worked as if he were chewing over her words. From the look on his face, he found them undercooked. "Of course I understand your desire to avoid dealing with the man.

But as unpleasant as that would have been, you were quite safe. And I would have made my way to you eventually."

Eventually. How comforting.

"When you finished toadying to the Regent, I suppose," she said with a huff. "How very reassuring."

Something ugly flared in his eyes, taking her aback. Yes, she'd called him a toady but he'd said she was witless. As far as insults went, the bout was a draw. Why had his gaze suddenly gone so frigid?

"What should I have done, my lady?" he asked in a hard voice. "Give him the cut direct? As it was, I likely offended His Royal bloody Highness by backing out of the conversation as quickly as I could in order to follow you. What more would you have me do?"

She stared at him, unnerved by the escalating tension between them. Something beyond his usual irritation with her drove him tonight, something elusive and yet powerful.

"Yes, of course," she said cautiously. "But when I saw Prince Ivan heading toward me, I simply couldn't bear the idea of him touching me. Not after what happened last time."

The seconds ticked uncomfortably by. Finally, Aden let out a weary sigh that flicked her guilt back to life. Even in the dim glow of the carriage lamp, she could make out the fatigue and strain on his handsome face, and knew she was partly responsible for it.

"I understand, but for God's sake, Vivien! The guests—most of whom you know—were packed to the rafters. And your admirers stood ten feet deep around you. I'm sure they would have been more than happy to protect you from the prince's advances."

She perked up. Was that jealousy she heard in his voice?

"Yes, I suppose that's true," she mused. "Lord Tumbler seemed more than happy to assist me."

When Aden's black gaze narrowed to suspicious slits,

Vivien had the unwelcome sense he guessed she was throwing out a feeler.

"Lady Vivien, you continue to make it very difficult for me to do my job."

Blast. Now he was back to calling her *Lady Vivien.* It was at times like this that she feared she was losing her touch. Or perhaps it was simply that Aden was immune to her, after all.

"Is that all I am to you? A job?" she blurted out.

Instead of answering, he lifted the curtain over the glass and looked out. It occurred to her that it was taking a rather long time to reach Blake House.

"Why is it taking so long to get home?"

"I asked the coachman to take his time returning you home. We are not finished with this conversation, Vivien. We must address the issue of your persistently reckless behavior, and I will not let you out of this carriage until we reach some kind of agreement on your safety."

Exasperated, she threw her hands in the air. "Must we keep harping on that? It wasn't as if anything really bad happened." She paused. Lord Tumbler might not agree with her. "Well, at least not to me," she finished.

Aden covered his eyes with a hand. "You had better tell me exactly what happened."

She didn't miss the long-suffering tone in his voice. "Oh, very well," she grumbled.

He obviously had no intention of kissing her, so she might as well tell him the entire silly tale and get it over with. Except for the hour she'd spent at the hazard table, the evening had become a farce and at this point her bed seemed infinitely preferable to a lecture.

"As I mentioned, Lord Tumbler was quite eager to escort me from the ballroom. I suggested the orangery because I thought it unlikely Prince Ivan would look there."

Aden raised his eyes to the roof of the carriage in patent disbelief.

"It was the perfect place to go," she said defensively. "No one else came in the entire time."

"And if Prince Ivan had found you, you would have been alone but for Lord Tumbler to protect you."

She opened her mouth to retort, but then closed it. *Drat.*

He waved his hand in a windmilling circle. "Never mind. Go on with your story."

Vivien crossed her arms over her chest and scowled, but complied. Halfway through the tale, she noticed that his mouth seemed to be twitching. A minute later, he pressed one hand to his lips as if holding something back. Finally, when she got to the part where Lord Tumbler rebuffed her offer of assistance, he burst into laughter.

And not just a chuckle, either. In fact, he was soon clutching his side, barely able to breathe.

"I don't see what's so funny," she said, indignant. "You certainly wouldn't be laughing if Lord Tumbler had tried to slobber all over you."

Aden's laughter had started to subside, but that set him off again. When she glared at him, he held up a hand. "Enough, Vivien," he managed to gasp out.

She stared at him, mystified. Aden did not strike her as a man who found the world a very amusing place, at least not to this extent.

"Have you been drinking?" she asked suspiciously.

"No," he choked out. "It's all you. You lured Tumbler away from the ball, pushed him into a fountain, and then offered to haul him out. If word does get out, the poor man will have to rusticate in the country for a year."

Suddenly, she saw an image of Lord Tumbler's outraged, dripping countenance staring back at her and she dissolved into helpless giggles. That started Aden off again, and it took several minutes before they were able to bring themselves under control. Vivien, wrung out by all the conflicting strains of the evening, finally subsided into a few watery giggles as she dabbed at her eyes with her gloved fingertips.

"Here, let me," he said, extracting a handkerchief. He leaned over and pressed her eyes dry with a gentle hand. She held her breath, trying not to tremble under the soft touch.

When he finished, he stayed close, studying her face. "Vivien, what am I going to do with you?"

His wry, exasperated tone brought a sudden rush of tears to her throat. Since Papa's death, no one in her own family had worried about her, or lifted a finger to protect her. Aden had, but his help probably stemmed from his innately chivalrous nature and sense of duty rather than from emotion. As foolish as it was, she longed to be more than an obligation, or a burden to be disposed of as efficiently as possible.

While she fiddled with the ties of her cloak, the only answer she could muster was a shrug. When his gaze sharpened, she looked down at her lap, unable to face his piercing inspection.

She heard him draw in a breath and then two fingers came up to her chin, tilting her face up to meet his gaze. As she studied the severe lines of his handsome face, her heart twisted with an aching, hopeless desire.

A surprisingly tender smile curved his lips. "My poor sweetheart, you've had rather a trying evening, haven't you?"

Oh, Lord. If he kept staring at her like that, with so much sympathy warming his eyes, she *would* start crying.

"I'm fine," she whispered. Except for the pathetic crack in her voice.

Slowly, the warmth in his eyes transmuted into a seductive heat. When his gaze dropped to her mouth, she could swear all that heat flicked a kiss of fire across it. Her lips parted in an involuntary gasp.

"Christ, Vivien," Aden murmured in a ragged voice. His gloved hands cupped her cheeks, tilting her face up another inch as he swiftly claimed her mouth.

And claim he did, slipping his tongue between her lips in a swirl of delicious, liquid heat. She tasted champagne and fire and a potent masculine energy that drove its way straight to her heart. With a searing delight, both startling and terrifying in its power, she threw her arms around his neck, flinging herself against him. He let out a smothered exclamation and fell back against the squabs, bringing her with him in a tangle of arms and legs. In fact, Vivien sprawled half on him and half on her knees on the floor of the carriage, but she refused to let go. She tightened her hold and hauled herself up, chest to chest.

Aden's arms tightened around her, holding her in an awkward embrace. He broke the impassioned kiss on a husky laugh. "Careful, my love. You'll hurt yourself."

My love.

Could any two words possibly sound more wonderful? Eyes half closed, she pressed little kisses along his jaw, relishing the hard slash of muscle and bone and his bristled skin against her lips.

"I don't care," she muttered.

"Well, I do." He reached down, palmed her bottom in his big hands, and lifted. She squeaked, grabbing at his shoulders as he pulled her right off her knees. He managed to scoop her up and turn her with effortless ease, plopping her down in his lap.

She blinked at the sudden change, electrified by the sensation of her bottom nestling on top of his groin. Her cloak had flared out around them, cascading onto the floor and leaving only two thin layers of fabric—silk and the finest linen—between her body and his. She could feel *all* of him against her—hard, muscular thighs, and an equally hard and very intriguing bulge pressing into her.

"There, now," Aden purred in a deep voice. "Isn't that better?"

"Ah, yes. Quite, thank you," she stammered. "I'm very comfortable."

Oh, Lord. She cringed at her idiotic reply.

"Good," he said with a ghost of a laugh. Circling his strong arms around her, he slowly pulled off one glove and then the other, tossing them onto the opposite seat. Excitement corkscrewed through her body, twisting everything into a shivery sort of knot.

"What are you doing?" she whispered.

"I can't feel your skin through my gloves," he said. "And I want to feel you."

"Oh. Yes, that m-makes perfect sense."

His mouth nuzzled the fragile skin at her temple, and she could feel the smile pulling at his lips. "You do want me to touch you, don't you, Vivien?"

Unable to speak, she nodded twice. Firmly.

"I thought so," he murmured with a dark satisfaction. Then his hand settled with a firm, reassuring pressure on her knee.

And not through her gown, either.

Vivien's eyes widened as she looked down, finally noticing that her tumble into his lap had rucked her gown and shift up to her thighs. Aden's long fingers carefully stroked her through her white stockings, the callus-roughened tips teasing her with a delicious rasp through the delicate material. She shivered and bit her lip as sensation streaked up her thigh and settled in at the secret place at the apex of her thighs.

Aden nuzzled her jaw and she shivered even harder. "Are you cold, my sweet?" he asked.

She arched her neck, giving him access to her throat. "No," she said in a dazed voice.

"Ah, then you are feeling modest. Let me take care of that."

He leaned forward slightly and pulled his domino around

them, covering them in a black sweep of fabric. Vivien blinked, disoriented by the contrast between what she saw— or couldn't see—and what she felt.

And she felt quite a lot.

"There," he said in a smug voice. "You are now the picture of modesty."

She turned and came nose to nose with him, slipping her fingers into his cravat. "Mock me at your peril, sir. I vow there will be consequences."

A predatory grin lifted the corners of his mouth. "Is that so, my lady? Why don't you show me?"

Tightening her grip, she pulled his head down. When his mouth settled on hers, the world slipped away and only he remained. As he parted her lips, gently exploring with his tongue, a sweet welling of emotion unlocked the secret spaces in her heart where she'd stored her hopes and dreams, carefully guarded for the day she would find the man to fit key to lock.

A voice in her mind quietly called her a fool, but she denied it, too entranced by Aden's kiss. Tentatively, she sucked his tongue into her mouth, toying with it in a delicious slide of wet heat. She acted on instinct, eager to please him, and the deep rumbling in his chest told her she'd succeeded. Emboldened, she slipped her hands around his neck and deepened the kiss, tangling her tongue with his in slow, luxurious play.

Under the cover of his cloak, Aden's hand gripped her knee as he plundered her mouth, returning her eager kisses. Her body seemed to sing under his touch, responding with an unfamiliar yet delicious heat between her thighs. As if sensing her reaction, his fingers moved higher, gliding upward to the top of her garters and stockings. When they touched her naked skin, she jerked, bringing her rump more fully into contact with his groin.

Aden hissed into her mouth. The arm around her shoulders tightened as he lifted his pelvis, grinding into her. She gasped and broke free, her back instinctively arching as she pressed into him. A wild, urgent need to feel *all* of that masculine hardness made her squirm.

He froze, his hand gripping the top of her thigh. His chest heaved as he struggled for breath. Desperate to feel more, she gave an experimental wiggle.

His hand clamped down, holding her in place. "Vivien, stay still," he ground out. "You don't know what you're doing."

She tilted her head back to look at him. His heavy-lidded gaze smoldered with a ravenous intent and his stark cheek-bones were flushed with bronze. His strong mouth, still damp from their kiss, was pulled tight, as if he restrained himself. And at every point where they touched, she could sense the struggle his discipline imposed on him. His big body seemed to shake with the effort, almost as much as she shook with a passion she refused to deny any longer.

Aden might not want her tomorrow, but he wanted her tonight. For now, that would do.

Tightening her fingers around the back of his neck, she tugged him down. He came slowly, as if reluctant.

"We've talked enough for tonight," she breathed against his mouth. Then she nipped his lower lip, sucking it into her mouth.

He jerked, then his entire body came to life, surrounding her with his brawny strength. Bending her over his arm, he ravished her mouth with a kiss that slid endlessly into another, forming links in a sensual, primal chain. Vivien moved against him, too, caught up in her urgent, spiralling need.

Without breaking the kiss, he flicked the enveloping cloak aside. One hand moved to her throat, briefly stroking it, then his fingers reached for the clasp of her gown. With a decisive tug, he pulled it aside, exposing the high slopes of her breasts.

She gasped and stilled, her heart pounding so hard it seemed to fetch up against her breastbone. Aden went still beneath her as well, except for the fingers that played across her shoulder and drifted down to the top of her low-cut stays. His hand tickled her through the lace trim as he launched a gentle but relentless exploration.

"I need to see you, Vivien," he rasped. "Let me touch you, if only for a few minutes. Then I'll let you go."

The dark need in his eyes and the hard cut of his mouth sent her heart racing, while a thread of trepidation whispered through her. But then his gaze grew tender, and he nuzzled her mouth with an affection that brought tears to her eyes.

Blinking them back, she broke away. Sitting up straight in his lap—she couldn't fail to miss the sensual hiss that escaped his lips when she moved against his erection—she slowly drew the soft fabric of her gown down over her breasts, letting it pool around her waist. That pulled a husky groan from his throat. With trembling fingers, she began to unlace the front ties on her stays.

When she fumbled with the strings, he brushed her fingers aside and closed a big hand over her breast. His thumb pushed down the top of her stays and her nipple popped out, already pulled tight and aching for his touch. With a satisfied rumble, Aden stroked his thumb back and forth over the tip.

Vivien gasped as sensation streaked inward from the rigid point, seeming to burrow deep within her body. She clapped a hand over her mouth to keep in the cry that threatened to escape.

Unbelievably, Aden let out a husky laugh. "Do you like how that feels?"

She glared at him—or would have, if both her brain and body weren't melting from the inside out. He gave her a smug grin. It should have been annoying, but instead made her giggle.

"That is a very silly question, Captain St. George. Of *course,* I liked it."

"Then you're going to *love* this."

His head bent and his mouth fastened over her nipple. Vivien froze, transfixed by the sight of his dark head at her breast and by the storm of sensations electrifying her body. She arched up and he slid a hand behind her back, both supporting her and bringing her body up higher to meet his questing mouth. Vivien couldn't hold back a moan as he tugged on her aching flesh, torturing her with supple strokes of the tongue. She'd never felt anything like it, and it made her truly dizzy with pleasure.

Groaning, she let her hand float up to the edge of her stays, weakly pulling at the stiff fabric to give him better access. He growled his approval as his other hand began to move up her thigh, once more trailing across her naked skin. Lost in the wet heat of his mouth and the sensual glide of his big hand, Vivien let herself sink into it, giving herself completely to his touch and to his strength, yearning for everything he wanted to give her.

It was *wonderful*.

But suddenly, the carriage lurched to a jarring halt that broke them apart. Vivien started to slide from Aden's grip, and grabbed at his shoulders as he pulled her hips against him.

"What the devil?" he snapped as he held her upright.

All trace of the lover instantly disappeared, replaced by a brusque man who swiftly plunked her down on the squabs and yanked her cloak across her chest. Then he planted himself in front of her as he reached for the door, bracing himself against the wall of the coach as it jerked back and forth.

Vivien struggled to break free of her seductive daze. She could hardly think, and her breath came in short gasps as she fought to sit up straight and yank her bodice over her breasts. But her cloak had tangled about her and the trembling in her hands made her clumsy.

Just as Aden's hand grasped the handle on the door, a pistol fired. It was so close to the carriage that Vivien's ears rang with the report. She clutched at the back of Aden's cloak as fear blasted through her, wiping away her daze.

Aden whipped halfway around and shoved her to the floor. "Be quiet," he hissed. "And stay down."

She blinked up at him, and her heart shuddered with a painful jolt. She didn't recognize the man staring down at her. His face was pulled tight in a stone-hard mask and his eyes had gone flat and deadly, like a snake about to strike its prey. In one motion, he turned away from her and flowed into a fighter's stance.

A second later, the door flew open. The carriage dipped down with a man's weight, but all Vivien could see from her inelegant sprawl was a hand pointing a large pistol. A scream began to bubble up into her throat, but between one eye blink and the next Aden lashed out and kicked the pistol from the intruder's hand. Then he launched himself through the door, barrelling into the intruder.

Grabbing onto the edge of the padded bench, Vivien pulled herself to her knees. Her stomach cramped with fear and she could hardly breathe, but she couldn't just lie on the floor waiting to be either saved or abducted again.

And she couldn't let anything happen to Aden.

Shaking like a dry leaf in a storm, Vivien scrabbled to snatch up the pistol. She couldn't believe it hadn't fired when it hit the floor, and she carefully pointed the barrel away from herself as she awkwardly struggled to a standing position. The blood rushed to her feet and her head swam, but she took a deep breath and forced it to clear. Papa had insisted years ago that she learn to fire a pistol, and she had no qualms in doing so if it would save Aden and his men.

Staggering to the open door, she cautiously leaned out of the carriage, leading with the pistol. They were on a small street, probably in Mayfair. A few houses had lamps shining in the windows, but it was almost impossible to distinguish where they were.

But the flickering carriage lights illuminated a horrible scene, and her heart lurched into her throat.

Aden's young groom lay in the street, blood pooling around him. The coachman struggled with a gigantic man dressed in a black greatcoat, while Aden was fighting two men who were doing everything they could to bring him to the ground. When Vivien saw the flash of a blade in the hand of one of Aden's attackers, she acted instinctively. Pointing the pistol into the air, she discharged it with a thundering crack.

Everyone seemed to freeze for a moment into a frightening tableau, but Aden moved first. Shaking off one of his attackers, he lashed his foot out with deadly force, striking the other man in the gut. The man staggered back into his comrade, but both men soon returned to the fray. By now Aden's entire body had become a deadly weapon, striking out repeatedly, his arms and legs moving in a blur of movement.

Half deafened by the noise of the pistol and coughing from the smoke of its discharge, Vivien fell to her knees still clutching the weapon. But she steadied herself against the door frame, her heart banging against her ribs. She quickly discarded the idea of running for help since she'd have to wade through a tangle of fighting bodies in front of the carriage step.

But in less than a minute Aden had sent the last of his attackers reeling to the ground, and the brute attacking the coachman broke away. Coming up behind Aden, he gave him a hard shove, smashing him into the side of the carriage. Aden staggered, and Vivien clutched at him to hold him upright.

By the time Aden recovered his balance, the blackguard had hauled his companions to their feet and they stumbled away into the night, picking up speed as they ran.

Peering after them, Vivien finally noticed a coach at the end of the street. Its lamps were dark and its outline was little more than a bulky mass, but the gang headed toward it at a dead run. A moment later they were on board, the driver yelling at the horses, the wheels clattering on the pavement as they made their escape.

"Christ, Stevens," Aden barked at the coachman. "Where the hell is your pistol?"

"Coming, Captain," the coachman called from the front of the carriage.

A few seconds later, the weapon was in Aden's hand. He stalked to the middle of the street and carefully aimed after the retreating coach. He stood with legs braced apart, a tall warrior about to wreak havoc on a side street in Mayfair.

But he didn't shoot. It was clearly too dark and the carriage already careened around a bend in the street. Slowly, Aden lowered his arm, as if doing so pained him. Then he turned back to the carriage and he looked straight at Vivien.

On his stark features, harshly illuminated by the flaring lamps on the carriage, she saw only fury and death.

Chapter Twenty-Five

Aden stared into Vivien's haunted eyes as the echo of carriage wheels faded and the quiet of Mayfair settled around them once more. His feet seemed riveted to the cobblestones, making it impossible to approach her. She hadn't fallen apart during the attack, but now she trembled so hard that her cloak fluttered in ripples of cascading velvet.

He held his ground, despite all his protective instincts screaming at him to snatch her into his arms. The cold, killing mood was still upon him and he didn't dare touch her, not until he knew he wouldn't crush her in a punishing, primal grip.

"Are you hurt?" he managed to rasp out.

She shook her head, still clutching the pistol. Thank God she'd had the presence of mind to fire the damn thing else they might all be dead.

He'd sensed something off-kilter while they'd been waiting for his carriage in front of Lady Bentley's mansion. It had sent a familiar, prickling chill along the back of his neck. A careful perusal of the street had yielded nothing, and neither Stevens nor Jem had seen anything amiss. But, unsettled by Vivien's reckless behavior and his own unnerving encounter with his damn father, Aden had let his emotions override his instincts.

And then he'd compounded the error by giving in to his ravenous desire for Vivien. Like a bloody idiot, he'd let down his guard and Jem's death was the result.

He took a deep breath, willing his heartbeat to settle as he wiped his grimy, blood-spattered hands down the panels of his coat. Vivien had almost been lost, thanks to his stupidity. From the look of horror on her face, she was just realizing that, too.

He tamped down his self-disgust, stalking over to where Stevens crouched next to the crumpled body. Jem had been a good, trustworthy lad, eager to serve with Aden. But to dwell on the loss now would serve no purpose. First, he had to get Vivien safely stashed and then deal with the results of the evening's debacle. Later, when he was alone, he'd think about Jem and how he had betrayed the boy's loyalty.

Stevens looked up, his features solemn with sadness and regret. "Sorry, Captain, but the lad's dead," he said, stating the obvious. "The bastard caught him smack dab in the middle of the chest."

Vivien let out a choking sob, but Aden refused to look at her. He couldn't bear to see the blame on her face.

With a sigh, the coachman came to his feet. "This is my fault, sir. I didn't even see the bastards, but I should have known better than to come this way. Too quiet and too dark."

"No, the fault is mine," Aden said. "I felt something was wrong, but I allowed myself to be distracted. The onus for Jem's death is on me."

From behind him, Vivien made an inarticulate protest. Reluctantly, Aden finally pivoted on his heel to face her.

She stood with one hand braced against the carriage, the other clutched around the pistol. When he forced himself to meet her gaze, he saw no blame on her face, only the remnants of fear and a tragic, pale sorrow.

He made to go to her, but she flinched. His heart stuttered, but he schooled his features to remain impassive. Keeping his movements slow and steady, he gently pried the gun from her fingers.

"I'm so sorry, Aden," she whispered. "This is my entire fault. If I hadn't—"

Something snapped in his head. "Christ, Vivien. This is not your fault any more than Stevens's. I'm the only one to blame for this bloody mess, and we all know it. So please don't take this on yourself. I don't need the burden of that on my conscience, too."

She gaped at him for a moment, her eyes wide and shocked. Then her eyelids fluttered as if she were blinking back tears.

He smothered a curse. What the hell was the matter with him to snap at her like that? If not for her, he'd likely be dead.

"My lady, forgive me," he said, gentling his voice. "I had no right to address you in such a manner. In fact, I should be thanking you for saving our lives."

She seemed to wrap her dignity around her like a cloak. "It hardly matters, Captain St. George, not with that poor boy lying dead at our feet. Apology is not required, nor do I expect one. I only wish for this horrible night to come to an end."

Her voice held a wintry, closed-off chill. No one would believe that just ten minutes ago she'd been going up like fire in his arms.

For some demented reason he wanted to argue with her, or snatch her against his body and hold her until she melted. She was in shock and needed comforting and a good cry, not harsh words. But he couldn't give those to her now, or maybe ever. This incident was a clear warning of the danger Lady Vivien Shaw posed to him.

And in doing so, she posed to herself as well.

But he'd deal with that later, too. Right now he had to get her safely off the streets, and then handle the consequences of Jem's death and the attack.

"Of course, my lady." He turned to Stevens. "My mother's house is only two blocks away. I'll take Lady Vivien there by foot." He handed the coachman the pistol he'd taken from her. "Once we load Jem into the carriage, go straight to Bow Street. I'll send word to Sir Dominic and we'll meet you there as soon as possible."

"Aye, Captain."

They loaded the body into the coach, Stevens once more his calm, professional self. The coachman had been in the Service for years, working first with Dominic and then with Aden. Because death was their constant companion, no agent could afford to let it deeply affect him or sway him from his purpose. Aden had always told himself that, but with each passing day he found it harder to remain unaffected.

And being near Vivien made it worse.

They exchanged a few more words and then the coachman swung himself up into the box and took up the reins. As the carriage clattered away, Aden turned to Vivien. She waited quietly, staring thoughtfully at the cobbled streets.

"What is it?" he asked in a quiet voice.

She looked up and glanced at the darkened houses on the street. "Why didn't anyone come out to help us? Surely they heard the commotion."

He let out a snort as he took her arm, guiding her over to the pavement. "It's late. And this close to the park, robberies have been known to happen. No one would want to take a chance on getting shot."

"Well, that's not right," she said with a spark of her usual fire. "Someone could at least have run for the watch."

"Yes," he responded dryly. "That would have been *very* helpful."

She shot him an irritated glance, but fell silent. He was grateful for that, even though he knew he should be making a better effort to reassure her. But he had too much to sort through in his head, including what this attack said about the most likely suspect and the blackguard's motives. The men who'd attacked them hadn't been the gutter scum who'd taken Vivien before. They were well armed and well trained, and they'd almost succeeded at their task.

The kind of men who would be in the employ of a wealthy and powerful prince immediately sprang to mind. Unfortunately, Aden still had no solid proof that Khovansky was the mastermind behind Vivien's abduction.

"How far are we from your mother's house?" Vivien asked in a hushed tone.

"Just around the corner."

She stumbled and bit off a sharp cry. He stopped, catching her in his arms. She felt so slight and fragile against him, and the muscles in his chest contracted with guilt.

"What's wrong, Vivien?"

She looked up and gave him a self-deprecating smile. "I seem to be missing a shoe."

He blanked for a moment. "You lost your shoe? Where?"

"Back in the coach, I think. I didn't really notice until I got down into the street."

He looked at her feet, peeping out from under her cloak. One dainty gold and white shoe covered one foot, while the other was pathetically bare save for her torn stocking.

Sighing, he swung her up in his arms. She uttered a protest, but he ignored it. "This is getting to be a habit with you. Why didn't you say anything, you goose?"

She clutched at the lapels of the coat and gave an apologetic shrug. "It didn't seem very important at the time. And I only truly noticed after you loaded that poor boy into the carriage. After that, I couldn't bear the thought . . ." Her voice trailed off, and he could hear her swallow against the gorge rising in her throat.

He gave her a reassuring squeeze. "Don't think about it now. It won't help."

She tilted her head back, trying to see his face. "Is that what you do?"

He nodded. "It's the only way I can keep moving ahead." At least that had always been the case until recently.

A few quick strides took them around the corner and onto his mother's street. By luck or by happenstance, her carriage had just pulled up in front of her house. The groom let down the steps, helping his mother to alight. When she turned to thank him, she caught sight of Aden coming swiftly toward them.

"My son! What in God's name?" she gasped, rushing to meet them. "Is Vivien harmed?"

"No, but we've got to get inside. It's not safe out here." As the words left his mouth, Vivien shuddered against him. She seemed to huddle even more deeply into his arms.

His mother nodded and issued a few terse commands to her groom, then she ushered them up the steps to her house. The door opened on Patterson's concerned face, and the next moment they were finally safe inside in the light and warmth.

But for how long?

Aden paced the floor of Dominic's study, counting his steps. Twelve to the bay window, and back again to the fireplace, back and forth, again and again while he waited for his chief to return from Lady Bentley's ball.

It seemed impossible that only an hour had passed since he'd whisked Vivien away from the ball like some enchanted princess. They'd even shared a kiss—much more than a kiss—that had awakened the beautiful princess from her sensual slumber. She'd come alive under his mouth and hands, and the memory of their brief interlude was seared into his memory.

But the tale had not come to a happy ending and he doubted

it ever could. Aden might be the son of a prince, but his bastard lineage and his dangerous profession meant he could never be the hero of Vivien's story.

He stopped in the middle of the room, forcing himself to remain still. *Christ.* He was turning into a complete fool, pacing back and forth like a character from a novel. The idea that Vivien had barely escaped injury or worse had blasted through his control and his ability to think clearly, making him a danger to himself and to her.

It was a situation he could no longer tolerate. If caring for a woman meant one's reason crumbled to dust, then Aden could afford no part of it.

The door opened and Dominic entered, casting him a swift, assessing glance. "It must be bad if you're wearing a path in my carpet," his chief commented as he crossed to the drinks trolley behind his desk. "I've never known you to pace before. Lady Vivien must be trying your patience yet again."

Aden stopped before the big desk, crossing his arms behind his back and staring down at the floor. He couldn't bring himself to look at Dominic while he delivered his news.

"We were set upon not far from my mother's house," he said baldly. "Jem's dead."

He kept his eyes firmly fastened on the pale pink and green roses knotted into the Axeminster carpet. A fraught silence seeped into the room, and Aden fancied the temperature dropped by several degrees. Unlike some spymasters who saw the death of any of their agents or functionaries as regrettable but unavoidable, Dominic didn't react well to any loss, no matter who it was. He braced himself, knowing he deserved the full force of his chief's anger.

Aden heard the clink of crystal and the splash of liquid into glass. A moment later, Dominic handed him a tumbler with a neat dose of brandy. "I'm sorry to hear that," he said quietly. "He was a good lad and I know you were attached to him."

An automatic denial came to Aden's lips, but the words didn't come out. Dominic was right. He had grown fond of Jem, seeing in him the makings of a good spy and an even better man. His loss would be keenly felt.

He stared into his mentor's face, not really seeing him. First John in that debacle in France and now Jem. When had Aden become so attached to people? And now Vivien. He didn't know what the hell he was going to do with her.

Walk away, before it's too late.

His gut twisted into knots at the very idea, which only told him how necessary that course of action had become.

"Sit down and tell me what happened. You'll have plenty of time to blame yourself later," Dominic said.

Aden repressed the impulse to hunch his shoulders like a disobedient boy. Dominic *always* knew what Aden was thinking, one of his more irritating traits. Then again, his chief's uncanny powers of perception were the reason he'd risen from humble beginnings to become one of the best spymasters the Service had ever seen.

They both settled into comfortable wing chairs on either side of the fireplace. Tersely, Aden conveyed the essentials, glossing over the sensual interlude in the carriage. By the time he finished, Dominic's impassive expression had transformed into one of skepticism.

"Let me try to understand this," he said. "Due to Lady Vivien's contretemps with Lord Tumbler, you thought it best to spirit her away from the ball with as little fuss as possible."

"Her contretemps, as you call it, left her somewhat disheveled. That would have surely caused comment if she returned to the ball. She was also reluctant to face Prince Ivan again."

"I assure you her absence was noted, especially by Prince Ivan. He was quite vocal about it, unfortunately."

When Aden cursed, Dominic cracked a brief smile. "Your

mother, of course, handled the situation very capably. She put out word that Vivien had suffered a relapse of her previous illness and that it had been necessary to take her home immediately. She also saw to it that Lady Blake left shortly thereafter, which supported her story."

"Did it work?" Aden asked doubtfully. Things were bad enough without adding a scandal on top of things.

"Hard to tell, but again your mother came to our rescue."

"What did she do?"

Dominic held up his brandy, letting the firelight strike amber glints off the crystal. Then he took a slow sip. Aden repressed a sigh, knowing his chief was playing him.

"Lady Thornbury engaged in a very public flirtation with the Prince Regent," Dominic finally said. "A few minutes into that little display, no one had a thought for Lady Vivien."

Aden shot upright, slopping brandy on his cuff. "She did what?"

Dominic sent him an ironic look. "You heard me. One of the regrets of my professional life is that your mother never joined the Service. I told her years ago that she would make a truly accomplished spy, but she turned me down."

Aden gaped at him, unable to decide what stunned him more—that Dominic had asked his mother to become a spy, or that she'd engaged in a public flirtation with his father. Aden and his mother never discussed the Prince Regent, but he'd deduced long ago that she'd come to despise the man for how he'd taken advantage of her as a young, naïve woman in an unhappy marriage, and for how it had affected Aden's life. The fact that she'd voluntarily put herself out in so forward a fashion . . .

"She did it because it was necessary," Dominic said, reading his thoughts again. "And she did it for *you*."

That idea stiffened every muscle in Aden's back and

shoulders. He loathed the idea of being beholden to his mother. It made him feel . . . vulnerable.

"I would suggest you get past it," Dominic said in an unsympathetic voice. He set his glass down on a small side table with a decided click, signalling the end of that part of the discussion. "So, we now have a second abduction attempt—and a much riskier one, given that the attempt was made while Lady Vivien was clearly well protected—"

"Not well enough," Aden interrupted.

"Well protected," Dominic repeated calmly. "Given that, who is now your likeliest suspect in the case?"

"Khovansky. He has unlimited financial means at his disposal and the influence to deflect any uncomfortable questions. Blake may be involved, but only in a peripheral way."

The image of Khovansky attacking Vivien the other night, bending her back over her brother's desk, flashed through Aden's mind. It had him clenching his fingers around the glass.

"You find Khovansky's obsession with Lady Vivien most disturbing, don't you?" Dominic asked in a deceptively casual tone.

Aden stared at him in disbelief. "And you don't?"

"Of course, but it's different for you. It goes much deeper."

Again, automatic words of denial sprung to his lips, but he managed to bite them back. There was no point. Dominic clearly knew how he felt, and this was the very issue Aden needed to raise anyway.

"Yes, which is why I need to remove myself from this case." He stared into the smoky depths of his glass, trying to find the right words. "My emotions have come into play. The last time that happened, John died in the bed of a French spy." A sense of failure rustled through him, closely followed by the first faint echoes of despair. "And now Jem is dead."

He raised his gaze to meet Dominic's. "I've become a danger to Vivien and to those around me. And even to myself," he said bitterly, recalling how Vivien's quick thinking had saved him. "Fool that I am, I almost got myself killed tonight."

"I'm pleased to hear you are opposed to that outcome," Dominic said caustically. "For the last several weeks, I've feared a slip into a melancholic and perhaps fatal decline."

Aden slammed his glass down on the side table. "Christ, Dominic! Do you think this is a joke? I almost got four people killed tonight!" He jumped up and began pacing the room again. "Don't you understand? My emotions are beginning to cloud my judgment. It's time to put someone else in charge of this case and get me as far away from anything to do with it as possible."

"You mean, get you as far away from Lady Vivien as possible."

Aden didn't bother to dignify that with an answer. After a minute or so, his chief unfolded his tall form from the chair and strolled to the center of the room, forcing Aden to come to a halt.

"Emotions are only a problem if we let them get in our way," Dominic said. "Properly channeled, they can both sharpen our senses and our skills, and strengthen our resolve to protect those in our care."

Aden turned that over in his mind for a few moments, then impatiently rejected it. "I don't work that way. I never have."

Dominic's green gaze glittered cold, like the hardest of emeralds. "Then learn to adapt. Lady Vivien needs you, and you remain the man most suited for this job."

When Aden opened his mouth to object, the other man's eyes blazed hot with anger. The sight was so startling, so unlike Dominic's ironclad, calmly ironic demeanor, that Aden involuntarily flinched.

"Are you so arrogant as to think you can walk away from this now?" Dominic snapped. "And what about Lady Vivien's feelings? Have you thought how she will feel when you abandon her?"

Aden stared at him, too disconcerted to answer.

"That is not a rhetorical question," Dominic growled.

"I haven't."

"Then I suggest you start. Lady Vivien is entirely vulnerable right now, but she does trust you. I would be most disappointed if you betrayed that trust by giving in to what is nothing more than a selfish impulse."

Irritation punched through Aden's surprise. "I'm trying to keep her *safe,* Dominic. Why can't you understand that? I'm no good to her if I can't think straight."

"Sooner or later you're going to have to learn to think *through* the muddle of your emotions, instead of around them. For years I've watched you cut yourself off from the people in your life, building a high wall around yourself. And for years it worked, so I allowed it. But it's not working anymore, Aden. So it's time to try something different."

Aden felt like a tongue-tied schoolboy confronted with a perplexing equation, one that defied understanding no matter how hard he tried. All he could do was stand, rooted to the floor, staring at Dominic as his frustrated mind tried to sort it all out.

"I don't know how to do that," he finally admitted.

The anger in Dominic's eyes abated. "Step back a bit if you must, but don't abandon her. Vivien needs you, whether you will it or not." He let his mouth ease into a sympathetic smile. "You always worry a problem like a dog with a bone, Aden. You'll figure this one out, eventually."

"I wouldn't be so sure about that," Aden muttered.

Dominic had started to move behind his desk, but stopped to cast him a sharp glance. "How do you think you'd feel if something happened to Vivien because you weren't there to protect her? Would that be acceptable to you, knowing you had walked away instead of doing everything you could to keep her from harm? How would you feel to lose her that way instead of standing your ground and fighting for her?"

Aden glared at him, hating his chief's blunt manipulation even as he silently acknowledged the truth of his words.

Surprisingly, Dominic glanced away, staring out the window into the black night. When he returned his gaze to meet Aden's, his eyes looked remarkably bleak.

"I *have* suffered the cruelty of such a loss," his chief said in a quiet voice. "And a man does not recover from it. He moves ahead, but always he drags part of it with him, forever holding him back."

A deep silence fell between them, broken only by the crackling of the fire. Aden had heard whispers of some great tragedy affecting Dominic's youth, but no one had ever had the nerve to broach the subject. He had assumed it little more than idle gossip fueled by Dominic's mysterious past, but now he saw the evidence right before him.

But a moment later, Dominic's discipline returned, his gaze cool. "I tell you this as a friend, Aden. If you walk away from this now, you will regret it for the rest of your life."

Aden nodded. He didn't have to like it—in fact, he hated it—but Dominic was right. "Very well. What would you suggest as our next step?"

"I'll take over the investigation into Khovansky, including any possible ties in this matter to Lord Blake."

"What the hell am I supposed to do?"

When a sardonic smile curled up the edges of Dominic's mouth, Aden could barely hold back a curse. Whatever was coming next, he wasn't going to like.

"You, my dear Aden, are about to take a wife."

Chapter Twenty-Six

Vivien jerked out of her uneasy doze with her heart pounding and her muddled brain struggling to make sense of her surroundings. But she couldn't seem to focus, couldn't remember where she was. Panic clawed her in its irrational grip.

"It's all right, Vivien," came Lady Thornbury's soothing voice. "You're at my house, remember?"

Of course.

Blinking, she took in the quiet elegance of Lady Thornbury's morning room, where they waited for Aden to return from Bow Street. He'd been gone for hours, and his mother had finally persuaded her to close her eyes and rest. Vivien had been convinced she couldn't sleep a wink but she'd quickly fallen into a restless slumber.

She flicked aside the cashmere shawl across her legs and swung her feet to the floor, done with her nightmare-addled sleep. Peering at the small clock on the mantel, she tried to focus her gaze on the delicate numbers on its face. No luck. Exhaustion dogged her, even more so than when she'd been kidnapped. The almost constant strain of the last few days—both physical and emotional—was taking its toll.

"What time is it?" she asked, hiding a yawn behind one hand.

"It's almost five o'clock," Lady Thornbury replied as she

stirred up the dying embers of the fire. Then she moved silently about the room, lighting several branches of candles. Vivien had to squint until her stinging eyes adjusted to the light.

"Aden . . . the captain hasn't yet returned?" she asked.

When her friend cast her a sharp glance, Vivien willed herself not to blush. Aden's manner when he had left her with his mother several hours ago had been brisk and sensible rather than loverlike. He'd carried her up to this room, issuing instructions to his mother as he went, then had deposited Vivien on the chaise and told her to *stay put*. If she hadn't been so shattered by Jem's death, Vivien would have bristled at his imperious tone. As it was, she'd wanted nothing more than to crawl into a dark corner, rest her head on her knees, and burst into tears.

"Aden has just come in," Lady Thornbury said. "That's what woke you up. You heard voices down in the hall."

Vivien smoothed a stray curl of hair back from her face, all too conscious that she must look far from presentable. She'd changed into one of Lady Thornbury's warmest dressing gowns hours ago and pulled her hair back in a long braid, but it would take more than that to make her less of a fright. She needed a decent night's sleep—several, in fact—and a respite from the fear and anxiety that dogged her every step. Unfortunately, that didn't appear to be on the immediate horizon.

Shoving her feet into the pair of cozy slippers that went with the dressing gown, she pushed herself up. A wave of dizziness swept over her and she staggered, banging her hip into the arm of the chaise.

As black dots flickered across her vision, she heard the door open and swift footsteps cross the room. Strong, familiar arms swept around her and lowered her carefully back onto the chaise.

"Take easy, slow breaths," Aden's voice said calmly in her ear.

She did as he said, sighing with relief at the feel of his steady hand on her back, stroking up and down her spine. Gradually, her vision cleared and her stomach settled.

"Thank you," she murmured, giving him a weak smile.

He inspected her with a somber gaze. As she stared back, taking in his handsome, fatigue-marked features, it came to her in a blazing rush that she only felt truly safe and at peace when he was near. On the heels of that alarming realization, it took all her willpower not to throw herself into his arms and burst into foolish tears.

But her feelings must have been evident, because something wary shifted in his gaze and his face went blank. His hand fell from her back and he rose and crossed to the fireplace, as if seeking its warmth.

"Mother," he said, "I think Lady Vivien could use a cup of tea."

"I've already rung for it." Lady Thornbury rustled up to him and placed a motherly hand on his cheek, turning his face toward her. "I think you could use a cup, too. And some breakfast."

"Coffee, more like it. And a fresh change of clothes," he said in a wry voice. "Bow Street is never a debutante's ball at the best of times, but in the middle of the night . . ." His nostrils flared with disdain.

"Lady Vivien, you look tired," he said, abruptly switching the topic. "Didn't you get any rest?"

She swallowed the lump in her throat from his cool tone. Why couldn't she remember that he saw her primarily as a responsibility, and not someone he wished a relationship with? After all the trouble she'd caused, Aden probably couldn't wait to be shot of her.

"Yes, although I imagine I look almost as bad as you do,"

she said, trying for a light tone. "But at least I don't smell like the inside of a guardhouse."

His eyes flashed with a quick gleam of appreciation and a smile lifted the edges of his stern mouth. It lasted only a second, but it lifted her spirits. It was ridiculous how much he affected her, a fact that did not bode well for her future peace of mind when her travails were over and he disappeared from her life.

"Mother, I need you to find suitable clothes for Lady Vivien for an extended trip into the country," he said, all business again. His rapid switches in demeanor were making her dizzy. "She cannot return home to pack and we must be ready to leave London within the hour," he ended on a decisive note.

Vivien gaped at him. "What are you talking about?"

"I will explain in a moment."

He turned his back to her, conferring quietly with his mother. Vivien crossed her arms over her chest and stared daggers at the back of his head. Of course he couldn't see her, but it made *her* feel better. Yes, she had a ridiculous crush on the man, but that didn't mean she liked it when he ordered her about like a child.

As she watched the two of them quietly confer, impatience finally overtook her. She jumped to her feet. Her head swam a bit, but she managed to keep her balance.

"Excuse me," she interrupted in a loud voice. "But since I am, apparently, going on a trip to the country, perhaps you might at least give a few details. Anything will do, really. Our destination, the reasons why—that sort of thing. Not that I mean to cause any trouble, you understand," she finished sarcastically.

Lady Thornbury, still looking as elegant and fresh as she did five hours ago, glided over to her with a placating smile. She scooped the cashmere shawl up from the chaise and wrapped it back around Vivien's shoulders.

"I know you're frustrated, my love," she said. "But Aden will explain everything. I must go off and see to the arrangements, but I'll return to you shortly."

She pressed a soft kiss to Vivien's cheek. "You must trust Aden," she murmured. "Everything he does is for your safety, and out of concern for your well-being."

Vivien grumbled something under her breath about pig-headed, arrogant men, earning her a grin from the older woman. She gave Vivien's arm a sympathetic squeeze and then hurried from the room.

Once Vivien had to face Aden on her own, some of her irritation-fueled courage leaked away. She was exhausted, anxious, and riddled with guilt over the death of his groom. The vision of the boy's body lying on the pavement, surrounded by an ever-expanding pool of blood, was not something she would ever forget.

And Jem's tragic death was at least partly her fault.

"Vivien, you're exhausted. Please sit down before you fall down," Aden said with a hint of exasperation. "I'll be happy to tell you everything, but I will *not* be happy if I have to pick you up off the floor or nurse you if you fall ill."

"I'm fine," she said emphatically. She wasn't, but he had enough burdens to carry without worrying that she was going to faint or fall into a decline. Still, she sat on the chaise as he slowly crossed the room to stand before her. She sensed the reluctance in him to be near her, and it made her heart curl in around itself.

"I'm so sorry about what happened to Jem," she said in a tight voice. "I'm so sorry about everything. You're only trying to help and—"

"No apology is necessary, Vivien. I know this evening's events were very distressing, but the best thing you can do is put them out of your mind. It serves no purpose to dwell on them, at least not now."

His firm tone of voice clearly told her the subject was closed. Just as clear was the effort he was making to repress his anger, whether with her or with himself she couldn't tell.

Not that it mattered. She blamed herself for all that had occurred these last few weeks, as much as Aden surely blamed himself. And all the ugliness of the present situation would likely stand forever between them, an insurmountable barrier to even the mildest of friendships.

She dug her nails into the sides of her legs, ruthlessly suppressing the impulse to cry. How selfish of her to worry about her own feelings when a young man who had tried to protect her lay cold on a mortuary slab.

"Very well," she said. "Then I suppose it's time for us to discuss what happened tonight. Who do you think was responsible for this latest attempt?"

His gaze flicked to the clock, his impatience obvious.

"I'm not going anywhere until you answer my questions," she said quietly.

Aden rubbed his forehead but finally nodded. He sank carefully down on the edge of the chair opposite, wincing slightly as he stretched out one leg. Absently, he began massaging his knee, as if it bothered him.

"Let me help get you started," Vivien prompted. "My abductor is obviously not Kit's moneylender."

Aden stilled a moment but then settled back into the chair, lazily crossing one long leg over the other. He appeared for all the world like a gentleman taking his leisure, save for the fact that he looked like he'd been rolling in the dirt—which he had—and that he sported an ugly bruise on his right cheekbone.

"Why did you come to that conclusion, my lady?"

She grimaced. "You must truly think I'm an idiot."

His eyes widened but she waved him to silence. "It doesn't matter. Kit has already paid the man eight thousand pounds. It would serve no purpose for him to abduct me now—or ever, for that matter. I was quite wrong to suspect him in the first place."

"The notion didn't completely lack merit, but I was able to deduce rather quickly that the person in question was simply making empty threats."

She glared at him. "You talked to him, and you never thought to tell me?"

He opened his mouth, closed it, and then opened it again. "Yes, I talked to him. And no, I didn't think to tell you."

"I'm deeply shocked. No, wait. I'm not," she said, showing her teeth.

That brought a snort of laughter from him. "Do forgive me, my lady. I will be sure to share all my investigations with you in the future."

"Splendid. Then you can start by telling me right now who you think is responsible for this."

"The greatest suspicion must now fall on Prince Ivan," he said. "I believe he was your first suspect, was he not?"

Vivien leaned both elbows on her thighs and dropped her forehead into her palms. "Yes, he was. But I convinced myself it was a ridiculous idea." She lifted her head and met Aden's sympathetic gaze. "He's a prince, for God's sake, and a visiting dignitary. Did he truly think he could get away with this?"

"He *could* get away with it and he still can, if we're not careful."

"Kidnapping me?" she asked, incredulous. "He wants to marry me, but how will that help? The laws against abducting heiresses and forcing them into marriage are quite strong." She thought for a second. "Not that I'm much of an heiress, but you know what I mean."

"I do." He sat up from his elegant sprawl and leaned forward, his gaze now fiercely intense. "But Khovansky doesn't just want to marry you, Vivien. He's obsessed with you, and I believe he'll commit any act, no matter how foul, to claim you."

She stared back at him as her weary mind tried to grapple with the bizarre situation. "I don't understand. He *knows* I don't want to marry him. Given how much I dislike him, why would he insist on acting in such a demented fashion? It doesn't make any sense."

Aden grimaced. "Obsessions like this never do because they're not rational. *He's* not rational, and he cannot accept your rejection. Khovansky's arrogance is compounded by the fact that he's a prince and an extremely wealthy and powerful man. I suspect no one has ever said no to him. Or if they did, they lived to regret it. You said no, which would only spur his determination to exert his mastery over you. Trust me, Vivien, the man is exceedingly dangerous."

Her chest grew tight with anxiety at the thought of falling into Ivan the Terrible's clutches. "Well, he *is* a toad so I shouldn't be completely surprised," she said, trying to not sound as worried as she felt. And as bad as it was, at least it meant Kit wasn't in any way responsible for her abduction, which was something. Still . . .

Vivien frowned. "I fail to see how my abduction will achieve Prince Ivan's aim. I have no intention of marrying him under any circumstances, and he knows that."

"You won't have a choice. Dominic is of the opinion that the next time the prince strikes he will take you out of the country—"

"What? Never!" Outrage propelled her to her feet.

Aden took her hand and gently tugged her back down. "Yes, I understand your outrage, but you won't have a choice. Not only will your reputation be ruined—"

"I don't care. I'd rather die than marry him."

Aden looked even grimmer than he had a few seconds ago.

"I fear that if Khovansky were to succeed, that might well be your only other alternative."

Her mind stuttered, refusing to make sense of his words. Then their meaning unscrambled, hitting like the kick of a pistol. "I . . . that can't possibly be true," she stammered.

When he hesitated, she shook her head impatiently. "It's my life. I have a right to know."

The grooves around his mouth deepened, telling her how much he didn't want to explain. She met his gaze, holding it so he would understand her intent.

"Very well," he finally said. "There are rumors about the prince that Dominic and I have yet to confirm entirely to our satisfaction."

"And those rumors are?"

"That he is guilty of murdering one of his servants, although it was never proven. But whatever did happen, his family went to great pains to cover it up."

Vivien closed her eyes, feeling nauseous. When she opened them, Aden carefully watched her, as if expecting her to fall apart. Who could blame her if she did?

"Is there anything else I need to know?" Her voice sounded little better than a croak.

"That's enough for now," he replied in a gentle tone.

Oh, God. There was more?

She steeled herself to hear it. "Tell me everything."

"It's not necessary."

"I want to know," she said doggedly. "I have a right."

His reluctance was evident, but he finally complied. "There have been rumors about his treatment of women. Ugly rumors. But they are as yet unconfirmed as well. Until such time as they are, I think it best not to discuss them."

The stone set of his face indicated he'd reached the limit of what he was willing to share. And given how queasy her stomach felt right at this moment, perhaps that was for the best.

"I see," she managed. "So, what you're saying . . ."

"I'm saying that we cannot allow anyone to know your whereabouts until Dominic can bring proof to the Russian ambassador that the prince is responsible for the attacks on you. Until that time, you must go into hiding."

With shaking hands, Vivien pulled the edges of the wool dressing gown tightly around her. The roaring blaze in the hearth filled the room with glowing warmth, but she was freezing.

And terrified, which irritated her immensely. Yes, it was an awful situation, but that was no excuse for going to pieces. "Would it not be better to stay in London and confront the situation? Go to the ambassador now? I can tell him what happened that night in my brother's study. That, combined with Sir Dominic's suspicions might be enough . . ."

She trailed off again as Aden grimly shook his head.

"It's not enough. Khovansky will simply maintain that your brother gave him to understand that his expectations were well founded, and that he simply acted on those expectations with the full intention of making you his wife." His mouth curled downward as if he'd just tasted something sour. "I'm sure the prince would make it clear to the ambassador that he would be more than willing to correct any misunderstandings by offering to make you his bride."

Vivien couldn't help scoffing at that. "Surely Count Lieven would not be so easily fooled!"

"Perhaps not. But Prince Ivan comes from one of the most powerful of the Russian ruling families. It's hard for us to understand just how influential that makes him."

Vivien frowned. "And that would excuse him from crimes committed in our country?"

Aden turned his palms up in a frustrated gesture. "The

British Crown will not wish to offend either the prince or the ambassador. Matters with the Russians are still in a delicate state. After all, it's been less than a year since an ambassador was even assigned from Russia to the Court of St. James." He shook his head. "Count Lieven will not appreciate such allegations being dumped in his lap without concrete evidence."

Anger and frustration drove her to her feet again. "The man can have me abducted, he can assault me, and in the process of trying to abduct me again he can kill a man, and yet there's nothing we can do about it?"

Aden rose to his feet, too. "Not right now. I understand the situation is frustrating, but Dominic and I both feel the safest course of action is to get you safely out of harm's way until the matter can be properly resolved."

She stared up at him. His eyes held a great deal of sympathy, but also determination.

"Where do you propose to take me?" she asked in a disgruntled voice. She didn't mean to sound ungrateful but she loathed the idea of running away.

"To a small spa town up north, near Buckminster. St. Clement is very quiet, especially at this time of year, and the clientele is mostly elderly and of limited means. It's far enough off the beaten path that the chances of anyone recognizing you are practically nonexistent."

Vivien could barely hold back a groan. She wasn't fond of country towns at the best of times, but this particular place sounded dreadful. "How delightful. And what will I do once I arrive in this idyllic spot?"

"Stay out of trouble," he said dryly.

"I never get into trouble, at least not on purpose," she protested.

He rolled his eyes, not even deigning to reply. Well, she could hardly blame him, but she wasn't quite ready to give in. "I fail to see how that would entirely eliminate the chance that someone might recognize me. If the point is simply to get me out of town, why don't I just retreat to my brother's estate in Somerset? Surely that's far enough away to suit your purpose."

"Because everyone within ten miles of the estate would know you were there. You are much too recognizable at the best of times. Besides, in St. Clement you will be living under a false name."

Her jaw sagged open. Surely she hadn't heard that correctly. "I beg your pardon?"

"I know it seems odd," he said, crossing to the bell pull in the corner. "But it's the best way to avoid detection."

Vivien was beginning to wonder if she'd fallen asleep again and was dreaming. If she was, it was certainly the oddest dream she'd ever had. "I don't really understand any of this."

"I know," he said sympathetically. "But your breakfast will be here in just a few minutes, and then you can have a nice cup of tea. You'll feel much more yourself after you've had something to eat and drink." He took her arm and steered her back to the sofa, ignoring the scowl she directed at him.

"Don't patronize me, Aden. I don't like it one bit."

A fleeting smile touched his lips. "I wouldn't dream of it, my lady."

She subsided onto the chaise with a grumble. Actually, now that she thought of it, she was rather hungry. She hadn't eaten anything since early last evening.

Aden stood over her, watching her with a faint smile on his lips. He looked so handsome and so powerfully masculine, even as fatigued as he clearly was, that her heart turned over in her chest. She had no idea how he truly felt about her, but she knew he would do anything to protect her, no matter the risk to his own safety—all while treating her with gentleness and a consideration she hadn't experienced since the death of her father.

Little wonder she'd fallen in love with him.

She blinked and went still. The phrase had slipped into her mind so easily, like a warm breeze fluttering past gauzy curtains in an open window. But once inside, it rocked through her with the force of a summer storm, settling in her heart with a sense of profound inevitability.

And with it came the sense of a kind of peace she'd never known.

But on the heels of *that* came a burgeoning fear, because once this was over and Aden was gone from her life, she knew such peace would disappear from her life forever.

"What troubles you, my lady?" he asked gently. He sat down gingerly next to her on the chaise, as if afraid to jostle her.

"Oh, nothing," she said brightly in a ghastly attempt to overcompensate. "Why do you ask?"

Now he stared as if her brain was leaking out of her ears, which it might well be given that inane remark.

"I've been pushing you too hard," he said. "Do you need my mother?"

There was little Lady Thornbury could do in this particular situation, and if Aden ever guessed how Vivien truly felt about him, he'd probably run screaming from the room. She'd never met a man so determined to keep himself at a distance from the people in his life. In all fairness to him, however, he had been anything but distant last night, before the attack.

"I'm fine," she said, giving him a reassuring smile. "I'm sure I'll be even better once I've had a cup of tea."

He rose and strode to the door, looking out into the hallway. "I don't know what's taking so long," he said with a scowl.

"I'm sure breakfast will be here soon. After all it's only five o'clock. The servants will hardly be up."

"We need to be getting on the road. I have no idea why it's taking my mother so long to pack," he groused.

"It's not as if I have clothes lying about your mother's house," she said patiently. "Why can't I simply go home, pack, and tell my family what's happening? Mamma will be bound to worry unless she hears from me soon."

He crossed to the window and drew aside the curtains, peering out into the street. "My mother will see Lady Blake later this morning and explain the situation. She'll also ensure that a story is put about town that you've gone to visit friends up north for several weeks."

Vivien frowned. It all seemed so unnecessarily complicated. "But why can't—"

She stumbled to a halt when a horrible thought struck her. When Aden cut her a narrow glance, she sighed. "Cyrus. He's part of this, isn't he?"

He turned to her, keeping his back to the window. The pity she saw on his face made her stomach twist.

"We cannot rule it out," he said. "For safety's sake, no one in your family can know exactly where you will be staying. Not that we think Kit or your mother has anything to do with this," he added hastily, taking in her expression. "But if they knew our plans, they might inadvertently reveal them, or—"

"Or Cyrus might blackmail it out of them by refusing to cover their bills."

Bitterness rolled over her in a great, choking tide. She had known for years that she could not depend on her family, but she had never expected to be so thoroughly betrayed. At the most critical juncture of her life, she felt entirely alone.

Aden came and sat next to her again. He looked down at her hands, clenched in a tight ball in her lap. Gently, he prised them free of each other, lifting one to press a soft kiss on the back. "You are not alone, my dear girl, although I know you must think you are."

She stared at him, stunned by his change in demeanor. His dark gaze, warm and steady, sent heat filtering back through her cold limbs.

"My mother cares a great deal for you," he said, "as does Sir Dominic. We will let nothing harm you, I promise."

She swallowed past the lump in her throat. "And what about you?" she whispered. "How do *you* feel about me?"

His lips parted as he drew in a hesitating breath. Then the door opened and his mother came in, followed by the butler rolling a cart.

"Breakfast has finally arrived, my dears," Lady Thornbury trilled in a cheerful voice.

Aden rose from the chaise and crossed to his mother, leaving Vivien once more crushingly alone.

Chapter Twenty-Seven

Vivien levelled another glare at Aden, although he certainly couldn't see it. He'd spent most of their journey with his long legs stretched out as much as possible in the cramped space of the travelling coach, and with his hat tilted over his eyes. How the man could sleep under these circumstances was beyond her, and her resentment swelled with every mile marker that passed. Yes, she could now admit she was madly in love with him, but that didn't mean he wasn't an immensely irritating man—both in his ability to adapt to any circumstance without apparent discomfort and in his all too obvious intention to have as little contact with her as possible. For the first hour of their journey, she struggled with a wounded sense of rejection as he'd done his best to shut her out. Now, hours later, all she wanted to do was box his ears and get out of the blasted carriage.

With a weary sigh, she pulled off the spectacles he'd made her wear and rubbed the dents on her nose. She still couldn't believe it necessary to wear so ridiculous a disguise, but Aden had insisted. He'd also insisted she wear the ugliest mustard-colored pelisse known to man, along with a bonnet with a poke so large she almost jabbed his eyes out every time she got in and out of the coach. That was *entirely* his fault, as she'd told him in no uncertain terms when he'd had the nerve to let out a long-suffering sigh at their last stop.

She peered out the window as dusk settled over the dreary November landscape. It would be full dark soon and she could only hope they would stop for the night. Surely even Aden wouldn't insist that the horses pick their way across rutted country lanes, risking everyone's life and limb.

Retrieving her reticule from where it had fallen to the floor, Vivien slipped the spectacles inside. She was sick of wearing them, sick of the mud and the dirt and, most of all, sick of Prince Ivan bloody Khovansky for placing them all in this terrible fix.

"Put your spectacles back on, Vivien."

Startled by the unexpected command, she jumped in her seat as the carriage hit a massive rut, bouncing her up in the air. She landed with a jolt and a stab of pain shot from her rump all the way up to her shoulders.

Aden, with his brawny physique, hadn't moved a jot. In fact, he was in the exact same position as he'd been for the last hour—arms folded across his chest and hat tipped over his face. How in God's name had he seen what she was doing?

"I thought you were asleep," she muttered, leaning forward to massage the base of her spine.

"I was, until you started making so much noise."

"I certainly wasn't. I was simply putting away these ridiculous spectacles. It's pitch-dark out, and I highly doubt anyone is peering into passing carriages in the hope of catching a glimpse of me."

He pushed up the brim of his slouched hat and stared at her. Despite her assertion, some light still glimmered low on the horizon, enough for her to see his cool gaze.

"Nonetheless, you will wear the spectacles at all times." He glanced at the gruesome bonnet, which she'd tossed on the seat some time ago. "As well as your hat."

"Perhaps you'd like me to wear them when I'm asleep, too. Just in case Prince Ivan jumps out of the closet or out from under the bed," she retorted.

"Vivien."

She couldn't mistake the quiet warning in his voice. With exaggerated care, she removed the spectacles from her reticule and placed them back on her nose. Then she mashed the bonnet down on her much-abused coiffure as she glared at him. "Honestly, I know we need to be careful, but you act as if there are villains hiding behind every rock and tree. And this disguise is ridiculous. I'm surprised your mother had clothing this ugly in her house."

Aden straightened up, twisting his torso in a stretch and then flexing his arms. Vivien's irritation stuttered and died as she watched the ripple of his well-defined muscles under his coat. Unlike her, the cold didn't seem to bother him. In fact, he'd slipped out of his greatcoat hours ago, piling it on top of her lap blanket to help keep her warm.

A stab of guilt had her mentally wincing. Despite his cool demeanor, Aden had done everything in his power to make her comfortable. Still, she wished he would explain what would happen when they reached the village of St. Clement. He'd mentioned something about *hiding in plain sight,* but hadn't explained the cryptic comment. In fact, she had no idea what would happen when they arrived at the inn—if they actually stopped for the night. Other than Aden's well-armed coachman and groom, they were travelling without any servants. Not having a maid to lend her some air of respectability in public seemed problematic, even if she was tricked out in a ridiculous disguise.

Aden narrowed his eyes at her. "The disguise is necessary, and you will wear it for as long as I tell you to."

She repressed the urge to stick her tongue out at him. "You are the most cautious person I've ever met. One might think you were a spy, with all this wearing of costumes and skulking about."

If she hadn't been looking right at him, and if the last dying rays of the sun hadn't chosen that exact moment to blaze across his face, she would have missed his unspoken response. But she caught the surprise that flashed across his features. Just as swiftly, it was replaced by a carefully blank expression.

Vivien peered at him, dumbfounded. But then all the small, disparate pieces of information she'd collected and stored in her memory rearranged themselves like puzzle pieces, snapping together with smooth precision. His reticence, his obscure military background, the gaps in his personal and family history, his uncanny abilities and remarkable physical skills. Even his relationship with Sir Dominic, whose dealings with the government always seemed so murky, suddenly sprang into focus.

"Oh, good Lord," she breathed. "You *are* a spy."

A muscle twitched in his jaw. "Don't be ridiculous. I'm a soldier," he said with what he must have thought was an astonished look.

Though his denial was immediate, even slightly incredulous, it nevertheless confirmed her suspicions.

"Oh, my God," she said, pushing her fingers under the spectacles and rubbing her eyes. The one man in the world she'd fallen in love with, and he was a spy. No wonder he worked so hard to keep her at a distance. From every lurid tale she'd ever heard, it seemed spies weren't keen on a life of domestic tranquility.

She opened her eyes and inspected him over the top of her spectacles. His expression was closed, and he'd folded his arms across his chest again as if trying to shut her out. If she had a particle of sense she would take the hint and mind her own business.

"Does your mother know?" she asked, ignoring her better instincts.

"This is a ridiculous discussion, and we are not having it," he growled.

Another revelation struck her with blinding force. "Oh, heavens! Of course she does. She can run rings around anyone in the *ton,* including Sir Dominic. It's no wonder she has so much influence in the political sphere. I've heard more than one man say Lady Thornbury would make a better prime minister than Liverpool." She thought about that. "I must say, I'm inclined to agree, since your mother is the most intelligent person I know."

Aden stared at her with a bemused expression. His mouth opened and then closed, rather like a fish thrown up onto a riverbank.

"But I can't imagine your father was very happy about your career choice," she mused. "Lord Thornbury was a terrible high-stickler, wasn't he? From what I've heard, spying is not considered a profession for gentlemen."

"That's enough," he finally snapped, his voice so cold it was a miracle she didn't freeze.

Vivien winced, annoyed at her own insensitivity. But the idea of Aden as a *spy* had truly knocked her back on her heels. "I'm sorry. I suppose you're not allowed to discuss these sorts of things. I promise I won't tell anyone. I'm actually very good at keeping secrets. Really, I am."

A moment later, the chaise clattered into the yard of a small coaching inn. But even over the noise of the wheels on cobblestone, Vivien swore she heard Aden mutter a truly stupendous oath.

Vivien rolled over on the lumpy mattress and squished up the even lumpier pillow, trying to get comfortable. She'd been lying awake for hours, every nerve in her body jangling with a frustrating combination of fatigue and agitation. To make matters worse, she was intensely aware of Aden bedded down on the floor on the other side of the room. Unlike her, he appeared completely undisturbed by their bizarre situation or by the hard floor that served as his bed. She supposed one learned to sleep anywhere when one was a spy, or perhaps he'd learned to do it in spy school—if there even was such a thing.

Not that she would ever know. Aden had refused to say another word about it, and had told her severely before leaving the carriage that she was to drop the subject and leave all the talking to him. Then he'd pulled out a plain gold ring and slipped it onto her finger. She'd stared at it, dazed by the implications. But she'd snapped out of it when he told the innkeeper they would be taking only one room, under the name of Mr. and Mrs. Edwards. Of course, she'd gaped at Aden like an idiot, unable to utter even a single word.

Which had probably been his plan all along.

"I'm sorry, but it's the only way," he'd said, not sounding the least bit apologetic. "We could not bring your maid, nor can I leave you alone to sleep. It's not safe."

Aghast, Vivien had darted a look at the sole bed, tucked under the eaves of the ancient-looking timbered roof.

"Where will you sleep?" she'd managed in a squeaky voice. Rationally, she agreed with his logic, but the idea of sleeping with Aden, even if only for show, made her skin prickle with rattled nerves.

Taking pity on her, he'd explained that he'd sleep on the floor, right in front of the door. She'd calmed down a bit after that but the rest of the evening passed in a strained atmosphere. They'd eaten dinner in almost total silence as Vivien was too distracted by what lay before her—both tonight and on the morrow—to pursue her curiosity over Aden's unusual profession.

Fortunately, he'd given her some privacy after dinner, going down to the taproom so as to allow her to wash and ready herself for bed. Returning a short time later, he'd retrieved one of the pillows from the bed, extinguished the candles, and stretched his long frame out on the floor, fully dressed and wrapped in his coat. Only then had Vivien flung off her dressing gown and scurried under the coarse but thankfully clean bed linens, grateful for the darkness that covered her silly blushes. After saying her prayers, she'd closed her eyes, so exhausted she was convinced she'd immediately fall asleep.

But she hadn't counted on her heightened awareness of Aden. And whenever she wasn't thinking about him, all her other worries circled in her brain like a crazed flock of swallows, diving and swooping endlessly until she couldn't think anymore. Every time she closed her exhausted eyes, an image of Jem's lifeless body imprinted itself on her eyelids. Between that and the horrible sense that her life had completely unravelled at the seams, Vivien began to wonder if she would ever fall asleep again.

Whispering the curse she'd heard Aden mutter when getting out of the carriage—and feeling a bit better for it—she rolled over, thumped the pillow again, and ordered herself to sleep. Finally, she settled, and the soft darkness closed around her. Vivien's eyelids fluttered shut, and she let out a quiet, slow breath.

And out of the depths of her mind, the image of Jem, bloodied and lifeless in the street, swam up at her with blinding force. Fear and horror enveloped her, squeezing the breath from her body.

She bolted upright, choking and gasping for air. In a blind panic, she propelled herself out of the high bed, thudding down onto the cold floor. Her feet slipped out from under her and she landed on her backside, letting out a startled yelp of pain.

"Christ, Vivien!"

She felt rather than saw Aden scramble up from his make-shift bed and cross to her with lightning speed. His arms went around her, pulling her up from her graceless sprawl. She peered up at him, but he was nothing but a large blur in the smothering darkness.

"Did you hurt yourself?" he asked in a worried voice.

She clutched at him, trembling from the shock of hitting the floor as well as lingering remnants of her awful vision. She couldn't seem to catch her breath to speak.

"Hang on," he said, gently lifting her onto the bed.

When his hands left her, she had to bite her tongue not to cry out. He moved as stealthily as a cat, barely making a sound as he crossed the room. Then she heard the scratch of a tinder-box and a candle flared into life. He carried the taper back, holding it in one hand as his gaze swept over her. As a blush spread to every part of her body his gaze fell upon, it occurred to her that the plain but finely spun cambric of her night rail afforded her modesty little protection.

She shifted, slanting a cautious glance at his handsome features, rendered even more starkly masculine in the glow cast by the small flame. Her heart contracted and she had to clamp down on the words trembling on the tip of her tongue, words that begged him to take her into his arms and hold her safe.

And even more dangerous words, too, ones that would reveal her true feelings. Ones that would ask him to do things no unmarried lady should ask a man to do.

He tipped her chin up, giving her a somber inspection. "Did you have a nightmare?"

How could a tone so gentle hit her with such blistering force? Swallowing a rush of tears, she gave a miserable nod. On top of everything else, now the poor man had to deal with a woman on the verge of hysteria.

"Did you hurt yourself when you fell out of bed?"

She had, but not in any place she felt comfortable discussing.

"A . . . a bit, yes," she stuttered. "But I'll be fine."

He frowned. "Did you get a splinter in your leg? These floors are rough. If you caught a splinter, we should get it out." He leaned down, bringing the candle with him. "Let me see." He began to carefully lift up her hem.

Shocked, Vivien clutched the fabric tightly around her knees. "It wasn't my knee or my leg that got hurt," she blurted out.

He frowned. "You made a hell of a thump when you fell. Where exactly *do* you hurt?"

She stifled a groan. "Never mind," she said through clenched teeth. "I'll be fine."

He stared blankly for a second, then amused understanding lit up his eyes. "I see. Do you want me to rub it for you?"

Her mouth dropped open at the scandalous suggestion. Even more scandalous, the notion darted into her head that she might very well like Aden to, ah, soothe her bottom.

"I hardly think that would be proper," she said in a breathless voice.

"Well, if you're sure," he said.

Blast him. She could hear the laugh in his voice. "Quite, thank you." There. Not even her old governess could have sounded as prim.

"Well, then, back to bed with you."

He slid his big hands under her calves and eased her legs under the covers. Then he tucked the bedding around her before smoothing back the hair that had escaped from her braid. The infinite tenderness of the gesture brought tears rushing back to her eyes.

"Hush. Don't cry," he murmured. "All will be well. I promise."

She blinked hard, annoyed with her weakness. Crying rarely solved anything, as she had learned after her father died.

"What do you need?" he asked. "Tell me, and I'll get it for you."

She stared up at him, the candlelight flickering in a soft, dancing blur and outlining his broad shoulders in its gentle glow. Her awareness contracted, focusing solely on him. A fierce longing rushed through her and swept away all her worries about the days ahead.

There was only tonight, and only Aden.

Vivien grasped the soft linen of his shirt where it gapped open across his chest and pulled herself up to a sitting position. He flinched a bit, eyes widening with surprise, but he didn't pull away.

"I need *you*," she whispered. "I need your body against mine, with nothing between us."

Shock flashed across his features. Not that she blamed him given what she'd just said, but the circumstances demanded swift and decisive action. Already, she could feel him mentally pulling away.

"Vivien, you don't know what you're saying," he rasped in a hoarse voice.

In answer, she stretched up and pressed her trembling mouth to his lips. She tasted him, using the tip of her tongue to gently probe the seam of his mouth. When she slipped in a fraction, he groaned low in his throat. His heartbeat accelerated under her palms and hers leapt in response.

For a few seconds, he allowed her clumsy caress, opening briefly and sucking her tongue into the hot cavern of his mouth. She whimpered and clutched at him, relishing the feel of his hard muscles under her fingertips.

Then he broke away on a gasp, retreating even as Vivien kept a firm grasp on his shirt.

"Christ," he rasped. "You're killing me. Do you have any idea how foolish this is?"

Stung by the harsh note in his voice, she let go. They stared at each other, both panting, his eyes glittering back at her with naked passion.

Then he seemed to clamp down on himself, struggling for the impassive detachment he so carefully cultivated.

It only made her determination flare like a torch.

With deliberate movements, she unlaced the ribbons on her night rail and let the fabric whisper open on her chest. Aden straightened up as a rush of color darkened his cheekbones.

"What are you doing?" he asked in a tight voice.

She forced herself not to roll her eyes. Either Aden was particularly dense when it came to this sort of thing, or she was very bad at it.

"I'm getting what I need." Her voice came out low and husky even to her inexperienced ears.

"I don't think . . ."

His voice died when she eased first one sleeve off her shoulder then the other, shrugging the soft cotton from her arms and letting it slither down to her waist. She pulled her hands from the sleeves, fully exposing her bare breasts to Aden's stunned gaze. He stood stock still. But at least he wasn't moving away, so she assumed she was making progress.

Of course, her heart was pounding so hard she just might faint, which would certainly be a humiliating way to end her first attempt at seduction.

She sucked in a deep, unsteady breath. Aden let out a quiet hiss, his eyes narrowing to an obsidian gleam as he took a step closer. Feeling both triumphant and terrified, Vivien reached behind her and began unravelling her braid with shaking fingers. That lifted her breasts up even higher.

"Wouldn't you like me to take my hair down?" she asked in a quavering voice.

He moved then, coming down on her so swiftly she almost did faint from the shock. He grasped her wrists and pulled them up over her head, capturing her beneath his hard body.

"Later," he said through clenched teeth. "You'll take it down later."

Chapter Twenty-Eight

Vivien's trepidation was quickly transformed into spiralling excitement as Aden pressed her into the mattress. The wooden frame of the old bed creaked beneath their combined weights. He was big and solid, and she loved the way his body covered hers. Instinctively, she'd parted her legs when he came down on her, and he was now wedged between her hips, his thick erection nudging her mound and belly. She couldn't help wriggling, catching her breath as she cradled him between her thighs.

His dark eyes went to half-mast when she moved, gleaming with sensual pleasure. His lips parted and he breathed out a sigh before lowering his head those final few inches to kiss her.

But he barely touched her lips—more a gentle brush, the prelude to a question. "Are you sure, Vivien? Be very sure, because there's no turning back from this."

She frowned. "Did you forget that I'm the one who just took off my nightgown? Was that not a clear enough indication of what I want?"

He stared at her for a long moment before letting out a strangled laugh. "Forgive me. I'm only a thick-headed male, and when it comes to sex we can sometimes get confused."

"How a man can get confused when a woman bares her breasts to him is beyond me," she muttered, now starting to feel embarrassed. An awful thought struck her. "You do want to do this, don't you? Oh, God, tell me you want it as much as I do."

Then she bit her lip, aghast at what she'd just revealed. Good Lord, she'd practically thrown herself at the poor man. She *had* thrown herself at him. What if he was only obliging her out of some misguided sense of pity or compassion?

Aden's half smile slid into a full-out grin. "I'd rather show you what I want. Let's start with your breasts, since you raised the subject first. Would that be acceptable to you?"

Cautiously, she nodded her head.

"Good." He inched down a bit, the movement dragging the length of his erection over the intimately sensitive spot between her thighs. Vivien arched into him, moaning with surprise as a gentle spasm contracted her inner flesh.

"Now, now," Aden murmured in a teasing voice. "You're getting ahead of yourself. I said we'd start with your breasts."

But then he flexed his hips, nudging her again in that perfect spot. She dug her fingers into his shoulders and closed her eyes, enjoying the tight sensation between her thighs. He was so big and hard. *Everywhere.* And she couldn't wait to feel him everywhere, too.

"Open your eyes, darling," he said.

Reluctantly, she dragged them open. As much as she wanted to look at him, with her eyes closed she could concentrate entirely on her burgeoning responses to his body.

Not that looking at him wasn't very pleasurable, too.

"Good girl," he murmured. "If only you were as obedient outside the bedroom."

Scowling, she pinched his shoulder. It was like pinching a block of wood. "That was a beastly thing to say, Aden. I always do what you tell me to do."

He braced himself on his forearms, gazing at her with an ironic lift to his eyebrows.

"Well, within reason," she amended.

"Let's get back to your breasts," he said dryly.

She had to repress the mad urge to giggle. "Yes, let's."

His gaze lowered to take them in, the nipples already flushed and starting to harden. She hated to admit it, but she tended to feel self-conscious about her breasts. They were rather small and the fact that she was so unfashionably slender didn't help much, either. Her stays did plump them up a bit—nothing like some of the other women in the *ton* who leaked over the tops of their bodices—but without them she knew they looked rather . . . lacking.

As Aden inspected her, Vivien started to get nervous. "Is something wrong?" she finally blurted out.

His gaze snapped up to her face. "What could possibly be wrong?"

She bit back a groan. Would she never learn to hold her tongue?

"My sweet." He dipped down and captured her mouth, gently sucking on her lower lip. Vivien wrapped her arms around his neck and opened to him, taking comfort from the soft tangle of their tongues.

Too soon, he broke away. "Are you feeling shy?"

She attempted a casual shrug, which wasn't easy when pinned beneath a dominating male.

"Tell me," he gently ordered. "I won't do anything else until you do."

"This is ridiculous," she grumbled as a hot flush climbed up her cheeks.

"Tell me anyway."

He seemed determined—and she knew just how determined Aden could be—so she gave in.

"My breasts. They're . . ." she trailed off, her cheeks blazing hot with embarrassment.

"They're what?" He looked confused.

"They're too small," she said through clenched teeth. "My modiste says I should have extra padding."

"Your modiste is an idiot," he scoffed. "And you're insane. You have the most beautiful breasts I've ever seen."

"You're not just saying that to make me feel better, are you?" Lord, she hated feeling so unsure of herself.

He shifted, keeping one long leg between her thighs but lifting his weight off her chest. "I'm telling you the truth, silly girl. But I do intend to make you feel better, too." He slid a hand over to capture her right breast, plumping it up between his long fingers. "Your tits are perfect, in fact. I could suck on them all night and still want more."

The deliberately crude words lanced through her like a bolt of electricity, pulling a startled gasp from her lips. But they made everything inside go soft, too. So did the sight of his tanned fingers on her pale skin as he softly stroked her breast.

"They're the perfect size," he murmured. "Just right for my hand and even better for my mouth. And I love your nipples. So pink, and look how hard they get when I squeeze them."

He pinched her nipple between the tips of his fingers, tugging softly. Vivien gasped, writhing as sensation streaked from the rigid tip to her core. Unconsciously, she lifted her hips, nudging her mound into his thigh.

"Sensitive, too, I see," he said. "And the stiffer they get, the more you'll feel. You're all cream and pink berries, my love. I can't wait to taste you."

Vivien writhed as he stroked and played with her flesh. Her body tightened with frustration, needing more than the light, teasing stroke of his fingers and the soft, wicked murmur of his words.

"Do all men talk so much while they're doing this?" she gasped.

Aden chuckled, ignoring her silly question, then gave her nipple a teasing pinch. If his leg hadn't been pinning her down, Vivien would have shot off the bed.

"You want more, I take it. Trust me, I'm happy to oblige."

Vivien sucked in a breath to scold him, but before she could utter a word, he bent and fastened his lips around her nipple. He pulled her into his mouth, sucking and drawing on the stiff tip. She shivered as he tasted and played, using lips, tongue, and even his teeth. When he nipped the tight, burning peak, she grabbed his hips and rocked against him, seeking relief from the tension pulling tight in her womb.

"Oh, oh, oh," she gasped, lifting into him as little ripples started pulsing deep inside.

With a hard suck, Aden pulled away. Vivien arched after him, desperate for the contact of his mouth. Gently, he pushed her down.

"Not so fast, sweetheart. I want you to enjoy this."

"I am enjoying it," she gritted out. "I'd like to keep on enjoying it, which I can't do if you stop."

His eyes glittered with seductive heat as he loomed over her. "I have no intention of stopping. But I would like to get the rest of your clothes off, and mine too, come to think of it."

"Oh, well. That makes sense, now that you mention it."

He made to shift off the bed, but then paused and leaned over to kiss her other breast. "I apologize for neglecting this one, but I promise I'll get to it shortly. And I trust we've answered the question of how I feel about your breasts."

Vivien gave a quick nod, blushing even hotter when he let out a quiet laugh.

"Good." He rolled off the bed and swiftly pulled his shirt over his head. A moment later, his breeches hit the floor. When he left his smalls on, Vivien let out a tiny sigh of relief. As exciting as all this was, it was rather intimidating, too. Aden had a powerful body, large, broad-shouldered, and layered with heavy muscle. His erection seemed to match the rest of his dimensions, by the looks of things. The linen obscured the details but not the size, clearly outlined through the fabric.

"And now for you," he murmured, gently tugging her night rail down her hips.

Feeling clumsy, Vivien helped him, trying not to flinch as he slowly drew the delicate cambric down her legs. He moved with great deliberation, his gaze devouring her and his mouth drawn into a hard, tense line.

"Christ," he said, almost prayerfully.

He tossed her garment in the direction of a nearby chair then brushed his hand down her stomach, stopping just above the golden thatch of hair at the apex of her thighs. His fingertips traced the pale blue veins running faintly underneath her skin, and Vivien trembled in response.

"You're like a fairy princess. So damn sweet and beautiful," he said, his voice falling to a husky rumble.

He stood by the bed, his expression registering a complicated mix of emotions. Something seemed to be holding him back, keeping him apart from her. The evidence of his body told her that he still wanted her, but his brow had darkened.

Vivien sat up, feeling shy but determined to prevent him from sounding the retreat. Not this time. "No one's ever called me a fairy princess before. I hope that pleases you."

Startled, his eyes darted to her face. "Pleases?" He placed a hand on his lightly furred chest. "Vivien, you stop my heart."

"Well, that doesn't sound good," she replied with a nervous chuckle.

As their gazes held, any impulse to laugh died on her tongue. Passion arced between them, desire rising on a hot tide. Succumbing to a need so much stronger than any she'd ever felt, Vivien lay back on the pillows. She drew her legs up, opening herself completely to him. His eyes narrowed to slits of dark intent, hawklike, as if sighting his prey.

His very willing prey, she might add.

"What are you doing all the way up there?" she whispered, holding out her arms.

Aden's lips parted in a heady smile. "Just enjoying the view, my sweet. It's an exceptionally fine one."

He reached out and slid his hands under her bottom, dragging her toward him. She yelped with surprise when he pulled her right to the edge of the high mattress. He spread her legs wide as they dangled, keeping her open by planting a hand on the inside of each thigh. In that position, she was even more exposed than before. It made her feel both vulnerable and confused.

"What are you doing?" she asked in a squeaky voice.

Another lascivious grin. "You'll see," he purred.

Mystification turned to astonishment when he dropped to his knees before her, cupped the globes of her bottom, and tilted her up. Then, while one big hand held her steady, the other spread wide her secret flesh, opening her to him even more.

It dimly occurred to Vivien that she should protest such outrageous manhandling, but any words she might have uttered strangled to death in her throat. It was the most intensely shocking and exciting moment of her life, which was saying a great deal, given the events of the last few weeks.

And then he gently parted her inner lips and came down on her with his mouth. The jolt of sensation that rocked through her lifted her straight off the bed. If Aden hadn't been holding on to her, she likely would have wound up on the floor.

"Oh, my God."

He pulled back. "Quiet, love. You'll wake the neighbors." He didn't bother to conceal the laughter in his voice.

Groaning, Vivien dropped back onto her elbows as Aden

moved in, slowly dragging the flat of his tongue across the wildly sensitive knot hidden in her blond curls. She felt the vibration in every nerve ending in her body, but especially deep in her womb. When he did it again, licking and then gently probing her with his tongue, she instinctively clamped her thighs against his shoulders as if trying to keep herself from falling apart.

His head came up and he watched her with glittering eyes, clearly enjoying himself. "Do you like it?" he asked as his finger gently rubbed through her damp folds.

When she didn't answer—likely because her brain was leaking out of her ears—he leaned forward and blew on her sensitive bud. Her muscles tightened another notch.

"Yes. God, yes," she gasped.

"I'm so glad." Then he spread her wide with his fingers again, leaning in to taste her once more.

Devour her, more like it. He licked her tender flesh, slicking his tongue into her sheath, then pulling back to fasten his mouth on her tight bud, sucking gently. As she moaned, writhing beneath him, he deepened the intensely intimate kiss. Pressure spiralled in a tight coil deep inside, then pulsed out in tiny, shivering spasms. She had, of course, been vaguely aware of the pleasures deep within her own body, but nothing she'd ever felt before came remotely close to this.

When he pressed his tongue hard against her stiff bud, Vivien almost jolted off the bed. Without lifting his mouth from her, Aden braced her legs over his shoulders and held her steady. She arched her back, throwing her arms wide and digging her fingers into the bedclothes to keep from flying apart.

"Oh, no," she sobbed, as the delicious pressure built to unbearable levels. "Stop, stop."

When Aden growled against her, she felt the vibration deep inside. "Like hell," he rasped. "You started this, Vivien, but I'm finishing it."

She wriggled beneath him, too excited to respond. But then his head came up.

"Unless you really want me to stop, that is," he said, sounding a little uncertain.

Vivien struggled up on her elbows, peering at him in confusion. Her mind was so dazed it took her a few moments to realize he was serious. Did he really think she wanted him to stop *now*?

"Aden, if you stop now, I'll beat you senseless with the poker." It didn't sound like much of a threat, given how winded she was, but it did the trick.

"Thank God," he muttered. "You had me worried."

She had to repress the impulse to laugh, but his consideration touched her deeply. Even as far as they'd gone, he would never force her to do anything she didn't want to do.

But when he pushed her back on the bed and stood up, her heart lurched. Was he stopping, after all? She'd simply die of frustration if he did.

After she beat him to death with the blasted fireplace poker, that is.

"I thought I told you not to stop," she burst out.

Aden winced at her shrill tone. "I'm not stopping. Trust me, Vivien. I'll get you there."

She was about to demand an explanation when he yanked down his smalls. Her mind went blank and the question died on her lips. He had called her a fairy princess, but he was a veritable god—a warrior god, at that. His lean waist, narrow hips, and powerful thighs were all on full display. Along with a *very* large erection jutting out from the nest of dark hair between his legs.

Vivien pressed a hand against her stomach, trying to quell the quiver deep inside. She couldn't decide whether to pounce on him or run screaming from the room.

"Don't worry," Aden said gently, clearly reading her thoughts. "It's not nearly as bad as you might think."

She dragged her gaze up to his face. The tight pull to his lips told her he was trying not to laugh.

"I have no idea what you're talking about," she said with as much dignity as a naked woman could muster. Part of her might be terrified, but she would cut her tongue out before she admitted it. After all, he was right. She *had* started it, and she intended to finish it, too.

His lips curved in a smile as he pulled her into his embrace. She let out a shivery moan when her stiff nipples rasped against the crisp hair on his chest.

"Liar," he whispered into her ear.

She ignored him, too caught up in rubbing her body against his. Fire seemed to ignite from every point of contact, and she couldn't help but luxuriate in the flames. She wrapped her arms around his neck and lifted one leg over his hip, bringing her mound into contact with his muscled thigh. She cried out as a voluptuous spasm rippled out from her core. For a few minutes, he let her rock against him, allowing her to build up the pleasure while his hands roamed over her body. He explored everywhere he could reach—fingers trailing down her spine to cup and shape her bottom, then drifting up to caress the sides of her breasts. All the while he murmured hot whispers in her ear, crude endearments and earthy praise that sent desire pulsing through her body.

Aden shifted and his erection slid between her thighs, dragging across her inner lips. Another bolt of sensation lanced through her. "Aden," she cried out, pulling herself tight against him.

Suddenly, Aden rolled onto his back, bringing her with him in a wild sprawl.

"You're ready, Vivien. I want you. Now."

She barely recognized his voice, so deep and guttural with lust.

He lifted her until she balanced astride him, her legs spread wide by his powerful body. They were plastered against each other, pelvis to pelvis, and she couldn't help rocking again, he felt so hard and wonderful beneath her.

Aden's hands clamped around her hips, holding her still. "That's delicious, love. But I want you to come while I'm inside you."

Planting her hands on Aden's shoulders to steady herself, Vivien stared down at him, too breathless to utter a word. He was so big and powerful beneath her, looking utterly the dangerous man he was. But his mouth—his beautiful mouth—was shaped in a tender smile, and his hands roamed over her body with a light, affectionate touch.

The enormity of the moment, the glory of it, swept through her, and she had to blink back tears.

"Ready?" he asked.

Unleashing a trembling smile, she nodded.

He guided her to her knees, positioned himself, then pressed her down so the tip of his erection nudged upward into her slick passage. Carefully, he pushed up even as she started the slow slide down. The delicate inner tissues burned, protesting the relentless stretch of his broad shaft. It was far from pleasant, but Aden soothed her with gentle murmurs and a soft, seductive play of hands over her breasts and belly, and along her thighs.

Finally, he was deep inside her. Vivien sat, awkwardly poised, trying not to wince as she adjusted to his invasion of her body. But as much as it stung, she couldn't help but be rocked by the indescribable intimacy of their connection, and by the mingling of lust and adoration on Aden's face. He couldn't seem to stop touching her, either, worshipping her body with his hands. That look on his face—so naked with emotion—in itself made the act worth it.

Then his dark eyes came into sharp focus and a line creased his brow. "Vivien," he finally said, "undo your braid."

It seemed an odd request at this point, but she was happy to oblige. Pulling the braid forward over her chest, she untied the ribbon at the end and began to unweave the strands.

"Take your time," he whispered. "I want to watch you."

Taking a deep breath—which caused the heat to flare brighter in his gaze—she nodded. Slowly, she unwound the thick strands, smoothing out any tangles. He watched intently, stroking her arms but holding his body still beneath her. The moment felt unbearably peaceful and sweet, the silence disturbed only by the sound of the low fire simmering in the hearth, or the distant closing of a door below in the inn.

By the time Vivien finished unravelling her braid, the burn between her thighs had eased, replaced by a rising need to move against him. She shifted, bringing her sex in contact with his pelvis. The swift cut of pleasure pulled a groan from her throat

"That's it," he murmured, spreading her hair over her breasts. "Move against me, sweet. However it feels best to you."

Tentatively, she began to rock up and down, searching for the closest fit. All the while, he played with her breasts, teasing the rigid tips and coming up on his elbows to lick her. When he sucked hard, pulling a nipple into his mouth, she sobbed with ecstasy and rocked forward.

Aden responded, surging into her. Heat swept through her body. Vivien opened her thighs wide and pressed down, concentrating fiercely on the tantalizing play of his hard flesh against her. But she needed more, and she sobbed out her need in incoherent bursts of words, clinging to his shoulders as she rocked. His head came up from her breasts and he buried his face in her neck, one hand moving down between their bodies.

And then he touched her, *right there,* right on the tight little bundle of flesh that ached with need. He slicked his fingers and rubbed her until she began to tremble in his arms. Contractions rippled from her womb, finally coalescing in luxurious spasms that pulled from her mouth a startled cry. When she arched back, letting the waves wash over her, Aden pressed a hot kiss to her breastbone, right above her heart.

Then, so quickly it seemed a blur, he pulled her up and off, falling onto his back and bringing her with him. He clamped his hands on her bottom and ground against her, his erection pulsing against her belly, spilling his seed between them.

And in the aftermath of that shattering moment, when everything that was to come was still unknown, Aden cradled her against his chest.

Holding her as if she belonged there forever.

Chapter Twenty-Nine

Vivien imagined she must look like the most pedestrian of wives as she strolled with Aden toward the spa in the center of the village of St. Clement—several years married, and with a husband who resembled nothing so much as a prosperous shopkeeper who'd brought his ailing spouse to partake of the waters. As far as anyone could tell, they were among the most boring couples on the planet.

Walking down the street with Aden, she realized how well he'd chosen his profession. He possessed a remarkable ability to fade into the background, obscuring his masculine strength and power with a slightly stoop-shouldered pose, quiet speech, and genteel but nondescript clothing. It was a remarkably simple and straightforward method of disguise.

As for her appearance . . . well, the less said, the better. She looked awful, decked out in muddy-looking colors, bonnets that managed to be both prim and enormously ugly, and those blasted silver-rimmed spectacles. Her family and friends would be aghast if they saw her so shabbily attired, and she winced whenever she caught sight of herself in a mirror. But Aden had insisted repeatedly that she needed to preserve her disguise, attracting as little notice as possible.

Engaging notice hadn't been a problem, since he'd practically locked her up in the house since they'd arrived in St. Clement. Confined indoors with only the servants and Aden to talk to— and he wasn't doing much talking these days—Vivien had finally put her foot down after four days, demanding she be allowed to leave the house.

She glanced up at the man escorting her down High Street. Aden's face still wore a grim, resigned cast, signalling he didn't much like her venturing out in public. Initially, he'd flat-out refused to escort her into the village. Vivien had lost her temper then, insisting that she'd lose her mind if she didn't have someone to talk to.

"You can talk to me," Aden had snapped over his paper at the breakfast table. "Or the servants. I'm sure they'd be happy to talk to you."

Vivien had reminded him that all the servants were in Dominic's employ as bodyguards, which made them doggedly watchful and reluctant to engage in conversation. Even the woman assigned to Vivien as her maid clearly saw her role more as guardian than servant, keeping watch like some modern-day Argus until Vivien felt ready to jump out of her skin.

"As for you," she'd stormed at Aden, "you've barely said two words to me since we arrived. I can't for the life of me imagine *why*," she ended on a sarcastic note.

He'd had the grace to flush a dull red. Since that fateful, glorious night at the inn, Aden had retreated into an even more irritating version of his impassive self, leaving Vivien to wonder what she'd done wrong. She'd tried to get an answer out of him, but he'd evaded any discussion of their fiery encounter, telling her they'd talk about it when she was safely returned to London. She didn't believe that for a minute, but she was too embarrassed—and hurt—to raise the issue again. That night had changed everything for her, and she'd thought Aden might possibly feel the same.

But with every passing day more doubt crept in, and Vivien began to fear she'd made a dreadful, soul-shattering mistake. Her long days and nights in the spacious manor house in St. Clement might be safe and comfortable, but for Vivien it was rapidly becoming a lonely and boring interlude in a life that had somehow ended up in the ditch.

At least Aden had let her out of her gilded cage this morning, and she was determined to make the most of it. If that meant ignoring the ill-tempered and overbearing man who might very well break her heart, so be it. If there was anything Vivien had learned over the years, it was how to hold her head high when her entire world was crumbling about her. Aden might have stolen her heart, but he would most certainly not steal her pride.

She stopped in front of a milliner's shop where two elderly women were inspecting the hats displayed in the window. The hats were quite ugly, but not nearly as ugly as the one Vivien wore, so as far as she was concerned they merited a look. But as she joined the other two women at the window, she heard Aden breathe out an exasperated sigh.

Forcing a pleasant smile on her face, she cast a glance at him over her shoulder. "Is something the matter, Mr. Parker?" she asked, emphasizing the false name they'd adopted. "Are you unwell?"

"Not at all, my dear. Why do you ask?" he responded in a terse voice.

She eyed his jaw. If it was any tighter, it would likely shatter into a million pieces. "I thought I heard you sigh, but perhaps I was mistaken." She adopted a worried frown. "Or perhaps it was your dyspepsia. You did have rather a large meal last night, with a second helping of roast beef. I'm convinced your doctor would not have been pleased."

"Oh, my," cried one of the elderly ladies, who had been shamelessly eavesdropping. She was tall and remarkably thin, with pale eyes and a kind face. "Too much red meat is *fatal* for dyspepsia. My dear sir, you must listen to your wife. Why, my poor husband was also in the habit of overindulging in his food." She let out a dramatic sigh. "The consequences were dire, and I'm afraid Mr. Simmons was taken from this life prematurely, God rest his soul."

Her companion, a stout, commanding-looking woman, rolled her eyes. "For heaven's sake, Sally, your husband drank himself to death." She held up a hand to forestall the other woman's protest. "Richard was my brother and I loved him dearly, but we all know he spent a good part of each day dipping too deep. Didn't make him any less of a lovely man, but there's no point in denying the truth of it."

Mrs. Simmons flashed Vivien and Aden an apologetic smile. "Yes, well, there's no need to air our dirty laundry in public, Dorothy. Besides, this nice young man doesn't look to be suffering from dyspepsia at all."

When the elderly woman ran a practiced and very appreciative eye over Aden's muscular frame, Vivien had to bite the inside of her cheeks to keep from laughing. Especially after she snuck a glance at him and took in the rigid cast of his features.

The other woman, the one named Dorothy, tilted her head and also ran an assessing gaze over him, obviously sizing him up as a prime piece of horseflesh.

"You're right about that, Sally. Dyspepsia doesn't seem to be the right diagnosis." She cast a swift glance at Vivien's hat and nodded wisely. "I'd be willing to bet your lord and master looks so sour because you're fixing to put a dent in his purse with the purchase of a new hat. And why shouldn't you, too? Miss Theresa makes the best hats in town, and you're clearly in need of a new one."

Vivien found herself unable to respond, mostly because she was trying desperately not to laugh. Aden, however, had gone from annoyed to grim, which made the whole situation even funnier. One of England's most dangerous spies, set back on his heels by two little old ladies.

"Dorothy, you're embarrassing the poor man," Mrs. Simmons gently scolded. "Whatever will they think of us? That is surely no way to greet newcomers to our fair village."

"Oh, Lord, I suppose you're right," the other woman said, comically scrunching up her nose. "You mustn't mind me at all, sir. As anybody in town will tell you, I will run off at the mouth at the drop of a hat."

"Please don't apologize," Vivien said. "We've only arrived in your charming village a few days ago, and we've yet to make anyone's acquaintance. I'm very pleased to meet you."

And as soon as the words were out of her mouth, she realized it was true. Two weeks ago, she could never have imagined craving the company of what appeared to be two genteelly impoverished country widows. But they had cheerful faces and spoke kindly and without affectation. If the last few weeks had taught Vivien anything, it was that many of the people in her life—including some of her family—were lacking in those wholesome virtues.

"Goodness, where are our manners, Dorothy," cried Mrs. Simmons. "We have yet to introduce ourselves. As you have no doubt already guessed, I am Mrs. Simmons. This is my sister-in-law, Mrs. Pettigrew."

Mrs. Simmons, for all her age, gave them a graceful bow, while Mrs. Pettigrew bobbed up and down like a friendly, plump robin.

"I'm very pleased to meet you," Vivien repeated with a warm smile. "I'm Mrs. Parker, and this is my husband, Mr. Parker."

Mrs. Pettigrew levelled a dazzling grin at Aden. "Yes, and a fine, strapping man you are. I've always had a soft spot for big men, like my dear, departed husband. It's a pleasure to meet you as well, Mr. Parker."

Aden finally shook of his irritated demeanor. "Thank you, madame," he said, bowing gravely over her hand. "The pleasure is mine, I assure you."

He extended another bow in Mrs. Simmons's direction. That lady pressed a hand to her thin chest and looked smitten. "Oh, Dorothy," she cried, "doesn't he have the most beautiful manners? He puts me in mind of my own dear Richard, who was the most charming man one could ever hope to know."

"When he wasn't jug-bitten, of course," Mrs. Pettigrew said in a cheerful voice. "But, as Sally says, there's no need to air all the dirty laundry in public now, is there?"

"Indeed no," Aden said with a solemn demeanor.

This time, Vivien heard the laughter in his voice. The knot in her stomach, the one that had been living there since they'd slept together, loosened up. She gave him a tentative smile and his lips quirked up in response. That smile actually reached his eyes, setting spark to the glow that had been a raging fire between them just a few nights ago.

But a moment later, the sober Mr. Parker again took up residence.

"My dear ladies," he said, addressing the two widows. "You must excuse us, but my wife must not stand out any longer in the chill. We should be on our way."

"Oh, you must be going to the spa," said Mrs. Pettigrew. "We're going that way ourselves. We'd be happy to escort you." She gave Aden a conspiratorial wink. "No one knows St. Clement better than we do. We can point out all the prosy old bores so you can avoid them."

"Oh, yes," Mrs. Simmons chimed in earnestly. "We know all the latest *on-dits* too. If you want to know *anything* about anyone in our fair town, you need only enquire with us. Why,

Dorothy is so good at winkling out information, you'd think she was a spy for the Crown."

"That is indeed a very useful talent," Vivien said in a strangled voice. She didn't dare look at Aden, knowing she would no longer be able to contain herself if she did. Instead, she simply took his arm and smiled as the two ladies fell into step beside her.

Unfortunately, her erstwhile husband's arm felt like a block of hardwood under her gloved hand. The muscles were bunched with tension, clearly signalling his irritation over the attention of her newfound friends. He may have been amused a few moments ago, but the brief display of warmth had vanished.

Fortunately, he had impeccable manners, for which Vivien was profoundly thankful. She was desperate for company and could hardly believe that two old ladies constituted a threat to her security. But to Aden, it seemed that everything under the sun was cause for suspicion. It seemed a tiresome way to live.

"You've clearly come to our little town to avail yourselves of the waters. I fancied you looked a little peaked," said Mrs. Pettigrew, giving Vivien the once-over. "Why, you're as skinny as a post and rather pale, my dear, if you don't mind my saying so."

"No, I don't mind." She didn't either. Vivien was used to the subtle cut and thrust of the *ton,* but a sudden vision of Mrs. Pettigrew let loose in that milieu, mowing down aristocrats like so many stalks of hay, sprang into her mind. She quite liked the idea, and suddenly life in the town of St. Clement didn't seem so dreary.

"My wife has been feeling poorly, which is why she will not be engaging in many activities or visits during our stay," Aden interjected in a voice guaranteed to dampen enthusiasm. "Her doctor insists she get plenty of rest and quiet."

Vivien stifled the urge to bash him over the head, but that

didn't mean she couldn't express her displeasure by other means. "Oh, but my love," she said in a soulful voice. "You remember that Dr. Hunter *insisted* I needed some wholesome activities and cheerful company to prevent me from falling into melancholy. Surely you have not forgotten how anxious I became the last time you tried to lock me up in the house."

Mrs. Pettigrew and Mrs. Simmons cast horrified looks first at Aden, then at Vivien. Vivien dared a sideways glance at her protector. Without moving a muscle on his face, he still managed to convey righteous outrage.

"You exaggerate, my love," he said stiffly. "You know that my first concern is always your well-being."

She could appreciate that, but his desire to hide her away from the world—even in so safe a place as St. Clement—was rather trying.

"He doesn't really lock me up," Vivien confessed to their companions. "But he does tend to fuss and nag quite a bit. I know he doesn't look it, but he's really rather old-maidish when it comes to my health."

"There's no need to bore our new friends with such trifling domestic details," Aden said. "But I'll be happy to discuss the arrangements for your continuing care when we return home."

Vivien clearly heard the implied threat in his voice, and it cheered her right up. In her limited experience, whenever she and Aden had a fight it usually led to kissing, and that had the potential to lead to other pleasant things.

Well, except for when they got attacked by a gang of ruffians, that is.

"What exactly are you suffering from, Mrs. Parker?" Mrs. Pettigrew asked with concern. "We have two very good doctors in St. Clement. On our recommendation, Dr. Puppleworth will be more than happy to see you."

"That won't be necessary," Aden hastily interjected. "My

wife is merely suffering from fatigue. She simply needs a good rest."

Mrs. Simmons winced with sympathy. "Do you have children, Mrs. Parker? I find children to be very fatiguing."

Vivien affected a wistful sigh. "No, I'm afraid my husband and I have been denied that blessing."

"Oh, look," Aden said, pointing across the street to a shop with a display of books in the window. "There's the circulating library. Perhaps we should go in and sign up while we're passing by."

The women ignored him.

"No children and suffering from melancholy, eh?" Mrs. Pettigrew said with a shrewd look in her kind eyes. "I think we know exactly what your problem is, Mrs. Parker."

"We do?" said Mrs. Simmons.

Mrs. Pettigrew leaned close to her sister-in-law. "Breeding problems," she announced in a penetrating whisper. She cut Aden another glance. "But I can't see that he's the problem."

Vivien could feel Aden's entire body vibrating like a tuning fork, but she was having too much fun to end his misery by bringing a halt to the discussion. "Alas, you have deduced our tragic situation," she said with a dramatic sigh. "My doctor is hopeful that the healing waters will restore me and allow us to fulfill our fondest wish." She finished by gazing at Aden with soulful adoration.

He gave her a tight smile, though his eyes promised retribution.

"You've come to the right place," Mrs. Pettigrew said gaily. "But you must take the waters every day, and put some meat on your bones, too. Which means you must come to tea with us on a regular basis. Our cook makes the best scones and plum cakes in the county."

"We should be delighted," Vivien responded before Aden could level any objections. Much to her surprise, she found the situation not only entertaining but strangely comforting. No one knew her, or had any expectations regarding her behavior. It was . . . a relief.

"Splendid," cried Mrs. Pettigrew. "And then we can introduce you to—"

"Dorothy," Mrs. Simmons cut in. "There's Mrs. Colman, waving at us from the apothecary shop."

"Oh, bother," Mrs. Pettigrew sighed. She gave Vivien an apologetic smile. "Forgive us, my dear. Why don't you go along, and we'll catch up to you in a few minutes."

After the two women hurried away, Vivien braced herself for a thorough scold. Instead, Aden simply gave her an arch look. "You're lucky I don't take you home right now and put you over my knee, *Wife.*"

She opened her mouth to retort but closed it when she realized his mock threat sounded a great deal more enticing than it should.

"Vivien, I understand you're lonely," he continued in a serious voice. "But you must be careful. It won't do for people to gossip about us. We're trying to maintain a low profile, remember?"

She gave him a little jab in the ribs. "Firstly, no two women could be more completely innocent. Secondly, we're in the middle of nowhere. How anyone could figure out who we really are is beyond me."

"You'd be surprised."

"Yes, I would be very surprised. You know how grateful I am for your concern, but I begin to think this is excessive. We must be entirely safe here."

He stopped in front of a tobacconist's shop, only pretending to peruse the window display. She could see his frustration in the hard set to his jaw and in the way the skin stretched over his cheekbones.

"Do you truly not think Prince Ivan will take the most

desperate of measures to achieve his aim?" he asked. "For all intents and purposes the man is mad, Vivien. You must never forget that, or you will come to a bad end." He cast her a brooding glance. "Do you understand? You are not to get too close to anyone in this village or share information like you did just now."

Her fragile, hopeful mood evaporated. "Yes, I understand. I am to be more like you. That shouldn't be too hard, because I'll just scowl at everyone and refuse to have civil conversations."

He started to scowl at her but then wiped the expression from his face. "Don't be ridiculous. I do nothing of the sort."

"You do. You close yourself off from everyone in your life, even your mother. Everyone can see how much she wants to mend whatever it is between you, but you keep pushing her away."

She pulled her hand from his elbow and made a great show of retying her bonnet. When she finished, she held onto her reticule with both hands so she didn't have to touch him again.

"I don't understand you," she said past the choking sensation in her throat. "You seem determined to push away anyone who wishes to be close to you." She forced out the sticky words. "Including me."

He grimaced and took her by the elbow, leading her around the corner and into the village square. It was fronted on three sides by shops and the town's only coaching inn, and by the pump room and spa on the other. Vivien tried to dredge up interest in the classically designed buildings, but frustration and a creeping sense of melancholy weighed her down.

And now Aden had obviously decided to reinstate the silent treatment. Good thing the waters at the spa were a cure for nervous ailments, because she would need at least a gallon to cut through her anxious and gloomy mood.

Or a large brandy when they returned to the manor house.

Aden's steps slowed as they approached the grand marble portico. "It's necessary," he said rather abruptly.

Her mind blanked. "What is?"

"It's necessary for me to keep a distance from . . . those who would be close to me."

Her heart constricted at his choice of words. "Why?"

"For my work. To maintain my focus."

She pondered that for several seconds, then rejected it with a growing sense of anger. "I still don't see why. Sir Dominic doesn't act like that, and he's a spy, too."

"Vivien—"

She flapped a hand. "Don't bother to deny it, and don't try to change the subject. The point is, Sir Dominic *does* have people in his life, and you don't."

When she stopped in the middle of the square, he was forced to come to a halt too. His expression—grim and haunted—caught her low in the gut. She realized for the first time just how wide was the chasm between them.

"Why are you like this, Aden? What happened to you?" she whispered.

For a few seconds, his eyes blazed with emotion, but soon he was again the man behind the impassive mask.

"Trust me, my dear," he said. "You do not want to know."

Chapter Thirty

Surprisingly, Aden enjoyed Mrs. Pettigrew's dinner party. Attending an evening where two-thirds of the guests were in their dotage turned out to be oddly relaxing and he'd enjoyed watching Vivien charm her way into their good-natured hearts.

More than once in the last few weeks, as he adjusted to the slower rhythms of village life, he'd found himself more at peace than he'd been in a long time. The only dangers that threatened were tumbling off one's horse or tripping over a loose cobblestone.

Or succumbing to the temptation that Vivien posed to his self-control. That *was* a considerable danger, both to his head and his heart.

Aden stood quietly by the front door of Mrs. Pettigrew's town house, on a small but pretty crescent at the top of the hill overlooking the village. His erstwhile wife was saying her good-byes to her hostess and Mrs. Simmons, who'd made good on their promise to take Vivien on as their special project. They'd introduced her to their friends, spent every afternoon with her at the spa, and had invited her and Aden to dine three times since their arrival two weeks ago. Their attentions had kept Vivien both busy and happy.

Initially, he'd opposed the friendships but had finally

decided it made sense to keep her occupied. Now she didn't constantly fret, or study him with a puzzled, almost lost expression in her big blue eyes. He knew Vivien still struggled to understand his silent retreat after their insanely misguided sexual encounter at the inn. He'd been the worst kind of fool to touch her, but she'd been so vulnerable and sweet and so bloody beautiful that he'd given in to temptation, swept away on a tide of emotion that made *him* feel vulnerable too.

A vulnerable spy usually ended up a dead spy, so that meant keeping his guard up and keeping Vivien out. Because whenever he touched her, his brain resembled nothing so much as runny French brie and his finely tuned instincts deserted him with unseemly haste.

So, he'd let her make friends and enjoy herself, and it had surprised the hell out of him how quickly she'd taken to village life. Without the demands of her selfish family dragging her down and safe under his care, she'd blossomed.

Not just blossomed. She sparkled like a glittering night sky, and Aden dreaded the moment she would no longer be part of his life. She'd radiated light and heat into the dark, cold corners of his soul, but both would disappear on the day he had to walk away from her.

That day was coming soon.

"Take care of our sweet girl, Mr. Parker," Mrs. Pettigrew said as she snugged Vivien's cloak up around her throat. "She's looking ever so much healthier, but the night air can be treacherous."

Aden smiled. "You may be sure of it, ma'am. My wife's well-being is always my first concern."

With a little jolt, he realized his practiced comments were actually nothing less than the truth. A world without her had rapidly become a world in which Aden was losing interest.

Vivien planted an affectionate kiss on Mrs. Pettigrew's

plump cheek. "You all fuss too much. I told Mr. Parker this morning that I've never felt better."

Mrs. Simmons nodded wisely. "I told you the waters and our clean, fresh air would clear up your little problem." She waggled her eyebrows. "In fact, I wouldn't be surprised if in the next several weeks we receive some very happy news."

Aden's brain stuttered. He truly was losing his edge. "What happy news?"

Mrs. Pettigrew and Mrs. Simmons both eyed him askance. Vivien seemed to be inspecting the plasterwork on the ceiling, perfectly conveying the silent message that he was an idiot.

He was, at least around her these days.

"You know," Mrs. Pettigrew prompted, directing a vague gesture at Vivien's midsection. "The *breeding* problem."

Aden felt himself redden. "Oh, that," he said in a faint voice.

"Yes, that," Vivien responded dryly.

"I suggest you go home and have a *discussion* about it," Mrs. Pettigrew said with a sly grin. "I'm sure the results will be very *fruitful*."

Mrs. Simmons clapped a hand over her mouth to hold back giggles as Aden hastily bundled Vivien out the door. He'd rather go unarmed into a den of cutthroats than discuss sex with a pair of elderly widows—especially sex with Vivien.

Who was still snickering when they settled into their waiting carriage.

"My dear Mrs. Parker," Aden gently mocked. "We need to have a chat about your new friends. I hardly think they exhibit the right tone of mind for a woman as genteel as yourself. Whatever would your mother say?"

Her smile dimmed. "My mother would be appalled to see me keeping such company, I'm sorry to say. She would no doubt label them vulgar mushrooms."

Aden had learned that only one thing had the power to truly

unsettle Vivien and that was her family—especially her mother. It didn't take a genius to deduce that Lady Blake had neglected her for years, and that Vivien keenly felt that lack of maternal affection.

"I'm sorry," he said. "I didn't mean to distress you."

She gave a sad little shrug and fell into a pensive silence. After a minute, her elegant eyebrows puckered together in a frown, and her fingers absently played with the tasselled ties of her cloak.

"What is it?" he asked. "Tell me, and I'll fix it."

Vivien let out a choked laugh that sounded more like a sob. "It's nothing. I'm just being silly."

Her weak attempt at a smile only made her look more forlorn. Aden ordered himself to let it go, but he loathed seeing her unhappy. She'd accused him of closing himself off from the people in his life, and that was true. But keeping her out had been a struggle from the first moment he'd laid eyes on her, and he felt the battle slipping away from him. It was a battle he'd started to want to lose, too. Anything was preferable to seeing her looking so lost and alone.

He moved across to join her. She jumped, staring up at him in surprise as he settled his arm around her shoulders. When she shivered, he pulled her close.

Tipping up her chin, Aden pressed a gentle kiss to her brow. "Tell me what troubles you, sweet. Let me help."

Her hands fluttered up to rest on his chest. The slender fingers, sheathed in soft, pale kid, trembled lightly against him as if part of her was afraid to touch him.

"I'm being a ninny," she whispered.

He bent his head to hear. "Why do you think that?"

She swallowed hard, like a child forcing back tears, and he wondered how long it had been since anyone had truly listened to her or put her needs first.

"I've been happy here," she said. "It's not that I've forgotten about Prince Ivan or that I've stopped worrying about my family. But it's been so peaceful, and everyone has been terribly kind and affectionate." She managed a wavering smile. "And Sir Dominic's servants spoil me to an outrageous degree. I find I'm becoming quite selfish, and I confess it concerns me. Some days I wish we could stay here forever."

She deserved spoiling, but only Vivien would worry about succumbing to it. That was part of her charm. Despite her beauty and her many talents, she was innately modest and kind, drawing others to her with a laughing ease that slipped past the most hardened of shields. Even Dominic's staff—all retired agents who now ran this safe house—had fallen victim to her charm. Every day, Aden watched them trip all over themselves in their eagerness to make her happy.

"You deserve a little spoiling," he said. "It should not concern you."

A sigh shuddered through her, vibrating from her body into his. "I'll miss it when we return to London. Life is so much simpler here."

She frowned, as if puzzling something out. It took all his restraint not to kiss away the frown lines creasing her pale brow.

"People here are so unaffected . . . and more honest than in London," she said. "I know that's not fair, and I am fortunate to have many dear friends there who care for me." She blew out an exasperated breath. "It doesn't make any sense, I know. People are people, wherever they are."

"It makes perfect sense. The *ton* has its attractions, but honesty and unaffected behavior don't number among them." He tapped her nose. "You know that, too. You're just too good-natured to say it."

She gave him a fleeting smile. "There's another reason I'll be sorry to return home."

He settled her more comfortably against him, relishing the feel of her lithe body back in his arms. "And what is that?"

She sucked in a deep breath, as if gathering her courage. "I'll miss you, of course. I'm afraid that once this is over, I'll never see you again."

The quiet yearning in her voice twisted his heart into knots. He closed his eyes, shaken by his own fierce desire to return her emotion.

Christ. He opened his eyes. "You don't know what you're saying."

She flinched and tried to draw away. He tightened his arms around her.

"Forgive me," she said. "I had no right to say that. You mustn't think I expect anything from you. You never said—"

He grasped her chin, forcing her to look at him. "You should expect things from me," he said in a harsh voice. "You deserve them. Unfortunately, I don't deserve you."

Her lips parted and she trembled in his arms. He knew what he should do—he should soothe her with kind words and platitudes, assurances that life would soon return to normal. But that wasn't what she needed. She needed *him,* and without the barriers he'd grown so adept at constructing. His mother, Dominic, his half siblings and friends, his fellow agents—those he could keep out.

But not Vivien. Not anymore.

He saw the pain of rejection in her beautiful, sad eyes. He recognized that look since he suffered from the same malady. He'd been plagued by it ever since he'd found out who he was—an unwanted child, the inconvenient bastard of a pitiful excuse for a man.

She scowled at him. "Really, Aden, for an intelligent man you sometimes say the most ridiculous things."

Her unexpected response pulled a rusty laugh from his

throat. No wonder he wanted her so much. No one else could make him laugh, or lighten his cares the way she did.

"I know, my sweet," he said in an apologetic tone. "Sometimes I even confuse myself."

The lonely expression faded from her eyes, and a bit of her sparkle returned. "Dear me, It would seem you should do something about that."

He tipped her face up, stroking her stubborn little chin with his gloved hand. "Any suggestions, Mrs. Parker?"

"You can start by kissing me, Mr. Parker."

Vivien barely noticed the carriage drawing to a halt in front of the manor house, too lost in the hot tease of Aden's mouth. When she'd worked up the courage to ask him to kiss her, for a horrible moment she'd thought he'd refuse. He'd embraced her to comfort her— he was very good at that—but she was afraid nothing could break through his wall of reserve.

But then his gaze had flared with desire. He'd taken her mouth then, swooping down with a passion that pushed her head back against his arm. His body enveloped hers, a cage of flesh and bone from which she longed never to escape.

Their kiss had quickly grown heated and wet, drowning her in pleasure. Her hands had crept up his chest, slipping inside his coat and fumbling for buttons. He'd stopped her by pulling her body tight against him even as he murmured a warning against her lips. But he hadn't broken away from her.

Until now.

"Vivien, I have no intention of making love to you in a carriage," he said in a firm voice. "That tends to not end very well, as you recall."

Well, *that* ruined the moment.

Sighing, she took his hand as he helped her down the coach steps. She'd had every hope of convincing Aden to make love to her again, but the opportunity had probably passed. Fuming irrationally about frustrating spies and men who kissed like the devil and then walked away, she stomped up the marble steps to the house and waited for him to open the door.

As he stood at her back—in fact, he pressed all along the length of her back—Aden let out a soft chuckle.

"Oh, ye of little faith," he murmured in her ear.

His breath tickled and she couldn't help shivering.

After a swift glance up and down the street, he unlocked the door and ushered her inside. As he helped her off with her cloak, MacDonnell silently appeared from the back of the house. Vivien smiled at the man who served as butler to the establishment and Aden's second-in-command. He was more than a simple servant, as was every one of the staff in this oddest of houses. They all superficially looked the domestic part, but they worked for Sir Dominic and their sworn mission was to protect her. If her maid was less than adept at fixing hair and the cook occasionally burned the eggs, it was a small price to pay for their vigilance and dedication.

"Would you like me to send Martha up, Mrs. Parker?" MacDonnell asked as he took her wrap.

Vivien smiled. Even within the house their fictional identities were maintained. She had initially objected, thinking it silly, but Aden had insisted.

"That won't be necessary," Aden replied. "I'll be helping Mrs. Parker tonight."

MacDonnell's left eyebrow ticked up a notch as he stared at Aden. Aden stared right back, as if daring him to issue a challenge. After a few seconds, the butler inclined his head and Vivien could breathe again. More than anything, she hoped Aden's directive meant what she thought it meant, but the last few weeks had taught her not to take anything for granted.

"Bunch of bloody old ladies," Aden muttered as he steered

her up the stairs and down the narrow corridor leading to the bedrooms. The house was silent, its peaceful atmosphere wrapping around them with sense of solidity Vivien could almost touch. She meant every word she'd said to Aden. Life in this house and in St. Clement had become a precious gift, and she dreaded the day when it would end.

When they reached her bedroom, Vivien turned and rested her back on the door.

"Are you coming in?" She studied him, unable to read the expression in his hooded eyes. So much about him confused her, but what she wanted from him rang in her heart with the clarion call of church bells.

He braced a hand on the door frame, hemming her in. "Do you want me to?"

Before she could answer, he feathered a kiss along her jaw. She groaned and tipped her head back, thunking it on the hard oak.

"Vivien, don't hurt yourself," he said with amused exasperation.

She fumbled behind her for the doorknob. "You'll just have to kiss it all better."

It took a few seconds for her to twist the knob because his mouth was back on her again, kissing the sensitive underside of her chin. But she finally managed to get it open and they stumbled in. Giggling, Vivien grasped the lapels of his coat to keep from falling even as his arms whipped around her to hold her up. She went up on tiptoe to brush her lips over his hard, beautiful mouth. Even as she reached for more, he wrapped his big hands around her shoulders and gently pushed a few inches between them.

"Are you sure?" he asked in a husky rumble. His gaze bored into her. "You know something of what I am and who I am, but only a little. I cannot tell you what will happen after we leave this place. All I can do is—"

She pressed her gloved fingers to his lips. "If you want to be with me as much as I want to be with you, then that is enough." It would never be enough, but if that was all she could have then she would take it and gladly suffer the pain that came later.

His eyes burned with a raw, sexual heat and something she prayed was more. Her body answered, desire beating in a heavy pulse in the secret places of her body.

"Christ, I could die from wanting you," he rasped as his fingers played with the old-fashioned ruffle on her bodice.

She smiled and drifted out of his reach. As she moved, she drew the gloves from her arms, pulling them off in a slow, deliberate slide. She knew he found her body attractive—even beautiful. Their night at the inn had been a gift of passion, freeing her from inhibitions and calling forth a sensuality she hadn't known existed within her.

Aden stood apart from her, legs braced in a wide, masculine stance, his hands clenched against his thighs. He seemed rooted to the floor, every muscle held rigid with exacting discipline. But his eyes tracked her with a predator's gleam.

Lazily, she undressed, easing buttons through loops, drawing out pins, untying tapes. Her gown whispered to the floor and then she kicked off her shoes. Next, she sat on a small padded bench and slowly lifted the hem of her chemise. With trembling fingers, she untied her garters and pushed her stockings to the floor.

When she looked up to meet Aden's gaze, the breath snagged in her throat. He hadn't moved but he looked ready to pounce. A nervous shiver snaked up her spine even as her body softened and grew damp, preparing for his invasion.

With a hesitant smile, she stood and turned her back to him. As she pulled the pins from her hair, letting it tumble free, she glanced over her shoulder. "I need help with my stays," she said, her voice a soft tremble.

He moved swiftly. His fingers undid her laces and he eased her stays over her hips and down her legs. As she stepped out of them, he let his hands glide up under her chemise, stroking his way to her bottom. He let out a soft growl as he shaped her. "You have a perfect arse, Vivien. Do you know that?"

She giggled, thinking it the silliest and yet somehow the most profound compliment she'd ever heard. But the giggling stopped when a big hand flat on the small of her back pushed her forward, forcing her to grab one of the mahogany posts on the old-fashioned canopied bed.

Clutching it tightly, she sucked in excited breaths as his hands roamed her body. He stroked her bottom, the backs of her thighs, and between her legs, teasing his fingers through the fluff of hair. His hands held her captive with pleasure, drawing moisture and heat from her body until she was slick and desperate for more.

Then he leaned in, brushing the hair from the back of her neck and planting soft kisses down her spine. She wanted to weep, overcome by the beauty of his touch. Aden's hands could kill—she'd seen the evidence of that—but with her, those hands had given only sheltering strength. Now they touched her with a tenderness that held a different kind of power, one that bound her to him forever.

When his fingers slipped between the folds of her inner lips, she gasped and clutched at the post, going up on her toes. Carefully, he parted her, slipping inside. Vivien moaned and pushed back, craving a deeper contact.

"Not so fast, love," he crooned, withdrawing from her.

She whimpered an incoherent protest. Gently, he turned her. His dark gaze burned, sultry and heavy-lidded, but a smile curved his lips.

Vivien scowled at him, crossing her arms underneath her breasts. "Don't tease me, you brute."

His gaze drifted to her chest. "I wouldn't dream of it. But I would dream of getting you out of the rest of your clothes."

A moment later and her chemise drifted to the floor. His hands returned to her body, stroking and playing even as she started pulling at his clothes, desperate to feel his skin against hers. She fought him until he finally capitulated with a hoarse laugh, practically tearing his clothes off while she climbed onto the bed, shaking with an unholy combination of lust and love.

When he joined her, they sank into the deep tester mattress, their bodies cleaving, their mouths a breath apart for a timeless moment, fraught and aching with emotion.

Then he began. He made love to every inch of her, tasting her, drinking her in, his mouth drawing one exquisite sensation after another. When he moved between her thighs, his fingers gently opening her for that most intimate of kisses, she felt his smile press against the inside of her thigh. He stilled, leaving her suspended and one step away from falling into a well of pleasure.

"What is it?" she managed, gasping with frustration.

When he didn't answer, she forced herself up on her elbows. He lay sprawled between her legs, his broad shoulders pushing her wide. Seeing him there, so naked and powerful, his fingers gently combing through her blond fluff, was insanely erotic. With that part of her brain that was still able to think—a very tiny part—Vivien judged it a wonder that she didn't swoon on the spot.

With a lascivious smile curling his lips, he patted her nest of curls. "I like to look at you, all golden and creamy white." Then his fingers carefully parted her. "And this part, too. So pink and wet, so pretty."

Then he leaned in and sucked, and Vivien collapsed with a moan on the pillows. He took her to paradise—twice—before crawling up her body. His face had taken on a hard cast, his gaze scorching her. Cradling her head under his arm, he scissored her legs wide with his powerful thighs. Then, with a smooth thrust, he entered her. Sparks of sensation shot up her spine and she arched to pull him more deeply into her.

His eyelids closed and intense pleasure swept over his face. Then he opened his eyes, trapping her in the fathomless depths of his entrancing dark gaze.

And he moved, riding her. Slowly at first, drawing her into a sleepy haze of passion. But it wasn't enough. She dug her nails into his shoulders, into his hips and buttocks, silently egging him on. As he rocked into her, grinding pelvis to pelvis, he lavished kisses on her cheeks, her mouth, her neck, her breasts—everywhere he could reach. His mouth devoured and yet cherished with a tenderness that filled up all the empty spaces, making her forget she'd ever been alone.

Finally, when they were both shaking, their bodies straining toward each other and toward release, he cupped her bottom, tilting her against him. Just an inch, just a fraction, so tiny a movement to bring so much pleasure exploding across her senses.

As she fell, her body dazzled by sensation, her mind and her heart seemed to leap across a shimmering void. Even in her daze, Vivien recognized it for what it was.

It was more than a leap of love. It was a leap of faith.

Chapter Thirty-One

Aden told himself to move even though every muscle in his body demanded he stay right where he was, on top of Vivien's sweetly curved body, his still twitching cock cradled against her belly. He was wrapped around her, crushing her into the mattress, but he felt as if he was the one who was surrounded. Her scent, her voice, and her touch had invaded him, wending through him with invisible satin ribbons to wrap themselves around his heart.

Christ.

He was in a great deal of trouble and without a clue how to extract himself.

Sighing, he rolled over on his back, taking her with him. She giggled at the change in position then draped herself across his chest, snuggling up like a fluffy kitten. She even flexed her fingers in his chest hair and purred, drawing her smooth leg up to rest alongside his hip. That had the unfortunate effect of pressing her damp nest of pretty blond curls into his cock. Yes, it was quite flaccid at the moment, but if Vivien stayed in that position much longer it wouldn't remain that way. If he had any brains left in his head—and he thought they might have exploded during his earth-shattering climax—he'd ease out from under her, cover her up with the bedclothes, and get the hell out of the house. As much as he wanted to be with her—for the rest of his life, he was beginning to suspect—that would be a huge mistake.

For him, of course, and most certainly for her.

He steeled himself to do just that when she pressed her lips to the center of his chest. That simple kiss jolted him, and he felt it take hold of his heart in a way no words could explain. Instinctively, he tightened his arms around her. His mind might know it was time to let her go, but his body had other ideas.

When she snuffled against him again, he couldn't hold back a smile. "What is that in aid of, Vivien?"

She rested her chin on his chest, gazing up at him. Her eyes shone with uncomplicated emotion, so clear, so loving, and so impossible.

"I like the way you smell," she said. "Is there anything wrong with that?"

"Given my level of exertion over the last hour or so, I'd say it means you're demented." He started to slip out from under her. "In fact, if you'll let me up, I'll have a wash." As excuses went it wasn't much, but it was better than nothing.

"Don't go. Please," she whispered, tightening her grip.

He bit back another sigh and subsided. They rested, skin to skin, beating heart to beating heart. All the while, he berated himself for being an idiot, and all the while his hands continued to stroke and play—combing his fingers through her thick, golden locks, watching them catch the reflected glow of the candles, and then drawing his hands over her burnished satin body. Soon enough it would end between them. For now, he would stamp the memory of her on his heart, a talisman during the hard, empty times his future surely held.

Just when he thought she'd fallen asleep, she stirred and looked up at him again.

"Thank you," she said quietly, her gaze solemn.

"For what?"

She crossed her hands on his chest, using it as a platform for her chin.

"For taking care of me and protecting me. And for this." A smile lifted the edges of her lush mouth. "Especially for this. It's quite the most wonderful thing that's ever happened to me."

"Exactly what do you mean by *this*," he said cautiously.

As soon as the words blundered their way out of his mouth, he knew they were a mistake.

Pushing against his chest, Vivien slowly sat up. Her hair fell in golden streamers over her pretty, pink-tipped breasts, and it took a masterful effort not to throw all common sense to the four winds and pull her back under him, sating himself in her beauty.

She considered him for several seconds, then seemed to reach a decision. "Aden, surely you realize how I feel about you."

God, he was not ready for this conversation. He would never be ready. "I'm sure you think you're fond of me, which isn't surprising under the circumstances."

She folded her arms under her chest in a classic defensive gesture. Unfortunately, her nakedness spoiled the intended effect since it plumped up her breasts into tempting mounds.

"And how would you define those circumstances?" she asked in a clipped voice.

"Vivien, I've saved your life more than once, and it's natural you should feel grateful. But gratitude can sometimes be confused with other emotions."

"I'm not a dimwit or a schoolgirl, Aden. I'm perfectly capable of identifying what I feel and what I don't feel. And of *course* I'm grateful to you. I'm grateful to Sir Dominic, too, but I'm not in love with him."

Such a simple word, yet it slammed through him with the force of a pistol shot. Though he'd known it was coming, nothing could have prepared him for its devastating effect.

He bit back the overwhelming temptation to respond in kind. "I never said you were a dimwit, sweetheart. But, in truth, we barely know each other. We've been thrown together in highly unusual circumstances—"

"Not unusual for you," she interrupted calmly.

"—unusual circumstances that have a tendency to heighten and confuse the emotions," he carried on doggedly. "I've seen it happen before, and rarely does the situation end well."

She pulled her legs up, bringing the linen sheet with her and covering her breasts. He'd miss them, but at least they wouldn't be distracting him. But with her big eyes, tumbled hair, and kiss-swollen lips, she looked like a woman who'd been well and properly shagged. A woman who'd enjoyed every moment of it, too, and was eager for more.

Instantly, Aden's cock twitched to life, more than ready to do her bidding. So much for not being distracted.

"Since you seem to know all about it," she said, "perhaps you'd be willing to answer one simple question."

He sensed a trap but couldn't see how he could avoid it. "What question?"

"How do you feel about me?"

Aden clamped down hard, refusing to allow any sign of inner turmoil to show on his face. "That's not an easy question to answer."

Vivien's chin went up in a defiant tilt. "I think it's a very easy question to answer. Do you love me, or are you merely fond of me?"

He sighed. "It is a great deal more complicated than a simple declaration of emotion, and you know it."

One side of her luscious mouth pulled down in a cynical slant but her eyes held a wounded, hollow look. "I see. You were simply taking advantage of a convenient opportunity to alleviate the boredom of this wretched situation. How foolish of me to assume otherwise, and how embarrassing for you that I misunderstood." She threw back the covers and began to slide out of bed. "I won't trouble you with my silly, over-wrought emotions a moment longer."

Aden snaked an arm around her waist, pulling her back into bed. She fought him, flailing her arms and legs in an effort to escape but he held her hard against him.

"You must be a dimwit if you think I would take advantage of you," he snapped. "I assure you there is nothing convenient about this situation or about falling in love with you."

She jerked once and then fell still, staring over her shoulder at him with a stunned gaze. Aden wanted to bite his tongue out. If he needed any proof that he had to get away from her, he'd just provided it. He *had* fallen in love with her, God help him. And it made him more vulnerable to making mistakes than he'd ever even imagined.

"You love me?" she asked in a tight voice as she twisted partway around in his embrace.

He sighed, feeling all the weariness of the last few months. Nay, years. "Of course I love you. How could I not? You're the most interesting woman I've ever met, despite your unfailing ability to get yourself into ridiculous situations."

She gave him a tentative smile. "I don't do it on purpose, you know. Things just seem to happen to me."

"Yes, I've noticed that trouble finds you on a fairly regular basis."

When she started to protest, he pressed a finger to her lips. "You're also intelligent, loyal, and generous to a fault, and it doesn't hurt that I could make love to you three times a day for the rest of my natural life and still not have enough of you."

She wriggled with pleasure, bringing her softly curved backside against his groin with predictably distracting results.

"You think I'm pretty," she said shyly.

He feathered kisses along the tender nape of her neck, and

she arched against him. "Pretty doesn't begin to cover it," he murmured.

She twisted fully around in his arms to meet his gaze. "Then why do you keep pulling away from me? If we love each other, then what is the problem?"

He frowned down at her. Where to begin? "Vivien, I wasn't exaggerating when I said I wasn't good enough for you. You can't begin to conceive of the life I've led . . . the things I've done, and the things I still must do."

"You're talking about your work?"

"Yes."

She rested her hands on his chest, staring earnestly up at him. "But surely you've done enough. You've been in the army for—"

When he shook his head in disagreement, she scoffed with impatience. "Very well. You've been a spy for almost ten years, is that not right?"

He nodded cautiously.

"Then I would say you've earned the right to retire from what must surely be a most dangerous profession. It's not as if you don't have other alternatives. After all, you're a St. George. Yes, I understand that you're a younger son, but—"

"I am not a St. George," he growled. "I have never truly been one of them, nor will I ever be."

She peered at him with confusion. "You're the son of Lord and Lady Thornbury. How can you not be a St. George?"

He released her as his gut twisted with bitterness. Sliding out of the bed, he snatched up his breeches and yanked them on. "Lord Thornbury was not my father."

Simply admitting it made bile rise in his throat. He fumbled with the fall of his breeches, avoiding her gaze until he'd buttoned himself. When he finally looked up, he couldn't read her expression.

"That is certainly unexpected," she said quietly. "But hardly unheard of." She hesitated, as if searching for the right words. "Did your fa—did Lord Thornbury know?"

"Yes." Aden couldn't bring himself to say anything more than that.

She nodded. "And yet he still acknowledged you as his son. That was kind of him."

A harsh laugh fought its way from his throat. "Hardly. He didn't have a choice."

Vivien frowned and brushed an errant lock of hair away from her forehead. She looked so beautiful, sitting amongst the rumpled bed linens. Beautiful and innocent, and not for him.

"What do you mean?"

Aden grimaced. "He had no choice because he had no desire to run afoul of my natural father. Lord Thornbury was anything but kind, I assure you. But he did not wish to embroil himself in the kind of scandal that would have resulted if he rejected me or my mother."

Vivien narrowed her gaze. "Aden, exactly who *is* your father?"

"The Prince Regent."

At the stunned expression on her face, his body went cold. There were many royal by-blows littering the land—he knew several—some of them of high rank. But those royal bastards hadn't had the shame of their parentage thrown into their faces on a regular basis, or seen their mothers treated with contempt by their husbands. But to his stepfather, Aden was a constant reminder of betrayal, and the old bastard had never let him forget it.

He retrieved his shirt off the floor, pulling it over his head while keeping his back to her. "And that, my dear, is why any sort of arrangement between us is impossible."

The bedclothes rustled and he heard Vivien softly pad across the floor. Her slender arms went around his waist as she rested her cheek between his shoulder blades.

"I am truly sorry for the pain your parents have caused," she said. "But their shame is not your shame."

He wanted to pull away from her but couldn't bring himself to do it. Her warmth, pressed all along his back, felt like heaven.

"I think you'll find that opinion to be in the minority," he said. "In my case, most of society would agree with my stepfather."

She moved around to stand in front of him, clothed in nothing but a bedsheet and looking impossibly beautiful. "But your mother is one of the most admired women in the *ton*. I'm not sure who knows the truth about your parentage—"

"Just about everyone," he interjected in a cynical tone.

"I've never heard even the *slightest* rumor, and I've been out and about in society for over seven years."

Now that she mentioned it, he couldn't remember the last time anyone had referred to his scandalous origins. And it *was* true that his mother enjoyed a very high standing in society, so perhaps the scandal had faded to a point where it no longer truly mattered. The shame and resentment had colored his life for so long—Aden couldn't even remember when he'd first learned who his father was—that perhaps his perception *was* distorted. Still . . .

"Aden," Vivien said, poking him in the chest, "you've essentially been away from London for ten years. Whatever scandal was attached to your birth has faded to the point of inconsequence. Besides, you're hardly the only illegitimate child of a prince. The Duke of Clarence has ten of them, and no one seems to give a fig about that."

Aden scratched the stubble on his chin. "That's all very true, but surely you can't expect me to believe it wouldn't be a concern to you."

She cast him such a look of disdain that he was tempted to shuffle his feet.

"Do you really think I'm that shallow?" she asked. "What have I ever done to give you that sort of idea?"

Brooding over her words, he wandered over to sit on the bed. Vivien gathered the trailing hem of her sheet and followed him.

"If I don't care about that sort of thing," she said in a matter-of-fact voice, "I don't see why you should, either."

Frustration started to build in his chest. Why could she not see how impossible it was? He'd chosen his path long ago, and it had forever marked him. She couldn't begin to understand what loving him would mean for her.

"It's not just my parentage that makes me ineligible for marriage, it's what I do." He gave her a hard stare, willing her to understand.

She adopted a patient expression. "Yes, you're a spy. But you won't be a spy forever, will you? I'm willing to wait."

Now she was trying to manage him. "Vivien, you have no idea what you're saying. The life I've led, the things I've done . . . it would be criminal for me to allow that to touch you. You are much too sheltered and innocent to understand—"

"Naturally, I couldn't possibly understand what you've done. Oh, wait, I could," she said sarcastically. "I saw it the night you rescued me. You stuck a knife into the ribs of that man outside the cave."

"Have you forgotten how you reacted when you saw that man? You almost fainted."

She rolled her eyes. "Of *course* I almost fainted. It was horrible. But I expect one doesn't rescue people from kidnappers by playing games with them. You did what you had to do, and I'm so grateful for that."

"Vivien—"

She held up a hand. "I understand that what you do is important. And I have told you that I'm willing to wait. Again, I ask you, what exactly is the problem?"

Aden clenched his fists against his thighs. He'd never expected her to be so bloody pragmatic about the whole thing. Christ, she was even beginning to make sense, and that scared the hell out of him. He couldn't bear the thought of her in danger or in any way tainted by what he did. And if he married her or even gave her a hope of marriage, he would surely put her in harm's way. His past would see to that.

He forced himself to harden his heart. "The problem is *you*, Vivien. You make this situation impossible."

Her eyes widened but she held her ground. "I don't understand."

"By loving you, by having you in my life, you make me vulnerable. And when I am vulnerable, it puts you in danger. That is not something I can tolerate."

Some of the color leached from her face. "Explain, please."

"A few weeks before you were abducted, I was on a mission in France with a small team of agents. We had worked together for years and knew each other as well as we knew ourselves. One man, in particular, was an old friend and my closest associate. His name was John, and he would gladly have given his life for me or for any other member of our team."

Aden paused, slowly opening his fists and smoothing his sweaty palms along his thighs.

"Go on," Vivien prompted.

He glanced up and nodded. "John had previously been in Italy for some weeks, and he had taken up with a woman there—a beautiful and accomplished actress. When he travelled to Paris to meet up with the rest of us, he brought her with him."

Vivien's fine brows arched up, but she said nothing.

"I objected, of course," Aden said, "but John would have none of it. He swore they were in love, and that she was exactly who she appeared to be. Nothing I said made any difference, and I finally gave up, but only on the understanding that he leave the Service at the end of the mission if he intended to remain with her." He couldn't hold back a bitter, self-mocking smile. "He loved her so much that he readily agreed."

Vivien flinched and pulled the sheet more tightly around her breasts. "I can understand that."

"Perhaps I can, too. Except John never got the chance to resign because his lover slit his throat while he slept. Then she stole the coded maps he was to carry back to England."

He ignored Vivien's choke of horror. "She was a spy for Bonapartists, you see, and had been using John all along. If I hadn't been so bloody stupid and so willing to give my old friend the benefit of the doubt, I would have seen that and found a way to expose her deadly charade. It was all just too neat and convenient, but I let John's emotions"—he corrected himself—"I let *my* emotions get in the way, and John's death was the result."

"That's not true, Aden."

She reached to touch him but he jumped to his feet, evading her. He couldn't bear for her to try to comfort him, not when he didn't deserve it.

"It is true," he said, crossing to the fireplace. He glanced at her, noting the way she shivered, and then tossed a log from the wicker basket onto the burning embers. After he got the flames roaring again, he straightened to face her.

"What happened to the woman?" she asked.

"I killed her."

Although Vivien's face paled, her expression changed very little. "I understand. You had no other choice."

He took two strides to reach her. "You understand nothing," he growled, grabbing her naked shoulders. "A man in my line of work cannot afford emotional involvements. He cannot fall in love and have a family. It would make him vulnerable, like

John. It would make *me* vulnerable, and I would make mistakes. Probably fatal mistakes."

Her eyes spit blue fire. "Are you comparing me to John's woman? A French spy and a murderess?"

"Of course not!" He gave her a gentle shake. "Don't you see? It's what I *feel* that's the problem. When I'm with you, I can barely think. Emotions are a liability. They're dangerous. *You're* dangerous to me, and I'm dangerous to you."

Her mouth flattened into a mulish line. "I do not accept that. I've never been so safe or happy as when I'm with you—despite the horrible circumstances."

He felt his mouth twist into a sneer. "Tell that to poor Jem."

She flinched in his grasp, and he let her go. He allowed his gaze to drift over her pale, slender beauty one last time, then pivoted on his heel and headed for the door.

"Aden, wait."

The barrier around his heart snapped into place, repelling the aching plea in her voice.

Barely.

He glanced over his shoulder. She stood in the middle of the floor, wrapped in her wrinkled sheet like a forlorn, haphazard goddess. The desolation in her eyes almost killed him. But when she started to speak he held up a restraining hand. "I'm sorry, Vivien. It's over."

As he shut the door behind him, he told himself it was for the best—for both of them.

Chapter Thirty-Two

Aden wearily climbed the stairs to Dominic's study after twenty-four hours on the road from St. Clement, with only his frustrated thoughts for company. But despite the continuous haring about in his brain, he remained convinced he'd made the right decision. Vivien would be safe with Dominic's guards surrounding her, and he would be better off away from her seductive pull.

The terse note he'd left explaining his sudden departure would infuriate her, but there was little to be gained in belaboring the points he'd made their last night together. They had no future and the sooner he was out of her life, the better. Vivien would get over him easily enough. She had numerous and perfectly eligible suitors, any one of whom would make a better husband than he would.

As for him . . . before Vivien, he'd never given his heart to a woman and he never would again. She'd claimed him and he would never be entirely free of those bonds. But there was only one thing he could do for her now—find the evidence necessary to send Khovansky back to his cold Russian lair and allow Vivien to return to her rightful place in society.

He stood for a moment at the study door, cudgelling his thoughts into order. His chief wouldn't be happy that he'd returned to London, but Aden had played babysitter long enough. It was time to bring this dangerous game to an end, and he couldn't do that while cooling his heels in some god-forsaken village up north.

When he finally opened the door he pulled up short, frowning at the sight of Dominic in close conversation with Griffin Steele, the remains of a breakfast tray on a low table between them. His chief looked up, a wintry expression collecting in his green gaze.

"The prodigal son returns," Dominic said. "Imagine my surprise to receive your note telling me you were abandoning your post."

Aden ignored the bait, instead nodding curtly to his cousin. "Griffin, how odd to see you at breakfast. A little early for you to be about, isn't it?"

Griffin leaned back in his chair and gave him a raffish grin. "You might think so, especially considering the delectable little pigeon I was forced to leave in my bed, but your superior's note was rather persuasive." He gave Dominic a smile that bordered on the malicious. "In fact, he ordered me to appear immediately. If I weren't such a trusting fellow, I do believe I would even consider the tone of the note to be rather threatening."

Dominic cast Griffin a derisive glance. "I simply gave you a little incentive. If there's anything I've come to realize over the years it's that you are a tad reluctant to inconvenience yourself, no matter how urgent the cause."

Griffin lifted a lazy shoulder. "Guilty as charged. I find it difficult to imagine exerting myself for any reason other than naked self-interest. Of course, when my dear cousin's well-being is at stake, I am always willing to make an exception."

Aden scoffed. "I'm sure. What the hell are you doing here, anyway?"

"One might ask the same of you," Dominic said darkly as

he sat down behind his desk. "I sent for Griffin as soon as I received your note."

"You see, dear boy," Griffin said, "I've recently come into receipt of some very interesting information. Dominic thought it best if I told you myself."

"I was about to send an express to you in St. Clement when your note reached me," Dominic said. "I only hope it's not too late to put effective safeguards in place."

A stab of alarm shafted through Aden's chest. "Are we speaking of information about Vivien?"

Dominic ignored his question, casting a critical eye over him. "You look the very devil, Aden. When was the last time you slept? And when *did* you arrive in London, anyway?"

Aden resisted the impulse to curse. "Just a few hours ago. I travelled straight from St. Clement by post-chaise, although I did stop at my rooms for an hour to change." His impatience got the better of him. "Which I told you in the note I sent round."

"Yes, your note, which failed to explain the reasons for your return." Dominic waved an irritated hand at Aden's incipient protest. "You can tell me all about it, but first get yourself a cup of coffee and sit down."

Aden stalked over to the silver coffee service and poured a cup. Fortunately, Dominic liked his coffee brewed strong as hell. Aden had a feeling he'd need several cups to get through this meeting.

"Does your information involve Khovansky?" he asked Griffin as he took a seat.

His cousin nodded. "One of my attempts to encourage honesty in some of my more reluctant sources has finally borne fruit. It would appear that the men responsible for Lady Vivien's abduction were members of the Campworth gang."

Despite the heat from the steaming cup of coffee he cradled

in his hands, a chill coursed through Aden's veins. "Borden Campworth?"

"None other," Griffin responded in a hard voice. "I think you'll agree this is not a good development."

One of the most notorious crime lords in England, Campworth ran an extensive network of smugglers, extortionists, and thieves. He also had several MP's and at least two members of the current government in his pocket, rendering him difficult to bring to heel. Dominic had been trying to bring the bastard down for years, with very limited success.

"Apparently, this source was able to confirm that Khovansky hired Campworth's men for both the initial abduction as well as the second attempt you managed to thwart," Dominic interjected.

Griffin nodded. "My source was also persuaded to reveal that another abduction is planned that will involve Khovansky himself."

Aden eased back in his chair, feeling a slight degree of relief. "They can try again, but they'll never find Vivien now. No one has ever uncovered St. Clement."

Griffin and Dominic exchanged a troubled glance, and Aden's alarm spiked again. "What?"

"Griffin's source was adamant that Campworth had information on Lady Vivien's location," Dominic said.

Aden shook his head impatiently. "That's impossible. I made certain of it."

"*You* did," his chief replied. "Unfortunately, Lady Vivien didn't. Apparently, she wrote to her younger brother once she arrived in St. Clement."

Aden rubbed his eyes, feeling sick. "Bloody hell."

"Indeed," Dominic said in a voice of doom.

"How did you find out?" Aden asked.

"Griffin sent me word last night that Campworth was involved. Unfortunately, I was out quite late and did not receive the news until I returned home after one A.M. I immediately checked with the man I had stationed at Blake House, who insisted all was quiet. That, however, failed to satisfy, so I tracked down young Kit Shaw at Brook's. He informed me, with some reluctance I might add, that Vivien had sent him a short note soon after her arrival, telling him she was safe. He also swore up and down that he'd told no one, including his mother and his older brother."

"Did he burn the letter?" Aden asked, dreading the answer.

"No."

"Christ!" Aden jumped to his feet and began pacing. What a complete and utter fool he'd been. It had never occurred to him that Vivien could do something so foolish, but she worried about Kit like a mother hen fretting over her chicks. He should have anticipated something like this and kept a closer eye on her, especially in those first days in St. Clement.

"And Khovansky? Where is he?" he snapped.

"He *was* staying at Osterley with the Jerseys, but I received a report not an hour ago from Kenilworth, who I'd assigned to tail the prince. Khovansky presumably took to his bed two days ago with a raging head cold, attended only by his valet. Kenilworth managed to get upstairs to Khovansky's bedroom early this morning and found that the prince was most definitely not on his sickbed. Unfortunately, Kenilworth found Khovansky's valet to be so terrified of his master that he was singularly useless in providing any coherent information."

Aden came to a halt in front of Griffin. "Any specifics on the time line?"

"My source said it was imminent. Given the state he was in when my men finished with him, I think it's safe to say we got everything out of him that we could."

Aden strangled the impulse to panic, forcing himself to think. "What happened to your source? You made sure he can't get word back to Campworth?"

"You may reassure yourself on that score, Cousin," Griffin said, rising to his feet. "No word will reach Campworth of any breach in his plans." He nodded to them and headed to the door. "I'll leave you professionals to do what you do best."

Griffin paused with his hand on the knob, glancing back at Aden. "I will hope for Lady Vivien's safety. She is a remarkable woman and deserves much better than to fall into the clutches of a man like Khovansky."

"No woman ever deserves to fall into Khovansky's clutches," Dominic commented once Griffin was gone. "But for now, we will concentrate on protecting Lady Vivien."

"I'm heading back north immediately," Aden said. "Vivien is well protected, but if I can get there before Khovansky, so much the better. I can catch the bastard in the act."

"That would be helpful, but I think our problems with the prince are a tad more complicated than that. It will require a political intervention as well, and that will take some doing."

"There won't be any need for political interventions when I'm through with him," Aden growled. "Are we done? I need to be on my way."

Dominic's only response was to wave him toward one of the chairs in front of his desk. Aden stared at him with disbelief. "Is this really necessary?" he snapped.

His chief sighed. "I could wish you to have more faith in me. I sent Kenilworth and another man north as soon as I received the report on Khovansky. They're more than prepared to deal with any problems until you arrive. Now, sit."

Muttering under his breath, Aden took a seat. When Dominic spoke in that tone of voice, there was little point in resisting. But the thought of Vivien, so far away and with Khovansky likely in pursuit, set panic to clawing at his guts. Though logic told Aden she was well protected, his heart told him he'd abandoned her precisely when she needed him most.

Dominic steepled his hands in front of his chin and subjected

Aden to a thorough inspection. "Why did you return? And do not insult my intelligence by stating, as you did in your ridiculous note, that you thought it necessary to move the investigation along."

Incredulous, Aden stared at him. "We're going to do this now? When Vivien is in danger?"

"If she's in danger, it's because of you. I realize the last few months have been difficult, but I didn't anticipate that your weariness, for lack of a better word, would cause such a lapse in judgment."

Aden flinched—only slightly, but Dominic caught it nonetheless. He allowed some of the cold ire to leave his face. "Aden, I ordered you to protect Lady Vivien until this matter was resolved. Not run off half-cocked when you came face-to-face with your emotions."

Aden bristled. "My emotions have nothing to do with it. I simply felt that—"

Dominic raised an imperious hand, cutting him off. "I'm sure you'd like me to believe that, but we both know it's not true. You find your emotions inconvenient, but they are not something you can ignore any longer."

"Christ, I'd like to," he muttered.

Dominic's spare features softened in sympathy. "My friend, despite what you think, denying your feelings only clouds your judgment to a greater extent."

"Like John's feelings clouded his judgment in France?" Aden flashed.

"John was outwitted by another agent, and a very good one. It happens. You, however, were not outwitted, nor did your affection for John fog your brain. You discussed the situation with him and gave him fair warning. The mistake was his, not yours."

Aden brooded over the memory of his friend, sprawled in his bed, naked and bloody. An equally ugly memory followed, that of a beautiful and false woman, John's killer, dead by Aden's hand. She was a good agent, yes, but not good enough to escape his brand of justice.

"It's the game," Dominic said softly. "Ugly, tragic things happen. Let it go."

"I'm sick of the game," Aden responded without thinking. He paused, stunned by the simplicity and truth of the words.

"As are we all. Now tell me why you left Lady Vivien."

Aden fell into obstinate silence, but Dominic simply raised an arrogant eyebrow and waited him out.

"All right," Aden finally grumbled, "I fell in love with her. Is that what you wanted to hear?"

Much to his surprise, Dominic grinned. "Yes, it is. And I take it she loves you."

"I believe she does," he said cautiously.

"Why, then, did you leave her?"

Aden gaped at him. "Christ, Dominic! You know what I am, what I'm capable of. You know my background, too. Vivien deserves better than me."

"What she deserves is a good man to love her. A man who is also strong enough to protect her from the wolves at her door."

Aden let out a harsh laugh. "Yes, but I'm hardly that man."

"Lady Vivien apparently does not agree. Nor, might I add, does your mother—a lady of great perception, as you know. I will add that I agree with your mother's assessment."

Dominic got up and rounded his desk, perching on the edge of its polished mahogany surface. Aden stared up at him, feeling both wary and exposed.

"Aden," Dominic started in a kind voice. "From a young age you have tried to bury your emotions. That was understandable given the way Lord Thornbury treated both you and your mother, never allowing either of you to forget her lapse in judgment. At that stage in your life, emotions were not your friend. You brought that attitude with you into the Service, and your ability to repress your feelings carried you through many a difficult situation. But in this case, denying them has led you astray."

Aden stared at his chief. "How so?"

"Put aside your fears, for the moment, and concentrate on what you feel for Lady Vivien. What does *that* particular emotion tell you?"

Aden tried to do as Dominic bid him, ignoring the pounding of his heart and the frantic rush of blood through his veins. No. He tried to *feel,* not think. What did his love for Vivien tell him to do?

He closed his eyes and groaned as the answer became brutally obvious. "I never should have left her."

"Exactly right."

Opening his eyes, he sprang to his feet. "I can't waste another moment."

Dominic nodded. "Go."

Aden grabbed his coat and hat, cursing under his breath. "I am an idiot. A complete, sodding idiot."

Dominic's sardonic laugh followed him out the door. "Of course you are. You're a man in love."

Chapter Thirty-Three

Vivien locked her travelling trunk, smiling at the servant Aden had assigned to protect her. "Thank you, Evans. Could you please ask Mr. MacDonnell or one of the footmen to come up and fetch this? I only have to finish packing my overnight bag and I'll be ready."

Evans, a lanky, capable woman, scoffed as she grabbed the trunk. "That won't be necessary, my lady. I'm just as strong as those fellows. I'm a better shot, too," she muttered as she hoisted the trunk on her shoulder.

Vivien could believe it. Evans might pretend to be a lady's maid but her talents clearly lay elsewhere. The older woman wasn't very adept at dressing one's hair or pressing a gown, but she'd watched over Vivien like a mother cat with a single kitten. Her quiet but supportive strength had been a blessing these last few days since Aden decamped for London without one word of warning.

Sighing, she folded a shawl and stuffed it into her portmanteau. Evans and MacDonnell vehemently opposed her departure, trying to thwart her every step of the way. She'd finally taken matters into her own hands, sneaking out yesterday to hire a post-chaise for this morning. MacDonnell had pitched a fit when Vivien told him while he was serving her yet another solitary meal in the dining room last night.

"My lady, you can't leave," MacDonnell had exclaimed, clutching a tureen of dumplings to his waistcoat. "You are to remain here until either Captain St. George or Sir Dominic returns or sends for you. It'll be my head if I let you leave. Besides," he added rather desperately, "I'm sure the captain will be back any day now."

She had politely responded by noting that short of locking her in her bedroom, there wasn't a thing MacDonnell could do to stop her. And if he *did* lock her up, she'd simply crawl out the window and down the trellis, then find her own way back to London on the common stage.

Eyeing her morosely, MacDonnell had finally agreed, with the stipulation that he and Evans go with her. Vivien was secretly relieved, since the idea of travelling alone was rather daunting. Only the dawning realization that she might be stuck in St. Clement for weeks had enabled her to overcome her doubts about disobeying Aden's strict written edict to obey every one of MacDonnell's orders.

We'll just see about that, Captain St. George.

Scowling, she shoved her nightgown into the overstuffed bag and sat on it to force it closed. Every time she thought about Aden's last words to her—and she thought about them every two minutes—the blood rushed hotly through her veins. His rejection had left her stunned, then annoyed, and then hot with humiliation and anger. It had taken all her willpower not to dash out of her room after him, but the knowledge that she would likely burst into tears when confronting him had kept her from doing so.

When she'd finally calmed down enough to think, she'd realized that Aden's reaction had made perfect sense—in a thickheaded, masculine sort of way. For most of his life he'd seen himself as an outsider. It didn't matter that he had the bluest blood in the land—and hadn't *that* revelation about his real father been a shock—he'd been deliberately rejected by the people in his life who most mattered. He felt unwanted and unworthy, the walking definition of a scandal, and someone who didn't deserve a normal life.

As she'd mulled that over, shivering in her cold bed, Vivien had succumbed to tears. Not for herself, but for the lonely little boy who'd managed to grow up into the best kind of man, and yet one who still believed nobody wanted him. After she'd cried herself out, she'd decided it was better to wait until the morning when she could tell Aden in the clear light of day that she had every intention of marrying him and that he'd best get used to the idea.

Which had obviously been a huge mistake. For several hours, she'd let the staff convince her that he would surely return, but eventually her instincts had told her the truth. If she wanted a life with Aden, she would have to fight for it and force him to confront the illogic of his rejection—both of her, and of the life they could build together.

She fastened the straps on the portmanteau and took one last look around the cozy, quaintly decorated room. It had been a refuge these last weeks, as had the town and the new friends she'd made. She'd already sent a note round to Mrs. Pettigrew saying that she and *Mr. Parker* had been called back to town but hoped to return soon. A month ago, she would have shuddered to have to lead such a quiet, uncomplicated life. But now her life in London seemed restless and empty, full of noise and motion but holding very little meaning. Here, she'd found contentment and happiness. With Aden by her side, she could envision building a life that had little to do with the empty glitter of *ton* life and everything to do with love.

Draping her pelisse over her arm, she hoisted her portmanteau and headed for the door. Balancing the heavy bag on her hip, she propped the door open with her foot and thumped her way into the hallway. But as she started for the stairs a loud bang sounded from below, followed by raised, angry voices and several vibrating thuds.

Alarmed, Vivien dropped her bag and rushed to the head of the staircase. Before she reached it, the sound of a harsh, familiar accent sent fear crashing through her veins. She pressed herself against the wall, keeping out of sight as she tried to catch her suddenly fractured breath.

Khovansky.

From the other horrible noises filtering up the stairs, it was clear he'd brought a whole band of thugs with him, who were now engaged in battle with MacDonnell and the footman.

She sucked in a tense breath, realizing she had only a few seconds to escape, either through one of the upstairs windows or by the hidden set of stairs in the closet in the back bedroom. Aden had shown it to her as a precaution when they'd first arrived, but now it looked like her best chance.

Keeping her back to the wall to avoid creaking floorboards, she crept away from the staircase. If she could get out, she'd run straight to Mrs. Pettigrew's house and hide there. Then, when darkness fell, she'd—

"Vivien, I know you're up there," called a familiar voice that brought her up short. "I suggest you come down right now, or else I'm afraid your servants will come to harm."

She rested her head against the wall, shaking with anger. She'd never liked her older brother, but at this moment she truly hated him.

"Vivien, come down right now," Cyrus barked.

"I heard you the first time," she yelled back.

She pushed herself away from the wall and took several deep breaths, trying to slow the mad tripping of her heart. She needed a clear head and strong nerves to get through this, although she had little idea what she could say to either man except *no*.

A bitter smile twisted her lips as she walked slowly to the staircase. Aden had said no to her the other night and look where it had landed her—alone, in trouble, and without him to protect her.

Her courage almost failed her when she reached the top landing and beheld the chaotic scene in the entrance hall. At least five rough-looking men in greatcoats milled about the small space, and both MacDonnell and Evans had been bound, gagged, and shoved against the wall. Over their gags, both sets of eyes glared fiercely at their captors. Davis, the footman, was stretched out on the floor, unconscious and with a bloodied mouth.

Standing off to the side stood Cyrus and Prince Ivan. Her brother looked rumpled and furious and, classically, extremely put out. The prince, however, simply stared up at her with an expression both calculated and triumphant, like a hunter who'd just run the fox to ground.

Spitting out a curse, Vivien flew down the stairs and rushed to Davis, mindlessly pushing her way past the two thugs standing over the unconscious man.

"Vivien!" Cyrus exclaimed in an offended voice. "I'll thank you to watch your language before the prince."

For a second, she gaped at him. Even the prince levelled an incredulous expression in her brother's direction, clearly thinking him an idiot.

"Sod off, Cyrus," she said through clenched teeth.

Ignoring her brother's idiocies, she carefully felt Davis's skull, trying to assess his injury. Fortunately, he moaned and his eyelids started to flutter.

"Lady Vivien, I must ask you to get up from the floor," Prince Ivan said in a cold voice. "Such behavior is not fitting in a woman of your station."

"And does it befit *your* station to employ thugs to pummel servants and engage in kidnapping?" she snapped. "I wonder what the Russian ambassador will say when I tell him exactly what transpired here today?"

Khovansky's gaze blasted her with cold rage. She resisted the impulse to shrink away from him and huddle on the floor. No matter what, she would not bend before him.

"For God's sake, Vivien, get up," Cyrus grumbled, casting the prince a wary look.

He reached down and pulled her to her feet, bringing his mouth close to her ear. "Do not make him angry," he hissed. "The man's quite demented."

She pulled away. "You're only discovering this now?" She didn't bother to lower her voice.

The prince regained his control. "My lady, I suggest we repair to your drawing room where we can discuss this situation like rational people."

"There is nothing remotely rational about this situation," Vivien retorted. She was proud at the steadiness of her voice, even though her insides quaked like a jelly mold. "You need to take these brutes and leave this house. Immediately."

The prince gave her a courteous little bow. "That is my intention, once we have come to an arrangement."

Crossing her arms over her chest, Vivien stared back, refusing to move or say a word.

Khovansky shook his head regretfully. "You force my hand, Lady Vivien. Please remember that everything that happens today will be a direct result of your actions."

He gave a nod to one of his men, a large brute with a twisted nose and misshapen ears. With a feral smile, the man hauled Evans up, holding her by the collar so her feet barely touched the floor. With a lightning fast motion, he struck her across the face with an open palm.

Evans's head snapped back as the sound of the vicious slap echoed through the hall. Vivien choked out a cry and instinctively leapt forward, only to be hauled back by her brother.

Prince Ivan tilted his head and studied Evans, still held in a punishing grip by his man. Above the gag, her red face had already started to swell but her eyes glowed with fierce defiance.

"Shall we go into the drawing room and chat, Lady Vivien?" Prince Ivan asked. "Or shall my men take your maid into the kitchen and continue with the lesson? I assure you, the results will not be to your taste."

Vivien's insides cramped with horror as she stared at the prince. "Where are the rest of the servants? The cook and the other footman?"

"They are in the kitchen. You may be sure that all your servants are safely confined. All of them," Khovansky added for emphasis.

Vivien's last, faint hope that one of Sir Dominic's men might have escaped withered.

"My dear lady, there is no need for any more harm to come to your servants," the prince said in a soothing manner. "If you will cooperate, all will be well."

"Vivien, don't be an idiot," Cyrus said, a pleading note creeping into his voice. He glanced at Evans then swallowed hard, looking rather ill. "Let's just go into the other room and talk. Please."

Vivien darted a glance about the hall, taking in the leering, ugly expressions on the faces of Khovansky's men. She had no doubt they would do exactly as their employer commanded and enjoy it.

Almost choking on her frustration, she nodded. "I'll do what you say, but only if you solemnly promise not to harm any of the servants."

Khovansky gave her another of his ridiculously formal bows.

"I want to hear the words, Your Highness," she insisted. "Promise they will come to no harm."

Behind their gags, both Evans and MacDonnell protested

incoherently. The thug holding Evans shook her in his grasp, like a cat shaking a mouse, until she fell silent.

Khovansky placed his hand over his heart. "You have my word as a prince," he said.

A shiver slithered up Vivien's spine. She would pay dearly for what the prince saw as an insult to his honor. That would come later, however. For now, she had to focus her thoughts on keeping the servants free from harm.

She nodded and turned on her heel, bypassing the large drawing room and leading the way to the morning room. It was small, which meant that most of Khovansky's thugs would be forced to wait in the hall. She wasn't entirely sure, but she thought she recognized a few of them from the night she was abducted. Simply looking at them made her mind want to freeze with panic, and she needed all of her wits at her call.

Cyrus and the prince followed her into the sunny, south-facing room. Khovansky closed the door behind him and, with a gracious sweep of his arm, indicated that Vivien take a seat. By his demeanor, one might almost think he'd come to make a polite morning call. That, more than anything else, *did* convince her that the man was truly insane.

Warily, she perched on the edge of one of the low armchairs. She loved this room, with its cheerful tones of cream and yellow and comfortable furnishings covered with gaily floral chintz fabric. A searing pain of regret flared in her chest as she remembered the breakfasts she'd enjoyed with Aden here, chatting to him over coffee and newspapers, falling more in love every day.

Those memories now served no other purpose but to taunt her.

Her brother lowered himself onto the chair next to her, peering up uneasily at Prince Ivan. Cyrus opened his mouth to speak, but Vivien cut him off.

"How did you find me, Cyrus?"

He flinched, but then brought himself under control. "From the letter you wrote to Kit."

"Kit did not betray me!"

Cyrus let out a bitter laugh. "Of course he didn't. He swore up and down he didn't know where you were, but I knew that to be a lie. The idiot thought he was protecting you when he was bringing us all to ruin." He cut her a defiant look. "He left me no choice, so I searched his room and found the letter."

Vivien pressed a hand over her stomach. Aden had warned her not to contact anyone, but she'd known Kit would be sick with worry if he didn't know she was safe. She'd only written him once, and strictly instructed him not to tell anyone where she was.

"You had no right to do that," she said in a tight voice.

"And you had no right to run away without a word to your family," Cyrus snapped. "Mamma was beside herself, as you can imagine. I've had to listen to her hysterics for two weeks now, not to mention dealing with all her creditors."

Vivien dug her nails into the cushioned arms of the chair. "If you were a truly affectionate brother, you'd protect me instead of using me as a means to pay off your debts and further your career. Papa would have been horrified to see how you've treated us."

"Our father was as big a fool as every other person in this family," Cyrus sneered. "And what did you expect me to do? Stand by and watch while the whole lot of you pulled the family name through the mud? Your own behavior, I might add, has been little better than that of a trollop."

"That is enough, Lord Blake." Prince Ivan's cold voice cut like a lash through the room. "You will not insult my future wife, even if she is your sister."

Vivien's heart stuttered. She knew what Khovansky wanted, but to hear him announce it so boldly robbed her of breath.

"Apologize to Lady Vivien," Khovansky said, never taking his eyes off Cyrus.

Her brother glanced at her, then at the prince. What he saw there obviously frightened him as much as it did Vivien. He gave her a stiff little nod. "Forgive me, Vivien," he said in a resentful voice.

Her mind finally broke free of the insanity of the moment.

"Prince Ivan, I have not agreed to marry you. I will return to London, if I must, but you cannot force my hand. Threatening or harming my servants will not achieve your desired result, since no minister will perform the ceremony once he learns that my acquiescence to your demands was achieved by duress."

Prince Ivan tilted his head, letting his gaze drift over her before extracting a gold-plated snuffbox from an inner pocket. Leisurely, he availed himself of a pinch then dusted off his hands before deigning to answer her. "Ah, but you will gladly acquiesce, my lady. You see, I hold your family's fortunes and future in the palm of my hand."

Shocked, Vivien stared at her brother. "Cyrus, what is he talking about?"

When he could barely meet her eyes, she grabbed his sleeve and shook. "Is it true?" she demanded.

Anguish flashed across her brother's face and Vivien's heart plummeted. A moment later, Cyrus shook off her restraining hand and shot her a haughty glare. "His Highness has generously taken on the burden of both Mamma's and Kit's debts. As you know, they are quite extraordinary. Combined with the mortgage on Blake House—"

"Which you took out to finance your blasted career," she said hotly.

"—and the cost of the repairs to the estate in Somerset,"

Cyrus continued, "we have been brought to a standstill. Without the aid of Prince Ivan, we should all wind up in debtors' prison."

"How much do we owe him?" Vivien asked in a horrified whisper.

The amount Cyrus named was staggering. Vivien's head swam, and she had to take several deep breaths to wrestle her panic under control.

"So you see, my dear Lady Vivien," Prince Ivan said, looking down at her with a hideously possessive glint in his eye, "your family owes its continued position in society—indeed its very existence—to me. Of course, when you are my wife, then your family will become part of my family. I shall do everything in my power to see them prosper. In fact, it will be my fondest wish to do so, because I know it will give pleasure to *you*."

She stared into his protruding, toadlike eyes and read the triumph there. The walls of the room seemed to close around her and she found it hard to breathe.

"Why are you doing this?" she whispered. "Surely there must be other women who would welcome your attentions."

One eyebrow shot up. "I should think it obvious. I love you."

"And this is how you show your love, by threatening my family and blackmailing me? That is the behavior of a cad, sir, not a prince," she exclaimed.

She expected him to bristle at the insult, but a chilling smile stretched his broad features. The malicious intent in his gaze made her stomach churn.

"Ah, Lady Vivien, I cannot tell you how much I look forward to our wedding. You are spirited, but you must learn obedience to your husband. I believe I will greatly enjoy schooling you into a properly behaved wife."

Bile rose in her throat and Vivien had to swallow hard to

keep from choking. She cast a desperate glance at her brother. "Mamma will never agree to this."

Grimly, Cyrus reached into the pocket of his greatcoat, pulled out an envelope, and handed it to her.

Vivien tore it open. Moments later, she crushed her mother's plea for her to marry Prince Ivan with shaking fingers. "Cyrus, what did you do to make her agree to this? Mamma knows how I feel about him!"

"I simply told her the truth," her brother replied.

"You mean you threatened her," she responded bitterly. "And what about Kit? He wouldn't stand by and just let this happen."

Cyrus barked out an ugly laugh. "He has no choice. Kit is halfway to debtors' prison, or worse."

Vivien stared at the crumpled piece of parchment in her fist. Her mind pushed her brother's words away, reeling with stunned disbelief. Desperately, she clutched at the one thing that could save her. "No. Captain St. George will never—"

Prince Ivan flung a hand out, almost hitting her in the face. "My patience runs out, Lady Vivien. Your brother has explained the circumstances to you and you will accept them. If you do not, ruin awaits your entire family."

He leaned down to her, his florid complexion flushing almost the shade of clotted blood. Vivien tried not to shrink away but she couldn't help herself. The insane arrogance of the man rolled off him, like the scent of a bitter, noxious herb.

"And if you value your precious captain's life," he said, his accent growing ever more guttural, "you will never mention his name to me again. I leave his life in your hands."

Cyrus pressed a hand to her arm, looking almost as desperate as she felt. "Come now, old girl. It won't be so bad. You'll be a princess. You'll never have to worry about money again, nor will Mamma or Kit." He gave her a sick smile. "And I'm sure the prime minister and Prinny will think it a splendid thing. Why, think of all the influence you'll have."

She pulled her arm away from him. "They can go to the devil."

The prince gave a careless shrug. "In any case, the arrangements are in place. I have already spoken to Ambassador and Countess Lieven. Naturally, they are thrilled. By this time, I would imagine the ambassador has already hinted to the Prince Regent of our impending engagement. The formal announcement will go out as soon as we return to London."

Dumbstruck with despair, Vivien could only shake her head in pointless refusal. The trap was steadily closing about her. Even if Aden had been here, she doubted he could have done anything to protect her.

As if he read her thoughts, the prince leaned in even closer, pinning her with a gaze that seemed purely reptilian. "If you are thinking that your dashing captain can help you, then I suggest you think again. You are mine, Lady Vivien, and I will allow no man to stand in the way of claiming you as my bride."

His acrid breath washed over her and she shrank back in her chair.

"Am I making myself perfectly clear?" he asked, his voice softly threatening.

She forced herself to nod as she heard the bars of her cage slide into place. They'd planned it too carefully—Cyrus and the prince—and she didn't stand a chance. And if she turned to Aden for help . . .

Aden.

He might not want to marry her, but she had no doubt he would again risk his life to help her. She also had no doubt Ivan the Terrible would carry out his vile threat. Given his immense wealth and power, he might well get away with it. But that didn't even matter. Only Aden mattered, and if he were hurt or killed trying to help her, Vivien could never live with that horrible outcome. Bleakly, she accepted the losing hand fate had dealt her and met Khovansky's maliciously triumphant gaze.

"I understand perfectly, Your Highness. That being the case, I wish to leave Captain St. George a letter—" She held up a restraining hand when he started to object. "You may read it. I simply intend to tell him that I have agreed to marry you and that I will be displeased if he tries to interfere in any way."

The prince gave her another flourishing bow, one that seemed to mock her. "Of course, my dear, whatever you wish."

Vivien crossed to the small writing desk in the corner of the room. She rummaged for paper and ink and then wearily sat down to write her note. As the words stuttered reluctantly from her pen, she heard the closing snick of the lock on the cage that had just become her life.

Chapter Thirty-Four

Aden walked slowly from the mews where he stabled his horses, reading the *on-dits* column as the bustle of stable hands and grooms swirled about him. As soon as his coach reached the outskirts of London, he'd had Stevens jump down to retrieve the papers. Though tempted to shove the reins into the coachman's hands and start scanning the columns of type immediately, the sick feeling in his stomach had held him back.

Now he couldn't avoid the truth any longer. It was there in black-and-white for the entire world to see.

> As has been rumored for weeks, a certain foreign prince will soon be making a formal announcement of his engagement to Lady V—. The family of the future bride is apparently in alt at the prospect of such a distinguished and wealthy connection.

He stopped in the middle of the lane and closed his eyes, letting the wave of despair swamp him. He'd failed Vivien and now he couldn't see a way to help her escape the trap she'd walked into. Even worse, she didn't even want his help, as her curtly worded missive had made clear.

A blast from a carriage horn jerked him out of his reverie. "Here now, guv, stand clear," yelled a coachman as he wheeled by in a barouche just inches from Aden's booted feet.

Aden grimaced and waved an apology. He folded the papers and shoved them under his arm, heading for the back entrance to his set of rooms. Despite the fact that he'd managed to get a few hours' sleep on his journey back from St. Clement, weariness unlike anything he'd ever felt dragged on his bones. It had nothing to do with the fact that he'd only slept a few hours in the last several days and everything to do with the fact that he'd failed Vivien. And despite what Dominic said, that failure *had* resulted from letting emotion get in his way. If he'd kept a proper distance from her none of this would have happened. He would have kept his mind on the job and brought Khovansky to heel days ago instead of indulging in the stupidity of falling in love.

A love Vivien wanted nothing to do with, as her letter made clear. Even now, tucked into the inside pocket of his greatcoat, it weighed him down. And he certainly wouldn't have to pull it out again to read since the words had scorched themselves into his brain.

She'd tersely explained that she'd decided to marry the prince after Khovansky assured her that he'd had nothing to do with her abduction or the subsequent attempt. Aden refused to believe she could be so easily duped, but what she'd written next had shaken him to the core.

> *I will not say that I do not have reservations about accepting Prince Ivan's proposal, but I have no doubt that he loves me. He will provide for both my security and*

my family's, and allow us to maintain our proper station
in life. You, more than anyone, will appreciate that.

Aden's gut had burned with shame when he read those
words, knowing he'd used the same excuse to push her away.
Now, because of his cowardly rejection, Vivien would spend
her life tied to a man she hated. If she'd given him even a hint
that she wanted to fight he would have dared anything to help
her, even invading Carleton House to demand his father's
help. But her missive stated in clear, cold terms that she
would reject any such interference, all but ordering him to
stay away from her.

From what his people had told Aden when he arrived in
St. Clement a day after Vivien's departure, she'd gone will-
ingly. Despite the initial ugliness when Khovansky and his
men had barged in, Vivien had seemed more than ready to
leave with the prince and her brother. That was the part Aden
couldn't fathom. Vivien was no coward. Short of putting a gun
to her head, Khovansky hadn't a hope in hell of forcing her to
do anything she didn't want to do.

Aden brushed by the porter with a curt nod and headed
for the stairs to his rooms.

"Captain, wait," the man called out.

Expelling an impatient sigh, Aden paused at the foot of the
staircase.

Carter, the day porter, hurried up with an apologetic smile.
"Begging your pardon, sir, but there's a young man waiting for
you in your rooms. He said it was an urgent matter and refused
to leave until you returned. Right worried the lad was, too, so
I thought it best to let him in since he says you know him."

"Who is it?"

"Says his name is Mr. Christopher Shaw."

A jolt of anxiety blasted away Aden's fatigue. He gave

Carter a brusque nod and took the stairs two at a time. He strode into his front room, tossing the newspaper and his hat in the general direction of the padded bench by the door.

"Thank God you're finally here," Kit said, jumping up from one of the wing chairs in front of the bay window. He tugged anxiously on the hem of his waistcoat. "I know I shouldn't be here but I couldn't think where else to turn. You've got to help Vivien before it's too late."

Aden studied the lad, taking in his hollow-eyed look and the way he hunched into his coat. Shaking his head, he crossed to the cold fireplace and crouched down to get a blaze lit.

"How long have you been waiting?"

"Since early this morning," Kit said, dancing with impatience. "I snuck out before anyone was up."

"You should have lit a fire. It's freezing in here."

"I wanted to, but I didn't how you'd feel about me breaking into your rooms," Kit said with a sheepish smile.

"You didn't break in."

"Well, not really. But—"

"A moment," Aden said, holding up a hand as he finished lighting the fire.

He went to the brass trolley and poured out two brandies. After handing one to Kit, he waved the young man back to the armchair and then propped his shoulder against the marble mantelpiece.

"Tell me why you're here, Kit."

"I tried to tell Vivi that she should go to Sir Dominic, but she refused. She said everything was fine and I was absolutely not to interfere. But I knew it wasn't right, and that's when I decided to come to you. You've got to help her." Kit's blue eyes, so like Vivien's that it hurt, implored him.

"She's made it clear she doesn't want my help," Aden said, trying not to sound bitter.

Kit looked puzzled. "When did you talk to her?"

"It doesn't matter. All I can tell you is that she seems set on her course and she asked me not to interfere." But even as the words left his mouth, Aden mentally disavowed them. He might try to believe that—Vivien clearly wanted him to—but it just didn't make sense.

Kit's chin tilted up with mulish determination. Aden had seen Vivien's delicate jaw adopt that angle any number of times and it never failed to enchant him, even when it signalled an impending verbal brawl.

The young man shook his head. "They're forcing her— the prince and my brother. She doesn't have a choice."

Aden's hand jerked, splashing some brandy over the rim of the glass. Carefully, he set it down on the mantelpiece. "Did she tell you that?"

"Of course not. Vivien never complains. All she said was that she wanted to marry Ivan the Terrible and that I was to mind my own business."

"She actually called him Ivan the Terrible?"

"Yes. She also got very upset when I threatened to speak to you. Got quite frantic about it, in fact, and she actually yelled at me to leave you alone. Can't remember the last time Vivi raised her voice to me like that."

Aden sank into the other wing chair, trying to get his weary brain to think. "Clearly I still don't understand her motivation. I know Lord Blake had tried to use your financial situation as leverage against her, but I thought you'd obtained some relief from that." He narrowed his eyes. "You haven't started gambling again, have you?"

"No!" Kit looked outraged. "I told Vivi I'd stop gambling, and I have."

"Then why is she doing this, if not to save you?"

Kit turned his palms up in a helpless gesture. "It's not just me. It's Mamma's extravagance, too. Her debts run into the thousands. And Cyrus has mortgaged the family pile to the hilt. All told, we're only one step away from falling into the River Tick."

"Yes, but why does that mean Vivien has to marry Khovansky?" Aden snapped. Christ, what had the poor girl ever done to deserve such a useless family?

"Because Ivan the Terrible bought up all our debt," Kit replied in a morose voice. "When Vivien disappeared, he went on a tear. He tracked down every penny and before we knew it His Bloody Highness owned us down to the last bottle of port in the cellar. Now he's threatening to have us all thrown into debtors' prison if Vivien doesn't agree to marry him." He grimaced. "The man's a lunatic, St. George. I'm afraid for Vivien."

Aden rubbed his forehead, furious with himself. If not for his blasted pride he would have figured it out straight off. "Of course she doesn't want to marry him. She can't stand the bastard." As awful as the situation was, an echo of hope reverberated in his heart.

He gave Kit a wry smile. "You can be sure I'll be calling on your brother today. I will not allow Lady Vivien to be forced into a marriage she doesn't want."

His mind leapt ahead, solving the problem. Dominic's help would be needed and Aden might very well have to ask for his father's assistance as well. The idea made him cringe, but that meant nothing when Vivien's life was at stake.

"That's all very well and good," Kit said in a cautious voice. "But what are you going to say to Cyrus?"

"That your sister is already engaged to me. That should do the trick."

Kit goggled at him. "You're marrying Vivien?"

"I am." Aden stood, energy pulsing through his veins. The way forward had suddenly become simple and clear, and he'd let nothing stand in his way. Vivien was his, and he'd known it in his heart for days. Only his childish fears, masquerading as caution, had kept him from acknowledging it.

Kit leapt to his feet. "I say, that's splendid." He grabbed Aden's hand and pumped it.

Aden bit back a laugh. He had the feeling he'd be spending a fair amount of time riding herd on Vivien's family over the next few years. "It's time to pay a visit to Blake House to give your brother the good news. Would you like to come with me?"

Kit grimaced. "That may be sticky since Ivan the Terrible has the place surrounded with his guards. Doesn't want Vivien slipping out."

"Then he's not as stupid as I thought," Aden said dryly. "But I imagine the guards are more to keep me out than Vivien in."

"But what are we to do? Cyrus is hosting a dinner party tonight for the Russian legation. After that, everyone's off to Lady Jersey's ball. Khovansky intends to formally announce the engagement in front of the entire blasted *ton*."

"Then your brother should expect a few extra guests for dinner."

Kit frowned. "What about all the guards?"

Aden smiled and grabbed Kit's arm, pushing him toward the door. "Not to worry. I know just the man to take care of that problem."

Chapter Thirty-Five

Vivien stared at her reflection in the glass over her dressing table. Outwardly, she looked no different than she had a few weeks ago except for the ghastly dark smudges under her eyes. Her features, her hair, the color of her eyes all were the same, although it hardly seemed possible. An earthquake had tumbled her world upside down when she found love in Aden's arms, and then when her life took its nightmarish plunge into Khovansky's rapacious grasp.

It didn't seem possible to remain unchanged after such a revolution, but only her eyes showed the markings of her passage. They stared back at her, dull and empty as they matched the strange sense of hollowness creeping into the very center of her being. She felt numb, and the only prayer Vivien had left in her soul was imploring that the numbness take permanent hold. Perhaps then she could survive marriage to a vile man determined to mold her to his will.

Ivan had told her that in so many words, promising a swift removal from England as soon as possible and a return to Russia where he would have her *all to himself*. He'd practically licked his lips when he'd said it, his eyes gleaming with a chilling combination of hatred and lust. He'd stored up every rejection and every humiliation he thought she'd inflicted on him, and was hell-bent on exacting his revenge. That revenge would carry on the rest of her life, and there wasn't a damn thing anyone could do about it.

Not even Aden.

She squeezed her eyes shut. Every time she thought of Aden her chest grew so tight she could hardly breathe. Only the knowledge that she kept him and Kit safe made it possible for her to go through with tonight's charade and to face the ghastly days ahead.

Her mother fluttered into the room. "My love, the guests are beginning to arrive. You don't want to be late for your own engagement party."

Vivien dragged herself to her feet. "Under the circumstances, it seems a reasonable response."

Her mother's smile faltered. "Vivien, I know the prince wasn't your first choice, but can't you reconcile yourself to this? After all, you will be a princess. Think of how delightful that will be!"

"Even if that prince is a complete lunatic?"

Her mother cast a frightened glance over her shoulder, as if someone was listening. For all Vivien knew, there might be a thug with his ear plastered to the door. Since they returned to Blake House yesterday afternoon, the prince had stationed his men everywhere.

"Vivien, be careful. You cannot afford to be overheard."

"Yes, Mamma." There was no point in discussing things with her mother anyway, since there was nothing either of them could do.

"Oh, my darling," Mamma said, taking her hands in a fond clasp. "Everything will be fine, I just know it. I'm going to ask the prince tonight if I can accompany you back to Russia. A daughter should have her mother by her side when she gets married, especially when she's moving so far from home.

Besides, I think it would be rather splendid to see the Court in St. Petersburg, don't you?"

Vivien couldn't begin to imagine her pampered, indolent mother making that kind of journey, nor did she wish to expose her to Prince Ivan's uncertain mercies. Still, it soothed Vivien's heart a wee bit to know her mother had made the offer.

"Thank you, Mamma. We will discuss it later, but we shouldn't keep the prince waiting." Ivan the Terrible had outlined in no uncertain terms that she was always to make herself available to him. The man wasn't to be her husband, but her jailer.

As they made their way downstairs her mother twittered and fussed like a sparrow, profusely complimenting Vivien on the diamonds and rubies the prince had sent earlier in the day. The terse note accompanying the necklace, bracelets, and earrings had explained that they belonged to his mother and that he expected her to wear them tonight. Baroque and ugly as sin, Vivien already hated them.

When they entered the drawing room half the guests had already arrived, including Ambassador and Countess Lieven.

"My dear, we began to wonder if you would be joining us this evening," Khovansky said as he bowed over her hand. When he straightened, Vivien had no trouble reading the ire in his protruding eyes.

"Nonsense, Your Highness," the countess said in her charming accent, slapping him lightly on the sleeve with her fan. "It's entirely appropriate for Lady Vivien to make a grand entrance. After all, she is the star this evening. She can do whatever she wants and we must all bow down before her."

Vivien gave her a grateful smile, wishing she could stick her tongue out at Khovansky. She was entirely sick of the way the man glared at her. If this kept up she would likely murder him within a week of their wedding. All things considered, hanging seemed the preferable option.

Doing her best to ignore him, she drifted about the room greeting their guests and forcing inane social chatter past her lips. Since she and Khovansky had not yet formally announced their engagement, no one referred to it directly. But she received many sly compliments and veiled congratulations. By the time they moved into dinner she felt ready to scream.

As she took her seat to the right of Cyrus, she glanced down the table, frowning. "Where's Kit?"

Now that she thought about it, she hadn't seen him all day. He was likely still smarting from the scold she'd given him last night, but he'd been hell-bent on asking Aden to help. Vivien had been numb with exhaustion and despair by that point, but Kit's dogged insistence that she go to Aden had broken through, pitching her into panic. She could bear many hardships, but Aden's death wasn't one of them.

"I was about to ask *you,*" Cyrus replied in a low voice. "One would think he could be present for his sister's engagement party." A sneer curled his lips. "Perhaps he's drowning his sorrows in one of those damned hells he's so fond of."

"Perhaps. I only wish I could join him."

Cyrus hissed at her to be quiet, but Vivien was spared the need to reply when the footmen began serving the soup. She managed to ignore her brother through that and the next course as well, focusing her attention on her seatmate, a kind and elderly baron who'd been a friend of her father's.

When the dishes from the second course were removed, Cyrus rose to his feet. Vivien's stomach clenched when he picked up his goblet of champagne and pompously cleared his throat. Her brother was going to announce her engagement, and there would be no going back.

She braced herself, smoothing out her features. A smile

was impossible, but her last shreds of pride urged her to avoid looking like she was about to lose her dinner.

"As some of you know," Cyrus began, "you have been invited here tonight for a joyous occasion, one that will mark—"

A loud crash echoed through the hallway, followed by several alarming thumps that cut Cyrus off. Everyone glanced at the door and then back at Cyrus. He stood with his mouth hanging open, staring anxiously at Khovansky.

"Please continue, Lord Blake," the prince said loudly from his place down by Mamma.

Cyrus raised his goblet again, but almost dropped it when another crash sounded. This time the door to the dining room shook as if something heavy had been flung against it. A few seconds later there was a dragging noise and then the double doors flew open and a tall man, dressed all in black, strode into the room. He stopped, narrowing his cold gaze right on Ivan the Terrible.

Aden.

Vivien's vision tilted sideways, her mind struggling to make sense of what she saw. She'd refused herself the luxury of wishing for a last-minute, daring intervention—Aden defying the prince, defying *himself* in order to rescue her. Rising to her feet, she stared at him, open-mouthed.

His gaze flickered down the table to find her, and a loving smile parted his lips. It stole the breath from her lungs, and Vivien had to clutch the edge of the table to keep from toppling over.

Verbal pandemonium broke out as everyone started shouting at once. Vivien winced when Cyrus bellowed loud enough to shatter glass. "How dare you break into my house," he stormed at Aden. "You will leave now, or my footmen will throw you out on the street."

"That's not going to happen, Cyrus," said Kit as he strode

into the room and stood shoulder-to-shoulder with Aden. "I've instructed all the servants to remain in the kitchen."

Cyrus began gobbling, incoherent with rage. Vivien's mother let out a shriek, flopping back in her chair as if about to swoon. Several of the men demanded answers from no one in general, adding to the chaos.

Khovansky, who'd been staring at Aden with an utterly stunned look on his face, finally sprang to his feet, roaring for quiet. The din cut off as sharply as a razor's cut, and a fraught silence fell over the room.

"Captain St. George," the prince snarled, "you have developed a most unwelcome habit of interfering in my affairs. You will regret that."

Aden shrugged. "I doubt it," he said with obvious contempt.

Khovansky's features turned a livid shade of purple as he cast a pointed stare out to the hallway.

"If you're looking for your merry band of thugs, you'll be disappointed," Aden said, glancing over his shoulder. As if on cue, Griffin Steele strode into the room, garbed in a swirling greatcoat and looking like a pirate.

"Everything under control?" Aden asked him with a faint smile.

When Steele lifted an arrogant brow, Vivien blinked. She had seen that expression on Aden's face more than once. Standing next to each other, she almost took them for brothers.

"Of course," Steele replied in a bored voice. "Hired brutes from the stews are hardly a match for my men. We've got them under guard in Lord Blake's study." He cast an ironic gaze on Cyrus. "Sadly, I fear his lordship's furniture is a little worse for the encounter."

Cyrus huffed with outrage again, but the Russian ambassador cut him off. "Captain St. George, I demand to know the meaning of this intrusion. And what is this talk of thugs and rescues?"

"Your Excellency," Aden said. "The prince is blackmailing Lady Vivien into an unwanted marriage and holding her entire family hostage. To prevent her from trying to escape, he recruited a criminal gang to keep the Blakes' prisoners within their own household."

With a snarl, Khovansky took a step toward Aden. "You will regret this action until the day you die, I promise you."

Aden barked out a short laugh. "I think not. By the way, my dear count," he added, turning back to the ambassador, "Prince Ivan was also responsible for Lady Vivien's abduction some weeks ago."

"These are outrageous accusations to make against a member of the Russian Court," the ambassador said in an austere tone. "You would be wise to have proof before making them."

"I have ample proof, enough to have the prince thrown into prison for a very long time if he were an Englishman."

"You will answer for those baseless accusations," Khovansky snarled. "I will see you hang if I have to go to the Regent himself."

Vivien let out a strangled gasp, clutching the edge of the table.

Countess Lieven glanced at her before directing her sharp gaze at Khovansky. "You do know who the captain's father is, do you not?" When the prince gave her a baffled stare, she gave an insouciant shrug. "Never mind. You will soon enough." Then she left her seat and rustled over to Vivien, taking her hand in a comforting grip. "Are these distressful accusations true, my child?"

Vivien shook so badly she feared her legs might collapse. With every inch of her being she wanted to tell the truth. But what would that mean for Aden? Would she precipitate his ruin, possibly even his murder?

She forced herself to meet Khovansky's eyes. The burning hatred and the demented threat she saw in his expression sent shards of fear slicing through her. Not for herself, but for Aden.

"Vivien, look at me," Aden's calm voice cut through her panic. She took a deep breath and met his gaze.

And lost her breath all over again when she saw the love in his eyes, shining on her like sunlight on Midsummer's Morn.

"My darling, you must trust me," he said. "I promise all will be well."

His tender gravity transformed the words into a vow, one that bound them together for the days and years to come. Vivien's heart unfolded like the pages of a book as she smiled back at him. For a glorious moment they simply looked at each other, and then he nodded, prompting her to speak.

"Yes, my lady," she responded to the countess. "Captain St. George speaks the truth. Prince Ivan was responsible for my abduction, and has threatened my family with financial ruin if I don't marry him."

Cyrus dropped into his chair and began moaning in unhappy chorus with his mother's hysterical tears.

The countess curled a lip at the prince before returning her attention to Vivien. "I take it that you have no wish to marry Prince Ivan, then."

"I never did, my lady," Vivien said firmly.

The older woman patted her hand. "Then you shall not." She turned to her husband. "My dear sir, under the circumstances I think it best our party leave. Immediately."

"Indeed, my dear." Count Lieven directed an imperious stare at Ivan the Terrible. "Your Highness, I will ask you to accompany us back to the embassy. We have much to discuss."

The prince had been frozen in place, staring at Vivien with

poisonous venom, but the ambassador's words cut him loose. "No," he roared, pitching himself down the table toward Vivien.

She barely had time to fling her arms up before Aden grabbed the prince from behind. He spun him around and drilled a fist into Khovansky's face, following it up with a punishing blow under the man's jaw. The prince's eyes rolled in his head and he dropped to the floor without a sound.

"Well done, Captain," muttered Countess Lieven.

Vivien let out a strangled, astonished laugh.

"I never could stand him," the countess whispered to her. "Dreadful, froggy-faced lout."

Not that there was any need to whisper, given the shouts and hysterical noises coming from the rest of the guests. Fortunately, Aden and Steele quickly exerted control and Vivien sank down in her chair to watch them restore order out of chaos.

After calling two footmen up from the kitchen, Steele oversaw the transfer of Khovansky's inert form to the ambassador's carriage. The countess, after hugging Vivien, hurried out with her husband and the other guests followed, obviously eager to begin spreading the gossip about the exciting conclusion of Vivien's aborted engagement party.

"Ruined. We're ruined," moaned Cyrus.

Vivien glared at her brother. "Do shut up, will you, Cyrus? If we are ruined, it's your fault."

She looked at her mother and Kit at the other end of the long, cluttered dining table. Mamma was weeping loudly into her handkerchief while Kit ineffectually patted her on the shoulder. "In fact, it's all our faults," Vivien added, "and it's time we start taking responsibility for our mistakes."

Cyrus jumped to his feet. "You can do whatever you want, but I won't stay here a minute longer and listen to this drivel."

As he stormed out of the room, their mother hauled herself

from her chair. "Cyrus," she bleated plaintively, rushing after him. "What are we all to do?"

Kit sighed. "I'd better go after them, if only to make sure Cyrus doesn't strangle Mamma."

"What a splendid idea," Aden said, coming in from the hallway. "And make sure everyone else leaves us alone. Your sister doesn't need any more upset."

"I'll take care of it." Kit grasped Aden's hand and wrung it. "Thank you, sir, for everything."

Aden gave him a wry smile. "You did well, Kit. I begin to have some hope for you."

When Kit laughed and left the room, Aden closed the door behind him.

Vivien sucked in a breath. Finally, they were alone. She stood up again on wobbly legs, grasping at the table to steady herself. Aden crossed the length of the room in long, loping strides.

"Easy, my love." He lowered her back into her chair. "There's no need to do anything. Just sit down and rest for a few minutes."

"I'm sorry," she said, hardly able to look him in the face. Suddenly, she was more nervous than she'd been all evening. "I don't usually act like such a wet hen."

Aden hooked an arm over the back of a neighboring chair and pulled it over. "You're no wet hen, Vivien. You're the bravest person I've ever met."

He gently removed the horrible, heavy pieces of jewelry from her neck and wrists and tossed them carelessly on the table, pulling a choked laugh from Vivien. Then he took her hands, turned them over, and planted a kiss, first on one palm and then the other. His handsome face grew blurry, and Vivien had to blink several times to clear her vision. He waited patiently, gazing at her with such tenderness that she found her throat closing on yet more tears.

She studied him, amazed at the change. It was Aden, and yet not. Or, rather, the Aden she'd always longed for him to be—open, loving, able to let her in.

"Is it really over?" she whispered.

He nodded. "The ambassador and his wife—who was splendid, I must say—will deal with Khovansky. As for his band of thugs, Griffin and his men are hauling them off to Bow Street. They will never bother you again, Vivien."

Her defensive walls finally crumbled. Despite herself, she couldn't hold back a few sobs of relief. The nightmare was finally over, at least for her. But for Aden?

She clutched his hands. "But you're safe, aren't you? Prince Ivan will not be able to harm you?" She couldn't hold back a shudder. "He made such horrible threats—"

Aden leaned in and pressed his lips to hers, teasing her mouth with tender kisses that slowly grew heated. He thoroughly explored her mouth, gently demanding she let him in. When she did, he claimed her, kissing her until she had to clutch at the lapels of his coat to hold steady.

When he finally broke away, his eyes gleamed with sensual intent and Vivien was gasping for breath.

"You're not to worry about Khovansky ever again," he said. "Do you understand?"

Still reeling from his kiss, she could only nod.

"Good." He gave her a rather stern look. "Not that you don't deserve a scold for what you did—or didn't do, I might say."

She shook her head. "What do you mean?"

"Goose," he said affectionately. "I mean for not sending for me or Sir Dominic right away. I know you agreed to marry Khovansky only to save your brother and me. Your intentions were noble, but unwise, to say the least."

"I didn't know what else to do. Besides," she grumbled, "you weren't very encouraging the last time we spoke, if you recall."

He grimaced. "I'm an idiot, and I apologize for that. I let my fear and my pride come between us, and only by the grace of God—and Kit—did we come around." He took her face between his hands. "I'll never leave you again, Vivien. I swear it."

Too overcome with emotion to speak, she leaned in to give him a kiss. They engaged in that very pleasurable activity until they were both breathless and heated.

Aden pulled back with a groan. "We've got to stop or I'll have you on the table with your heels up in the air. I hardly think Lord Blake would approve."

She giggled. The sound of her laughter made her dizzy, since only a few hours ago she'd believed she'd never laugh again. "What happens now? I'm very happy to be free of my engagement, of course, but it does leave my family in a terrible pickle."

"We're going to get married and find a place to live, regardless of what happens to your family. There are some nice little terraces going up around Cadogan Square that might do very well."

Vivien grabbed the front of his coat. "Truly?"

He frowned. "Yes. We're going to get married, so what did you think?"

"But what about your work? Can you simply walk away from that?"

He kissed the tip of her nose. "Trust me, I'm ready. Besides, there are other things I can do to help Dominic and the government that don't require me to skulk around the Continent in disguise. From now on, the only skulking I'll be doing is under the sheets with you."

She smiled, patting his chest. "That sounds lovely, but . . ."

"But?"

Vivien anxiously chewed her lip. Aden tipped her chin up.

"Out with it, my love."

"It will be a financial burden, but Mamma and Kit will have to live with us."

He stared at her with mock horror.

"Well, they will," she said defensively.

Aden waved an insouciant hand. "Not to worry. I have a plan. You'll simply have to support us at the gaming tables."

She scowled at him. "I will not!"

He laughed. "Sweetheart, I'm by no means poor. I inherited a tidy sum from my aunt some years ago, and I've had a great deal of success investing it. I won't do a thing to help Cyrus, but I am well able to provide for the rest of your family."

Vivien was about to throw her arms around his neck when a horrible thought darted into her head.

Aden rolled his eyes. "What now?"

"What will your father think of all this?" she blurted out. "I've created such a horrible scandal and God knows what people will say about me and Prince Ivan. Will the Regent be displeased if you marry me?"

"Darling, I'm his by-blow and the result of one of the more lurid scandals in the *ton*. How upset do you think he could get? Besides, if he does have any objections, my mother will deal with him."

She stared at him doubtfully. "Really?"

"Yes, really." He stroked her jaw. "Did I not promise weeks ago I would take care of you?"

"You did, but it works both ways."

"What do you mean?"

"I'm going to take care of you, too," she answered, tapping him on the chest for emphasis. "You need a bit of fussing over."

He shook his head, looking a bit dazed. "My love, I think I have been waiting my entire life for someone to fuss over me."

"Good. From now on we take care of each other."

"Now that you mention it," he said, pulling her onto his lap. "There *is* something I'd like you to take care of."

"So I see," she said, laughing with a joy so encompassing she could barely contain it. "Or, rather, *feel.*"

She shifted to get more comfortable, and Aden drew in a sharp breath. "I think I have the perfect solution to your problem," she murmured.

"Splendid," he replied, nuzzling her throat. "Then I suggest you get started immediately."

Epilogue

Thornbury House, Berkeley Square
December 1814

Dominic Hunter stood inside the doorway to the ornately formal drawing room, allowing himself to bask in the happy scene playing out in front of him. His schemes usually came to fruition, but rarely had he taken such pleasure in the outcome as he did now.

He heard the rustle of silk behind him and then a small, gloved hand slipped into the crook of his elbow.

"Goodness, Dominic," said a gently lilting voice. "Why are you hovering in the doorway? Don't you want to congratulate the bride and groom? After all, they would never have reached this moment without you."

He smiled down at the diminutive and comfortably plump middle-aged woman, still lovely after so many years, who'd come to stand beside him. "I have the feeling that Aden and his new wife would have found their way to each other somehow, Lady Tait. I merely gave them a nudge in the right direction."

She rolled her eyes. "That's not what Anthony told me. And why, my dear, do you insist on calling me *Lady Tait* when we're in public? It's ridiculous to be so formal. You know very well I'm only twelve years older than you."

Dominic smiled at her comically wry expression. "Yes, but you've been more of a mother to me than my own mother ever had the chance to be."

Her eyes softened as she tugged him down to plant a soft kiss on his cheek. "Thank you, Dominic. You know the special place you will always hold in my heart." Her glance cut over to Aden and Vivien, standing in the center of the room greeting their wedding guests. "I hope you will find your happiness someday, just as that lovely couple has."

A dark, familiar pain rustled deep within him. Dominic barely acknowledged it, having learned to live with it long ago.

"This makes me happy," he said. "To know that Aden is where he truly belongs. It has been many years in the making, and no man deserves it more."

Lady Tait let out a ladylike snort. "Dominic, you know very well—"

A deep, masculine voice cut her off. "Linnet, Dominic is much too old for you to be scolding him, don't you think? And in public, no less. You'll set all the gossips to buzzing."

Breathing a sigh of relief, Dominic turned to greet his former guardian and mentor. "Sir, it's a pleasure to see you. It's been much too long."

Sir Anthony Tait's upright form barely showed any concession to his age, although his hair was liberally sprinkled with gray and his lean face had grown craggier with the years. But his clear, hazel gaze still gleamed with the intelligence and sharp perception that had made him one of England's most formidable spymasters.

Lady Tait glowered at her husband, obviously intending to cow him. She failed miserably. Firstly, she was so much shorter than he and, secondly, her love for him lit up her features. Dominic had lived with the Taits for several years as a lad, and he knew better than anyone the strength of their feelings for each other. He'd been privileged beyond measure to be considered a part of their family.

"I was merely reminding Dominic that he's not too old to find his own happiness. Surely you can't disagree with that," Lady Tait said, trying to sound severe.

"My dear, I make it a strict policy never to disagree with you," her husband replied.

When her mouth dropped open in disbelief, both Dominic and Sir Anthony laughed. Lady Tait drew herself up to her full height—which barely reached the center of Dominic's chest—and snapped open her fan.

"If you two gentlemen will excuse me," she said in an imperious voice, "I intend to make my congratulations to the bride and groom. Anthony, do not keep Dominic trapped here while you prose on forever about government business. We're at a wedding, not a meeting at the Home Office."

"Yes, my love," Sir Anthony replied in a dutiful voice.

Lady Tait muttered something about *stubborn men* under her breath, but Dominic didn't miss the smile lurking about her lips as she sailed off.

"She has a point," Sir Anthony said. "It's long past time for you to get married and start a family of your own. Whatever happened in the past should not—"

Dominic narrowed his gaze in warning.

The older man studied his face for a few moments and then sighed. "Very well. But since we are speaking of family, do we expect Griffin to make an appearance today?"

"No. The Prince Regent is expected shortly. I can't imagine Prinny would welcome the proprietor of London's most notorious gaming houses to his son's wedding, especially since His Royal Highness also happens to owe Griffin a considerable sum of money. Besides," Dominic said, glancing around at the genteel assemblage, "this is hardly Griffin's style."

"It could be," Anthony replied. "You're not giving up on your plans to reform him, are you?" He gestured toward the happy couple, now making their way in a leisurely fashion about the room to greet their guests. "Griffin deserves this as much as Aden does."

"I know," Dominic said. "And I'll see that he gets it."

He'd made it one of his missions in life to help men like Aden and Griffin, the bastard sons of the royal princes, the ones who'd been tossed aside by their fathers. Men who'd had to fight for every last scrap of dignity and self-worth, just like Dominic had been forced to do.

Sir Anthony gave a thoughtful nod. "Griffin is a more challenging case, as I'm sure you realize. His loss has been profound."

The darkness inside Dominic rustled again, a reminder that it would not be forgotten.

"Don't worry," he replied in a grim voice. "I have every intention of reuniting him with his mother." That, in fact, would be a hell of a task since Griffin's mother had been lost to all of them for twenty-eight long years. "I'll find her, even if I have to search every corner of England to do it."

"Do you think he noticed how nervous I was?" Vivien asked, wrinkling her pretty nose in dismay. "I'm afraid I sounded like a complete ninny."

They watched Aden's mother steer the rotund figure of the Prince Regent across the cavernous drawing room toward Edmund, Aden's half brother. Edmund had graciously offered Thornbury House as the setting for their wedding breakfast, especially once he'd been apprised that Prinny would be attending. Aden had winced when his mother had insisted on including his father on the invitation list, but the old fellow had been quite helpful in smoothing over lingering problems with the Russians, outraged that a gently bred Englishwoman and his son had been the target of such a sinister plot. The entire episode had been the biggest scandal of the Season, and only the fact that Aden had claimed the ultimate prize—Vivien's love—made the subsequent gossip and fuss remotely tolerable.

But with Vivien by his side, Aden could put up with anything.

"My darling," he said, smoothing his hand along the back of her silky-soft neck, "you've met my royal parent several times over the years. Why should today be any different?"

She shivered under his caress even as the expression in her beautiful blue eyes conveyed both laughter and disbelief. "Because today is our wedding day, silly! And the Prince Regent is now my father-in-law. It's all rather a bit much to take in, don't you think?"

He shrugged. "I suppose I've gotten used to it. Besides, he can't be any worse than your family, can he?"

Vivien glanced across the room where Cyrus was trying to toady up to the Regent. "I'm sorry we had to invite Cyrus, but I think your mamma was right. It would have generated even more gossip if we'd left him off the list."

Aden dropped a swift kiss on her rosy mouth, not caring for one moment if anyone saw him do it. Vivien was his wife, now and forever, and he would kiss her wherever and whenever he chose. Besides, she looked so delectable in her gold dress trimmed with lace and cut temptingly low across the bodice, it was a wonder he didn't carry her off into an empty room and have his way with her.

"You're not to worry," he said. "Cyrus and I have come to an understanding." Namely, that Cyrus was to stay the hell away from Vivien or face Aden's wrath.

"I'm sure," she replied in a dry voice. Then she tilted her head, her gaze running over him in a way that made his blood instantly heat.

"What?" he asked, his voice going low and husky.

"I was just thinking of Mr. and Mrs. Parker, and what they would think about all this."

Aden slid his hand from Vivien's neck and trailed it down her arm, making her shiver again. He entwined his fingers with hers. "I certainly know what Mr. Parker would be thinking right now."

"Oh, yes?" she asked, her eyes sparkling with so much love and laughter that Aden could barely contain his own happiness. To know that this woman was his to adore to the end of their days was a joy and a freedom he'd never thought to experience.

"He'd be thinking about their *breeding problem,* and how best to resolve it," he said.

"How odd. I believe Mrs. Parker would be thinking the same thing."

Her lips parted and the tip of her pink tongue touched the corner of her mouth. Aden instantly turned hard, which wasn't very convenient, under the circumstances.

Vivien's sapphire gaze turned smoky with desire. "Do you think Mr. and Mrs. Parker might be able to slip away for a few minutes to discuss the problem? Without anyone noticing?"

Aden grinned. "I'm a spy, my love. I do this sort of thing for a living." He cast a swift glance around the room, sizing up the quickest route of escape as he slipped an arm around her waist. "Just leave everything to me."

Dear Reader,

Thank you so much for reading *Secrets for Seducing a Royal Bodyguard*, book one in The Renegade Royals series. I enjoyed sharing Aden's and Vivien's story with you, along with teasing you with hints about Dominic Hunter's story, which began in my novella *Lost in a Royal Kiss*. Dominic will be a consistent thread throughout the series as he helps my heroes secure their rightful places in society.

One character you might also have noticed is Aden's cousin, Griffin Steele. As soon as he appeared on my computer screen, Griffin was the type of character who took hold and pushed me in some unexpected (and fun!) directions. I'm thrilled that Griffin's story, called *Confessions of a Royal Bridegroom*, is coming up next.

Griffin is the illegitimate son of Chloe and Prince Ernest from *Lost in a Royal Kiss*. He's the classic Regency reprobate, living his life by his own reckless code, and the heck with what anyone thinks of him. Naturally, given the type of man he is—dangerous, charismatic, and rebellious—I had to give him a heroine with the strength and intelligence to stand up to him.

That's where Justine Brightmore comes in, and I'm happy to say she's one of my favorite heroines. When Griffin finds a mysterious baby on his doorstep, he hasn't a clue what to do with it. But Dominic Hunter does, and he sends the prim and practical Justine to lend a helping hand. Justine thinks Griffin is nothing but trouble, and she firmly intends to keep a safe distance. But Griffin's convinced that Justine's starched exterior conceals a passionate and beautiful woman, one he's determined to reveal—whether she wants him to, or not!

Confessions of a Royal Bridegroom will be released in April 2014. Please read on for an excerpt. You can also stop by my website to keep up with all the news about subsequent books in the series, read more excerpts, and enter my fun contests. You can find me at www.vanessakellyauthor.com.

After seven long years, Griffin Steele was a sinner's breath away from casting off the millstone around his neck, the one that dragged at the few shreds of decency in his dark soul.

"I trust everything is to your specifications," said Madeline Reeves in her smoothly seductive tones. "Lizzie, Rebecca, and I went over the terms quite carefully, and I believe we've done a more than adequate job of addressing your concerns." Her full-lipped smile offset any hint of criticism that her words might have conveyed.

Griffin glanced up from the document to the woman who managed his brothel and who had once graced his bed. Madeline was a statuesque beauty, dark-haired and sloe-eyed, with a languid sensuality that masked a keen business mind and a cardsharp's instincts. She was also, despite her profession, thoroughly decent and one of the few people Griffin had elected to trust in his life.

He responded to her challenge with a nod. "I know the terms seem more demanding than are justified, given our relationship. I also know you see the reason for it." He allowed the document to settle with a whisper of fluttering parchment onto his desk. "Am I wrong?"

Madeline's smile tilted up at one corner in wry understanding. "No, you're not wrong. You're never wrong, are you?"

Griffin had to repress a bitter laugh, covering the emotion her remark had engendered with a languid smile. "My dear, you flatter me, but I trust you see the reasoning behind my insistence on your ability to meet my terms. At least in this particular instance."

"I do." Madeline's lovely features shifted ever so slightly, transforming her from one of London's most sought-after courtesans into a canny businesswoman. "If we could not demonstrate our ability to manage The Golden Tie according to your terms, then we would never be able to maintain our financial independence and treat the girls with a modicum of decency. I know how important that is to you."

She leaned forward to place a hand on the polished countertop of his Chippendale desk, her burgundy gown, beautifully tailored to showcase her magnificent figure, rustling with the soft slide of expensive silk. "I won't let anything happen to the girls, Griffin. You have my word."

"I know I do, and I am grateful to you."

He was, too. Madeline and her new partners—all women who worked in his brothel—were a key part of his plan to achieve his freedom.

Griffin had long wanted to shed The Golden Tie. He'd only saddled himself with it because he'd been unable to tolerate the brutal treatment meted out to the girls by the brothel's former owner—a foul excuse for a man named Paulson. The pig had done nothing to protect the girls from disease, pregnancy, and beatings from the customers. The man had, unfortunately, also owned The Cormorant, the first gaming house Griffin had acquired and the foundation of his wealth and influence. Though Griffin had only wanted the gaming house, he'd found himself taking the brothel on, as well.

Not that he was a saint. He'd taken full financial advantage of the opportunity—on his terms, of course—but now he was eager to rid himself of a responsibility he'd never wanted. Too often, in the years since he'd arrived in London, he'd seen the ruination of women, mistreated and then discarded by the sorts of men who frequented establishments like The Golden Tie. His own mother had suffered a similar fate. Griffin's father had the bluest blood in the land, but to his mind the man was less than a scraping of mud from a bootjack.

"Griffin, is something wrong?" The keen understanding in Madeline's eyes jogged him even more than her words.

Waving a negligent hand, he rose to his feet to signal an end to their interview. "Not in the least, my dear. I'll have my solicitor look over the papers later today, but I'm sure everything is in order. We should be able to sign off in a few days." With a smile, he rounded the desk to offer Madeline his hand. "I wish you the best of luck, Mad. I know you'll make a go of it."

She rose with the sinuous grace that had entranced so many. Madeline was tall, enough so that she could almost look him straight in the eye.

"Would you, perhaps, like to celebrate the completion of our deal?" she purred, her velvet-brown gaze glittering with satisfaction and invitation. "Once more for old times' sake?"

Her voice brushed along his nerves, pleasantly arousing. At one time, Griffin would have responded to that siren call with alacrity. But he'd left Madeline's bed months ago, as much from a growing ennui as a reluctance to mix business and pleasure. For a moment, he allowed himself to consider the invitation, knowing that Madeline would be more than willing to do all the work. But then that dark, dissatisfied part of him that had been pushing so hard of late, the part driving him to step far away from his current life, reasserted itself. He didn't have to say a word, either. Madeline, ever sensitive to his emotional nuance, saw the answer on his face.

"Ah, well," she said, not sounding all that disappointed. "I thought not. Truly, Griffin, you are turning into a monk. And we haven't seen you next door in three nights. I do hope you don't intend to take yourself off to some dreary mountaintop in Scotland, or hole up in a ridiculous hermitage on one of your uncles' estates." She let her gaze drift down over his body. "That would be such a waste."

He grinned at her. "Now, you're simply flattering me, and you know I'm immune to that sort of thing."

She was about to retort when a quick knock on the door cut her off. Before Griffin could call out permission to enter, Tom Deacon opened the door and barreled into the room.

Griffin raised his eyebrows in a pointed question. His business manager might be several inches taller and outweigh him by three stone, but Tom knew better than to charge into his office without permission. Combined with the scowl on the man's blunt features, it suggested that something had disturbed his normally unflappable right-hand man.

Tom came to a halt in front of the desk, practically stepping on Griffin's toes. The space was small enough that Madeline had to sit down in order to avoid getting squashed between the two men.

Griffin's office, once the room from which he'd managed the gaming hell that had graced this part of Jermyn Street, wasn't large. He'd closed The Cormorant only a few months ago, converting the building back to its original use as a private dwelling, but he'd seen no point in moving his office to a more spacious room upstairs. From here, Griffin could still monitor the comings and goings in his household and the brothel next door, connected by a small, conveniently placed passageway right outside his office door. Tom's bulky form and his obvious agitation filled the room, making the walls seem to close in.

Sighing, Griffin moved around to the other side of his desk

and waited. Tom was a man of few words to begin with, and it rarely served to push him. But after several seconds of watching Tom's jaw tick under the impact of some obviously perturbing stimulus, Griffin finally lost his patience.

"Are we going to stand here like a pair of chawbacons, or are you going to tell me why you're so disturbed?" Griffin asked with some asperity.

Tom's jaw worked again, as if chewing over a gristly piece of beef, but he finally spit words out. "It's a baby. A baby in the entrance hall."

Griffin's mind blanked for a second. "A baby?" he repeated, sounding rather like a chawbacon after all. "In my house?"

Some of the girls did occasionally succumb to that particular hazard of the profession, but Griffin always set them up off the premises. Babies weren't exactly good for this sort of business.

Tom unleashed a grim smile. "Aye. And, apparently, it's yours."

Griffin strode down the hallway toward the front of the house.

"If there's one thing you can be sure of," he snapped over his shoulder at Tom, "it's that this baby is *not* mine. I've been very careful with that sort of thing, I assure you." Given his lamentable parentage he'd be damned if he spread his seed around with such careless abandon.

"I'm just telling you what the boy who brought him said," Tom retorted. "I'm not sayin' it's true, am I?"

"I should bloody well hope not," Griffin muttered. Even so, he couldn't help counting in his head, thinking of whose bed he'd been warming about nine months ago. A few moments of rapid reflection confirmed what he'd thought. He'd been sleeping with only Madeline back then, and he'd sure as hell had not gotten her with child.

Still, some enterprising or desperate woman might try to pin the charge on him, hoping to squeeze him for money. Griffin's reputation when it came to matters of a sexual nature was exaggerated. He was more discriminating than anyone gave him credit for, unlike Prinny and some of his other royal uncles who couldn't seem to resist an attractive bit of tail to save their lives. Griffin also made a point of never sleeping with a woman whilst in his cups. He'd learned early on that losing control of oneself only led to trouble. On the few occasions when he did indulge in drink, he generally did it in private, or with the few people he trusted to have his back.

He pushed through the baize door and into the entrance hall. A moment later he practically skidded to a halt, with Tom almost ramming him in the back.

There was a baby, all right. It was wrapped in a white blanket, resting in a commodious straw basket, which someone had plopped into the middle of the tiled hall. Griffin couldn't actually *see* the infant from where he stood, but he could hear its woeful crying. Its thin wail climbed up into a higher register, rapidly transforming into a lusty, keening lament that bounced off the plastered walls to make everyone wince.

"Nothin' wrong with that set of lungs," Tom observed in a sour voice.

Griffin resisted the impulse to jam his fingers in his ears as he inspected the other stranger. A small boy of not more than ten years of age, clearly a street urchin, stood by the basket, shifting uncomfortably as he rolled his ratty cap between nervous fingers. Hovering behind the boy with a pained look on his narrow features was Phelps, Griffin's manservant and factotum.

"What the hell is going on?" Griffin asked in a voice loud

enough to be heard over the wailing. "Phelps, why in God's name would you let these brats into the house?"

"Couldn't really stop the boy, Mr. Griffin," Phelps said with a helpless shrug. "He slipped right under my arm before I could say nary a word."

Griffin turned to the urchin. Despite his scruffy appearance, intelligence gleamed in the lad's eyes, along with a wary curiosity. Nor could he fail to note the way the child's gaze jumped from point to point, obviously taking in the highly polished wall sconces and the brass hardware on the doors.

"Don't even think about it," Griffin said in a dry voice.

The boy's eyes widened in an imitation of innocence. "Got no idea what you're talking about, guv."

"I'm fairly sure you do. Now, tell me who you are and why you brought this child into my establishment."

Just then, the baby's cry kicked up to a deafening level. Tom actually did stuff his fingers in his ears.

"Hellfire and damnation, Phelps," Griffin exclaimed. "Pick the child up and keep it quiet. I can barely think with that racket going on."

Phelps, a wiry, capable man who once owned a rough-and-tumble pub in Covent Garden, backed away, putting up his hands as if warding off an attack. "Sorry, sir. I'm afraid I'll drop it. Never did go in much for babies."

"Phelps, you raised a daughter, remember? She works in this very house. Surely you held her on more than one occasion," Griffin replied, exasperated.

"Aye, and I loves her like my life, but I didn't much enjoy holding her, neither. Not when she squalled like that."

"Pro'lly just needs its nappy changed," observed the boy with the trenchant wisdom of one who had younger siblings.

Griffin turned to Tom, who backed right up to the baize door looking even more panicked than Phelps.

"Oh, for Christ's sake," Griffin muttered.

He crouched down beside the basket. It had been years since he'd held a baby, but he supposed he'd not lost the knack of it. Growing up in his uncle's vicarage in the wilds of Yorkshire, he'd spent many a lonely afternoon in the kitchen with the housekeeper, Mrs. Patterson, a kind woman and the closest thing to a mother Griffin had known in those days. She'd had an inexhaustible supply of grandchildren, and she'd sometimes enlisted his help when she had to take care of one or another of the brood. Without any siblings of his own, Griffin had never minded. He'd spent many a bleak winter's day by the fire, rocking a fractious baby to sleep while Mrs. Patterson bustled about with her cooking.

"Now, what's all the fuss about," he murmured as he carefully peeled the soft blanket away. A very red, unhappy face peered up at him, its mouth pursed with infant outrage. The baby sucked in a breath and waved its little fists in the air, obviously preparing to let out another wail of complaint, so Griffin quickly slipped his hands under the small body and lifted, standing upright in the same motion.

"Here, none of that," he said in quiet voice as he shifted the child to rest more comfortably against his chest.

The baby's cry wavered and then abruptly cut off, replaced by several rather shattering sobs that sounded more like a case of the hiccups. Tears clung to its dark eyelashes and it still looked miserable in that heartrending way of babies. But at least it had stopped lacerating their ears.

"Huh," grunted Tom, inching cautiously forward, as if fearing the baby might leap up and bite him. "Never took you for the motherly sort."

"It's not exactly advanced mathematics," Griffin said before turning his attention back to the lad who'd delivered such an unusual package. "What's your name?"

"Roger. What's yours?" the boy asked with a nervy curiosity that put Griffin in mind of a squirrel.

"Griffin Steele, at your service. Now, perhaps you'd like to tell me what this is all about."

Roger gave a satisfied nod. "You're the nob I was supposed to find. I've got a message for you."

"I'm not a nob," Griffin replied automatically. If there was one thing in the world he did *not* want to be taken for, it was an aristocrat.

Roger glanced around the hall and then raised his eyebrows, investing the look with a polite skepticism that would not have been out of place in the finest drawing rooms of the *ton*.

Griffin sighed. "Well, get on with it then. Who's trying to dump this baby on me and claim that I'm its—" He broke off, shaking his head. "Is it a boy or a girl?"

The boy lifted his shoulders in an insouciant shrug. "Beats me, guv."

Muttering under his breath, Griffin gingerly pulled up the infant's lace-trimmed robe. He couldn't fail to notice that the garment was fashioned of the finest lawn, nor that the matching cap was trimmed with lace.

"A boy," he said, hastily tucking the material back around the obviously well-fed body.

Everyone in the hall seemed to let out a collective sigh, as if they'd all been dying to know the answer.

"Now that we've ascertained that pertinent fact, perhaps you can tell me what you're doing with him, and why you brought him here," Griffin said, gazing sternly at Roger.

The boy opened his mouth to answer, but the words died on his tongue when the green baize door swung open and Madeline swept into the hall in all her sultry glory. Roger's gobsmacked expression was one that Griffin had seen on much older faces more times than he could count.

He cuffed the boy on the shoulder. "None of that. You're much too young to even be looking."

Madeline rustled across the hall to join them. "Goodness, is this little one truly yours, Griffin?"

"No," he replied, trying not to growl with irritation. "But if everyone will kindly stop interrupting me, I might be able to find out who he *does* belong to."

Madeline was staring at the baby with a surprisingly maternal look on her face. "Well, he seems very sweet." She gently stroked the now-drowsy baby's rounded cheek.

"Good, then you can hold him." Griffin swiftly transferred the baby into her arms. She looked startled, but accepted the burden without protest.

"Now, you were about to say?" he prompted Roger.

"I haven't a clue who the brat is, Mr. Steele," the lad said. "Never saw him before a half hour ago. A lady said she'd pay me a 'alf a quid if I delivered him here, and waited to make sure you got him."

Griffin blinked at the ridiculous sum the boy had been offered. "Did she say why?"

"Nah. Just said I was to deliver the basket straight to you and no one else. She was right certain about that. Said you, and only you." Roger scratched his dirt-smudged nose, looking thoughtful. "Figured you must be the kid's dad, she was that insistent."

"Then she didn't actually say I was the boy's father."

"Come to think of it, no."

"And how were you to get paid for this little errand? Were you to meet her afterward?" Surely this mystery woman would not be so foolish as to pay a street urchin *before* he performed his allotted task. If she hadn't, then Griffin could use the boy to track her down.

Roger gave him a gap-toothed, knowing grin, obviously comprehending exactly what Griffin was thinking. "Sorry, Mr. Steele. The lady already paid me. She walked me right up to your door and said she'd wait outside while I went in."

After a moment's surprise, Griffin exploded into action, bolting across the hall and yanking the door open. He ran down the few steps onto Jermyn Street, fairly quiet this early in the day. A few carts lumbered down the street and several plainly dressed persons, probably servants, hurried about their business. Griffin cast a swift glance in both directions, but the only possible lead to the mystery woman was an enclosed black landau that was bowling swiftly down the cobblestones to round the corner only a second later.

Cursing, he strode back into the house. "What did the woman look like? Did she come in a carriage?" he rapped out.

"Don't know. She wore a veil," came the clipped answer from Roger.

"And what about the carriage?"

The boy gave a nod. "Aye. She found me in Piccadilly. We rode to the top of the street, and then we got out and walked the rest of the way with the baby." He looked thoughtful. "Wondered why we just didn't drive up to your doorstep."

"I imagine she didn't want anyone looking out the window and sighting her carriage," Griffin replied, feeling more frustrated by the moment. Whoever the mystery woman was, she'd taken great care to hide her identity while at the same time making sure the baby was safe.

"Did you notice anything particular about the carriage?" Madeline asked the boy after casting a worried glance at Griffin. "A crest on the side, or unusual markings?"

"It was black."

Griffin pinched the space between his eyebrows. "Thank you for that trenchant observation. Anything else?"

Another careless shrug of the boy's bony shoulders was the only answer.

"Too smitten with the blunt that lady gave you to pay attention to anything else, I reckon," Tom said with sarcasm.

"I reckon you're right," Roger replied with a grin. "Can you blame me?"

"No, I suppose not," Griffin said. "And you're sure you never saw this woman before?"

"Aye."

"And there's nothing else you remember."

Roger blinked rapidly several times, which seemed to aid the process of extracting a final bit of information from his brain.

"Aye, she did. She said to make sure you read the note in the basket, and not to lose the ring, neither."

Griffin hunkered down beside the basket and rummaged through the blankets. They were of white wool, soft and well made, finished with satin ribbon. Like the baby's clothes, they were scrupulously clean and obviously expensive. It appeared that someone cared a great deal about this infant.

He fished out a folded note, sealed with red wax. He tucked it into the waistband of his breeches and continued his search, digging through the blankets until he got to the bottom of the basket. Finally, he extracted a small, black velvet bag cinched shut with a drawstring. He untied it and upended the contents into his palm.

A ring rolled out. A heavy signet ring, worked in thick gold and with an intricate design carved into its face. Griffin slowly straightened up as he examined it.

Tom let out a thoughtful whistle. "That cost more than a bob," he said, leaning close to inspect it. "What do you figure the markings for?"

Griffin held it up, trying to catch the light coming in through the arch window over the front door. "It looks to be a family coat of arms, maybe Italian. I can't be precisely sure until I get it under a magnifying glass."

"How do you know it's Italian?" asked Phelps in a hushed voice, as if someone might overhear them.

Griffin glanced around. The little group in the hall had inched closer, eagerly straining to see the ring and obviously caught up in the bizarre drama. Even Roger seemed enthralled, creeping close to gaze at the heavy piece of jewelry. Or so Griffin thought, until he felt a flutter of movement near the back of his coat.

"I don't think so." He grabbed Roger by the wrist and pulled the boy in front of him. "You've already picked enough pockets today."

The boy let out a dramatic sigh. "Can't blame me for trying, guv."

"Oh, yes we can," barked Tom, seizing the boy's shoulder and propelling him toward the front door. "To think you would try to fleece Griffin Steele, of all people. If you don't have anything more to tell us, you little blighter, you can be on your way."

Tom glanced at Griffin, silently asking permission.

"One more thing," Griffin added. "Roger, if you ever see this veiled woman again, I want you to follow her until she arrives at her destination, and then come report to me." Not much hope of that happening, but he might as well cover off every eventuality he could.

He nodded at Tom, who fished a shilling out of his pocket and gave it to the boy.

"There will be more of that if you come to me with useful information," Griffin said.

Roger tipped his threadbare cap, gave them one last gapetoothed grin, and slipped out the door.

"Open the note," Madeline prompted as she gently bounced the baby up and down in her arms.

Griffin glanced at the expectant faces of his staff. "Everyone loves a mystery," he murmured, shaking his head. He didn't. He hated mysteries and all the drama that came with them.

He slipped the ring into a pocket and then extracted the small note from the waistband of his breeches. The paper was heavy, obviously of good quality. Slipping his finger under the wax, he gently peeled open the note. The handwriting was clear and feminine, and the message contained only a few lines.

> *The child's name is Stephen. His life is in grave danger. I beg you, Mr. Steele, to keep him safe until I contact you again. May God bless you!*
>
> *A friend*

Naturally, the note lacked any other identifying marks. That would have been far too easy.

"What does it say?" asked Tom with a curiosity he rarely displayed.

"That the baby's name is Stephen and that we are to keep him safe until further notice," Griffin said, repressing the impulse to curse.

"Well, that's a right proper mystery, ain't it, Mr. Griffin?" said Phelps in a voice of wonder. Clearly a mystery that Griffin's employees found quite enjoyable. He didn't share the feeling.

"It is," he replied in a grim voice. "Phelps, I want you to find Dominic Hunter. I don't care if you have to drag him out of his damn office in Whitehall or from the deepest pits of hell, but do not come back here without him."